# The Centhini Story
## the Javanese journey of life

Conceptualised by Kestity Pringgoharjono
Translated from New Javanese by Dr Soewito Santoso
Photographs by Fendi Siregar
Captions and maps by Kestity Pringgoharjono

Project Editor: Lee Mei Lin
Designers: Lynn Chin Nyuk Lin and Jailani Basari

Copyright © 2006 Marshall Cavendish International (Asia) Private Limited
Photographs © Kestity Pringgoharjono

Published by Marshall Cavendish Editions
An imprint of Marshall Cavendish International
1 New Industrial Road, Singapore 536196

All rights reserved

No part of this publication may be reproduced, stored in a retrieval system or transmitted, in any form or by any means, electronic, mechanical, photocopying, recording or otherwise, without the prior permission of the copyright owner. Request for permission should be addressed to the Publisher, Marshall Cavendish International (Asia) Private Limited, 1 New Industrial Road, Singapore 536196. Tel: (65) 6213 9300, fax: (65) 6285 4871. E-mail: te@sg.marshallcavendish.com

The publisher makes no representation or warranties with respect to the contents of this book, and specifically disclaims any implied warranties or merchantability or fitness for any particular purpose, and shall in no events be liable for any loss of profit or any other commercial damage, including but not limited to special, incidental, consequential, or other damages.

Other Marshall Cavendish Offices
Marshall Cavendish Ltd. 119 Wardour Street, London W1F 0UW, UK
Marshall Cavendish Corporation. 99 White Plains Road, Tarrytown NY 10591-9001, USA
Marshall Cavendish International (Thailand) Co Ltd. 253 Asoke, 12th Flr, Sukhumvit 21 Road, Klongtoey Nua, Wattana, Bangkok 10110, Thailand
Marshall Cavendish (Malaysia) Sdn Bhd, Times Subang, Lot 46, Subang Hi-Tech Industrial Park, Batu Tiga, 40000 Shah Alam, Selangor Darul Ehsan, Malaysia

Marshall Cavendish is a trademark of Times Publishing Limited

National Library Board Singapore Cataloguing in Publication Data
Santoso, Suwito.
The Centhini story : the Javanese journey of life / translated and condensed from the original Serat Centhini by Soewito Santoso ; photography by Fendi Siregar ; additional text by Kestity Pringgoharjono. — Singapore : Marshall Cavendish Editions, c2006.
p. cm.

ISBN-13 : 978-981-232-975-2
ISBN-10 : 981-232-975-7

1. Indonesia — History — 1478-1798 — Fiction.   I. Siregar, Fendi, 1949-   II. Pringgoharjono, Kestity, 1974-   III. Title.   IV. Title: Centini.

PR9500.9
828.9959803 — dc22        SLS2006026566

Printed in China by Everbest Printing Co Ltd

Front cover: The *segoro-wedi* (sand-sea) in the caldera of Mount Bromo
Page 1: A fisherman waits for his catch on the Serayu River
Page 4–5: Prambanan temple at sunrise
Page 6–7: Gateway to the Jalatunda well, Dieng Plateau
Page 12: The main gate to Jumprit Spring, the source of the Progo River
Page 394: The kingdom of Mataram gate, Kota Gede
Back cover: Relief on a wall of the Borobodur temple
Endpaper: Detail of a page from *Serat Centhini*, showing the *Hanacaraka* script

# The Centhini Story

## the Javanese journey of life

Based on the original *Serat Centhini*
Translated and condensed by
**Soewito Santoso**

Photographs by
**Fendi Siregar**

Additional text by
**Kestity Pringgoharjono**

# contents

8 foreword

12 introduction

## 28 the pre-adulthood journey
- 32 jayengresmi
- 66 jayengsari and ni rancangkapti
- 84 mas cabolang

## 182 the adulthood journey
- 186 mangunarso, anggungrimang and nyi rancangkapti
- 190 seh amongrogo
- 236 seh amongrogo, the husband of nyi tambangraras
- 268 jayengresmi, jayengrogo and kulowiryo
- 336 nyi selobrangti and cethi centhini
- 342 jayengresmi and jayengrogo
- 346 nyi turido and nyi rarasati

## 350 the post-adulthood journey
- 352 ki arundoyo and nyi malaresmi
- 366 seh amongrogo and nyi tambangraras
- 378 jatisworo and ragasmoro

## 382 the arrival
- 384 ki bayi panurto and nyi malarsih
- 386 seh amongrogo and nyi tambangraras

392 family tree
396 glossary
398 index
400 acknowledgements

## foreword by
# kestity pringgoharjono

"You are mad!" Those were the very words of Adji Damais when I told him in late 2003 about my intention to have *Serat Centhini*, an epic 19th-century work, translated and condensed into English. As a highly respected cultural expert and historical observer, his advice and views mattered greatly to me. But while the idea was mad, Mas Adji gave his support instantly. He saw an urgent need to make an important part of Indonesia's rich culture accessible to not only a new generation of Indonesians but to a broader audience as well, and recognised that this project—to capture the essence of *Serat Centhini* and present it in a more contemporary manner—has a role to play. He provided me with many insights and much guidance, without which this project would have been fraught with many more obstacles.

For the project to move forward, however, it was crucial to have access to expert knowledge. It is sad to say that there is little academic interest in and new research being done about the literary heritage of this fabulously diverse country called Indonesia. But from the late Ibu Hilmiyah, library administrator of the Mangkunegaran palace, I learnt of Dr Soewito Santoso. I discovered that although Dr Soewito was retired, he is highly regarded in international academic circles as an expert in Javanese literature. But the question was whether he would be happy to get involved in this project.

I am sure that when I first called him to talk about my idea, he must have been surprised that someone a little older in age than his grandchildren would be bold enough to ask such an eminent expert to play a central role in her project. But the Javanese hierarchy of *bibit*, *bebet*, *bobot*—or lineage, rank and wealth—was on my side. My husband's grandfather was well known to Pak Wito and their relationship allowed me to put forward my proposition. Pak Wito agreed that *Serat Centhini* needed to be preserved, but he politely declined my invitation because of his age. We agreed to meet in Jakarta to discuss a supervisory involvement, but thank God, the path was shown for him to play that central role I had always envisioned. He proved himself wrong about old age being a concern. In the end, it was his passion that drove him to share his special gift and knowledge with all of us in this book. For this, I am sincerely grateful.

The great words of *Serat Centhini* are incomplete, and can never be understood, without the pictures. Mas Adji suggested Fendi Siregar, a true artist renowned for his work in Indonesia and abroad. Here again, fate and Indonesia's three degrees of separation as opposed to Oscar Wilde's six played its part.

When we finally met in Singapore, we discovered that Pak Fendi knew my mother socially. That helped open up our conversation and I soon realised that he was the only one who could take on the gruelling task. For it was not just a matter of photographic skill and artistic composure, it was also about living and breathing the project. How else would one discover whether the locations in *Serat Centhini* actually exist? There are no detailed maps to rely on and no GPS satellite navigation system… just the odd wise man giving such directions as "over the hill and walk for two hours till you come across a large banyan tree with an odd looking trunk and you will find it". The patience, the determination and the excitement of finding that elusive mountain or rare grave or capturing a ritual hardly seen these days are what drove Pak Fendi on his own personal journey. The gift of his pictures is wonderfully captured for posterity in this book.

 Managing this project has given me the opportunity to gain a deeper appreciation of my own culture and heritage as well as the privilege of receiving a crash transfer of knowledge from Pak Wito, the guru of Javanese literature and culture. Not only that, over the years, I have made strong friendships with Pak Wito and Pak Fendi. Although we belong to three different generations and live in three different continents, we all share the same dedication—to preserve our great heritage in this book, *The Centhini Story*. Again, it was passion that helped overcome the obstacles of distance and the generation gap.

And while many are no longer around to tell their stories—like the last master kris smith, whose lineage goes back to the Majapahit kingdom, and the caretaker of a holy person's grave, who died in the aftermath of a tragic earthquake that struck in May this year—their stories will live on in this book. The gifts and richness of the island of Java are tempered and balanced with God's other secrets, oftentimes manifested in our earthquakes and volcanic eruptions and other challenges which may not allow us to preserve them for a future generation. I hope that *The Centhini Story* in its own way will preserve some of those gifts, if not in life then in record.

We are honoured to be able to present this book as a precious record of our great heritage. The mortality of people and of places that have been built and destroyed should still maintain a red string, a link, for the generations to come. It is my deepest hope that this book will be of benefit to all.

London, August 2006

## foreword by
# soewito santoso

In the name of Allah, The Most Merciful and Compassionate.

**When I heard** about an attempt to publish *Serat Centhini* in English, I was very much moved. Clearly ringing in my ears again and again were the words of my late guru, Professor Dr R. M. Ng. Poerbatjaraka: "Mas [as he always called me], should anyone wish to publish *Serat Centhini*, get involved." Not only that, he had two more requests: "Keep working on the *Sutasoma Kekawin* until it is finished. After that, work on the *Ramayana Kekawin*; I have done the translation for this, but it is now missing."

He gave me these messages when I visited him at the Military Hospital in Jakarta in 1964 where he was being looked after. I was about to leave for Canberra, Australia, to take up the position of lecturer in Old Javanese Language and Literature at the Australian National University. At that time, I was indeed working on the manuscript of the *Sutasoma Kekawin*. It was to be the basis of my Ph.D thesis at the Faculty of Arts, University of Indonesia, and Professor Poerbatjaraka—an icon in the study of Old Javanese Language and Literature—was one of my supervisors. When he passed away a few months later, I realised his words were his last wishes, and that I had unwittingly and unknowingly taken it upon myself to fulfil them.

Sixteen years later, I fulfilled two of those wishes with the publication of the *Ramayana Kekawin*. The *Sutasoma Kekawin* was published three years before, in 1977. Not bad, considering that the two *kekawins* (a term widely used to describe poems written in Old Javanese, the language in use from approximately the 8th to the 15th centuries) mentioned are the longest, most beautiful and most difficult to work on in the treasury of Old Javanese belles-lettres. Besides, I was also giving lectures and presenting papers at international seminars. Looking back, it was indeed a feat.

As for *Serat Centhini*, the message was clear enough—that I should only get involved, not initiate. And so I simply waited and turned my attention to other aspects of Javanese literature, namely those relating to the *Babad Tanah Jawi* (The Chronicles of Java) and Islam. When I reached middle age, I felt an emptiness inside. As a child growing up during the Japanese Occupation and having to take part in the *Sie-nen-dan* exercises, I lost the opportunity to learn to read the Qur'an. And when I was at high school, I was occupied with guerilla warfare escapades. This feeling of emptiness did not abate but became overpowering with the realisation of sins acquired from my atrocious behaviour then, albeit with the excuse of fighting for the independence of the fatherland and protecting the common people from colonial oppression.

At long last, after more than forty years, news about *Serat Centhini* finally came. But what could I do? I was already in my late seventies, and had less strength and energy to tackle anything massive. But when I went to Jakarta and looked at the situation very closely, I felt a strong need to close the gap, one not yet undertaken. I was to write a condensed version of the original work in both English and Bahasa Indonesia. I knew it would not be an easy task to translate the work from New Javanese into two languages and condense an epic some 3500 pages long to one-tenth its length. Moreover, the condensed version had to attract not only the curiosity of the common reader it had to be of enough value to entice academics to embark on further study of the original text. For that purpose, the language had to be smooth and fluent, not swaying and turning like the stride of a *serimpi* dancer moving to the rhythm of the gamelan music. Furthermore, it should contain as much material of the original work as possible so as to whet the appetite of those intent on unravelling the riddles and mysteries contained in it; riddles and mysteries hidden in the layers of time gone by and in a culture that is already at great variance with that of today. To dig them up, we should be like the archaeologist in the field and work not with a bulldozer but with a hoe of accuracy and patience.

However, what I have done with this condensed version might only be to show the sites to be dug, with few clues and little guarantee of success. Nevertheless, I pray to God The Almighty to grant me strength and the ability to bear the burden. Finally, I supplicate humbly that His Blessings be bestowed to our revered and esteemed Prophet Muhammad PBUH (Peace and Blessings Be upon Him). May God be willing and accept our prayers.

Canberra, August 2006

introduction by
# soewito santoso

## Java in the 19th century
**Mataram kingdom and the Dutch East India Company — contact and friction**

History at the beginning of the 19th century recorded a great war in Europe. Napoleon Bonaparte had become the Emperor of France and was extremely feared by the whole of Europe. With the exception of England and Russia, almost all nations on the European continent were subdued. The Netherlands was integrated into France.

Over in Southeast Asia, in 1810, the island of Java was ruled by Governor General H. W. Daendels, who was rapidly making preparations to defend the Dutch colonies against the British. To fund the defence reforms and colonial administration, he sold land that rightfully belonged to reigning kingdoms at the highest possible price. For example, all the lands in the regency of Probolinggo in East Java were sold to a Chinese called Han Ti Ko for one million dollars. He also toughened labour regulations, which highly disadvantaged the people of Java. So radical were the measures that they were abhorred by his own people, those back in Europe and those settled in Java, and more so by the kings and princes of Java. Napoleon Bonaparte recalled Daendels in 1810 and replaced him with Jan Williams Janssens. Janssens, however, could not make use of the defence reforms to protect them from the assaults of the British, who began to assert itself under the leadership of Lt. Governor General Thomas Stamford Raffles.[1]

On the ranks of the Javanese princes, we see the sultans of three kingdoms—Bantam (Banten), Cirebon and Mataram. Mataram was the most powerful and had the largest territory, which extended from West Java to East Java. The Dutch East India Company, in seeking to establish strongholds in Java, always endeavoured to play one Javanese power against another. For instance, by giving assistance to the Sultan of Bantam against Sultan Agung of Mataram, it obtained the lands south of Batavia (Jakarta). Within Mataram kingdom itself, uprisings broke out after the death of Sultan Agung. By taking the side of the

[1] Vlekke, B. H. M. *Nusantara*. Harvard University Press, Cambridge, 1945, p200–541

sultan against the rebel prince Trunojoyo, the Company obtained the lands along the north coast of Java. As the princes lost access to the sea and overseas trade, so too did they lose their power. The Dutch became more and more entrenched in Java. Additionally, the Chinese rebellion (1740–1748), which started in Batavia but finally extended also to Central Java, made the Sunan Paku Buwono of Kartasura—the capital city of Mataram after the rebellion of Trunojoyo—lose a great deal of land and power. Along with this loss of land and power, the role played by the princes and the Javanese people in the economic field also became insignificant.

**Tradition and Islam**
It was only in the field of culture that the foreigners did not interfere and so, the traditions that were passed down from the ancestors showed no signs of decay. Those traditions are what have lately been called the 'magnificent legacy of the forefathers'. What it means, however, nobody can yet define accurately and comprehensively. One can say that the Borobudur temple is a magnificent heritage, that the wayang (shadow play) is a magnificent heritage, likewise the *Mahabharata* and the *Ramayana*, and various other things. Moreover, because so much time stands between when these things were created and the present time and because there was little contact between the cultural elements of the past and those of the 19th century, these elements of culture became hidden in riddles and mysteries and have been very difficult to unravel.

The academics of today have done a great deal to unravel the mysteries, but the results are not satisfactory due to lack of funds and expertise. The mysteries are also too deeply buried in the sands of time. The situation today is so different from that of our ancestors who were closer to the product of the culture of the age they were in. Thus in matters related to the construction and design of temples, if we were to compare the temples of Central Java with those of East Java, the differences between them are so obvious that the disparity must have been conducted conscientiously. That is why a Dutch scholar who studied the temples mentioned that the differences between them were deliberate, requiring a high degree of craftsmanship. He used the term 'local genius' for those who set out to do things differently. They made the changes by using local cultural elements, so that little by little elements of foreign cultural products were replaced with local ones, which were already adjusted for the benefit of both sides. Certainly, these changes were not easy to make and a local genius is not just anyone indeed. A Javanese wise man would say that that kind of man is one endowed with God's blessings… blessings given in the form of guidance, inspiration, patience and intelligence. It happened in every field of civilisation, for instance, in architecture as well as in literature.

Let us look at the temples of Borobudur and Prambanan. By worshipping the Buddhas and Budhisattwas, our Buddhist ancestors obtained religious guidance. Further guidance from Buddha the Enlightened One can be gleaned from the reliefs of the Jataka stories carved on the walls of the Borobudur. Likewise were the followers of

| **introduction** |

Hinduism, who received guidance by worshipping the images of Brahma, Vishnu and Shiva. By paying attention to the reliefs of the Kresnayana and the Ramayana on the walls of the Prambanan temple, they saw examples of how to perceive good from bad and vice versa, and learnt which deeds brought misfortune and which brought prosperity. If we look more closely at the temple buildings, the reliefs intricately carved on them and the ornaments that adorn them, we can conclude that the contents (religious teachings and guidance) and the container (buildings, carvings and ornaments) have been integrated harmoniously to create a superb image.

And now let us contemplate the following question. If one already owns something that is good, beautiful and useful, would one be prepared to part with it and take on something else that is lesser known? Most people will say no. The local genius, however, will take the question more calmly. He will consider the matter deeply, explore the pros and cons of doing it, and finally ponder whether the action would enrich or beautify those already accomplished.

This was the situation that arose when Islam and its attendant culture came to Java's shores from India and Arabia. Surely, the Moslems wanted to offer their religion and everything else that came with it to the people who were still embracing Hinduism and Buddhism, even though those faiths had already been adapted to suit local conditions. Not surprisingly, the Moslem missionary faced great difficulties. So great were they that a most serious discussion concerning the new religion took place at the court of Demak. In a conference between the Wali Songo[2] and the Sultan of Demak, Sultan Syah Alam Akbar, the *walis* (saints) reported that the fortunes of the people of Java began to decline with the fall of the Hindu kingdom of Majapahit. The land was plagued by many mishaps, crops failed consecutively, people lived in poverty and as a result, Islam had no chance to take root and develop. The Sultan then asked the counsel of saints for ideas that would solve the problems and bring good fortune back.

Sunan (an honorific literally translated as 'the highly esteemed one') Kalijogo, a young *wali* amongst the nine saints in the Wali Songo, then asked permission to speak: "Milord, give me permission to speak. For a long while, I have been pondering upon the problems we are facing and I have attempted to do my utmost to pray for Allah's guidance. One night, in my meditations, I heard a voice say: 'My son, Kalijogo. If you want the good fortune of the country to return, restore the old traditions. Choose elements from the old culture that can be used to enrich the new.' Milords, these were the very words I heard. With your wisdom, explain for all of us to hear its meaning." On hearing those words, the saints fell silent. Although Sunan Kalijogo

---

2 The word 'Wali Songo' is a collective term for a group of nine eminent Javanese saints who were responsible for the initial spread of Islam in Java in the 15th century. They are Maulana Malik Ibrahim, Sunan Ampel, Sunan Bonang, Sunan Drajat, Sunan Giri, Sunan Gunung Jati, Sunan Kalijojo, Sunan Kudus and Sunan Muria. Of these, Sunan Giri and Sunan Kalijogo are mentioned in this publication of *The Centhini Story*. There are actually more than nine (*songo*) saints (*walis*) in Javanese history and they are just as well respected as those in the Wali Songo for their role in spreading Islam further. Of these subsequent generations of saints, Sunan Tembayat and Seh Domba are mentioned here.

was the youngest amongst them, they felt that he had proven himself to be highly knowledgeable especially in matters concerning Islam and culture. The message he put forward to them was not easy to read. To return to the old traditions would mean a return to Hinduism and Buddhism. Furthermore, the worship of idols inherent in them constitutes a great sin in Islam. The saints could not find an answer and only shook their heads. What did it mean to choose elements from the old to enrich the new?

Sunan Kalijogo spoke again, very cautiously: "Milords, again I ask your indulgence for my misbehaviour. We have to admit that so far, the drum (*bedhug*) in our mosque has only made the people deaf (*budheg*) towards the teachings of Islam. Can we not place the gamelan beside the drum?" Most of the saints shook their heads in disapproval. Put musical instruments in a mosque? Impossible! He continued: "Milords, Buddhists and Hindus have helped us build the mosque [of Demak] in many ways, by cutting down trees and transporting the wood from the forest to the city. Is that not taking elements of the old to build the new? If the gamelan is regarded as an old element of our culture, could we not read the name of Allah upon it to make it rightful for us, since we can make cooked meat rightful to eat by pronouncing the *basmallah*[3] upon it? Could we not make other things rightful in the same way? If the drum cannot open the people's ears to listen to the teachings of our religion, why can't we play the gamelan and allow the people to dance and sing to glorify Allah The Almighty? Furthermore, since it is a requirement to say a mantra before entering the courtyard of a temple, is it not possible to pronounce the *kalimah sahadah*[4] before entering the precinct of a mosque in order to listen to the gamelan? If the gamelan, which we have already made rightful cannot be placed in the mosque, why can't we build a special place for it in the mosque compound? When people are in the mosque and enjoying the sounds of the gamelan music, we have the opportunity to tell them more about our religion. Isn't it so that since they have already pronounced the creed, they have the right to receive more teachings? Besides, if our ancestors the kings and queens of Majapahit made *sraddha*[5], why can't the Sultan make the same offering and call it *hajat dalem*, the king's ceremonial sacrifice to pray for Allah's blessings and mercy? Wouldn't all these encompass borrowing elements from the old culture to enrich the new? Let the old customs become the container and the new elements of faith the contents. What we have to do is make the container fit the contents."

---

3 The word *basmallah* refers to the phrase *bismillah hirrahmanir rahim*, which means 'In the name of Allah, the Most Merciful and Compassionate'. Muslims pronounce the *basmallah* before doing anything, be it at the start of a meal or upon entering a home.

4 The *kalimah sahadah* is the Islamic Creed, which reads 'There is no God but Allah and Muhammad is His messenger'. It is the declaration of faith towards Allah and His prophet.

5 *Sraddha* are offerings made to the souls of ancestors. The offerings are presented in the form of a rice-mountain symbolising the Mandhara Mountain, which was used to churn the ocean of milk to produce the *amreta* (the elixir of life) for the welfare of the country and its people.

"*Alhamdulillah! Allahu Akbar!*" (God be Praised! God is Great!), called out the saints in unison. Sunan Kalijogo's speech, which flowed like flood, had washed away their doubts and hesitations.[6]

With praises of tribute in their hearts, the saints worked very hard making preparations for the big festival of *sraddha* the Islamic way, with the sound of the gamelan music inviting people to come. And the people responded overwhelmingly. They came in groups and throngs from every corner of the kingdom. Anyone who wished to enter the mosque compound was asked to pronounce the *kalimah sahadah*, the expression of faith towards Allah and His prophet. They came every day and the queues were long with no end in sight. And if someone asked them where they were heading for, the answer was always: "To the capital city, to see the Sahadatain."[7] And when they went home, they brought with them the good news about the mission of the prophet of Allah, Muhammad by name and whose birthday would be celebrated at the mosque of Demak-Bintoro on the twelfth of the Javanese month of Mulud.[8]

To remove the impression that the *hajat dalem* was an attempt to get rid of the *sraddha*, the saints introduced a ceremony for the dead. It was not only to be performed by the nobility but by everyone. And it would be performed every year in the eighth month of the Javanese calendar, called Ruwah, the month of the souls. The ceremony, which was to be held from the middle to the end of Ruwah month, was called Nisfu Sya'ban[9] and that is the name down to the present time. Today, we might say that the

above: *Gamelan players in the Grand Mosque of Yogyakarta. They are preparing to play the gamelan called Kyai Gunturmadu for Sekaten, the festival that celebrates the birthday of Prophet Muhammad. The festival dates back to AD 1477 when the Grand Mosque of Demak was built. The integration of religion and local cultural elements, such as the gamelan orchestra and wayang, is one of many reasons for the successful spread of Islam in Java and is attributed to Sunan Kalijogo's unique way of spreading Islam. It is only in Java that one would find musical instruments in mosques.*

6 Notosoeroto. *Wat is Sekaten* in Indonesie 5, 1951-1952

7 'Sahadatain' is the other name for the *kalimah sahadah*, which is the Islamic Creed. It is from this word that the name of the festival celebrating Prophet Muhammad's birthday, called Sekaten, is derived. During the time of the Mataram kingdom, however, the festival was called Sahadatain. It was only later, when Mataram was divided into the kingdoms of Surakarta and Yogyakarta, that the festival was given the name of Sekaten.

8 Mulud is the third month in the Javanese calendar system (equivalent to the month of Rabiul Awal in the Islamic calendar). There are twelve lunar months in a Javanese year, each having either 29 or 30 days, which roughly parallels the Islamic calendar. The Javanese calendar system was originally based on the solar cycle. However, in AD1633 (1555 AJ in the Javanese calendar), Sultan Agung decided to change it to a lunar-based system. Although the Javanese calendar follows the lunar system of the Islamic calendar, it is not the same. The Javanese system is a combination of Javanese, embedded with Hindu influences, and the Islamic calendar.

9 The month of Sya'ban is the eighth month of the lunar year in the Islamic calendar (Ruwah month in the Javanese calendar) and the month immediately preceding the holy month of Ramadhan. Moslems try to do more good deeds than usual in this month and some would fast. The 15th night of the month is most special. On this night, Moslems pray, recite the Qur'an, praise God and make a great deal of supplications to God. In addition, the Javanese celebrate Nisfu Sya'ban in the second half of Ruwah month by sending offerings and prayers to their ancestors in their graves. This is done as a symbol of their respect and remembrance of the dead.

saints and their followers made conscious adjustments to elements of the old culture, Islamised them at the same time and implemented the changes into all stages of life and all walks (or strata) of life. And what do the stages of life and walks of life in the Javanese community of old mean?

It is generally known that the people of Java, and Bali in particular, received considerable cultural and social influence from India. Amongst these are what are called the *catur-kasta* (the four social strata) and the *catur-asrama* (the four stages of life). These two systems are thought to be divinely decreed and cannot be changed or broken. It needs to be noted also that amongst human beings, there are many believed to be incarnations of gods and deities. This was the reason behind the existence of the deification of man, which then developed into ancestor worship. In the course of time and via interaction between people of various cultural backgrounds, society in Java and Bali underwent drastic changes. Much of the original system has been forgotten; even then they are sometimes still latent in people's minds. For instance, in the ancient Hindu era, a person from the *sudra* caste was forbidden to engage in learning or studying. Today, with the introduction of compulsory education by the government, the prohibition does not legally exist anymore. In Java, religion(s) has also contributed to changes in the social order. In the rural communities, people might still say that they come from *sudra-papa*, the most sinful and lowest stratum of the community, and at the same time boast about their academic achievements, wealth and social status. This goes to show that they do not know what the word *sudra-papa* really means.

The origin of the *catur-kasta*, or the four social strata, is as follows. When The Supreme Deity in the Hindu pantheon wanted to create human beings, he first created the *brahman* caste from his head. A *brahman*'s duty on earth was to study and teach; they are the administrators of the world. Secondly, he created the *ksatriya* caste from his chest and arms; their job on earth was to protect the world, especially the *brahmans*. Thirdly, he created the *vaisya* caste from his stomach, whose duty on earth was to produce food for the world and trade. Last of all, he created the *sudra* caste from his legs, whose duty on earth was to support the three other higher classes by carrying out all their orders. For a person in the *sudra* caste, all his life should be always and only in the service of the *dwijas*—or 'twice-born', the collective name of the members of the three other castes—so that the four stages of life in fact does not apply to him.

The *catur-asrama*, or the four stages of life, is as follows:
- The first stage, which occurs between the ages of six and twelve, is called the *brahmacarin* (student). At this stage, all members of the first three castes start learning the Vedas (books of knowledge) with a guru.
- The second stage is that of *grhastha* (householder). A *vaisya* should marry and do his job to produce food for the world. He is also expected to put into practice everything he has learnt from his teacher. If there is something he does not know how to perform, say a certain ceremony or ritual, he can seek the assistance of a *brahman* called *purohita*. A *ksatriya* at this stage, though not required to marry

just yet, is obliged to study until the age of eighteen years. At this stage, the study concerns defence and public administration as well as religious matters. A king or nobleman very often has his own *purohita* to advise him on all matters of life, especially those that are complicated and harder to solve. At the age of eighteen, a *ksatriya* has to marry. After that, a prince, for instance, can succeed his father and become king. Examples are abundant. In the *Ramayana*, Prince Rama is expected to be crowned king after he marries Princess Sita. In the *Sutasoma Kekawin*, Prince Sutasoma is advised by his father the king to marry so that he can succeed him as ruler of the kingdom. However, Prince Sutasoma refuses and escapes to the forest to do penance and study with a *wanaprestha* (forest dweller).

- The third stage is that of the *wanaprestha*. When a householder has seen the birth of his grandson, he knows that his time to go to the forest has come. He has to leave his family and live in the forest to continue his study with older *wanapresthas*. His wife is allowed to accompany and serve him. When he has attained a high level of knowledge, then it is time to take on the fourth stage, that of a *sannyasin* (wanderer).
- A wanderer is not permitted to own anything which is part of the earthly realm. He has to leave his wife behind and may not stay at any one place for any length of time but wander around until death comes. If his life lasts longer than the clothes he wears, he may not put on other clothes but live as a *digambara* (naked wandering priest).[10]

So far we have talked about the *catur-kasta* and the *catur-asrama* but nothing yet about the knowledge that can be used as guidelines in life. Every caste has its own duty to carry out in every stage of life. To fulfil their duty, everyone has to know the objectives of life and how to accomplish them. The objectives of life, called the *catur-warga*, comprise wealth (*artha*), sex (*kama*), duty, good deeds, religion and law (*dharmma*) and union with God (*moksa*). The first objective in life is to gather wealth so as to be able to set up a household, which is the second objective. With a successful household, one has the opportunity to lead a good life in accordance with the *dharmma*. Finally, the *dharmma* will release man from the bondage of this world and return them to the abode of the Godhead.[11]

There exist many books that concern themselves solely with providing knowledge about the *dharmma* for every caste in the social strata. But there also exist books that contain everything from *artha* up to *moksa*, shortcuts if you will. Two examples of the latter are the *Ramayana* and the *Mahabharata*, which provide all kinds of knowledge ranging from lovemaking to marriage to warfare. In Javanese literature, *Serat Centhini* is one such book that contains all the knowledge.

---

10  Basham, A. L. *The Wonder That Was India*. 3rd revised edition, Taplinger Publishing Co., New York, 1968, p159-60

11  *ibid* p138-59

All that has been said above should be regarded as necessary because they explain the social make-up of the people of Java (and Bali for that matter) which goes back to Indian life and culture of yore. Without them, it would be almost impossible to understand the contents of *Serat Centhini* fully and correctly. As was mentioned earlier, we have forgotten much about the past and as links with the past are lost, the picture blurs. When questions arise and answers are not forthcoming, misunderstanding occurs. Many of the tales and accounts in *Serat Centhini* cannot be understood clearly without understanding the cultural context of the time. Take, for instance, the protagonists'— Seh Amongrogo and his wife Nyi Tambangraras—existence in the *alam walikan* (spirit world) after the former was sentenced to death by drowning at Tunjungbang (Red Lotus) Bay. In Islam, one who lives in the incorporeal world cannot meet or communicate with people from the corporeal world. In *Serat Centhini*, however, Seh Amongrogo and his wife are able to meet family members on the earthly plane. This idea or possibility can only be perceived logically when seen and understood in the Hindu and Buddhist context… that the world of the human being and the world of deities exist in the same sphere.

Another example concerns the idea of reincarnation, unheard of in the teachings of Islam. Seh Amongrogo and his wife—already in the incorporeal world—meet Sultan Agung of Mataram, who is doing penance on Telomoyo Mountain and is known as Panembahan Anyokrokusumo Sidowakyo. Seh Amongrogo makes known his wish to become king so as to help mankind further. Sultan Agung advises them to incarnate into male and female bee larva respectively. He then eats the male larva while Pangeran Pekik, his brother-in-law, consumes the female one. Consequently, Sultan Agung has a son and Pangeran Pekik, a daughter. When the children come of age, they are married to each other. The son then succeeds Sultan Agung, which is the fulfilment of Seh Amongrogo's wish. Reincarnation is not known in Islam, but it is a very important pillar in the teachings of Hinduism and Buddhism. It is not surprising then that Stutterheim, in his book about Islam in Indonesia, visualises Islam as it is practised in Indonesia as a blanket with holes through which elements of Hinduism and Buddhism can be seen.[12] One could say that this is the view of a non-Moslem scholar and the opinion of an outsider.

Let us now go back to the efforts of the nine saints and their followers to make Islam more acceptable to the people based on the ideas of using the old to enrich the new and the container fitting the contents. When observed from the view of an insider, it looks as if the opposite has taken place. The container is Hinduism and Buddhism, whilst the contents is Islam. In his doctoral thesis, P. J. Zoetmulder examines the existence of pantheism and monism in Islam through Sufism. What is presented in it is very close to the original material in *Serat Centhini*, which in the framework of the *catur-warga* is the fourth stage of the objective of life. And why was it close to

---

12  Stutterheim. *Cultuurgeschiedenis van Indonesie*. Vol. 3, J. B. Wolters, Groningen, 1951–1952

the original material? The reason is because Zoetmulder uses the views and books of Moslem Sufis. Nevertheless, we need to remember that Father Zoetmulder was a non-Moslem theologian and so we must still keep open the possibility for contrary views from Moslem Sufis.[13]

Readers of this publication should realise that I cannot dwell too much on one topic in this introduction but offer a kind of roadmap, or guidelines if you will, for the curious adventurer. This is because the subject matter in *Serat Centhini* is so great in their number and variety—covering all knowledge that is needed for attaining the objectives of life in all the stages—that students of Old Javanese literature call it the encyclopaedia of Javanese knowledge. That knowledge is composed in and disseminated via the many chains of experiences encountered by various kinds of people, every one of them a seeker of *artha, kama, dharmma* and *moksa*.

## The Islamisation of traditional literature

Literature serves as a repository for man's life experiences. Since the beginning of civilisation, man has attempted to record his experiences of life for the purpose of passing them on, whether intentionally or not, to the generations to come. Before any system of writing was invented, the transfer was done orally in the form of stories and then later in the form of pictures etched on the walls of caves or stones. From pictures, the ideas changed into symbols and finally into a script. The process and progression from oral literature to a written one took a long time; it was a journey which progressed step by step with the stride of civilisation itself. Furthermore, we must take into account that environment has always played a great influence on the people and progress of the culture. As well, communication and the exchange of experiences between groups of people create opportunities for elements of culture to merge with one another.

At this point, assume that I am a puppeteer. I will hit the puppet chest with a cudgel and say: "*Swuh rep nda tatita, genti kang cinarita* (Let it be silence, leave the past and let us begin with another story)." I would say this just to prevent the mind from drifting too far away into the old days. And so, let us now talk about the traditional literature of the Javanese, particularly the ones that are inherited from the 19th century.

For sure, the literature would already have in them many cultural elements by virtue of the people's interactions with groups from other different environments, which consequently produced a different form of culture. For instance, the arrival of people from India in Java in the first century AD, which resulted in further development and strong growth of the original indigenous Javanese culture, is symbolised with the arrival of a prince from the Saka tribe in India called Aji Saka and two attendants,

**above:** *The principal writing material in Java before the advent of paper was the* lontar *(long palm leaf). Leaves of the tal tree are first dried and treated. Letters are carved on them with a sharp knife, then rubbed with a charcoal dye to make them stand out. It is probable that palm leaves were already in use in Bali from the time of the earliest written records.*

---

13  Zoetmulder, P. J. *Pantheisme and Monisme in de Javaansche Suluk literatuur.* Nijmegen, Berkhout, 1935

Setya and Tuhu. Because of a misunderstanding between the attendants, they fell into a fierce fight which led to their deaths. Aji Saka recorded this incident for posterity by creating the Javanese script. Now, what better allegory can be thought of to describe the flowering culture than the origin of the Javanese script? With the advance of Islam in Java, the Aji Saka story took on a slight transformation with great repercussions. In the Moslem version, Aji Saka was referred to as the companion of the prophet Muhammad who stopped in India en route to Java and on this journey, he wrote the *Mahabharata*, the *Ramayana*, the *Arjunawiwaha* and other books. At present, we know that the Javanese script is derived from the Pallava script. As well, these books come from the Hindu-Javanese literary treasury. Nevertheless, with this story, the Moslems of Java have always believed that the books were the work of a companion of Prophet Muhammad who was definitely a Moslem. As such, those books should be regarded as Moslem literature.[14]

From the above we can see that the saints and their followers worked tirelessly to provide a new face and image to Hindu and Buddhist cultural elements in accordance with Islamic principles. Take, for instance, the change of the *sraddha* ceremony from an ancestor worship ritual into an occasion that celebrates the birthday of Prophet Muhammad. Also, the date of the *sraddha* was changed from several years after the death of a certain king or queen to the twelfth of the month of Mulud in the Javanese calendar. Very often, those changes would have already taken place before they were brought to Java, but still they were warmly received. It is not surprising then that the relationship between Moslem and Javanese traditional literature was an extremely friendly and intimate one, especially those stories that told of the heroes of Islam, for example, the story of Amir Hamzah, the *Panji* stories, the *Mahabharata*, the *Ramayana* and many others.

In the 18th century, in the Mataram kingdom's capital city of Kartasura—later on Surakarta—the court poets did not differentiate any more the origin of the stories. For example, Yosodipuro I (1729–1788) wrote *Serat*[15] *Rama* and *Serat Menak*, the Javanese version of the *Ramayana Kekawin* and the Amir Hamzah story respectively. Yet in another book, the *Serat Cabolek*,[16] he even included the Dewaruci story (which originated from the Hindu-Javanese literary works of the 8th to 16th centuries AD) and sought to explain it from the Moslem point of view. In the same book, he also mentioned Seh Amongrogo, the main figure in *Serat Centhini* who was sentenced to death by drowning by Sultan Agung for breaking the Islamic law.

14a. Winter, Sr. *Aji Saka angajawi*. Semarang, 1886
  b. Santoso, Soewito. *The Islamization of Indonesia/Malay Literature in its earlier period* in The Journal of the Oriental Society of Australia, 1971, Vol. 8, #1 and #2

15 The word *Serat* in the titles of Javanese literary works is an indication that the work was written in New Javanese, the language in use from the late 17th to the 20th centuries. *Serat* is also commonly taken to mean 'story'.

16 Soebardi, S. *The Book of Cabolek*. The Hague, M. Nijhoff, 1975

| introduction |

# Serat Centhini (The Centhini Story)
## A product of the 19th century?

I start this part with a question. Why was the book named after someone whose role and position in the story is so insignificant? Centhini is only a *cethi* of Nyi Tambangraras, the daughter of Kyai Bayi Panurto and the wife of Seh Amongrogo. In the Javanese language, *cethi* means both 'maid' and 'maiden'. Those three other characters are more important than Centhini, in their roles as well as their standing in the story. Why then was her name chosen as the title of the story? There should be some significance to it, which unfortunately is still hidden from us. We do not know a lot of things, one of them being the relationship between the maid and her mistress. But as far as I can remember, those who come in contact with *Serat Centhini*, whether just a casual reader or a student of Javanese literature, without exception always regard or understand the *cethi* Centhini more as the maid-servant than the maiden-companion of pure heart and mind of Nyi Tambangraras. It is a demeaning view, I think, and one that leads to much misunderstanding. The common perception of a maid's role is that of servitude, where menial services are provided in return for a fee. To see Centhini in this light is debasing for her, as her role is more significant for she was devotedly faithful in taking her mistress Tambangraras to a 'higher' level of spiritual development.

above: *An open page of a volume of Serat Centhini, courtesy of the library of the Surakarta kingdom. Although the original work no longer exists (some believe it was torn into shreds and found under the king's deathbed), it is fortunate that exact copies were made in the late 1800s.*

In all probability, it was Prince A. A. Mangkunegoro III, the crown prince of the Surakarta royal place—and the inspiration behind *Serat Centhini*—who made the choice to name the book as such. The word *serat* was chosen perhaps because there were already other books in the Sasono Pustoko (library of the Surakarta palace) that revolved around Seh Amongrogo and Nyi Tambangraras, namely *Suluk*[17] *Seh Amongrogo* and *Suluk Tambangraras*. Perhaps he chose *serat* to make the new book distinct from the others.

As to why he chose to name the book after a maid, we should look more closely at the role of a *cethi*. In the *Ramayana Kekawin*, the fate of Rama, Sita and Laksmana is determined by the whisper of Manthara, a *cethi* of Queen Kaikeyi. The maid Manthara was reminding Kaikeyi of the promise of King Dasaratha. But instead of Rama being crowned king and ruling the country, Rama—together with his wife Sita and his

---

17 *Suluk* books are books that contain teachings about Islamic mysticism (Sufism) as the way to get on the path to the One (God). In such books, everything is dedicated to God and there is no mention whatsoever about 'worldly' matters, be they sexual or otherwise. While some sections of *Serat Centhini* contain *suluk* (mystic) teachings—such as Kyai Ageng Karang's teachings to Seh Amongrogo and the latter's teachings to his wife Nyi Tambangraras—it is not a *suluk* book as it contains ideas that are not congruent with the teachings of Islamic mysticism.

younger brother Laksmana—are banished to a forest for twelve years, where they were miserable and constantly in danger, and finally forced to wage war against the demon-king Rawana. In the *Serat Rama*, the Javanese version of the *Ramayana Kekawin* and the work of the court poet Yosodipuro I, Manthara is not mentioned any more. She is forgotten even though her whisper is still recorded and its consequence still constitutes the main component of the Rama story.

When I was in primary school, I read a work of Kalidasa written in the Javanese script. It was the *Sakuntala* (published by Balai Pustaka). I came across the story again when I studied Old Javanese at high school. Of Kalidasa, however, I got to know him better through his plays and poems when I was lecturing at the Australian National University. In all his plays, including the *Sakuntala*, the role played by the *cethi* in both roles of maid-servant and maiden-companion was really very important.[18]

Contemporary to Kalidasa, other writers are also known, among them Vatsyayana who wrote the *Kamasutra*. Even before Kalidasa, prominent playwrights such as Bhasa and Sudraka are widely esteemed. These two lived two or three centuries before Kalidasa, yet they proved to be exemplary leaders in the field. Bhasa had been an acclaimed figure in his own right. Sudraka, however, was not acknowledged by scholars in Indian drama, but there is enough evidence to show that for centuries a play titled 'Mrcchikatika'[19] was attributed to him. One translator rendered it with just 'The Clay Cart', another with 'The Little Toy Clay Cart' because the little clay cart was a toy. The role of the clay cart is indeed very small and insignificant in the 'Mrcchikatika' when compared with the other actors, which includes a prince, a merchant, a courtesan and a band of robbers. And yet the clay cart, the little toy, is taken as the title of the play. Hence, it can be concluded that naming a work of art after something insignificant in terms of its role and position in it was familiar practice, though perhaps one not very common at that time.

In 1939, Zoetmulder wrote an article[20] arguing that perhaps Centhini's position as Tambangraras' maid on the one hand, yet being allowed to sit in on the teachings of Seh Amongrogo to his wife on the other, made her an idol for the common reader who could identify themselves with her. My view though is that her presence at the time of instruction was not a favour but a duty, namely to be near her mistress at all times.

If there is truth to the discussion above, then a question comes to mind. Who came up with the title for the story? Was it the prince or his team of court writers?

---

18 Mirashi, V. V. and Navlekar, N. R. *Kalidasa—date, life and work*. Popular Prakashan, Bombay, 1969

19a. Pendleton, Oliver, R. *Mrcchikatika, the little clay cart: A drama in 10 Acts, attributed to king Sudraka*. Greenwood Press, Westport (Connecticut), 1975
  b. van Buitenen, J. A. B. *Two plays of Ancient India*. New York and London, Columbia University Press, 1968
  c. Sharman (ed.) *The Little Clay Cart: An English translation of the Mrcchikatika of Sudraka, as adapted for the stage by A. L. Basham*. State University of New York Press, Albany, 1974

20 Zoetmulder, P. J. *Iets omtrent de naam Serat Tjentini* in Het Triwindoe Gedenkboek M. N. VII, Soerakarta, 1939

The question comes up because apparently when three volumes had been finished, the prince was not satisfied with the work, in particular those parts related to sex which he felt were not satisfactorily dealt with. It seemed that the prince knew about the *catur-warga* and wanted all that was known about it to be written. Coincidently, two court writers—R. Ng. Yosodipuro II, who was sent to explore the region of West Java, and Kyai Ngabehi Sostrodipuro who was sent to Mecca to study Islam more deeply—had returned so that the whole team could work together. Yet up to Volume 5, the prince was still discontented for the same reason and so decided to write the erotic sections himself up to Volume 10. With Volume 10 finished, the original people of the team continued to work on the remaining two volumes.[21] When I compared the erotic content in the first five volumes with those in Volumes 6 to 10, I could fully agree with the prince that they were not satisfactory.

It is not surprising then if Prince Mangkunegoro III was dissatisfied with the way the erotic sections were dealt with. In all probability, the writers of *Serat Centhini* were reluctant to discuss the matter at length, being renowned Moslems of high ranking in knowledge and they felt uneasy to be involved in such matters openly. On the other hand, the prince himself—who might have had some knowledge about the teachings of the *catur-warga*—would have considered the book to be incomplete without the inclusion of the *kama* section. Not including the *kama* section might even bring about disasters and calamities to the kingdom and its people because in those parts, the worship of the phallus—the symbol of prosperity and abundance—is implied. An agricultural country cannot afford to leave out fertility rites. There are ample references in *Serat Centhini* of these fertility symbols, for instance, the statues of Kyai Drepa and Kyai and Nyai Gaprang. In addition, the life of the girl-dancers cum prostitutes (*ronggeng*) that are told in *Serat Centhini* are also reminders of the courtesans in ancient India and the geisha of Japan up to the present time, whatever changes it has undergone. These precepts and conducts are things to be avoided by Moslems as they are believed to generate sin of the highest degree. Yet, on the other hand, they must be preserved. Thus, there was no option left for the prince than to take the matter in his own hands. And since the naming of the story was motivated by tradition and the sex related sections were also under the influence of Indian heritage, for example, the *Kamasutra* or *The Anangga Rangga*, I am convinced that it was the prince who had decided on the title of *Serat Centhini*.

Within this framework of the four stages of life and to highlight the prince's regard for the erotic sections and his insistence on including such details in *Serat Centhini*, I will put forward an example. At the court of Surakarta, there still exists an official called *canthang balung*, whom the public only gets to see at royal parades. Clad in peculiar clothing, he leads a group of female dancers and can be seen dancing and making funny movements. His position in the court civil service

---

21  Soebardi, S. *The Book of Cabolek*. The Hague, M. Nijhoff, 1975

is not clear and remains a mystery for everyone even until today. Although articles concerning his role and origin have been published, none has been conclusive. In fact, no one has thought of linking him to Vidusaka, a funny character in the plays of ancient India whom students of Indian literature call the buffoon or royal jester. Vidusaka, who is very close to the king or prince, is given the position of 'superintendent of the courtesans'. To put it plainly, he is head of the royal prostitutes. In connection with this idea and in all probability, this *vidusaka* figure might also be similar to the *panakawan* in Javanese shadow play. The word *panakawan* literally means 'a close friend [of the king or prince]' and like the figure of *vidusaka*, the *panakawan* is also a funny figure.

I will now put forward one more question, although there are more to be asked but it is not the place to raise them in a condensed version. The question is: Can *Serat Centhini* be classified as a product of the 19th century? According to the introduction in Volume 1 of *Serat Centhini*, Karkono edition,[22] the writing of the story began in the year 1814 at the order of Prince A. A. Mangkunegoro III, who later became the Sunan Paku Buwono V. I regard this information more accurate than that given by R. M. Arya Sumahatmaka[23] who gives 1826 as the commencement year. Whatever the case, from these dates, it can be concluded that *Serat Centhini* was indeed written at the beginning of the 19th century.

However, if we consider the materials that have been incorporated into it, it can be assumed that the story of Centhini already existed long before that. For instance, in *Serat Cabolek* (The Story of Cabolek), another work of Yosodipuro I, the story of Seh Amongrogo's death by drowning at Tunjungbang Bay is already mentioned. Moreover, the manuscript of *Suluk Seh Amongrogo*—attributed to Rangga Sutrasna—was already in the collection of the library at the court of Surakarta. Finally, Poerbatjaraka indicates that the main part of the story of Centhini originated from *Serat Jatiswara*.[24] There are many more books included or simply mentioned in *Serat Centhini* such as the *Dewaruci*, *Lokapala*, *Sastra Jendra*, the story of Aji Saka, and the chronicles of Prambanan and Pengging. Most of these books were already in existence while some others were contemporary works. Likewise were the Arabic books that were used in the instruction of *fikh* (Islamic jurisprudence) and mysticism. With these in mind, it is probable that what the writers had to do was to simply compile all the components already in existence and then perhaps render them into poetic form. As such, it is reasonable to ask whether *Serat Centhini* is a product of the 19th century.

---

22  Partokusumo, Karkono. *Serat Centhini latin*. Yogyakarta, Yayasan Centhini, 12 Vols, 1992

23  Soemahatmaka, R. M. A. *Ringkasan Centhini (Soeloek Tambangraras)*. Based on a script written by Reksapoestaka, M. N. and published by Balai Pustaka, 1981

24  Poerbatjaraka, Prof. Dr. R. Ng. *Kapoestakan Djawi*. Djakarta, Djembatan, 1952

| **introduction** |

**Life is a journey**

That life is a journey is public knowledge. It is also public knowledge that history is the record of the life experiences of successive generations. And if ethnic groups and nations come together and exchange their experiences of life and their stories, passing them on when they returned home, the result is enrichment for all.

It is just like the files in a computer, which can be taken out or fitted together at will. That is why the literary works of art of the past were cast in the form of a frame story. *Serat Centhini* is no exception to that rule. The outer frame, taken from the *Babad Tanah Jawi* (The Chronicles of Java),[25] is the story of Sultan Agung and Sunan Giri Parapen. Within this frame, stories of the journeys of Sunan Giri's children are inserted. In turn, within the stories of their journeys, a plethora of legends, traditions and teachings of all kinds—ranging from how to behave properly in social gatherings to ways of attaining communion with The Supreme—are told. The sons and daughter of Sunan Giri—Jayengresmi, Jayengsari and Rancangkapti—are not mentioned in the *Babad Tanah Jawi* and so it can be definitely asserted that they are not historical figures, unlike Sunan Giri for whom there is much evidence attesting to his existence.

The experiences of life, however diverse, are in fact the experiences of mankind in the different stages of life, from the younger years up to the stage of searching for divine union (*artha, kama, dharmma* and *moksa*). It is with this in mind that I wrote this condensed version of *The Centhini Story*. The story—which charts not only the physical journey of two princes and a princess after their kingdom was invaded but also their spiritual and mental growth—is set out in three stages of life, which I have named 'The Pre-Adulthood Journey', 'The Adulthood Journey' and 'The Post-Adulthood Journey'. The presentation of the story is very different from the original work, which was not structured in this way as it was written in the form of poetry and song.

The Pre-Adulthood Journey is the journey of young travellers, young both in terms of age and their mental and spiritual development. In The Adulthood Journey, the main characters are grown up and we come across a greater variety of older travellers, each in different stages where the development of their soul is concerned. One might be older in terms of age but still spiritually less advanced than someone younger. In the third stage, The Post-Adulthood Journey, the travellers are physically advanced in age and their souls are highly developed. I have chosen to conclude *The Centhini Story* with a chapter I call 'The Arrival'. The final stage is not a journey anymore but the end of the journey or the point of arrival. It is, in other words, the meeting of the weary soul with The Supreme Soul or The Creator.

---

25  Meinsma, J. J. (ed). *Babad Tanah Djawi*. Den Haag, 1899–1903

# the pre-adulthood journey

- jayengresmi
- jayengsari and ni rancangkapti
- mas cabolang

### JAYENGRESMI: GIRI TO KARANG

1. Ruins of Majapahit kingdom
2. Naga temple, Panataran temple complex
3. Lodhaya forest
4. The water nymph
5. The battle of the dragon
6. Kyai Ageng Selo
7. Woro Surendro, the beauty of Prawoto
8. Grand Mosque of Demak
9. Kawisworo of Panegaran hermitage, Pekalongan harbour
10. Seh Sekardalimo, Slamet Mountain
11. Wasi Singgungkoro, Mount Cereme
12. The golden girl of Tampomas Mountain
13. Ki Ajar Sugandha of Mandalawangi, Mount Gede
14. The secret of longevity
15. Ruins of Pajajaran kingdom, Salak Mountain
16. Hermitage of Karang, Karang Mountain

### JAYENGSARI AND RANCANGKAPTI: GIRI TO PEKALONGAN TO SOKOYOSO

1. Kyai Amatsungeb
2. Baung Waterfall/Singosari temple/Kidal temple
3. Tosari and surroundings/Mount Bromo and Tengger area
4. Ki Ajar Satmoko, Semeru Mountain
5. Seh Wahdat, Argopuro Mountain
6. The holy virgin/the book *Kadis Markum Baslam*, Raung Mountain
7. Banyuwangi, the place of perfumed water, Ijen Mountain
8. Ki Hartati, the merchant from Pekalongan, Ragajampi harbour
9. Pekalongan
10. Dieng temples

**MAS CABOLANG:** SOKOYOSO TO WIROSOBO TO SOKOYOSO

1. The girls of Manut village
2. Ki Naradi, the hermit of Arjobinangun, Cilacap via Serayu River
3. The Wijoyokusumo flower, Nusakambangan island
4. How the Progo River got its name, Sindoro Mountain
5. The *bedoyo* pool, Mount Sumbing
6. The riddle in Tidar, Mount Tidar
7. Temples of Borobodur and Mendut
8. Mataram
9. Ki Ajar Sutiksno of Kepurun
10. Prambanan temple
11. Panembahan Romo and the stages of knowledge
12. Woods where the *kalang* people live
13. Tembayat
14. Pajang
15. Majasto
16. Girimarto
17. Sukuh temple, Lawu Mountain
18. Ponorogo
19. Selawung
20. Majenang, Wilis Mountain
21. Wirosobo (and back to Sokoyoso)

# Jayengresmi

FROM GIRI TO KARANG

It was evening. The night was young, just after the Isya (evening) prayer. The king, Sunan Giri Parapen, was sitting in the audience hall attended by his *santris* (disciples) and followers. Amongst them were Raden Jayengresmi, a son with one of his concubines, and Raden Endrasena, a student of Chinese descent.

Raden Endrasena had come to Giri kingdom from China with the intention of studying religion with Sunan Giri, who was known even in China as 'king of the religious saints of Java'. Together with some 200 men who accompanied him, he trained the *santris* of Giri in martial arts and they soon became a mighty defence force. So devoted and loyal was Endrasena that Sunan Giri regarded him as his own son and gave him control over the security force of the kingdom.

Raden Jayengresmi was also devoted to his father but in a different way. Already, at his young age, he was very well-versed in matters of religion. There was no question too difficult for him to answer and no element of religious service that he could not do to perfection, so that without doubt his devotion to God was showing in all his behaviour. He was so intelligent and wise that his father gave him the opportunity to assist him in the instruction of religion. That evening, he sat in front of his father with head bowed low as if touching the floor. He was very calm and there was no trace of anxiety on his face. Not so was Raden Endrasena, the hero of the victorious first clash of arms against the Mataram kingdom, who was glowing with confidence and pride.

Sunan Giri was in deep thought. He was despondent, but now and again his eyes flashed with pleasure. Now and then he looked at his son, his head bowed low; and then he turned to Endrasena, looking vigorous and powerful. What a difference between them—one so calm and peaceful, the other most forceful, almost fierce in his appearance. Deep down in his heart, he had the feelings of a king of faith. He knew he

opposite: *A mosque built on the ruins of the 15th-century Giri kingdom. Though not from the Giri period, the mosque is still used by the local people. The steps in the foreground lead to an ancient pool.*

held power—the power to determine the fate of his people as well as the power of faith that was capable of leading the world to its final goal.

Raden Jayengresmi lifted his head to glance at his father and said: "Milord, grant me permission to speak." Sunan Giri replied: "I give you permission to speak, my son. You look so gloomy even though with Allah's consent, we have broken the army of Mataram many times superior to ours." Jayengresmi continued: "Forgive me again, milord! In my opinion, this fighting between Giri and Mataram doesn't need to happen. Does milord forget the words of Sunan Ngampeldenta or does my honourable father forget his own prophecy passed on to Sultan Adiwijoyo of Pajang? Forgive me a thousand times, milord! I'm afraid you have transgressed your rights and squashed your own words. Furthermore, Pangeran (Prince) Pekik [of Mataram] is a descendant of Sunan Ngampeldenta and an emissary of the sultan of Mataram." He refrained from speaking further and bowed his head.

Sunan Giri was taken aback by those words, surprised that his son dared to speak so frankly. His words were most respectful, but they pierced sharper than a sword. Then he remembered clearly Sunan Ngampeldenta's message: "Sunan Setmata (Sunan Giri I) is allowed to establish himself as *raja waliyullah* (king of faith)." He recalled Sunan Setmata, also known as Sunan Giri Gajah Kedaton, ruling over the kingdom of Demak for forty days only to release the kingdom from unwanted influences of Hinduism and Buddhism. Sunan Giri also recalled plainly King Setmata passing the death sentence on Seh Siti Jenar for breaking the Islamic law. All these were done in the name of religion and conducted in his capacity as Defender of the Faith. Sunan Giri's own words of prophecy at the assembly of princes of Java resounded loudly in his ears—that with Allah's consent, the ruler of Mataram would conquer the whole realm of East Java including Giri.

far left: *The tomb of Sunan Giri Parapen in Sidomukti village, Gresik District, East Java. Hundreds of pilgrims visit his grave every day to pay their respects by reciting the holy Qur'an. The brick structures in the foreground are the remnants of graves.*
middle: *The entrance to Sunan Giri's tomb. In Java, the tombs of holy men deemed to have wielded great influence in spreading Islam were made to look stunning. Here, intricately carved wood painted in striking colours frame the entrance.*
left: *A view from the top of Giri Kedaton hill. The furthermost cluster of roofs is the Sunan Giri Tomb complex.*

Raden Endrasena, sensing a wavering in the king, spoke up: "Milord! I understand fully the words of Prince Jayengresmi, but I beg you not to hesitate. It is not the time for that. The battle and victory of yesterday showed that Allah is in favour of all your intentions. If evening had not fallen and we did not have to perform the Maghrib (sunset) prayer, I'm sure we would have defeated the army of Pangeran Pekik. Tomorrow, I will attack them again with might and means and even if they retreat to Mataram, I will go after them and hopefully capture Sultan Agung as well."

Sunan Giri became more and more perplexed. At length, he said to Raden Endrasena: "It is up to you and the people. I will comply with whatever you decide to do. But note that from now on, the city of Giri will be known as Sokaraja. I will now retire to the meditation room to implore God's order. Dismiss the audience and always be on guard." Raden Endrasena perceived the king's last order as approval for him to destroy the troops of Mataram. To him, the change of name from Giri to Sokaraja also confirmed that the king was on his side. Instead of returning home to rest, he made further preparations for battle the next day.

Raden Jayengresmi, however, felt differently. He believed that his father, in wanting to acquire worldly power, had undermined his religious position as 'king of saints'. He also believed that his father was delighted with their victory over Pangeran Pekik, since he took Sokaraja to mean 'the city (*raja*) of joy (*soka*)', referring to the previous day's victory. Inside him, a battle waged between his love for his parents and his love for God, The Creator and Sustainer of the World. He loved his parents because they raised him with care and love. So his love for them was based on obligation and gratitude. Furthermore, God has enjoined children to love their parents, especially their mother. To him, his love for God was the highest goal of existence; how sinful it would be if he left his parents. In his view, his father had taken the wrong path, one that would lead the entire family to deny God's decree and cause him to break his own prophecy. Does he have to obey his father? No! He will go and leave infamy but will stay devoted to his parents and pray for their well-being and God's forgiveness wherever he may be. "My Lord, grant me good guidance. Grant peace and well-being to my parents. Bestow on them Your mercy." His prayers kept his lips wet and his strides steady to leave the bloodbath that was to come.

Let us return to the king who had confined himself in his meditation room, praying to God for His mercy and direction. He was in gloom, which was why he renamed the city of Giri to Sokaraja. The word *soka* means 'gloom' or 'despair', although both Endrasena and Jayengresmi took it as synonymous with *suka*, which means 'joy'. They thought Sunan Giri was happy when he changed the city's name. While Endrasena took it as an approval of his gallant exploits and achievement, Jayengresmi saw it as uncharacteristic of a religious saint. And while Endrasena prepared his troops for battle, Jayengresmi fled the city, cutting off all ties with his parents and family, though with a bleeding heart.

Outside the palace walls, the impending conflict made the common people fearful. One man gathered his family and left the city with belongings packed in bundles. On seeing him, his neighbours followed suit. In no time throngs of men, women and children were leaving the city to escape the approaching war and brutal rampaging looters.On the street, three *santris* were seen running, two to the east and the third in the opposite direction. They met at a crossroad. Buras, the oldest of the disciples, asked: "There you are, Gathak and Gathuk! I'm looking for Master Jayengsari and Mistress Rancangkapti. Do you know where they are?" They answered: "No, brother! We are looking for Master Jayengresmi. People say he went westward on his own." Said Buras: "Quick! Go west after him. I will look for the young masters." Even without Buras' advice, they would have gone that way, not only out of fear but also by instinct for they came from Cirebon, a place far, far west of Giri.

In the middle of a forest stood a leafy banyan tree. There was neither grass nor undergrowth beneath it, only a few flat stones neatly grouped together as if prepared for weary wayfarers. On one of the stones sat a man. Judging by his clothes, it was clear he was from the upper class. He looked dejected, but his eyes shone with the peace of having surrendered to God. He was Raden Jayengresmi. He had walked more than half a day with no particular direction in mind, just going where his feet took him. In the beginning, when he was still wavering between his love for his family and his devotion to God, his steps were uncertain. He walked aimlessly through the streets of Giri, but the moment he decided to leave his lot in God's hands, he took the only one direction he knew—to the west, towards the *kiblah* (direction of the Ka'bah in Mecca).

He had entered the forest at the crack of dawn, welcomed by the warble of fowl and birds singing the glory of the day. He was tired by the time he came across the banyan tree and the flat stones seemed to invite him to take a rest. He chose the biggest stone so that he could sit cross-legged. Uttering the word of gratitude *Alhamdulillah* (God be

above: *A forested area on Giri Kedaton hill.*

Praised!), he sat facing the *kiblah*. In an instant, he plunged into silent remembrance of God and his limbs relaxed. His lips, initially whispering the *istighfar* (plea for forgiveness), gradually ceased to move when he fell into deep meditation.

Gathak and Gathuk happened to wander into the same forest. Once in a while, they called out their master's name, their only refuge: "Master Jayengresmi! Help us! We are lost!" At other times, they supplicated to God: "O God, let us find our master." Their cries and prayers were carried by the wind and bounced back and forth by the trees. Whether it was an act of nature or God's intercession, at length their cries reached Raden Jayengresmi and woke him up from his meditation. By concentrating his mind fully, he guided his attendants to the shadows of the banyan tree.

"Master, finally... we find you! Don't ever leave us again! Wherever you go, let us always be with you. Don't leave us behind. Not ever!" Gasping for breath, they stumbled to where their master was seated. Said Raden Jayengresmi: "Gathak and Gathuk, be calm. Praise God with gratitude and ask for His mercy". They fell to the ground moaning: "*Alhamdulillah*! O God, forgive us!" Raden Jayengresmi left them lying there, knowing that they had fainted from excitement and relief. Since their arrival at Giri, they had been his attendants. They served him night and day with sincerity, learnt to read and understand the Qur'an and prayed at the mosque with him. It was not surprising that they were so attached to him.

The sun was already leaning to the west when Gathak and Gathuk began to stir. Before even opening their eyes, they complained in unison: "I'm starving!" Gathak sat

## the pre-adulthood journey

up suddenly and exclaimed: "Gathuk! Where are we? Why are we here? We haven't been here before!" Gathuk also jumped up, but he was unable to reply and just ran to and fro. Finally they became aware of the presence of their master, who was still sitting calmly on the stone. They fell down on their knees and said: "Master! Where are we? We're starving, our tummies are rumbling all the time!" Raden Jayengresmi said: "Gathak and Gathuk! Be calm and sit down. I will tell you where we are." Gathak sat in an instant but not Gathuk who was still standing and complained: "Brother Gathak, how can I sit down? If I sit down, I might never be able to get up again. I'm so hungry!" Jayengresmi advised: "God The Merciful is the best Provider for all His devotees, even in this forest. If you make use of your nose, you will find food. Now leave. Use your nose and eyes." Said Gathuk: "Brother Gathak, the master is always right. Now I can smell durians, mangosteens, mangoes." Gathak warned: "Be careful, Gathuk. Tigers usually keep watch for ripe durians." Replied Gathuk: "Tigers? Hah! If I meet one now, how unlucky it will be! It won't be the tiger that eats me. I will devour him raw, flesh and bones. I'm starving, you hear?" They left to look for the aromatic durian. Not only did they find durians but also mangoes, star fruits and rambutans, which they gathered for their master. Gathak placed some fruit on a banana leaf and offered them to Jayengresmi, who took a star fruit and two rambutans. Apparently, it was enough to quench his thirst and still his hunger.

Then Raden Jayengresmi spoke again: "Now, tell me what has happened to my brother and sister and why you have come to look for me." Gathak said: "Have mercy, master! After Jeng Sunan retired to the meditation room, Raden Endrasena made preparations for the battle for the following morning, the final showdown with the army of Mataram. The people were confused and started to leave the city. We looked for you everywhere. Someone told us you didn't return from the audience." Gathuk interrupted: "We wanted to be with you, master. On the crossroad, we met brother Buras. He told us to go west after you while he looks for master Jayengsari and mistress Rancangkapti in their rooms. When we reached the outskirts of the city, shots were cracking and the battle was already underway. We didn't find any food on the way; everybody looked after themselves. We only drank water from the vessels along the road." Gathuk related his own sufferings and was almost in tears when he recalled how hungry he had been. He wanted to stop, he said, but fear kept him going. Gathak added: "We stopped for a while to rest because Gathuk couldn't go further. So many people were leaving the city. When I turned back to look at Giri, the sky was red and smoke was whirling to the sky. People said Giri was on fire and the battle had started. We decided to leave the main road and look for you in the forest."

Raden Jayengresmi was deeply moved by their sufferings. But his heart bled when he heard that the city was ablaze and the people were

running in confusion to escape the devastation. He mumbled to himself: "The strive for worldly power and wealth always brings destruction and distress to the common people." His head hung lower and lower, his lips breathing the *istighfar*. When he looked up, his attendants had finished eating and he said: "Gathak and Gathuk! Let's go!" "Where to, master?" they asked. Raden Jayengresmi replied with determination: "To the direction of the Ka'bah, the place of security."

## 1 The ruins of Majapahit in Mojokerto

After walking for several hours, they arrived at the ruins of the ancient capital city of Majapahit. They entered a portal and inspected what was left of the buildings. At length, they sat near a pond enclosed by a wall of stones. The water was flowing over, as if telling them that the time for the Asyar (late afternoon) prayer had come. After washing their hands, face and feet, Gathuk made the call to prayer and they then recited verses from the Qur'an by heart.

The call to prayer was heard by Ki Parwa, caretaker of the ruins. After exchanging salutations with the visitors, he related a little of the history of the place they were in. The pond was the bathing place of the princess of Campa, the queen of King Brawijaya. Pointing out her grave, he explained that she had converted to Islam. Ki Parwa then brought them to the Brahu temple, adding quietly: "This is where King Brawijaya used to pray. There is a full moon tonight and it is a very propitious moment to meditate on The Supreme." Since early that evening, the princess of the night had shown her glory, first thrusting through the leafy tops of the trees and when she reached the higher spheres, nothing could stop her from penetrating every niche and corner of the temple.

below left: *A view of Wringin Lawang Gate in Trowulan, Mojokerto, East Java. Located in Jatipasar village, it is believed to have been the gateway to the capital of the Majapahit kingdom and is one of many ancient remains found scattered in different villages in Trowulan District. Its construction resembles a temple split in two, with a path through the middle.*
below right: *Detail of Wringin Lawang Gate.*

# the pre-adulthood journey

The atmosphere was mystical and sublime. Raden Jayengresmi agreed to spend the night there. It was dawn when he finally came out of the temple. He took leave from Ki Parwa and continued his journey.

## 2 The Naga temple of the Panataran temple complex

They walked for hours and stopped only when they came across a temple complex near Panataran village at the foot of Kelud Mountain. The main temple was lofty, consisting of terraced structures built on top of one another, with the topmost structure at the eastern end. The walls were engraved with scenes from the Rama story, including that of the monkey army building a bridge to span the sea between India and the island of Ceylon, called Langka in the story and the seat of the demon tyrant Rawana.

One of the smaller temples was the Naga (Dragon) temple, so called because of

top left: *Segaran Pool in Segaran village, Trowulan District. The pool was part of the Majapahit kingdom's irrigation system, which included a network of dams and canals. The water comes from a spring located on the southern side.*

top right: *The tomb of the princess of Campa, Segaran village. Dating to AD 1448, historians believe it to be the grave of a princess from Champa (today's Cambodia and Vietnam), who married the last king of Majapahit. The tomb is located at the eastern end of Segaran Pool.*

bottom: *The Brahu temple. It is believed the cremations of several of Majapahit's rulers, including that of King Brawijaya, were carried out here. Made of brick and reaching a height of 16 metres, it was built some time during the Majapahit era (13th to 15th century).*

a huge dragon engraved on its walls. It was so huge that it surrounded the body of the temple. There is a story in the *Mahabharata* of deities and demons churning the milk-sea to find the *amreta* (elixir of life). To churn the sea, they used the Mandhara Mountain as the rod and the dragon Basuki as the rope to spin the mountain. The deities placed themselves at the tail end of the dragon, leaving the demons no choice but to take their place at its head. After much churning, a nymph appeared with the *amreta* in a jar. The Naga temple is a replica of Mandhara Mountain and every year, the king of Majapahit would stay in the temple and meditate in front of a jar of water. His meditations transformed the water into the elixir of life, which would be released into streams throughout the whole kingdom for the people to enjoy its benefits.

Another small temple of some import is the 'temple with the date'. It is called thus because an engraving of the Javanese year 1292 AJ can be seen just above the entrance. The date presents some important clues for historians and archaeologists.

left: *The Candi Naga (Dragon Temple) is one of many temples in the Panataran temple complex, the largest and most important Hindu temple complex in East Java. Covering almost 1.3 square kilometres in Panataran village, the complex is dedicated to the god Shiva.*

right: *The temple with the date, also called 'the dated temple'. This is one of the more prominent buildings in the Panataran temple complex. The Javanese date of 1292 AJ, engraved above the entrance, translates to the year AD 1370.*

## 3 Kyai Gaprang and the forest of Lodhaya

Raden Jayengresmi left the Panataran temple complex with mixed feelings and a discomfort created by the loss of the grandeur of the past blended with his own uncertain future. After a long walk, they came to the village of Gaprang, named after two statues that stood alongside a road. Now, Kyai Gaprang—holding his huge phallus, a symbol fertility and longevity—and his wife Nyai Gaprang are seen to represent the male and female principle. The union of the two was regarded as beneficial for the whole community. Hence, people came from far and wide to pay homage and give offerings in return for a good harvest or a child or two. Gathak and Gathuk seemed very much impressed with what they saw but kept silent because they could not imagine how the worship of the phallus could bring about an abundant crop.

Moving on, they reached the forest of Lodhaya and entered it. There, in its midst, they found a structure with walls of plaited bamboo and a thatch roof. Inside it was a gong called Kyai Pradhah. They met the caretaker who explained that the instrument

was always included in the gamelan orchestra, which would be played at wedding feasts or celebrations commemorating the birth of a son. People revered and feared Kyai Pradhah, believing that its exclusion from the orchestra would lead to some sort of calamity.

Leaving the forest, they soon came to a village called Pakel. It was almost twilight and they decided to spend the night in a hut. Nearby was a pond with water so clear it seemed to invite them to purify themselves for the evening prayer. Soon Gathuk made the call to prayer, but he felt strangely uneasy and dared not raise his voice too loudly. After prayers and as he and Gathak were resting, they heard voices outside. But when they looked out, all they saw were tigers sleeping on the ground. Trembling with fright, they approached their master and whispered: "Master, we are doomed! We are surrounded by tigers. There is no escape. If the tigers come inside they will surely attack us and we will become a mass of flesh and blood!" Raden Jayengresmi countered: "Gathak and Gathuk! Where is your faith in God The Almighty? Nothing can happen without His consent and He is the best Protector of the faithful. So don't worry, go to sleep. I will keep the watch." They returned to their sleeping place, not daring to make a sound or move a muscle. Raden Jayengresmi did not sleep but stayed awake, praying for their well-being and that of his parents, brother and sister. The night passed uneventfully.

The next morning, Gathak and Gathuk heard voices again, but this time there was no trace of sleeping tigers. Instead they saw three men talking among themselves. Shortly after, they had a visit from Ki Carita, the village chief. He had heard from the men about the visitors' stay in the hut and concluded that they were of good lineage and great spiritual power. After exchanging salutations, Ki Carita introduced himself: "Master! I am Ki Carita, the village chief. I'm extremely amazed to hear that you stayed

far left: *The statues of Kyai and Nyai Gaprang in Gaprang village, Kanigoro District, East Java.*
middle: *The annual bathing ritual of Kyai Pradhah Gong in Sutojayan village, Blitar Regency. The man in the centre is holding the sacred gong. This ritual commemorates the 1st of Suro, the Javanese New Year, a day considered sacred by many Javanese. Bathing the gong in flowered water and incense is believed to ward off disease and misfortune for society. The tradition is believed to have been founded by a respected ancestor called Pangeran Prabu.*
left: *After the bathing ritual, the gong is kept in a special room in this house. Note the stone tigers that guard the house.*

in the hut. Very few people are brave enough to spend the night here. Please accept the food I bring for you as a token of welcome and respect." Raden Jayengresmi replied: "Well, Ki Carita! We are wandering *santris* from Giri and I thank you heartily for your welcome and the delicious meal."

As they ate, he asked Ki Carita about two bundles that he saw hanging in the hut. The village chief explained that they contain clothes believed to be the property of Nyai Loro Kidul, the Queen of the South Seas.[1] About the tigers in the night, he said: "They are the Queen's attendants. They take the form of humans during the day but at night appear as tigers and guard the hut." He then pointed to a *pakel* (a fruit, like a mango) tree that grew in front of the hut and said: "That tree was planted by the king of Mataram, Panembahan Senopati. Every time it bears fruit, the fruit would be presented to the king of Mataram. That is also why this village is called the village of Pakel."

## 4 The water nymph

The sun was only a pole-length high when Raden Jayengresmi and his attendants took leave from Ki Carita. They travelled in a northeast direction and stopped at Tuban at midday to pray. They rested under a tall *kapok* (silk-cotton) tree near a well. When Raden Jayengresmi approached the well to take ablution, the water in it swelled up to overflowing but settled back to its previous level when he finished washing. After prayers, they continued on their journey in a northwest direction.

---

1 In the story 'The Battle of the Dragon' (p44–48), Nyai Loro Kidul is known as Ratu Angin-angin, the Queen of the South Ocean, which presently is known as the Indian Ocean. She is known as Nyai Loro Kidul in the story 'Preparations for the Wedding' (p102–103). In the story about Mount Dlepih (p254–255), she also reigns over the South Ocean and is known as Nyai Ratu Kidul.

At nightfall, they stopped when they came to a pond retained by a wall of yellow stones. Raden Jayengresmi decided to rest there because the pond reminded him of his younger sister, Rancangkapti, who would swim in a pond similar to it. That night, the memory of her kept him awake. To while away the time, he started to meditate, rightly entering into deep remembrance of The Almighty. Suddenly, there appeared before him a beautiful lady dressed in ancient court clothes. Greeting him with folded hands, she said: "Milord, have mercy on me. Your prayers have disturbed my attendants. They become restless and nervous." He asked her: "Milady, who are you?" The lady replied: "I am the daughter of the late King Brawijaya of Majapahit, Ratu Mas Trengganawulan by name. As I could not embrace the new religion, The Supreme Deity appointed me to be the guardian of the spirits of the Bagor forest and its surroundings. This pond is my bathing place."

In the morning, Gathak and Gathuk asked their master: "Master, we heard you speaking with someone last night. Who was it?" Replied Raden Jayengresmi: "It was Princess Trengganawulan, the nymph of the pond. She is the guardian of the forest of Bagor and its surroundings. Let us do the Subuh (morning) prayer and then prepare to leave."

## 5 The battle of the dragon

Without wasting any time they set off, traversing plains and rivers and penetrating undergrowth. They were in the district of Grobogan in Central Java when they met an old man in a forest clearing. On his shoulders were bamboo containers filled with unfermented palm juice. Feeling thirsty, Gathak and Gathuk approached the man, who introduced himself as Ki Jatipitutur, chief of Kesanga village. Raden Jayengresmi asked him: "Brother! Do you have any stories to tell about this area?" He replied there were and began to tell the story of King Joko, the bachelor king who ruled over the kingdom of Mendhangkamulan:

❁ *One day, as King Joko was hunting in the woods alone, he came across a dragon doing penance. Not pleased with what he saw, he shot the dragon with an arrow and it died instantly. Then he heard a voice from nowhere, saying: "Well, King Joko! I admit you are a powerful king, but your temper does not befit you. You will be punished by the Supreme Lord for killing me." The voice fell silent and together with it the corpse of the dragon vanished. Nature responded in uproar—rain and hail fell in torrents, trees were uprooted and rivers swelled and rumbled like thunder.*

*The young king ran to and fro looking for shelter. In the end he came to a village called Sangkeh, where the widow Kasiyan and her young daughter Dyah Rarasati lived. As suddenly as it fell, the rain stopped. The sun came* up, its light glittering in the pools of water and creating a magical display, which attracted the king's attention. Just then, Dyah Rarasati came out of the house. She had no make-up on her face, yet she was glowing. Her slim body was neither short nor tall, just the right height, and her brown skin glowed in the sun's rays. She walked to the barn and joined the womenfolk who were pounding rice. Without uttering a word, she took a pounder and joined them at the pounding block. As she placed her left leg on a sack of rice, the lower part of her sarong rode up her legs and exposed her legs. The young king was so fascinated by the sight that he unconsciously murmured the asmaragama formula (spell for the art of sexual relations). The king and the girl ejaculated at the same time. Rarasati's pet hen then pecked at the fallen sperm, which united with Rarasati's egg inside the hen. When the king came to his senses, he felt embarrassed with his inability to control his emotions. Feeling dejected and ashamed of himself, he returned to his home.

The hen laid an egg, which Kasiyan kept in a rice basket. Every day she would take some rice from the basket to cook, but strangely instead of being depleted, there would always be more rice in there. Believing the egg to be a magical one and hoping for the same effect, she brought it to the rice barn and placed it on top of a heap of rice. She became most hopeful when she discovered that the rice basket was not as full as before and assumed the barn would be

left: *The dragon symbol engraved on the door of Sunan Giri's tomb. The* naga *or dragon is a mythical serpent in Javanese belief and is usually represented in respected and sacred places such as temples and tombs. Note the shape of the Javanese dragon, which is different from the dragons of Chinese and Indian folklore.*

*filled with rice.* But what a surprise she had when she went to the barn. There, on top of the rice, was a huge dragon. Before she could run away, the dragon spoke: "Mother Kasiyan, do not be afraid. I will do you no harm. Go to the king and tell him what has happened. He should know what to do." So the widow and her daughter, with the dragon not far behind, went to the chief minister who was not amused by what he heard. But what could he do except to report the episode to the king?

King Joko was sitting on the verandah of his palace enjoying his breakfast when he saw the procession coming his way. On seeing the dragon at the back, his first thought was that it had taken his chief minister and the ladies hostage and he became angry. Aiming his bow and arrow at the dragon, he barked: "What's this... a dragon taking my people hostage?" The chief minister then said: "Milord, this dragon wants me to bring him to your presence. He says he has some information to give milord." Retorted the king: "What, a dragon talking like a human? What an outrage!"

The dragon started to talk: "Pardon me a thousand times, sire, if your humble servant makes this commotion. I do not want to create any confusion but just to have an audience with you, milord!" King Joko said: "You speak well. Make it short and then leave or I will kill you." Making a homage-like gesture, the dragon said: "Milord, I am your son." He then related the whole story, beginning with the king killing a dragon, his visit to the widow Kasiyan's village and his uncommon experience with the girl.

In his heart, the king admitted that the dragon had told the truth, but he had to save face in front of his people. So he said: "Your story is really outrageous. It's impossible for human beings to have an animal as a son. However, God is Omnipotent and I am a great king who protects his subjects. I will say this: I will acknowledge you as my son if you can fulfil two conditions—kill my enemy, the white crocodile of the South Ocean, and find my future queen. Go now and do not cause any harm to my subjects." The dragon replied respectfully: "Milord, give me your blessings. I will rather die and be smashed into a thousand pieces than return without proving the truth of my words. I ask your leave now." And he disappeared in an instant.

The dragon made his way below ground only to reappear at the coast of the South Ocean where he thunderously announced his presence and challenged the white crocodile to meet him in a duel to the death. The crocodile was the manifestation of King Dewatacengkar, who having been defeated by King Joko was flung into the depths of the South Ocean. There, he was transformed into a vicious white crocodile. On hearing the dragon declare that he was the son of his foe, the crocodile emerged from the water and a terrible fight quickly ensued. For days and weeks they fought with all their might and means, yet not one of them seemed to get the upper hand. The fury of the fight did not escape the attention of the Queen of the South Ocean, Queen Ratu Angin-angin, who showed up to watch the duel. She had vowed to crown as king for a certain period whoever could kill the crocodile. For days and weeks they fought without resting even for one minute. In the end the crocodile—which was much older than the dragon—was defeated and turned into a hill, called Argalima Mountain.

Queen Angin-angin was delighted with the outcome and addressed the dragon kindly: "Well, my son! I have vowed that whoever can kill my enemy, the white crocodile, will be crowned ruler of my realm for a while. As you are the winner, I will give you my daughter Nyai Blorong as wife and declare you King of the South Ocean." But the dragon replied: "Milady! I am a messenger of King Joko, who has ordered me to kill the white crocodile and find his future queen. I've only accomplished the first task and so cannot accept your generous offer." The queen continued: "My dear son, you have proved yourself to be a worthy and obedient son of King Joko. Do not worry. I am decreed by The Supreme Lord to be the King's future queen. So you have fulfilled your objectives. Now I will declare you as King of the South Ocean and give you the name Joko Linglung Tunggulwulung. Marry my daughter and live happily for

left: *Bleduk Kuwu geyser in Kuwu village, Central Java. It erupts in an explosion of mud, followed by a plume of white steam every one or two minutes, bringing up salty, yellowish water from the bowels of the Earth. According to legend, the geyser is connected to the Indian Ocean in the southern coast of central Java. People believe this is the spot where Joko Linglung emerged after meeting Queen Angin-angin on the southern coast.*

*a few months. Then leave her here and return to your father. Report everything to him and tell him that I am waiting for his call."*

*The coronation and wedding took place soon after. At the appropriate time, Joko Linglung took leave to return to King Joko. Queen Angin-angin said: "It will be better for you to travel alone so leave your wife here for the time being. Do not return the way you came. Take another route!" Joko Linglung agreed and soon he was on his way, passing underground through the regions of Pasundan, Kuwu, Crewek and Mendhikil. As he neared the city of Mendhangkamulan, he continued his journey overland. When he met King Joko, the king acknowledged him as his son and gave him the region of Tunggulwulung to rule over. And like all fairy tales, the dragon and his wife ended up living happily ever after.*

The following morning, Ki Jatipitutur accompanied Raden Jayengresmi to see what was left of Joko Linglung's home in Tunggulwulung. Said Jayengresmi: "My brother, I am very thankful to you. Your friendship has helped me become aware of God's mercy and kindness. But the time to part has arrived and I beg your leave." Ki Jatipitutur replied: "I am the one who should thank you for keeping me company. It's not very often that I get visitors to share my solitary life in this lonely forest. I wish you a fruitful journey ahead."

## 6 The teachings and prowess of Kyai Ageng Selo

It was dark when they arrived at the village of Selo and the right thing to do was to look for a place to spend the night. They went straight to the house of the caretaker of the royal graves of Selo. His name was Ki Pariworo and he received them warmly.

The next morning, Ki Pariworo told Raden Jayengresmi: "I am a great grandson of Ki Ageng Getaspandowo and that is why I was appointed by the sultan of Mataram as caretaker of the heritage of the Mataram dynasty." Raden Jayengresmi said: "Then I have come to the right person. Please share with me the teachings of the esteemed ancestors so that I may find some guidance in life."

Ki Pariworo said: "Well, many of the teachings come from Kyai Ageng Selo. The teachings are called *pepali*, meaning 'words of advice to be taken into account for a peaceful life'. There are too many to mention them all and also, some of them are too difficult to carry out in life. So I think it's good enough to select a few—for instance, be kind to others; do not be vainglorious; do not be greedy for worldly things; do not be quarrelsome—and practise them as much as possible.

"You should know that a real man is one who is always considerate and whose actions are not obvious because he is aware of his kindred around. 'Kindred' is, in fact, the whole world, the entire creation of God. Furthermore, we should regard ourselves like the leaves that float on the surface of the ocean; wherever the current flows, we

follow suit. There is no place for personal wishes or desires. That is the metaphor for man and his Creator. Man should not follow his own passions but put his trust in God's hands and follow the principles set out in the holy Book."

After a while, Raden Jayengresmi asked: "I heard that Ki Ageng Selo was eminently powerful. Be so kind to tell me more." Ki Pariworo said: "Ki Ageng Selo used to work in the fields after the late afternoon prayer. He was in the field one fine cloudless day when the weather suddenly changed. It began to drizzle and the sky clapped with lightning and rolled with thunder. Suspicious about the strange occurrence, he prepared himself. When lightning flashed again, he uttered *Subhanallah* (Glory be to Allah). An old man appeared out of nowhere and attacked him furiously. He grabbed the man and tied him to a *gandri* tree (a durable hardwood tree used as building material). The man tried to escape but could not and was put into an ironclad jail in the capital city of Demak. Some days later, the man's wife visited him. Carrying a vessel containing water, she threw the vessel against the wall. There was a terrible explosion and the old couple disappeared. The story goes that Ki Ageng Selo had captured thunder. Up till today, the *gandri* tree still emits fire and people are advised to take the flame home to protect against the attacks of thunder. Even the king of Mataram keeps a flame from the tree in his palace and if it happens to go out, he will make sure it is replaced. I myself have personally brought the flame to the palace."

Raden Jayengresmi stayed with Ki Pariworo to listen to all his teachings. When the time came for him to leave, he expressed his heartfelt gratitude to the priest and continued with his journey.

above (both): *The grave of Kyai Ageng Selo in Selo village, Tawangharjo District, Central Java. Pilgrims visit the grave, mostly on Thursday nights, to pay their respects as well as to ask for blessings. Ki Ageng Selo is also believed to be the great ancestor of the kings of the Mataram kingdom, which was the predecessor of the Surakarta and Yogyakarta kingdoms. As such, members of the Surakarta royal family still visit the grave before any ceremony to ask for blessings.*

# the pre-adulthood journey

right: *The engravings on this door panel show Kyai Ageng Selo capturing thunder. The panel was once the door of the Demak Mosque, but it has since been removed and is now displayed in the Demak Mosque Museum located inside the mosque complex. A copy of the panel now fronts the mosque entrance.*

## 7 Woro Surendro, the beauty of Prawoto

Raden Jayengresmi and his companions strode fast towards the northeast. The sun was peeping over the horizon, creeping wearily along the mountain slopes as if not fully awake. Their journey took them across paddy fields into leafy woodlands and through swampy wetlands until they reached the slopes of a mountain in the region of Undakan. From there, they could see the village of Prawoto, but it would only be in the early evening when they reached it. At Prawoto, they stopped at a pool, took ablution and performed the late afternoon prayer. Raden Jayengresmi then sat under a tree, while his companions massaged his legs and sang hymns softly.

The head of the village of Prawoto was Ki Darmojati. His wife was Nyai Darmowati. Their daughter, Woro Surendro, was slim and shapely and walked in a most elegant manner. Not surprisingly, her name was on every young man's lips and she was known as the beauty of Prawoto. That evening, she was at the field picking vegetables and fruit; her basket was already filled with chillies, string beans, star fruit and mulberries. Sweat flowed down her flushed cheeks but did not make her less beautiful. Instead, she looked more radiant. Ni Woro did not go straight home but went to the pool to wash the food. To her surprise, she saw three men sitting at the edge of the pool. As if she had seen the devil itself, she turned around and quickly ran home. Before she could reach the front door, she called out: "Father, there are three men at the pool." Without stopping, she ran straight to the kitchen. Ki Darmojati followed her and said: "It looks like we will have guests. Prepare dinner and you, Menok (as her parents call her), pick up some fruit while it is still light." Replied Woro: "I have done so, father. I will help mother in the kitchen."

At the pool, Raden Jayengresmi asked Gathak and Gathuk: "Why did you shout out just now?" They replied: "Oh, master! It was an overwhelming sight. A very beautiful girl appeared, but she ran away. We believe she might be the pool fairy or a famous dancer." Just then, they heard footsteps and Ki Darmojati appeared in front of them and introduced himself: "Welcome, master! My name is Darmojati and I am the village chief of Prawoto. Be so kind as to let me know your name. Perhaps I can be of some help." Raden Jayengresmi said: "Uncle, my name is Jayengresmi. I'm a *santri* from Giri and these are my companions, Gathak and Gathuk." Ki Darmojati replied: "Well, sir, the sun has almost set. If you don't mind, please spend the night with me and my family at our humble place." Asked Jayengresmi: "Uncle, is your house the one with the huge portal?" Ki Darmojati said: "No, sir. That is the former palace of Sultan Prawoto of Demak. This village is named after him. He had two palaces, one in the city of Demak and the other in this village. During the rainy season, Demak floods over and the king would reside here in Prawoto." Jayengresmi said: "Uncle Darmojati, I thank you very much for your invitation. Since there is still time, I would like to see the palace grounds first." Ki Darmojati obliged and took them to the palace.

After the evening prayer, they sat in the *pendopo* (front hall) where they enjoyed drinks and snacks served by Nyi Darmowati and Woro Surendro. After introducing his family to the guests, Ki Darmojati asked his daughter to welcome Raden Jayengresmi and seek his blessings for a good husband." Jayengresmi thought to himself: "This girl is extremely beautiful and she reminds me of Rancangkapti." She approached him with folded hands and spoke: "Master, welcome to this humble place and I beg your blessings." Jayengresmi answered: "Thank you for your welcome, Woro, and may The Almighty grant you a handsome and caring husband."

above (both): The Grand Mosque of Demak. The mosque stands as a symbol of the founding of Java's first Islamic kingdom by Sultan Raden Patah at the end of the 15th century and is where the walis (saints) discussed many subjects. According to legend, it was built by the Wali Songo (Nine Saints of Java) in one night through supernatural powers. Some 2,000 people visit the mosque compound every day to pray, except during the fasting month of Ramadhan.

left: The Bobot (heavy) Stone. The base is made of rock so heavy that no one has been able to lift it. The stone is believed to have been made by Sunan Kalijogo, one of the Wali Songo, for the Demak Mosque. However, it was not used as the building of the mosque had been completed by the time it was made. By virtue of it being made by a saint, it is considered sacred and so people place offerings on it.

## 8 Demak Mosque, the first mosque built by the saints of Java

They talked until dawn broke. Leaving the company of his hosts, Raden Jayengresmi and his attendants proceeded to the mosque of Demak. It was Java's first mosque and one built by Moslem saints. There were many people around, but no one recognised him as the son of Sunan Giri. Feeling relieved, he went straight to the verandah where eight ornamental pillars from Majapahit stood. The portal of the mosque was engraved with a chronogram, which read *kori roro gawening wong* (two doors built by a man) and indicating the year 1429 AJ in the Javanese calendar. There was also a relief, in gold, of a bolt of lightning on the door of the mosque; it was a *sengkalan memet* (concealed chronogram), which read *papatra kinarya rupa gelap* (a graphic design portraying a bolt of lightning) and rendering the year 1441 AJ, which was found under the door.

When they entered the mosque, they felt serene and a sense of devotion towards The Almighty welled up within them. Inside were four main pillars, each two fathoms in diameter and very tall. The northeast pillar was peculiar; it was made of wood cuttings bound together and believed to be the work of a Moslem saint called Sunan Kalijogo. Just then, Raden Jayengresmi saw reed grass growing under the pulpit, which no one else could see. He was very much touched, as it was a sign from God about his future.

## 9 The sage Kawisworo of Panegaran hermitage

From Demak, the *santris* proceeded to Mount Murya to visit the tomb of the saint Sunan Murya, which people called the Muryapada grave. They stayed one night with the caretaker and in the morning, took leave and headed for the port of Pekalongan.

After a long walk, they saw boats and other kinds of vessels loading and unloading goods. Raden Jayengresmi hoped to see his brother and sister disembarking from one of the boats, but they were nowhere to be seen. He felt empty inside and whispered: "My brother and sister, where are you now? My Lord, have mercy on them. Let me meet them. *Amin* (Amen)." He wandered listlessly away from the shore, stopping only at night and leaving early in the morning without any particular destination in mind. He and his attendants walked until they arrived at the foot of Mount Panegaran.

It so happened that the sage Kawisworo was sitting on the verandah of his house when he had the sudden feeling that visitors were heading his way. He reflected deeply for a moment and saw in his mind Raden Jayengresmi wandering aimlessly at the foot of the mountain. He ordered his student Wasistho to invite them to stop by. Wasistho hurried down the hill and spoke respectfully to Raden Jayengresmi: "Well, sir! My guru is the sage Kawisworo of Panegaran hermitage. He knows about your circumstance and invites you to come by." Jayengresmi agreed and together, they climbed up the steep pathway to the hermitage.

When they reached the gate, the hermit was there waiting and he said: "My son, I know you are not happy. What is it that worries you so much? I think it is best for you to stay here with me for a while to calm down. Perhaps together we can pray for a favourable solution." Raden Jayengresmi paid homage with folded hands and said: "Reverend guru! I'm very worried about my brother and sister. When Giri fell, I was separated from them and have not heard anything about them since."

They stayed at the hermitage for some days, receiving knowledge from the reverend priest. One day, the hermit said: "My son, the time for you to leave has come. Go south to Mount Slamet. There you will find Seh Sekardalimo, a son of the last king of Majapahit, who has already embraced the Moslem faith. He was a student of the late Sunan of Tembayat, who in turn was a student of Sunan Kalijogo." Jayengresmi replied: "Reverend guru, thank you so much for your hospitality and for your teachings. I will leave right away with your blessings."

## 10 Seh Sekardalimo and the execution of Seh Lemah-abang

Over on Mount Slamet and sitting by the edge of a pond was Seh Sekardalimo with his students, Ki Maklum and Ki Sabar. Nearby was a mosque, surrounded by flowers in full bloom. Seh Sekardalimo said to his students: "Well, Maklum and Sabar. Clean the mosque and spread out the best mats you can find because soon we will have a very important guest." He had not long to wait as Raden Jayengresmi appeared a moment later. Seh Sekardalimo beckoned the *santris* to approach closer. Jayengresmi stepped forward and made homage with folded hands. Seh Sekardalimo said: "My son, I greet you. I have been waiting for you for some time." Jayengresmi replied: "Thank you, reverend guru! I beg for your blessings so that I will be able to carry out everything you instruct me to do." Seh Sekardalimo continued: "My son, whatever you do, do so with care and patience. Do not forget to do your supplications to God The Almighty and pray for His mercy. Your prayers will be accepted when the moment is right. Now, I will tell you about what my late guru, the saint Sunan Tembayat, said about the conference of the Wali Songo."[2]

---

2 At the conference of Moslem saints, Sunan Giri Gajah Kedaton ordered Sunan Tembayat to fetch Seh Lemah-abang. However, Seh Lemah-abang refused to attend the conference and said to Sunan Tembayat: "Seh Lemah-abang is not in, but God is." Sunan Tembayat reported to Sunan Giri that there was no Seh Lemah-abang, only God. Sunan Giri then ordered him to invite God instead. This time, Seh Lemah-abang said: "Well, God is not in but Seh Lemah-abang is". Sunan Tembayat reported this reply to Sunan Giri, who then ordered him to bring both Seh Lemah-abang and God to the conference. This time, Seh Lemah-abang obliged and went to the conference. But by acknowledging himself as God, Seh Lemah-abang was considered a traitor to Islam's belief and thus sentenced to death.

"There was a conference of Moslem saints presided by your great grandfather, Sunan Giri Gajah Kedaton. As chief of the Moslem saints, he had invited them to make a presentation of their perception of the Truth. Everybody had their say, but Seh Lemah-abang's explanation of the Truth as the mystic union of Creator with creation led to a terrible fight of words amongst those present. In the end, Seh Lemah-abang and his followers were sentenced to death. For three days their bodies were left on the ground, but there were no signs of decomposition. On the third day, Seh Lemah-abang's voice was heard expressing greetings to the saints and especially to Sunan Giri. Finally, the voice said: "Goodbye, O king of saints." And with that, the bodies disappeared. Well, my son, although Seh Lemah-abang may have attained perfection of knowledge, many of his followers did not. That was why he was to blame and had to pay for his mistakes with his life."

## 11 Wasi Singgungkoro in Mount Cereme

The wayfarers from Giri tavelled further until they came to a hermitage founded by Wasi Singgungkoro, believed to be a son of the last king of Majapahit. When the Majapahit kingdom fell into oblivion, he set sail in a proa and floated out to sea until it washed up on the shores of Cirebon. He walked to Mount Cereme and built a humble cottage on its peak. That was the place where he made penance and devoted his mind and soul in the service of his Lord. And the result was for everybody to see. The hermitage became a lovely sanctuary where everything found its peaceful refuge. Even animals—wild and brutal elsewhere—became peaceful; lions and tigers lived quietly alongside reindeer, goats and other mammals.

Arriving at the cottage, Raden Jayengresmi and his companions were overwhelmed by its tranquillity. The serenity of the place seemed to penetrate into his heart, calming his emotions and driving away all weariness and worry. Then he saw the priest beckoning to him. Paying homage with folded hands, he walked forward and said humbly: "O holy saint, I beg your mercy for disturbing your peace. You remind me of my guru, the reverend Seh Sekardalimo of Gunung (mountain) Slamet hermitage." Ki Wasi answered: "I know your guru and you are not the only one who comes here in consternation, only to find his longings and desires fulfilled. Yet all depends on one's efforts and resoluteness. What is it that makes your heart perturbed and upset? Tell me everything, so that you will be free from all grief and misery."

Raden Jayengresmi poured out his grief: "O holy sage, my heart is troubled by the loss of my brother and little sister. When Giri fell, they escaped in the confusion of the night and since then I've not heard anything about them. Where should I go to find them?" Ki Wasi replied: "For the time being, be satisfied with what I'm about to tell you. They are well and in good health, but it will be a long time before you meet them. It is best for you to stay here to strengthen your mind and body. I will tell you when to go further when the time comes."

opposite: *A view of Slamet Mountain in Banyumas, Central Java. It is the highest mountain in Central Java and the second highest in Java island after Semeru Mountain.*

the pre-adulthood journey

above: *This is Losari's fishermen's harbour in the northern port of Cirebon, which lies on the border of West and Central Java. Fishing is a traditional way of life in this coastal city, which is famous for its batik influenced by Chinese and European patterns.*

One day, Raden Jayengresmi asked about the *wuku*. Ki Wasi explained: "*Wuku* is the Javanese almanac. It is used to predetermine the ominous times of the year based on the days of the week. If we know which days are inauspicious, then we can plan things ahead successfully. Listen carefully as it is very complicated and not easy to understand." He then spoke about the thirty *wukus*, beginning with the *wuku* Watugunung and ending with the *wuku* Sinto. It was so complex that Jayengresmi felt a great admiration for the hermit. Ki Wasi then talked about the *naga jatingarang*, the special knowledge for determining the appropriate time for doing certain things, such as travelling. It was believed to be in the form of a dragon, a creature that is seen to represent great danger. The dragon's position on the four points of the compass moves every three months, so that in one year its position changes four times, in the end returning to the starting point. To avoid dangers, one has to keep clear of directly confronting the dragon's position.

The hermit then said: "My son, there is nothing else for me to teach you. Instead, I would like to ask a favour of you. I've lived far too long in this world and I would like you to show me the way to attain the perfect death. In my meditations, the deities have told me that a young Moslem saint will help me find the right way. I think you are that person." Raden Jayengresmi responded: "Well, my reverend guru has told me of this matter. There is nothing for you to do other than to embrace Islam, brought to us by the prophet Muhammad, peace be upon him. I will lead you in saying the *kalimah sahadah* (declaration of faith). With Allah's approval, you will attain bliss." He held Ki Wasi's hands and helped him declare the two admissions—'There is no god but Allah and Muhammad is His Messenger'.

When it was perfectly said, Ki Wasi revealed his last message: "Keep this in mind, my son. In the hermitage of Karang, in the region of Banten, resides a Moslem saint called Seh Ibrahim ibn Bakrim. Go there and study with him. He will advise you to go to Wonomarto, where Kyai Bayi Panurto has his place of learning. When Kyai Bayi asks you to marry his daughter, do so as it is the only way all your wishes will come true, including your wish to meet your brother and sister." With these words, the sage passed away and his body vanished. Raden Jayengresmi felt little need to stay any longer. He ordered Gathak and Gathuk to follow him to Karang.

## 12 The golden girl of Tampomas Mountain

Before long, they reached the foot of Tampomas Mountain in the region of Priangan. After walking up a footpath, they saw a mosque surrounded by a pool. The sage in residence was Seh Trenggono. He lived with his wife, Sitoresmi, and daughter, Roro Ruhkanti, a teenage girl of extreme beauty and elegance. She was famed throughout the region as 'the golden girl', with 'golden' referring not only to 'precious' and 'beautiful' but also to her silk-like fairness of skin. She was like a budding flower, just starting to open its delicate calyces for all to see. At her age she had already shown great interest in learning, especially in the study of religion and its requirements such as praying, fasting and reciting the holy Book.

One day, after the late afternoon prayer, Seh Trenggono and his family were collecting fruit in the backyard when a disciple informed him of the presence of strangers nearby. Before hurrying down to meet them, he asked his wife to prepare food for them and ordered his daughter to pick more fruit and vegetables. When he saw the wayfarers, he said: "Welcome to my humble dwelling, my son. I'm happy that you have come. Do not be shy and please feel as if you are in your own home. Please tell me your name and where you come from."

Raden Jayengresmi answered: "Thank you, sir. I am Jayengresmi, the son of Sunan Giri Parapen, and these

below: *Tampomas Mountain, northern West Java. Near its peak is a sacred shrine said to hold the remains of Prabu (King) Siliwangi of Pajajaran kingdom. The kingdom was in its glorious period during his reign but gradually declined with the rise of Islamic influence.*

are my companions. I've been travelling all over to find my brother and sister." Seh Trenggono said: "Giri is very far away and you must be weary. It will be best for you to stay here for a while."

Raden Jayengresmi accepted his invitation and soon they were sitting comfortably in the *pendopo* of his house. When Sitoresmi and Roro Ruhkanti brought hot drinks and snacks, Seh Trenggono said to them: "Sito and Ruhkanti, come forward. This guest of ours is none other than the son of Sunan Giri Parapen. I have already accepted him as my son and as brother to Ruhkanti. Please show your respect and welcome him." To Raden Jayengresmi, he said: "My son, this is my wife Sito and my daughter Ruhkanti. Regard my wife as your own mother and Ruhkanti as your own little sister." Sitoresmi came forward and touching his hands with folded hands, said: "Welcome to you, my son." Then Ruhkanti took her turn; lowering herself to her knees while paying homage with folded hands, she said: "Welcome, my brother. Make yourself comfortable." Jayengresmi looked at Ruhkanti and tears welled in his eyes. Seeing her kneeling in front of him had reminded him of his sister, Rancangkapti. At length he spoke: "Thank you, auntie, and you, little sister. I am so happy that God has brought me here."

After dinner, Raden Jayengresmi asked his host to show him how to become serene and at peace with himself. Seh Trenggono obliged and said: "All right, my son, but I will share the teachings with you in a more interesting manner. I will clothe them in *wangsalan*, a kind of riddle hidden in words. To find the teachings, you have to solve the riddle first, not just once but three or four times. The first thing to do is to find the hidden meaning of the words. For this, you need to have a good knowledge of the Javanese language. Next, you have to find the sentence composed by the hidden words. Then you need to understand the meaning of the sentence. The final stage is to find and understand the teaching hidden in the *wangsalan*.

"Let us consider this riddle—*puspa ranu, wit namaning bujangga gung*. The first stage is to find the hidden meaning of the words. *Puspa* is flower and *ranu* is water, so together it means 'a flower that grows in or on water'. Such a flower is the lotus. Now for the second part of the riddle—*wit namaning bujangga gung. Bujangga* is snake; *bujangga gung* is a huge snake, a naga or dragon. Then you have to find a tree or plant that has a name which includes the word 'naga'. This would be the *nagasari* tree. But the riddle is still not solved, as there is no meaningful connection between lotus and the *nagasari* tree. Let us look at the lotus; it has calyces like any flower, but where are they? They can be found in the word *nagasari*. The word for 'calyces' in the Javanese language is *slaga*. Thus you find the word *naga* hidden in the word *slaga*. The composition of the words is the calyces of a lotus flower (*slaganing kembang trate*) and the teaching is hidden in those words." He paused for while and then carried on.

"What is the teaching behind the calyces of a lotus flower? Well, a lotus grows from the muddy depths of water. Its calyces, though always in touch with the water, never becomes wet. Now listen carefully. A man living in this world should behave like the lotus. Even though all the necessities of life are supplied by the world, one's life should

not be influenced by the world. In other words, one should detach oneself from the world. In this way, one will find peace and tranquillity."

As Seh Trenggono said those last words, so too did he breathe his last breath. Raden Jayengresmi cried out loud: "My uncle, sir! Why do you leave me so soon? I need more instruction and guidance." Then he heard Seh Trenggono's voice: "Don't be disappointed and sad. I'm not dead but have merely moved from one world to another. Now that I'm not with my family, please look after your aunt and Ruhkanti." The voice faded away.

After her father's death, Roro Ruhkanti became more eager than ever to study the religion and abide by its principles, such as fasting and observing the Tahajjud (optional late night prayers), with the result that her face shone more brightly. Her mother and Raden Jayengresmi prayed earnestly that God might give her a caring and exemplary husband. One day, Roro Ruhkanti asked Raden Jayengresmi: "My brother, would you mind teaching me about the *Martabat Tujuh* (Seven Stages of Creation)?" He replied: "Sure, my sister. There are seven stages of emanation—*akadiyat*, *wahdat*, *wakidiyat*, *alam arwah*, *alam mithal*, *alam ajsam* and finally, *insan kamil*. The first three stages are immaterial, that is, without mass. The remaining four stages are of the material realm." He then explained the meaning of immaterial and material. By the time he finished, the sun was already setting.

Meanwhile, the sultan of Cirebon had heard of Seh Trenggono's death. He was not married and sent his chief minister to ask for Roro Rukhanti's hand on his behalf and to bring her to the palace without delay. Because he was part of the family, Nyi Sitoresmi consulted Raden Jayengresmi. He advised her to accept the proposal, since Ruhkanti would become the mother of future kings of Cirebon. And so, preparations

above (both): *Cirebon Keraton Kesepuhan (The Sultan's Palace). The Sultan of Cirebon's palace (left) and its gated entrance (right) were built in AD 1529. As the Cirebon kingdom still exists, the large square in the palace grounds is used for public gatherings and traditional ceremonies.*

for the journey for the queen-to-be and her mother began, and mother and daughter departed early the next morning. When they had left, Raden Jayengresmi felt little need to stay any longer at the hermitage. He ordered Gathak and Gathuk to prepare to continue their journey to Karang in the region of Banten.

## 13 Ki Ajar Sugandha of Mandalawangi

When they arrived at the foot of Mount Gede, they started to scale the Mandalawangi peak. On a plateau along the way, they saw an old man working on a field and enquired politely: "Excuse me, grandfather. Can you tell us the name of this village and who the village chief is?" The old man was astonished to see them and replied: "Master, this village is called Mandalawangi and the chief is Ki Ajar Sugandha. If you want to see him, please wait here for a while. I will inform him of your arrival first." Without waiting for an answer, he ran back to the village. Ki Ajar ordered him to bring the visitors to him without delay. The old man hurried back to the field and spoke breathlessly to Raden Jayengresmi: "Master, Ki Ajar invites you to come. Please follow me!"

After the usual salutations, Raden Jayengresmi told Ki Ajar about the situation he was in. Ki Ajar advised: "If you want to find your brother and sister, you have to be patient. It will be a while before you can see them. The time to be reunited with them is when all three of you have attained the high position of religious scholar and are knowledgeable in religious matters. For the time being, stay here or tell me where you want to go. Perhaps I can be of some assistance."

Replied Raden Jayengresmi: "Sir, I want to go to Karang, but I don't know the way." Ki Ajar said: "Oh, the hermitage of Karang is very far away. It is in the region of Banten, almost at the western end of Java island. The sage there is Kyai Ageng Karang. He originally came from Arabia and is of high learning. I heard his wife died while giving birth to their son. From childhood, the boy was already inclined towards religion, but he ran away from home all on his own one day. His father was very sad and is still waiting for him to return. I think he will be very happy to have you there. It is best for you to study with him." Jayengresmi said: "That is my very intention, uncle. I should go without delay." Ki Ajar spoke again: "No, no, my son. You don't know the way, so let me take you to the border of the old Pajajaran kingdom tomorrow. Moreover, tomorrow is a propitious day to travel."

So Raden Jayengresmi stayed with Ki Ajar Sugandha. They passed the night discussing all kinds of topics. They set off early the next morning. When they reached the village of Gandhok, Ki Ajar said: "From here, the ruins of the kingdom of Pajajaran are not too far away. Keep to a northwest course and you will be there without trouble. I must take leave from you here. Go straight ahead and do not look back until you have taken seven steps. I wish you a fruitful journey." They shook hands and parted. Jayengresmi did as told. After seven steps, he turned to wave goodbye, but the sage was no longer in sight.

# 14 The secret of longevity

The weather in the Bogor region is always cool and fresh and very conducive for plants to grow. Not surprisingly, fruit and vegetables are abundant and flowers, especially roses, grow wild everywhere in clusters. At the time the three *santris* from Giri were there, the roses were blooming, their sweet scent spread far and wide by the wind. In Bogor, too, rain falls almost every day from noon to nightfall. That particular afternoon was no exception.

The *santris* were walking on the dykes of a rice field when it began to rain. They saw a shack with a thatch roof of palm leaves and walls of bamboo, and ran there for shelter. Its owner, Ki Wargopati, was surprised to see them and exclaimed: "My God, who are you, master? I'm amazed that an outsider has reached this region safely for the paths are slippery, and the forest and undergrowth are full of wild beasts and venomous snakes." Raden Jayengresmi replied: "Well, uncle, whether a situation is difficult or easy depends on one's self. If one has the resolve, everything will be satisfactory. If there is no courage to face difficulties, nothing can be achieved. By the way, we are *santris* from Giri going to the hermitage of Karang in the Banten region. We have come to see the ruins of the kingdom of Pajajaran first."

Ki Wargopati was filled with admiration as he listened to Raden Jayengresmi speak and thought to himself: "This is not an ordinary man. His face shines and his words are so true and convincing. I think he is of noble origin." Aloud, he said: "Master, my name is Wargopati. I am the chief of this village. It is almost dark and it is raining, so please spend the night with me. My family and my fellow villagers will be delighted to have you. Look, my house is not far away. You can see it from here. What do you say?" Raden Jayengresmi replied: "I thank you for your hospitality, uncle." In a single file, they began to walk on the dykes and head for the village. But the rain had made the dykes slippery, causing Gathak and Gathuk to fall off a few times.

As soon as he reached home, Ki Wargopati beat the drum and shortly after, a crowd of men and women were gathered there. While the womenfolk helped Nyi Wargopati prepare food and drinks, the men cleaned the house and the mosque. Raden Jayengresmi and his companions had a bath and changed into fresh clothes. Soon they were sitting on mats in the front hall, where a feast had been laid out for them. Gathak and Gathuk noticed that all the side dishes, though prepared differently, contained fish and they asked their host if there was a reason behind it. Ki Wargopati answered: "No, nothing mysterious. It is only because I like this particular type of fish. The flesh is firm, yet soft and very tasty."

When the late afternoon prayer had been performed, Raden Jayengresmi asked permission to stay in the mosque. While there, Gathuk put a question to Ki Wargopati: "Excuse me, uncle. How old are you?" Laughing heartily, Ki Wargopati answered: "I am 92 years old. Why do you ask?" Gathuk replied: "I am very much impressed because you don't look your age. Moreover, you are still so strong and healthy. What is your secret? Please, if you don't mind, tell me the secret of longevity. Perhaps I too can learn how to stay young and healthy." Ki Wargopati replied: "Oh, there is nothing to it really. What you must do is perform the *puji dina* every day of the week. It is a kind of religious observance; you could call it the prayer of the day. But most importantly, you must do it regularly and continuously." Gathuk became more spirited and asked: "How do you do it, uncle? What are the words of prayer to be said?" Ki Wargopati smiled and said: "All right then, my boy. Listen carefully."

So Gathak and Gathuk moved closer to Ki Wargopati and listened to his words: "As you know, there are seven days in a week. Begin on a Friday, as was practised by our beloved Prophet Muhammad, peace be upon him. You fast for 24 hours and say the words *ya qawiyyu* 103 times during that period; the reward is Allah's mercy. The second day is Saturday. As practised by Caliph Usman, do not eat and sleep for 24 hours, but say *ya fatah ya rojak* 103 one times; the reward you get is the respect of everyone. The third day is Sunday and as was observed by Caliph Umar, do not smoke or chew betel for 24 hours, but say the words *ya hayyu'l qayyum* 103 times; the reward is that neither danger nor calamity will cross your path. The fourth day is Monday. As was practised by the prophet Isa, do not eat fish for 24 hours, but say the prayer words *ya rahman ya rahim* 103 times; the reward is that all your wishes will be fulfilled. The fifth day is Tuesday. As was practised by Caliph Abubakar, you must not eat or sleep for 24 hours and the prayer words to be said 103 times is *subhana maliki'l kudus*; the reward is that you will get the favour of Allah. The sixth day is Wednesday. As was practised by the prophet Abraham, you must not have salt for 24 hours. During that period, say the prayer words *subhana maliki'l khahar* 103 times; the reward is that all your sins will be forgiven. The seventh day is Thursday. As was practised by Caliph Ali, do not drink for 24 hours, but say *ya khabiru ya muta'al* 103 times; the reward is good health and strength in all undertakings. Whoever practises the *puji dina* faithfully will be rewarded with success in this world and the next." Gathak and Gathuk expressed their profound gratitude to Ki Wargopati.

## 15 The ruins of Pajajaran

Early the next morning, Ki Wargoparti took the *santris* to see the ruins of the Pajajaran kingdom. Upon seeing a large pool with water overflowing, Gathak and Gathuk could not help but take off their clothes and plunge into the fresh water. Ki Wargopati said to Raden Jayengresmi: "Master, this pool is what is left of the kingdom. Still, it has a very important legacy. There is the story of a married man who was childless but had a child after bathing in the pool several times. And there is a flat stone at the side of the pool called Kyai Selagilang, the holy flat stone. People say that their wishes come true after praying there."

Raden Jayengresmi said: "Uncle, now that I have seen the ruins, allow me to proceed to Mount Salak." On hearing that, Ki Wargopati fell to his knees and said: "Master,

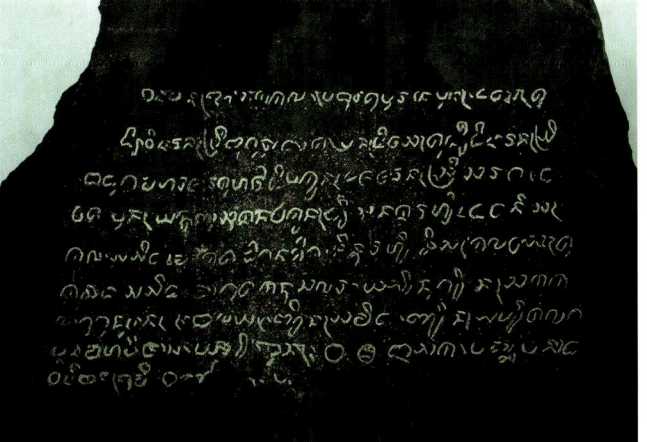 

allow me to accompany you to the mountain. I will bring my men and help you build a hermitage there." Jayengresmi replied: "As you wish, uncle. I don't mind." So Ki Wargopati gathered some men and they went to Mount Salak. They worked very hard to build a hermitage on a plateau on the western slopes. Water flowed everywhere, though never very rapidly. At some places, small waterfalls filled pools and irrigated the paddy fields and vegetable gardens. When the hermitage was ready, Ki Wargopati and his men returned to their village. There was no one left except the three *santris* from Giri. The serene and tranquil atmosphere inspired them to become more devoted in their worship.

## 16 The hermitage of Karang

Over at the hermitage of Karang in the region of Banten, there lived a man called Seh Ibrahim ibn Abubakar. He was also known as Kyai Ageng Karang. He was lonely and sad, for his wife had died while giving birth to their only son years earlier and that son had left home more than ten years ago in search of adventure and to study with gurus. Alone in the world, Ki Ageng devoted his life to improving the lot of his followers.

One night when everyone was fast asleep and in the serenity of the late night prayer, Ki Ageng heard a voice say: "Kyai Ageng, don't be too sad. Be most patient because your son will not return to you. However, God is Most Compassionate and He will grant you His mercy in another way. A son of Sunan Giri Parapen called Raden Jayengresmi will come to you and take the place of your own son. He has just founded a hermitage at Gunung Salak. Signs of his sainthood are already apparent now. Go to him and bring him here. Later on, your son will unite with Raden Jayengresmi." The voice faded away. Ki Ageng was filled with gratitude.

He set off for the hermitage on Mount Salak the next morning. Using his magical powers, he arrived there very quickly. He looked around in amazement, for he was there

*above left: The Batutulis stone in the Batutulis Monument complex, Bogor, West Java. The Kawi script, an ancient Sundanese language, tells of Sundanese history and culture. The area around the complex is believed to be the location of the capital of the Hindu Sunda kingdom, which reigned in the western part of Java island (from 7th to 16th centuries).*
*above right: The complex also houses a stone that bears the footprints of Prabu Siliwangi, who ruled over the two kingdoms of Sunda and Galuh, later known as Pajajaran. There are many remains from Pajajaran that await further study.*

opposite: *Sunset view of Karang Mountain on the western tip of West Java.*

not too long ago and it was covered by dense forest and wild undergrowth. And now a flourishing hermitage was in its place. Many *santris* were working in the field, planting rice, vegetables and flowers. Fruit trees were flowering, a few already bearing fruit. The drizzle watered the plants. Flowers bloomed everywhere, brightening the atmosphere. What impressed him most was the fact that although many people came, no one left empty-handed. Everyone went home with all kinds of foodstuff in their hands. Ki Ageng heaved a sigh of relief and expressed his gratitude to God: "*Alhamdulillah! Allahu Akbar!* (God be praised! God is the Greatest!)"

Just then, Raden Jayengresmi and his companions appeared before him with folded hands and greeted him respectfully. They walked together to the hermitage, where they sat facing each other in the front hall. Ki Ageng said: "My son, I have come here at the order of The Almighty to take you home to Karang. Let Gathak and Gathuk take care of the hermitage for a few months; they can join you in Karang later on. What do you say?" Replied Jayengresmi: "Sir, your wish is my command. I agree to go with you." Ki Ageng meditated for a second, then held Jayengresmi's hands and they disappeared from sight. At length, they arrived at Karang safely.

One morning, Ki Ageng asked Raden Jayengresmi: "Well, my son, tell me everything about your experiences since leaving Giri. Talking about it will help you feel better." Without leaving out a single point, Jayengresmi told Ki Ageng everything… about his sorrows and heartbreaks and the learned people he met along the way. What Ki Ageng said was true—relating his experiences did relieve his anxiety. Not only that, it also strengthened his trust in his new-found father, the great cleric of Karang.

Ki Ageng responded: "Do not worry! Put your trust in Allah The Almighty. Life and death, health and illness, prosperity and poverty—these are not acts of man but Allah's will. Do not doubt whatsoever. *La haula wa la quwwata illa billah* (There is no power or strength but with Allah). Every second of man's life can be compared with being in the centre of the agony of death. It is as though he is sailing in the ocean of Allah's mercy. Whichever direction one faces, no shore is in sight. However to a man of wisdom, after a short voyage, he is already on dry land. You must be aware that the ocean of Mercy looks very calm; there are no waves or swell and so many are not aware of any danger. They leave the boat and straightaway plunge into death, never reaching land. When you cross the ocean of Mercy, my son, you always have to be alert and watchful. At any cost, don't leave the boat filled with all its outfits. The parable of the boat is Purity, the rudder is Strong Resolve, the sail is Pure Heart, the compass is the Guidelines of the Guru, the provision is Consciousness, and the movements of the boat, whether forwards or backwards, is Allah's mercy. With all these outfits on hand, the shores of God's mercy will soon be in sight."

Raden Jayengresmi listened attentively. Meanwhile, time strode along by the seconds and minutes until the time for the Zuhur (midday) prayer came to pass.

# Jayengsari and Ni Rancangkapti
## FROM GIRI TO PEKALONGAN TO SOKOYOSO

## 1 Kyai Amatsungeb

After fleeing Giri, Raden Jayengsari, his sister Rancangkapti and a *santri* called Buras walked until they arrived at the village of Sidocremo. Said Kyai Amatsungeb, the village chief when he met them: "Master, I am so happy to have you here. If you don't mind, stay with us for good. Should messengers from Pangeran Pekik of Surabaya come here, I will protect you from them. Do not worry!" Raden Jayengsari replied: "For the time being, yes, we will stay with you. I do not want to cause you any trouble." Kyai Amatsungeb had received them because he was deeply indebted to Jayengsari's father, Sunan Giri Parapen.

However, Raden Jayengsari remained very worried because the village was too close to Surabaya. That night when everybody was fast asleep, he told Buras of his intention to leave the village. Rancangkapti was fast asleep and so Buras carried her on his back. Even though he was not married, he treated her like his own child. Buras knew his two masters very well, having worked many years in the service of their father.

Raden Jayengsari led the way and by the next morning, they were already in a forest resting under a big banyan tree. When Rancangkapti woke up, she was a bit confused and asked: "My brother, where are we? Last night we were in a village, why are we in a forest now? And brother Jayengresmi is not here. Brother, I'm afraid. Let's go home back to mum and dad." Raden Jayengsari was sad to hear those words. He could not tell her about the calamity that had fallen on their family and the fire that had destroyed the court of Giri, as he thought she was too young to understand the situation. He, too, had thought of his parents with pain and sadness but could not share his feelings with her. So he said: "Little sister, do you forget that it was you who wanted to look for our

opposite: *A sunset view of the Bali Strait. Sailing boats with a large triangular sail and an outrigger, called proa, are still used by fishermen today.*

brother. We haven't met him yet, so why do you want to return home? Have a little patience and do not worry. We will find him. Then we can go home together, the three of us." Rancangkapti was appeased. Meanwhile, Buras took out the provisions he had brought along. When they had eaten, they continued on their journey. They walked during the day and rested in villages at night.

## 2 Man-eating crocodiles

A few days later, they came across Grati Lake. It was infested with crocodiles of all sizes. While they brought fear to Rancangkapti, the animals in the trees brought cheer to her. She asked her brother to tell her everything about the crocodiles, the monkeys and the birds, as well as the flowers, trees and plants, all the while running from one place to another.

When she was out of breath, she sat down and said to Buras: "Mind you, Buras! The crocodiles here like to eat lazy boys. So said my brother and he's very clever, you know. So if you don't want to carry me on your back, be careful as the crocodiles will get you." Buras replied: "Is that so, princess? I will carry you on my back, I promise. I am very scared of crocodiles." Rancangkapti laughed and laughed, thinking she had really made Buras afraid. Continued Buras: "But princess, I also know that crocodiles like to eat crying babies. You must be very careful, too." Rancangkapti kept silent for a while, then answered: "Buras, you want to scare me, don't you? You must know Buras, that I am not a crybaby. I'm a big girl now and a very nice girl, too." Buras said: "All right mistress, you win." With a smile, she said brightly: "Of course, I win. Now what do you have for me to eat?" Buras replied in a serious tone: "Princess, when I looked around, the rambutan tree said to me, 'Buras, take my sweet rambutans to your mistress'. The *duku* and the banana trees asked me to do the same. So just to please them, princess, have a bite of each of them. Otherwise, they will get mad at me and beat me with their big twigs." Rancangkapti said: "All right Buras. I will have pity on you." She took some fruit and ate them. When she finished, she took a rambutan and gave it to Buras: "Buras. This is for you... your pay for carrying me on your back!"

Thus the meal went by in a very pleasant way. Rancangkapti did not ask for rice, eating only fruit to please the trees. They then continued their journey. Finally, they reached the region of Malang, where they came across the Baung waterfall and visited the Singosari temple.

When they arrived at the village of Sisir, they rested at a well with clear water that flowed from a small temple. From the strong scent of incense still wafting in the air, they knew there were many people worshiping there. Said Rancangkapti: "My brother! Give Buras some money to buy perfumed incense. I want to give it to mum as a present." Raden Jayengsari was very much moved by her words and tears rolled down his cheeks. Wiping off the tears, she asked: "Brother, why do you cry? Are you hungry?" He answered: "No, dear! I'm not crying. Dust comes into my eyes. Blow

# jayengsari and ni rancangkapti

on them." Rancangkapti said: "Look up! I'll pronounce my formula... 'The old man is riding on an elephant, his creese [*kris*, a kind of dagger] is very small." Then she blew into his eyes and said: "Now they are back to normal. You don't cry anymore." The three of them left the well and pushed further until they came to the temple of Kidal, the oldest temple of the Singosari era. They climbed up to get a closer look at its carvings and by the time they were done, evening was near.

## 3 Tosari and surroundings

They spent the night at a village and the next morning, they were on their way to the Tengger region. Raden Jayengsari thought that his brother might have taken refuge there. Passing the village of Pasrepan, they arrived at Tosari village on the southern slopes of the Tengger range. While looking for a place to stay, Buras met Ki Buyut Sudargo, one of the chieftains of the village. Ki Buyut asked: "My son, who orders you to look for lodgings?" Buras answered frankly: "My master is the son of Sunan Giri Parapen. He and his sister are looking for their older brother." An astounded Ki Buyut replied: "My son, your master is a real noble. He is the son of the king of saints. I'll beg them to stay with me." Upon meeting Jayengsari, Ki Buyut invited them to stay with him. After they had bathed, prayed and eaten, Jayengsari asked his host: "I saw a mountain peak burning at night. What is it and can we see it?" Ki Buyut said: "Milord! That is Mount Bromo. At night, its peak seems to be alight. At daytime, it is not so obvious. I will take you there tomorrow."

The next morning, Ki Buyut took them to the mountain and they viewed the crater. After that they went to the caldera plateau, called the *segoro wedi* (the sand-sea).

*above left:* Singosari temple in Malang, East Java. This 14th-century building is one of many monuments built in memory of Kertanagara, the last king of Singosari, and is dedicated to the Hindu god, Shiva.

*above middle:* Detail of Kidal temple, Rejokidal village, Malang. It is a memorial shrine for King Anusapati, another ruler of Singosari. On its walls are images of Garuda, the bird deity in Hindu mythology and also the carrier of god Vishnu.

*above right:* Baung waterfall, Kebun Raya (National Park) Purwodadi, north of Malang.

# the pre-adulthood journey

*above left: Mount Bromo. An active volcano located in East Java, it is sacred for those who believe the eruptions symbolise God's anger.*

Looking east, Raden Jayengsari saw a hill covered with flowers and enquired: "Ki Buyut, what is that hill?" Ki Buyut replied: "That is the hill of Ngardisari. It is where Ki Ajar Satmoko, the chief of the district of Tengger, resides. He still adheres to Brahmanism and has many students, both men and women." Jayengsari then asked: "Ki Buyut, can you bring me to him? I would like to know what Buddhism and Brahmanism are all about." He replied: "My pleasure, milord! But we better return home now. The sun is already leaning to the west and it will be evening soon."

## 4 Ki Ajar Satmoko

*above right: A view of the spectacular Tengger caldera from Mount Bromo. The caldera is Java's largest with its 10-kilometre sea of sand. Inside it is a sacred area called* poten. *During the annual Yadnya Kasada ceremony observed by the Tenggerese people, offerings of flowers, fuit, vegetables and rice are thrown into the crater.*

After breakfast the following morning, Raden Jayengsari, Rancangkapti, Ki Buyut and his wife departed for the village of Ngardisari at the foot of Semeru Mountain. While they rested at the outskirts of the village, Ki Buyut went ahead to meet Ki Ajar Satmoko. Their arrival was not announced, yet Ki Ajar already knew that important people would be visiting him. He asked Ki Buyut to bring them to his home. After a meal, Ki Buyut and his wife returned to Tosari. Jayengsari stayed back to talk with Ki Ajar. Rancangkapti was kept entertained by some *endangs* (female attendants).

Ki Ajar said: "Throughout the region of Tengger, people worship the God Brahma, whose abode is the burning crater of Mount Bromo. Once a year, they throw offerings into the crater. Here in Tengger, too, when a boy wants to marry a girl, the boy will take her comb and show it to his parents, after which the parents will take over the arrangements. When everything is agreed upon, the wedding proceeds at the bride's parents' house. The village chief proclaims them man and wife by sprinkling holy water from an engraved copper cup." Thus was the information Ki Ajar gave concerning marriage. That discussion was followed by other things concerning the life and religious practices of the Tenggerese. In return, Raden Jayengsari gave a discourse about Islam and the religions brought by all the prophets of Allah. He explained the pillars of the faith and all of its aspects in detail, as well as the Qur'an and other ceremonics. At the end, Ki Ajar concluded: "My son, while the practice of Islam, Buddhism and Brahmanism are different, the aim is the same—to worship God The Almighty." Jayengsari bowed in agreement.

Rancangkapti, with tears flowing on her cheeks, cried out: "My brother, the weather here is too cold for me and brother Jayengresmi is also not here. Let us leave to look for him." Ki Ajar consoled her: "My dearest young lady, be patient and don't worry. Your brother is fine. You will meet him but only after he finds a beautiful wife. She will bring you presents, fine jewellery and many clothes." With that, she stopped crying. Raden Jayengsari asked: "Sir, if you don't mind, tell me where to find my brother." Ki Ajar replied: "I cannot tell you that because it is still kept secret by the gods. But I can tell you that all your efforts and troubles will benefit you and bring you success in life, my son. Continue your journey to the east." Jayengsari said: "Since that is the case, permit me to take leave." Ki Ajar replied: "I wish you all the best, my son. For good luck during your travels, don't look back for the next seven steps you take." Jayengsari made homage with folded hands, took his sister's hand and went his way.

They walked a long time through woods and undergrowth, crossing rivers, wetlands and paddy fields. The sun was setting by the time they reached a lake at the foot of a mountain. There were many birds flying in the sky. Raden Jayengsari rested on the

*below: The Tenggerese are the descendants of a Majapahit princess and a man who fled the kingdom to avoid converting to Islam. Unable to conceive, they prayed to the god of Bromo to grant them children. Their wish was granted on the condition they sacrifice their youngest child. Before he was thrown into the crater, he asked his parents for some food. This act of giving food is commemorated every year with the Yadnya Kasada ceremony.*

green grass while Rancangkapti ran around and picked wild flowers. She seemed not to feel tired any more. The beautiful view and sweet scent of flowers had given her energy. Suddenly, a bird cried out loud and startled her. Looking up, she was surprised to see a big fish and lobster plummeting from the sky and shouted: "Brother, a lobster and a fish are falling from the sky! Buras, be quick! Catch them!" Like a lion pouncing on a lamb, Buras swooped down and in the wink of an eye, he had the lobster and fish in both hands. But Rancangkapti behaved as if she was the one who caught them. Out loud came her orders from her little lips: "Brother, give Buras some money to buy salt. And you, Buras, wash the fish and lobster quickly, and buy salt and vegetables. I think the fish is best grilled. The cook at Giri said that if you wrap fish in vegetables, the vegetables will taste like fish... very yummy."

The two men, years older than she, felt no need to object. Buras washed the fish and lobster, sprinkled them with powdered salt and wrapped them thickly in cassava leaves. He made a fire from twigs and dry branches of wood that Jayengsari had collected and soon, the air was filled with a delicious aroma. Buras turned them over a few times and cut some banana leaves. When his stomach began to growl, he was sure the food was ready. He put them on the leaves and served them to his master and mistress. The wind cooled the hot food, allowing Jayengsari and his sister to begin their meal. Rancangkapti said: "Buras, taste the wrappings. See whether it is as good as the fish itself." Buras quickly put the leaves into his mouth and nodded his head in agreement. He had not finished the wrappings when Jayengsari and Rancangkapti had their fill and handed down the leftovers to him. Rancangkapti warned: "Be careful, Buras. Slow down a bit, the fish has a lot of sharp bones." Buras could not reply because his mouth was full. He could only nod in agreement and pleasure.

After a short rest, they continued their journey. At nightfall, they stayed in a hut on stilts in a paddy field. The moon was full that night. Raden Jayengsari was on his own, praying for the welfare of his lost brother, parents and his little sister.

## 5 Seh Wahdat

Their journey thereafter took them through mountains and plains. They went from Bangil eastward until they reached the slopes of Mount Argopuro where they stopped to rest. They saw a peacock proudly spreading its tail to display its grandeur. The birds in the trees sang as if to accompany its performance. Rancangkapti clapped her little hands to applaud the scene. The peacock made a bow and then walked away gracefully. Raden Jayengsari then said: "My sister, I saw some houses on that slope. Let's go there to ask for directions."

They found a hermitage belonging to a sage called Seh Wahdat. He knew that a son and daughter of Sunan Giri Parapen would visit him and so he waited for them at the gate. When they arrived, he said: "Jayengsari and Rancangkapti, welcome to the humble hermitage of Argopuro. I am Seh Wahdat and I know everything about both of

above: *A cornfield on the sacred Mount Argopuro in Probolinggo Regency, East Java. The locals believe that the Rengganis peak on the mountain is where Ratu Rengganis, one of King Brawijaya IV's concubines, went into exile and lived until she died. She became the holy spirit who protects the mountain area and the people. Offerings are given to her every year.*

you. Come, stay with me for a few days." Paying homage with folded hands, they came forward and fell on their knees: "Reverend Sir! I beg your pardon for disturbing your peace." Seh Wahdat replied: "No, no my son! You and your sister are welcome here. You must be very tired and hungry from so long a journey. Please come in and have your repose in the hermitage. Everything is ready and whatever you have in mind, you will get." Buras thought to himself: "How could he say that everything is ready? I want to eat rice with salted fish and roasted dried meat. I don't see anyone here, not one soul. Who will prepare the food?" The sage interrupted his thoughts and said: "Buras, go inside. See whether everything you want is there." Buras thought: "He knows my name, too!" On entering the house, he saw every imaginable food and drink, not to mention his salted fish and roasted dried meat. Bowing low and with clasped hands, he went out of the house and said: "Master! Everything is ready. Please come in, I will serve you."

Raden Jayengsari and Rancangkapti stayed with Seh Wahdat for several days. They learnt a lot from him, including the *Sifat Dua Puluh* (Twenty Attributes of Allah). At the end of the sessions, the sage reminded Jayengsari to stay close to the teachings of the *sunni ulamas* (religious scholars of the Sunni sect of Islam).

One morning, Seh Wahdat told them: "My children! You have been studying with me for some time. It is now time for you to continue your journey. Go to Raung Mountain where you will meet a lady hermit. Stay with her a few days. When the time comes, she will advise you to go to Banyuwangi to meet Ki Hartati, a merchant

| the pre-adulthood journey |

from Pekalongan. If he invites you to join him, accept his invitation. Obey him. When he and his wife pass away, donate their wealth to the poor and needy. Then go to the Perahu Mountain via the Bhismo Mountain. There you will find the hermitage of Sokoyoso where the sage Ki Ageng Sokoyoso lives. He has reached the rank of a *waliyullah* (friend of God) and is also known as Seh Akadiyat. He has a son called Cabolang, who left home and is now living dangerously, but he will realise his mistakes and return to his parents on his own accord. Later on, he will grow up to become a great *ulama* (religious scholar). Study with Ki Ageng and follow all his instructions. You will meet your brother when you have established yourself at the hermitage of Wonontoko. Now, with my blessings and best wishes, you have to leave." Jayengsari and Rancangkapti fell to their knees and paid homage at his feet. Then they left, their eyes brimming with tears.

After travelling for a few days, they arrived at Raung Mountain where they rested by a lake. From where they sat, they could see the Strait of Bali and vessels moving in all directions, their sails flying in the wind and shining brilliantly in the sun. A river flowed from the lake to the sea, turning and twisting like a silver dragon. On its banks were settlements and fields flush with rice in all stages of growth. Birds perched on branches chirped noisily as if addressing Rancangkapti who had come to visit them. A peacock spread its wings and tail and bowed low in front of her and she responded with a hearty laugh. Then it turned around and walked up the slope. Rancangkapti spoke: "Brother, get up! The peacock wants us to follow her. She seems to be telling us there is a hermitage up there." Buras thought: "This mistress of mine is a real jewel. She seems to know the language of animals." Rancangkapti ordered: "Buras, don't just stand there. Let's go." The two older men gave no reply but followed her steps. Soon, they came across a beautiful garden surrounding a pond. In the middle of the pond was a *bale kambang*, a floating temple. To get there, they had to cross a rattan bridge.

below left: *Raung Mountain, one of Java's most active volcanoes. At over 3,330 metres high and located on the eastern tip of Java in Banyuwangi, it is visible from the island of Bali.*
below right: *The Bali Strait. This 2.5-kilometre wide strait separates the islands of Java and Bali.*

## 6 Diah Tan Timbangsih, the holy virgin

The lady hermit who lived on Raung Mountain never married and so the people call her the 'holy virgin', even though she was given the name Diah Tan Timbangsih at birth. She knew beforehand that Raden Jayengsari and Rancangkapti would visit her and so was ready to welcome them: "Welcome, my children! Come straight ahead!" The youngsters and Buras stepped forward and greeted her with folded hands. She then took Rancangkapti's hand and led her inside. When they were seated in the sitting room, Jayengsari told her that they had come on the advice of Seh Wahdat. Diah Tan Timbangsih said: "You must know that Seh Wahdat is my brother in faith. Therefore, you must behave with me in the same way you did with him. So feel at home the same way." The youngsters spent their days listening to her teachings.

## 7 The book *Kadis Markum Baslam*

One day, the holy virgin told Rancangkapti that she decided to become a hermit after reading the book *Kadis Markum Baslam*. She related the story to the little girl:

*Long, long ago there were four kingdoms ruled by three brothers—King Lawammah, King Amarah and King Mutmainah—and their sister Queen Sufiyah. Except for King Mutmainah, the siblings did evil things every day. Each had a great army and nobody, save for King Mutmainah, dared oppose them. No wonder the three evil monarchs hated him vehemently and joined forces to crush him.*

*This was their plan: King Lawwamah and his black army would be the main attacking force and make the first thrust from the centre. King Amarah's red army and Queen Sufiyah's yellow women's army would make their assault from the right and left flanks respectively. Slowly the allied forces got the upper hand over King Mutmainah. And when King Lawwamah's weapon hit him repeatedly, followed by King Amarah's colossal club and Queen Sufiyah's rapid stabbing of her sword, King Mutmainah fell to the ground. Gathering all his strength, he shouted his battle cry, "La haula wa la quwatta illa bi'llah" (There is no power or strength except God's). He then swung his magic whip around, hitting his three opponents with one sweep. They fell to the ground with not the slightest power left and begged for mercy. King Mutmainah said: "Only God The Almighty can grant the mercy you ask for. So I will help you to meet Him right away." And with one mighty stroke, he wiped the three devils out from the surface of the Earth.*

*The world shook from the clamour of jubilation from all its inhabitants: "King Lawammah is dead! King Amarah is doomed! Queen Sufiyah is extinct.*

## the pre-adulthood journey

*The world is saved. Long Live King Mutmainah!" The shouts reverberated throughout the realm in waves, filling the air with both joy and despair—joy from the oppressed masses and despair from the evil monarchs' daughters, amongst them were Princess Salasiyah and Princess Rifangi. As was the custom of old, the womenfolk and the wealth of the defeated became booty for the victorious side. But the two princesses would not surrender freely. And so when the victorious King Mutmainah entered the royal audience hall to claim his booty, he found them sitting on thrones with a dagger in their hands, ready to kill themselves. They shouted: "Enough! Not one step further or we will kill ourselves." He stopped at the entrance and said: "Don't be too hasty. I will not harm you. I want you both to be my wives, to reign with me over the whole world with love and prosperity." Replied one of them: "Slayer of my parents! There is no love between you and us, only hatred and enmity, the worst of its kind." Replied the King: "Well, princesses, your fathers and aunt fell heroically in combat, fair and square. Let bygones be bygones. Let us build our own future and happiness and rule the whole kingdom together with justice and righteousness." With bitterness still in their voice, they answered: "All right, O knight! We will marry you on one condition... that you revive them. Take it or leave it!" For they believed that if their parents lived again, there would be a chance to defeat the king and no need to keep their promise.*

*King Mutmainah was dumbfounded as he knew that evil would prevail if he revived them. He was deep in thought and kept silent for a long while until Princess Salasiyah woke him up with her harsh voice: "Well, my arch enemy! What do you say? We can't wait any longer." The king answered: "If I meet this condition, will you marry me unconditionally? Give me your word." The princesses answered in unison: "Yes, we will marry you unconditionally. We promise to be your queens." King Mutmainah was not stupid for he had thought of a plan—he would revive them and then put them in the strongest and most secure jail ever; so long as they are kept behind bars, they would not be able to do any harm." And so he revived his enemies only to imprison them for life. The princesses could not go back on their word and married the king. And as no evil was present, they lived happily ever after.*

The holy virgin ended her story with these words: "My children, listen carefully. The moral of the story of *Kadis Markum Baslam* is this. The evil kings and queen are the low passions in men. If you can control the evil side, you can surely find happiness in life. That is why I chose celibacy." Rancangkapti replied quickly: "Holy guru, give me your blessings to follow your steps, to become a lady hermit." Diah Tan Timbangsih embraced her and said: "No, no, my child. That is not your destiny. You have still a long story to write. Don't worry. Learn to control all your five senses and everything will be all right. Keep in mind that God's reward for a married woman is seven times greater than for an unmarried one. This is what Allah says about the purpose of creation: 'I don't create men and jinns, except to worship Me.' (Q, 51, 56). So only faith and devotion to Him and acceptance of fate are the pre-requisites for a happy life on this Earth and in the Hereafter. And what is written for you, my child! You will marry and if that happens, remember the story of *Kadis Markum Baslam*. And you, Jayengsari! What do you think about the story?" Raden Jayengsari answered: "Holy guru, the message is clear enough. We have to keep evil under control with all our might and means." She nodded in agreement and thought: "This young man has all the qualifications of a saint."

A few days later, on a bright morning, the holy virgin said to the youngsters: "My children, the time has come for you to leave for Banyuwangi. Go with my blessings. I will always pray for your safety." They paid homage at her feet and went their way into the unknown future without fear. Only Buras lingered a little and spoke: "Milady, I ask your leave and some provisions for the journey." She replied with a smile: "All right, I'll give you two coins. Whenever you use them to buy food or any other provisions, they will return to your pocket with no loss to the vendor." Buras expressed his gratitude and quickly ran after his master and mistress. Keeping her smile, the holy virgin retreated into her house.

## 8 Banyuwangi, the place of perfumed water

It was a long walk to Banyuwangi. They stopped in the day only to pray and passed the nights in villages. Finally, they arrived at a market in Banyuwangi. Buras bought provisions and paid with the coins he received from the lady hermit. After serving food and drinks to his master and mistress, and while waiting for his turn to eat, he put his hand into his pocket and felt the coins there. He mumbled with surprise: "The holy virgin spoke the truth!"

From the market, they went south. By evening, they reached the village of Nglicin at the top of Ijen Mountain. The view from there was superb. The water in the Strait of Bali glittered in the evening sun. Boats great and small were like toys tossed around by the waves. Even the big rolling waves of the South Ocean were in view. The mountains around the town of Banyuwangi looked like robust figures bathed in the rays of the sun tinged with gold.

Not long later the sun begun to sink, hiding behind the western mountain range. As the moon became brighter, the wanderers seemed to fall into a spell and they lost all sense of time. They did not sleep well that night. Early the next morning, they moved south again and stopped when they saw a magnificent temple made of white stone (marble). Raden Jayengsari and Rancangkapti sat under a *nagasari* tree looking with wonder at the white marvel. She asked her brother: "Brother, is that a temple? Why is

# the pre-adulthood journey

above (both): *Ijen crater. This crater lies inside the Ijen Volcano Complex, which consists of a group of volcanoes. The crater has a wide mouth with a diameter of 1 kilometre. Within it lies a turquoise blue crater lake, the world's largest and most acidic. Ijen is famous for its labour-intensive sulphur mining industry where workers dig for the mineral from active vents.*

it built of white stone?" Jayengsari replied: "Yes, my dear sister, it is a temple. It is also the first time I'm seeing a temple built of white stone." Meanwhile, Buras served the breakfast he had bought from a stall nearby. As they ate, they kept their eyes locked on the temple.

Then an old man clad in a jacket and loincloth approached them. Welcoming them, he said: "My name is Menakluhung and I am the caretaker of the temple. What is the purpose of your visit? Is it to meditate or just to look around?" Raden Jayengsari replied: "We are *santris* from Giri. My name is Jayengsari and this is my sister Rancangkapti." "And I am Buras, the servant," Buras said introducing himself. Jayengsari continued: "This temple is extraordinary. Temples are usually built of black stone but this one is white. Who built it, uncle?" Ki Menak replied: "According to legend, this place was once the Blambangan kingdom during the Majapahit era and was ruled by King Menakjinggo, also known as Urubismo. He was very powerful because he owned a special weapon, a club made of yellow iron. Any enemy, no matter how mighty it was, would lose all its power on seeing the club. This temple was where the king worshipped his Godhead. It was formerly called Candi Macan Putih (White Tiger Temple). Nowadays, people call it Candi Sela Cendhani (Temple of Marble)."

Raden Jayengsari remarked: "Uncle, the soil here is very fertile, the vegetation grows well and the port is busy." Said Ki Menak: "You are correct, sir. In the old days, Blambangan kingdom was very prosperous. Many trading boats still stop here on their way to and from the island of Bali. In fact, at this moment, I have a guest at home. He is Ki Hartati, a merchant from Pekalongan. I think it is best that you meet him, sir."

## 9 Ki Hartati, the merchant from Pekalongan

Raden Jayengsari felt a strange sensation when he heard the name, for had not Seh Wahdat advised him to join Ki Hartati? Without hesitation, he agreed to meet the merchant and in a single line, they followed Ki Menak to his home. They waited at the gate while Ki Menak went inside to meet Ki Hartati. "My brother," he said, "I bring home guests, wanderers from afar, a young man and his sister." Ki Hartati said: "Oh, my brother! Perhaps that explains the dream I had last night. In the dream, I was given a young rooster and a little hen. Where are they, brother? Let's bring them in."

Ki Hartati hurried out, followed by Ki Menak. When he saw the youngsters, he felt they were not ordinary people and that they were perhaps of noble origin. He said: "Welcome, my children. Come here and sit with me." They stepped forward and paid homage with folded hands and said: "With your blessings, we are well." Ki Hartati continued excitedly: "Let's go inside. Please tell me about yourself and don't worry. Regard me as your own father who has not seen you for a long time. My children, last night I had a dream of getting a young rooster and a little hen. I have no doubt that both of you are the answer to my dream. My name is Ki Hartati and I am a merchant from Pekalongan. I've been married for many years, but my wife can't conceive. My brother Menakluhung, is it not so that these children are my children? My brother, you have the knowledge and you know how to explain dreams. Tell me what my dream means, brother!" In response, Ki Menak explained about the ways to unravel the mystery of dreams and agreed that Ki Hartati was correct in thinking that the rooster and hen in his dream were indeed the children. Ki Hartati was so happy that tears flowed down his cheeks and he embraced them: "You hear that, my children? You are my Godsend children. Come with me to Pekalongan to meet your mother."

When they arrived at Pekalongan, Ki Hartati ran to his wife and said: "My dear wife! Welcome your son and daughter! I met them in a dream. They are indeed sent by God, the answer to our prayers. I'll explain further later on." Nyi Hartati embraced them warmly. With tears in her eyes, she said softly: "Welcome home, my children. As your father said, you are the children of our dreams." She took their hands and brought inside. Then the stories were told. The children related their flight from the war stricken city of Giri until they rested at Candi Sela Cendhani. Ki Hartati told them about his dream at Ki Menakluhung's home and Nyi Hartati related her long, lonely nights and of her supplications to God for children. All that had changed for the better. *Subhanallah!* (Glory be to Allah!).

As the children grew older, so too did their parents. One day, Nyi Hartati fell ill and never recovered despite Rancangkapti's care and love. She was so devastated she fainted. The old Ki Hartati, who loved his daughter very much, asked Jayengsari to see to the funeral arrangements while he took care of her himself. He whispered into her ear: "My precious, wake up. Don't despair. You have to pray for your mother to help her attain a good place in the presence of the Lord." By and by, Rancangkapti came to her senses and prostrated at her father's feet: "Father, pardon your foolish daughter! But I beg you not to return to the *pendopo*. Let my brother handle everything. Sit with me while I prepare the flower arrangements. Let me not lose sight of you." Ki Hartati nodded and sat where he could see her. He observed with satisfaction the way she handled the flower arrangements and the offerings for her mother. He was also pleased with Jayengsari whom friends of the family had praised for the excellent way he handled the funeral proceedings. With contentment, he noticed that both of them had grown up to his expectations, perhaps even more. He had the feeling that Jayengsari would do every job he was asked to do well. Rancangkapti, too, gave him nothing to worry about. He realised they were ready to lead their own lives in a world full of harshness and problems. With a smile, he whispered to himself: "God be praised!" Tears rolled down his cheeks.

Days changed into months and the months into years. More than two years had gone by since Nyi Hartati passed away and the 1000-day commemoration of her demise was near. One morning, Ki Hartati spoke softly to them: "According to my calculations, next Friday will be the day to commemorate your mother's death. If, by any chance, the time comes for me to go, then the first thing you have to do is distribute all of my wealth. Take a portion for yourselves and give the rest to the needy and the poor. Then go to Sokoyoso to study with Ki Ageng, who is also known as Seh Akadiyat and is about to become a saint. Finally, lay me to rest beside your mother." On the verge of weeping, Rancangkapti fell onto her father's lap and he embraced her lovingly: "Rancangkapti, my dearest little daughter. I don't want your tears as a token of your love and care for me and your mother but your consciousness as a virtuous daughter towards her parents. When I pass away, all my pious deeds stop except those that still benefit other people and children who are willing to pray for the abolition of our sins. This is what I expect from both of you. The fate of your parents in the hereafter is in your hands."

The Friday they were waiting for came and the ceremony went smoothly. After some of the guests had gone home, Ki Hartati retired to his room to rest. Not long afterwards, a brilliant light radiated from the room; it was so bright that those present were amazed and yet concerned. Jayengsari hurriedly entered the room to investigate. When he came out, he announced that Ki Hartati had passed away. *Inna lillahi wa inna ilaihi raji'un* (Indeed we come from Allah and to Him we will be returned). Ki Hartati had known of his impending death and left instructions for his funeral. His wealth and belongings were given away in accordance with the teachings of Islam. All that his children and Buras had to do was express their appreciation to those who were at the funeral. When it was all over, Jayengsari said: "Little sister, as our father wished, let us go to Sokoyoso." Rancangkapti rose to her feet and said: "All right, brother. Whatever you say."

At the break of dawn, they were at the foot of Perahu Mountain. Without resting even a minute, they started to climb and the air became colder. After a long walk up

above left: *Ragajampi harbour in Banyuwangi, East Java. In* The Centhini Story, *this is where Ki Hartati, Jayengsari and Rancangkapti departed by boat for Pekalongan.*

above right: *Pekalongan village, located on the northern coastal plain of Central Java. As well as being the main port in Central Java for the export of sugar, tea and rubber, it is known for its batik and textile production.*

the footpath, they saw an old man working in a field. Buras approached him: "Kind grandfather, can I trouble you for a moment? My master wants to know what village this is and who the village chief is." The old man said: "Bring me to your master first." Buras brought him to his master and mistress. When he saw them, he felt in his heart that they were no ordinary people. Greeting them respectfully, he asked Jayengsari: "Are you the master of this young man?" Jayengsari replied: "Yes, uncle! We want to go to Sokoyoso but have lost our way." The old man said: "Well, young man, my name is Ki Gunawan. Who are you and where do you come from?" Jayengsari replied: "Uncle, forgive me for not introducing ourselves first. We come from Pekalongan and we were the children of Ki Hartati, the merchant." Ki Gunawan asked: "You said you were the children of Ki Hartati. What happened to him?" Jayengsari then explained the situation: "Forgive me, uncle. I am Jayengsari and this is my sister, Rancangkapti. My mother passed away three years ago, then my father just a few days ago. His last wish was that I go to Sokoyoso to study with Kyai Ageng."

On hearing that, Ki Gunawan embraced Jayengsari and Rancangkapti, saying: "*Inna lillahi wa inna ilaihi raji'un*. My children, I'm a very good friend of your father. We were like brothers. I used to work with him. Your father always helped me by giving me money, but I was never successful. So I decided to leave the problems of trading and find peace in the mountains. If you are the children of my late brother, then you have to think of me as your uncle. Stay with me for a few days. Later, I will take you to Kyai Ageng Sokoyoso." Jayengsari took his sister's hand and followed Ki Gunawan home, with Buras not far behind.

## 10 Sokoyoso

After sightseeing in the Dieng region for a few days where they saw the Dieng temples and the well of Jalatunda, Jayengsari and Rancangkapti did not want to return to Ki Gunawan's home and asked leave to continue their journey to Sokoyoso. But Ki Gunawan objected: "No, no! You don't know the way to Sokoyoso. I said I will take you there and talk to Kyai Ageng. Once he accepts you and you feel comfortable, then I will go home." How happy they were to find such a wonderful and reliable guide.

To cut the story short, they arrived at a field in the region of Sokoyoso and saw an old man working there. Buras walked towards him and called out: "Excuse me, uncle. Can I intrude for a moment?" The old man looked up and saw Buras coming towards him, followed by two men and a girl and asked: "Are you together with those behind? I seem to know one of them. I'm Rogotruno, one of the chieftains of Sokoyoso." As they drew closer, he recognised Ki Gunawan and called out: "Well, Ki Gunawan. I never expected to see you like this, visiting us with your children! Do you want to see Kyai Ageng?" Ki Gunawan replied: "Yes. I wish to see him. Is he well?" Ki Rogotruno replied: "Yes, yes. Please wait while I inform him." He hurried to the village to tell Ki Ageng of the visitors: "Ki Ageng! Ki Gunawan and his children want to see you. They are waiting outside the village." Ki Ageng remarked: "Rogotruno! You know very well that Ki Gunawan has no children. He doesn't even have a wife. Show him in."

Ki Ageng Sokoyoso turned to his wife and said: "Nyai, be prepared. God has sent us children as a substitute for our lost son, Cabolang. Be happy!" Nyai Wuryan wiped away the tears that had welled up in her eyes. Her husband had once said that God would give her children to replace her lost beloved child who left her some time ago. Now, her husband tells her to be happy and why shouldn't she? Holding back her tears, she replied: "*Alhamdulillah!* Kyai! *Allahu Akbar!* (God is the greatest!)." She then went to the kitchen to prepare some food for the visitors.

Ki Ageng was also anxious to meet them. When they appeared in the front hall, he welcomed Ki Gunawan: "Welcome, brother. I'm very happy that you come with your children, really happy. Please have a seat." Ki Gunawan replied: "Thank you, Ki Ageng. You know very well that I don't have any children. These are the children of Ki Hartati. Both Ki and Nyi Hartati have passed away, but not before instructing them to study with you." Ki Ageng said: "*Inna lillahi wa inna ilaihi raji'un* (Indeed we come from Allah and to Him we will be returned). Well, children, the message your parents gave is correct. I'm a very good friend of theirs, perhaps more than that. We are like brothers. When we were young, your father, Ki Gunawan and myself wandered around looking for experiences of life, suffering and sharing good times together. By the way, please feel at home and tell me your names."

Jayengsari paid homage and said: "I beg your pardon, Ki Ageng. I am Jayengsari and this is my sister, Rancangkapti. Indeed, my father had ordered us to study with you. Now we surrender ourselves to you. Whatever you decide, we will abide."

Meanwhile, Nyi Wuryan entered the hall followed by some servants carrying food and drinks. Jayengsari and Rancangkapti paid homage with folded hands. Nyi Wuryan said to Rancangkapti: "My dearest daughter, come with me. Let your father sit with the men. Rancangkapti stood up, paid homage to the elders and said to her brother: "Brother, permit me to go inside with *ibu* (mother)." He replied: "All right, sister."

When Rancangkapti had eaten, Nyi Wuryan asked her to rest and lie down beside her. As she stroked Rancangkapti's hair, she asked her to talk about herself and that was how she learnt of her true identity as the daughter of Sunan Giri Parapen. By the time she finished relating Ki Hartati's death and the light that accompanied his demise, she had fallen asleep. Nyi Wuryan left the room quietly and whispered what she learnt to her husband. She then returned to watch her daughter with love.

Then Ki Ageng said: "Brother Gunawan, for your information, your son Jayengsari is the son of Sunan Giri Parapen and not the biological son of brother Hartati. Let Jayengsari himself tell you his story." Turning towards Jayengsari, he said: "My son, Rancangkapti has told your mother her story. It is now your turn. Do not worry! I'll cover your identity. No secret has to exist between us." So Jayengsari told them everything, from the time Giri fell until he met Ki Hartati at Banyuwangi on the advice of Seh Wahdat. Ki Gunawan was amazed to hear destiny unfolding itself. Ki Ageng then said: "Brother Gunawan! Be my witness. From this moment, Jayengsari and Rancangkapti are my children. Tomorrow, I will proclaim this matter to everyone in the region of Sokoyoso." Ki Gunawan gave his agreement. So too did the people of Sokoyoso.

left: *The Arjuna group of temples on Dieng Plateau in Central Java. Dating back to the 8th century and located 2,000 metres above sea level, they are the first temples ever built in Java. There are five small temples in this group; shown from left are Arjuna, Semar and Srikandi temples. The Dieng Plateau is actually the caldera of a collapsed volcano and was once the site of several hundred Hindu temples.*

# Mas Cabolang

FROM SOKOYOSO TO WIROSOBO
AND BACK TO SOKOYOSO

## 1 The dream

"My dearest, you have been unusually quiet this morning. What is the matter? In fact, you have not been your usual cheerful self for many days. Tell mum, perhaps I will be able to help you." Replied her daughter: "Mother! I'm sorry. Forgive this unfortunate daughter of yours..." She could not continue. Tears began to roll down her cheeks and at length, only her sobs were heard.

Her mother became extremely distraught. It was most unusual to find her sweet daughter, the cheerful flower of the village, to be in such deep distress. She embraced her child and caressed her long black hair. She said: "My dearest! Tell me everything that worries you. Don't make me worry unnecessarily." Daughter: "I'm sorry, mother! Last night I had a dream." Mother: "Well, my child! A dream is a product of fantasy..." Daughter: "No, mother, this dream isn't a fantasy. It's different. I usually forget my dreams when I wake up in the morning, but this dream doesn't seem to want to go away. I try to forget it but I can't. Whether I'm awake or asleep, it stays as if glued to my mind." Mother: "My child, tell me about it! You'll feel better." Daughter: "All right, mother! In the dream, I met a handsome young man claiming to come from Sokoyoso. He came to me to express his love." Mother: "Aha! Forgive your mother, I forget that you are already grown up. Don't worry! I'll talk to your father. For sure he will make inquiries about this young man from Sokoyoso." Daughter: "Mother! That is not the problem! In the dream, my friends were fighting over the same man. Even the boys from our village are crazy over him. Bejo is always singing the tune 'Rindu' (Missing You). Surti and the other girls are singing 'Bapak, Ana Maaling, Malinge Maling Atiku' (Father, There is a Thief Stealing my Heart). Mother, how can I compete with so many

opposite: *A Jathilan dance performance at the Reyog Dance Festival. The festival is held every year on 17 August in Ponorogo Regency in conjunction with the Indonesian Independence Day celebrations. Jathil is the name given to the 'feminine' partner in a homosexual relationship. In the past, boys would perform this role and be similarly made up and dressed. These days, though, girls take on the role of* jathils.

beautiful girls when even the boys are in the race? Perhaps it's just my fate to be always troubled by unsuccessful love."

This story did not happen in one village but also in other villages and even in cities far and wide. The account of the handsome young man continued to grow, troubling the minds of unmarried girls as well as young widows who already had a taste of sexual love. Even the boys were out of their minds. The tale became flavoured with erotic details. The name 'Mas Cabolang' was on everybody's lips. The rumour was that Mas Cabolang had left his parents in search of life's experiences. Well, what kind of experience would a young handsome man want? For sure, it would have to do with love and all the questions and problems that come with it. It is absolutely true that love has its questions and problems, questions that invite other questions. Love's problems are equally numerous. Adam was cast away from paradise because of love and from then on, the problems of love just grew and grew out of proportion.

It was true that Mas Cabolang, accompanied by his four *santris*, left home late one night when his parents and the other disciples at the hermitage were fast asleep. They headed southwest and reached the region of Purbalingga at daybreak. There they took their repose at the house of Ki Sarono, the chief of the village of Dukuh. Mas Cabolang expressed his wish to visit the grave of Seh Jambukarang, an ardent missionary of Islam, who according to legend was one of the sons of the last king of Majapahit. So the next morning, Ki Sarono brought him to see Ki Saroyo, the caretaker of the grave. Ki

*below:* *The grave of Mahdum Cayana, Seh Jambukarang's son. The grave is located at the foot of a hill in Makam village, Banyumas, in Central Java. His father's grave, which is of similar design, is located at the top of the hill. On the steps is the caretaker of the grave.*

Saroyo explained the etiquette to follow when visiting the graves of eminent religious teachers, one of which was not to linger around but leave the place once they have paid their respects. Mas Cabolang and his attendants observed the rule perfectly and when they prayed to bid their leave, they heard a voice say: "Well, my son! I'm very pleased with you. Whatever you wish for and desire, may God be agreeable and I give you my blessings for your further exploits." The caretaker was amazed to hear those words as such things had never happened before. Without delay, Mas Cabolang took leave and headed towards the region of Banyumas.

## 2  The girls of Manut village and the waterfall of Surowono

The long journey made them hot and tired, and when they heard the sound of a waterfall, they quickly headed towards it. How lucky they were! Along the way, they met a group of girls drawing water from a pool using bamboo tubes as tall as them. The girls became very confused on seeing the five men, of whom one was so perfectly handsome. They felt abashed and blushed but could not take their eyes away from Mas Cabolang. Nurwitri, the youngest amongst the *santris*, struck up a conversation by pretending to ask for the name of the place they were in. One of the girls answered: "Brother, the village up there is called Manut (Obedient and Docile) and the waterfall here is called Surowono (Place of Brave Encounter)." Nurwitri responded playfully: "Oh, I see. So you girls are obedient and docile... in other words, available?" The girls did not reply but smiled and gave coquettish glances before running back to the village.

The men continued their way to the waterfall. Although the sun was already very low, the day was still bright. They turned a curve in the footpath and came across a sight so beautiful that they immediately uttered *Subhanallah!* (Glory be to Allah!) in thanks. For in front of them was a rainbow, its colours clear and bright. Water plunged from a height of eight fathoms, spraying water like heavy raindrops, every one of them deflecting the rays of the setting sun and revealing all their glorious colours. Below, they saw the water rush into a river and flow between the trees of a forest, as if splitting the forest into two. They washed and feeling refreshed, walked to the village. It was called Temon (Meeting Place) and not Manut, as the girl had said. That night, they stayed with Ki Dati, the village chief. The next day, they proceeded in the direction of Banyumas, passing through the villages of Pancasan and Kemawi. They came to a big river, the Serayu, where Mas Cabolang got the idea of taking a bamboo raft to get to the coastal city of Cilacap.

above: *A typical home in Temon village, near Banyumas in Central Java. The 'forked horn' ornamentation on the roof is said to symbolise the buffalo, regarded throughout countries in Southeast Asia as the link between heaven and earth.*

| the pre-adulthood journey |

## 3 Ki Naradi, the hermit of Arjobinangun

Ki Naradi exclaimed: "My son Cabolang! You say you come from Sokoyoso. I have a friend there from my younger years, Seh Anggungrimang. His wife is Siti Wuryan. Do you know them?" Replied Mas Cabolang: "Yes, Kyai, they are my parents." He walked forward to pay homage at the man's feet. Ki Naradi embraced him and helped him up. Thus was the conversation between Mas Cabolang and Kyai Naradi, the hermit from Arjobinangun.

Ki Naradi had found the group sitting under a banyan tree and invited them to his hermitage. After they had washed up and eaten, they sat in the *pendopo* and continued their conversation. Asked Ki Naradi: "Well, my son. Did you come here on the orders of your parents or on your own will?" Ashamed to admit that he had run away from home without their consent, he kept quiet and bowed his head low. But Ki Naradi already knew what Mas Cabolang had done and said: "Ah well! Don't worry. You can continue with your ways. It's just like fire. At the point of flaring up, whatever you do to prevent it from flaring up will fail. But in the long run, it will become more powerful and shining, like iron after being burnt in fire."

The next morning, accompanied by Ki Naradi, Mas Cabolang and his attendants visited the Limusbuntu cave, which was said to be the dwelling place of a demon king in ancient times. Then they took a boat to Karangbolong to see a hill of white stone (marble) protruding into the sea. From there they went to Ujung-alang to see a mosque built entirely of stone. As was the case with other mosques in the area, it faced east and came with a kitchen and a room for ladies to pray. There was also a well, guarded by a statue of a big boar. Nearby was a grave, believed to be that of a Moslem disciple by the name of Santri Ayub.

below left: *The entrance to Limusbuntu cave. The cave is situated on the northern part of Nusakambangan island, which lies just south of Cilacap region in Central Java.*

below right: *Masigit Sela, the Stone Mosque. Located in Ujung-alang on the western part of Nusakambangan island, it is filled with coral and limestone stalactites and stalagmites. Hermits continue to use the mosque to meditate and pray for blessings.*

## 4 The Wijoyokusumo flower

From the mosque, they went to Cuwiring Mountain. Looking east from the peak, they could barely make out a group of three islands shrouded in fog. Ki Naradi then related a story of the islands, which today is called Bandung island: "In ancient times, the islands were once a pot where King Kresna kept a magic flower called the Wijoyokusumo. The story goes that a dead person would return to life if the flower was placed above his body, but it would only work for those who died before their time. King Kresna was adviser to the Pandavas during the Bharata war. When the war was over, they released all their weapons into the sea, believing that the presence of weapons would hinder their attainment of bliss. This story was told in the *Swargarohanaparwa* (The Book of the Attainment of Bliss), which formed the concluding part of the *Mahabharata*. When King Kresna threw the pot and flower into the churning waves of the sea, the pot turned into the three islands of Bandung. The magic flower grew on one of the islands where it is guarded by some parrots. Till today, it is believed that the flower can also strengthen the power and rule of a Javanese king. As such, whenever a king is to be crowned, he would always send a messenger to the island to retrieve the flower. If the deities were in favour of the chosen king, the mission would be easily accomplished. Otherwise, the waves of the South Ocean would swallow the messenger up."

When they reached home, Ki Naradi said: "My son, the monsoon will come shortly and cause destruction. I'm not asking you to leave, but for your own sake and safety, you must go now. Take seven steps forward and don't look back." Mas Cabolang paid homage and took the seven steps as advised. Suddenly, and without being aware of anything, he and his *santris* found themselves on a mountain peak from where they could see the Java Sea. They looked around and saw a well and a grave in the shade of a big banyan tree.

far left: *The 'kitchen' inside the Stone Mosque. The cube-shaped white stone is hollow and used by hermits to store rice and other food. The misshapen stone just above it is likened to a boar's head and marks the location of a well. Water from here is used for ablution and cooking.*

left: *Santri Ayub's grave inside the Stone Mosque. Santri Ayub is believed to be a disciple of Sunan Kalijogo, one of the Wali Songo who helped spread Islam in the area. Hermits visit the grave to pay their respects to the disciple.*

# the pre-adulthood journey

right: *Karangbandung island, where the Wijoyokusumo flower is said to grow. The flower exists only for those who can see it and whoever can see it is believed to be the chosen one, the one destined to be king. People today still believe in this flower as the Surakarta (Solo) and Yogyakarta kingdoms still exist. This tiny island lies east of Nusakambangan island.*

## 5 How the Progo River got its name

The water of the spring bubbled out of a cave and flowed into a stream of clear water. While Mas Cabolang was wondering where they were, a man appeared and introduced himself as Ki Kentol Gupito. He was the caretaker of the spring and the middleman between the spirit of the well and the people wishing to make offerings there. Ki Gupito explained: "This place belongs to the region of Jumprit, named after the man who first lived here. The grave under the banyan tree is his grave and has become an offering place for people far and wide." He then related the story of Ki Jumprit:

*Ki Jumprit lived along the Progo River. He suffered from an incurable disease and had tried all kinds of potions and creams to cure himself but none worked. One night, while he was meditating on the Supreme Deity, he heard a voice say: "Well, Jumprit! If you want to be cured, go to the spring of this river and bathe in it until the disease disappears. The water is extremely cold and you must persevere." Desperate for a cure, he left immediately. Every step brought him severe pain and agony. His feet were swollen and blood and pus oozed from the wounds on his body. But his faith in the words of the Supreme Deity kept him going. At length, he reached the place, weak in body but strong in mind and let himself fall into the pool. He didn't know how long he was in the water; it was as if he was unconscious. When he 'regained' consciousness, he got out of the pool and to his astonishment, felt extremely well. He stood up to look for food, which he found aplenty. While eating, he inspected his*

left: *This is Jumprit spring of the Progo River. The structures at the far end are the entry gates to the spring. This is a sacred place for Buddhists who visit every year on Vesak Day, which commemorates the birth and enlightenment of the Buddha. Pilgrims collect water from the spring and carry it on a 5-kilometre procession from Mendut temple to Borobodur temple.*

*body. The wounds had disappeared and there were only traces of sores, which although black, were neither painful nor filled with pus. He fell to his knees and prostrated many times to thank the Supreme Deity. Then with growing conviction, he immersed himself again in the healing water. It was icy cold, but for him it was just fabulous, peerless blessing from God. And so he proclaimed: "From this day, I call this river* **pera raga (sound body and mind).**" *By and by, people pronounced it* **peraga or Progo.**"

Ki Gupito added: "That is also why people come to make offerings to Ki Jumprit."

## 6 The *bedoyo* (dancer's) pool

They moved fast and without any significant obstacles or constraints, arrived at the foot of Mount Sumbing. The cold air penetrated their bones. The *santris* made a fire and sat near it. Its flames were reflected in the water, trembling as if agitated by the cold. Fascinated by the reflection, Mas Cabolang took off his clothes, plunged into the water and began to chase the fluttering flame. For sure it disappeared, as if floating away with the waves, but he continued to swim after it. Nurwitri, the youngest attendant, did not dare enter the water but was brave enough to wash his face with it. Cupping his hands, he scooped water and poured it over his face. Droplets of water fell like sharp needles on the other three attendants—Polokarti, Kartipolo and Saloko—and they jumped away. Only when they were asleep did Mas Cabolang come out of the water. He put on his clothes and sat down to meditate, stoking the fire from time to time.

# the pre-adulthood journey

Suddenly, the figures of a man and a woman emerged from the pool. The man was very handsome and the woman strikingly beautiful and apparently very adept in dressing and making herself up. All their movements were gentle and gracious. The man introduced himself: "Well, my grandson! My name is Candikyudo and my wife is Dyah Rantamsari. She was formerly a *bedoyo* (dancer) in the court of King Brawijaya of Majapahit. Now listen carefully. I prayed to the Supreme Deity to bless this pool, as I would like to leave it as a legacy for the younger generation. The Supreme Deity has accepted my prayers and gave this message: 'Whoever is strong enough to bathe in this pool on the night of Anggoro Kasih [Selasa (Tuesday) Kliwon] will be rewarded.' For instance, whoever looks at that person will fall in love with him or her as all of the person's movements and actions will be gracious and full of charm. The Supreme Deity then named this pool 'the pool of the court dancer' because my wife was once a *bedoyo*." Mas Cabolang paid homage with folded hands and the figures slowly faded into thin air. By then, it was dawn. Birds and other wild beasts were crying out to give their greetings to the new day.

When they woke up, Polokarti noticed something different in the appearance of his master and remarked to Kartipolo: "Have you noticed that our master looks more attractive this morning? Even Nurwitri has changed; he looks more feminine and beautiful. Perhaps the water in the pool had something to do with it." They descended the mountain but had to move very fast as girls and young widows, even women with husbands, wanted to follow the handsome Cabolang and the beautiful Nurwitri. They took a short cut through a forest and passed the villages of Ngadirejo, Keparakan and Temanggung in the region of Kedu.

below: *Sendang Bedoyo (Dancer's Pool). The pool is located at the foot of Sumbing Mountain. Even though much of the water in the pool has dried up, people still place offerings of flowers and fruit for the holy spirit that guards it. As well as burning incense and praying, they will drink the water from the pool in the hope of receiving rewards.*

# 7 The riddle in Tidar

Meanwhile, at the hermitage of Tidar, the ascetic Seh Wakidiyat addressed his four female students—Kismani, Brahmani, Aniladi and Jahnawi: "Well, my dearest! We will have an important guest soon, so clean the hermitage, roll out the best mats and make yourself as beautiful as possible. Prepare food and drinks as your visitor has gone through some difficult times." The girls immediately did as ordered by their venerable guru and took special care to make themselves beautiful. They had many questions. Who was this important guest? Why should they look lovely and adorable for him? What was the intention of their guru… was it to snare a handsome young man for them or to lure a powerful ascetic to the hermitage? Still, they did everything possible to look radiant.

When they were ready, they presented themselves to the priest for inspection. With a smile of approval on his face, he said: "At the foot of the hill you will find five people heading to this place. One of them is most handsome. I want you to invite them here." The girls paid homage with folded hands and left to carry out the order. One of the visitors was very good looking, the priest had said. This thought and the anticipation of a pleasant encounter made them walk even faster. The small footpath was no hindrance at all as they were used to it. They knew very well every hole or stone that might hamper their way.

True enough, they met the young men midway. Both groups were impressed with what they saw. Mas Cabolang and his friends felt as though they had met the fairies Suprobo, Wilutomo, Ratih and Rarasati as they left heaven for Indrokilo Mountain. In Mas Cabolang, the girls felt they had met Witaraga, the honourable handsome priest of Indrokilo. Even with dust and sweat on his body, all they saw was the brilliant and glorious face of that powerful priest. Said one of the girls: "Honourable wayfarers! Seh Wakidiyat, the hermit of Tidar, is aware of your presence and invites you to his place." Mas Cabolang replied, somewhat agitated as he came out of his daze: "Oh! Pardon me a thousand times! Forgive me for not responding accordingly. I thought I saw divine fairies. The invitation of the priest of Tidar is my command. Let's go!"

Seh Wakidiyat welcomed them heartily: "Welcome to the hermitage of Tidar! If I'm not mistaken, your name is Cabolang and you are the son of Seh Anggungrimang and Siti Wuryan. I studied with your father under the same guru, hence our close relationship. Stay with me for a while. When the time comes, you will have to continue your journey to Wirosobo. From there, you will return to your parents at Sokoyoso." Mas Cabolang replied: "Thank you, guru! I put myself in your hands."

So Mas Cabolang stayed with Seh Wakidiyat at the hermitage. Every day, he moved in the company of the girls who fascinated him. He could not escape their charms. The girls, too, could not free themselves from the poisonous arrows of the God of Love, which could make one suffer from lovesickness. And for sure this attraction did not elude the attention of the hermit.

## 8 The temples of Borobudur and Mendut

Along the way, Mas Cabolang recalled the happy times with his wives, who were like the angels in the abode of Indra. The difficulties and loneliness he encountered on his journeys had sharpened his desire to return to the conveniences of life with them. It was only when he came to a forest that his heart could beat in rhythm with the warble of birds and the sound of nature. By virtue of his upbringing as the son of a great ascetic, his lips mumbled formulas of praise and gratitude towards The Almighty. *Allahu Akbar! Allahu Akbar! Allahu Akbar!* (God is The Greatest!).

His steps were guided by faith and stopped only by a stupendous sight, for in front of him loomed an impressive stupa. Although there were already signs of decay due to the ravages of time, the stupa of Borobudur, since its foundation ten centuries ago had always been able to instill feelings of adoration, peace and security among Buddhists and non-Buddhists, with the exception of people without faith.

Mas Cabolang walked up the temple steps and inspected the reliefs on the walls, which recounted tales from the Jataka stories (stories of living beings who later became the Buddha after living according to religious guidance) and those of noble people who travelled around looking for knowledge and life experiences. He felt inspired when he stopped in front of a Buddha statue with its hands in the *dharmmacakra* position, which denotes the Buddha instructing the people to live according to the teachings and guidance of the Creator. The Buddha appealed to humanity to follow his path

below: *The Borobodur temple in Central Java is considered to be one of the Seven Wonders of the World. Built in the 8th century, its walls and balustrades cover a total surface area of 2.5 square kilometres. There are 72 openwork stupas around the temple's three circular platforms. Each stupa contains a statue of the Buddha.*

towards *nirvana* (heaven). Likewise, Rasulullah (the Messenger of God) Muhammad, who ordered his followers to follow his way of life as an example, which was none other than the implementation of the teachings of the holy Qur'an. Tears welled up in his eyes and rolled down his cheeks. As the sun was setting, Mas Cabolang decided to pass the night in the temple. Later, a full moon shone brightly against a blue cloudless sky, its beauty almost perfect. And on Earth, amongst the Buddha statues and whilst his attendants were snoring, Mas Cabolang was deep in contemplation.

They left the temple the next afternoon and headed for another temple in the village of Mendut. The Mendut temple was smaller than the Borobudur temple and its ground

plan was like that of a mosque. The wayfarers inspected the building and were most impressed with the fine carvings of lotuses, upon which rested a figure of a goddess. At the entrance wall, they saw a relief of a mother surrounded by children; she was the goddess Hariti, a symbol of motherhood and prosperity. And upon entering a room, they were most surprised to see another Buddha statue in the *dharmmacakra* position. To its right and left were statues of Buddhisatwas (Buddhas-to-be). Mas Cabolang decided to stay overnight in that room in the temple. Their next stop would be the bustling city of Mataram.

## 9 Mataram

### 1) The cemetery of Kota Gede

In Mataram, Mas Cabolang and his attendants stayed with a young religious official called Amat Tengoro. He was not married and lived with his elderly mother. Neither was he rich, and so he would gratefully accept whatever help Mas Cabolang's *mangunah* (magical power) could bring to help ease his situation a

*above left:* The Borobudur temple is awash with elaborate reliefs such as this.
*above middle:* The relief on this wall of the Mendut temple depicts the goddess Hariti.
*above right:* A statue of the Buddha in the *dharmmacakra* pose, Mendut temple. On the wall to its left and right are the statues of two Buddhisatwas (not shown in the photograph).

# the pre-adulthood journey

above (both): *The Kota Gede Royal cemetery. In the 16th century, Kota Gede was the capital city of the Mataram Islam kingdom. Its first king was Panembahan Senopati. The graveyard complex, about 5 kilometres southeast of Yogyakarta, is where the king's family is interred. Thousands of pilgrims visit the site every year. Visitors, including children, are required to wear traditional Javanese clothes, such as batik breast cloth for women and* blangkon *hat for men.*

little bit more. For as the son of a great cleric, Mas Cabolang had studied with his father and attained special powers along the way.

Ki Amat Tengoro was very popular with the people because he was always ready to help, whether it was by giving tuition in Qur'an reading or helping out on important occasions, such as the birth of a baby where he would read the story of the Prophet's life. On such occasions, Mas Cabolang and Nurwitri would also help out by playing the *rebana*.[3] In addition, on Thursdays when the late afternoon prayer was over, they could be seen at the cemetery of Kota Gede placing flowers on the graves of the kings and dignitaries of the Mataram kingdom.

## 2) The secret to the heart of a woman

One day, after the evening prayer, Ki Amat Tengoro, Mas Cabolang and his *santris* met Ki Amongtrusto, the leader of a troupe of dancers in Mataram, who had invited them to dinner at his home. At the front yard of his house, they were met by a bevy of beautiful girls in colourful clothing. The lower part of their dress was batik, whilst the upper garments comprised breast bands and silk stoles. Mas Cabolang whispered to Ki Amat Tengoro: "Brother, who are these beautiful girls?" He replied: "My brother, in Mataram, they are called *ronggeng*, professional dancers always ready to entertain people in any way possible. They are also called *ringgit* (money) because their services can only be had with money. When all the requirements are met, they can be enjoyed here or elsewhere." Mas Cabolang smiled with understanding and said: "If this is the case, then Ki Amongtrusto's invitation has two purposes—to develop friendship and to promote the skills of the girls." When they met, Ki Amongtrusto disclosed his objectives: "Well, my

---

3 *Rebana* is a type of drum. The smaller ones, which can be held in the hands, are of two types—those with metal cymbals around the edge (tambourine) and those without cymbals. It is usually the girls who use the tambourine. In *The Centhini Story*, there is no mention of cymbals at all, only that one drum is big and the other, small. The big drum is usually too heavy to hold and so is placed on the lap.

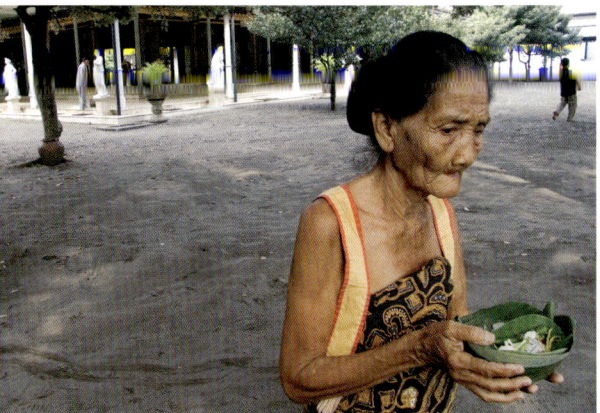

dear Cabolang! Don't be shy. They aren't my daughters but professionals." Mas Cabolang thought: "In this case, Ki Amongtrusto is also a professional pimp."

The dinner was superb, the more so because it was served by attractive women whose voluptuous bosoms would peep out as they bent over. All their movements were aimed to stimulate passion. After dinner, Ki Amat Tengoro and the *santris* took leave and the dancers returned to the waiting room. Only Mas Cabolang and Ki Amongtrusto were left and between jokes and laughter, they talked about women. Mas Cabolang asked: "Uncle, how do you keep a woman loving you so that she will not look at another man?"

Ki Amongtrusto answered: "The secret lies in the body of the woman or by way of a formula. This knowledge comes from a Moslem cleric called Ki Lukmanu'lhakim. There are nerve points on a woman's body which can be used to trigger amorous sensations. Where these points are depends on the date of the Javanese calendar. There are two parts in a month, each corresponding to the waxing and waning of the moon. The first to the fifteenth of the month is the period of the waxing moon; the sixteenth to the end of the month is the period of the waning moon.

"If you want to make love on the first night of the month, start by kissing her forehead; on the second, kiss her navel; on the third, press her left and right feet; on the fourth, press her left and right arm. If you make love on the fifth night, you start by kissing both her breasts. On the sixth, begin by kissing the point between her eyebrows; on the seventh, kiss the point between her breasts; on the eighth, kiss both her lips starting with the upper one; on the ninth, press both her thighs. On the tenth, start by kissing her belly; on the eleventh, kiss her nose. If you make love on the twelfth, start by caressing her shoulders; on the thirteenth, kiss both her breasts like on the fifth. When you make love on the fourteenth, kiss her lips whilst stroking her face. On the fifteenth and last night of the waxing moon, start by kissing her eyebrows. If carried out gently and lovingly, all these can excite her greatly and give enormous pleasure, one that ends in orgasm. The woman will

*above left:* A court servant wearing a batik breast band and silk stole. Nowadays, such dress is only worn during special rituals as well as on court and ceremonial occasions. The woman is carrying an offering in her hands.

*above right:* Batik is an integral part of the lives of the Javanese people. As traditional dress, women wear kebaya, a long sleeved blouse made from silk or other fine material, and jarit, a long cloth of batik wrapped around the lower part of the body.

*following page:* A relief from the Borobodur temple depicting an act of lovemaking.

| the pre-adulthood journey |

opposite: *This is the late Ki Empu Djeno Harumbrodjo, the 15th descendent of a famous kris maker of the Majapahit kingdom and the last great* empu. *An* empu *is a master kris smith who can make a kris sacred by 'filling' it up with spiritual powers, ranging from bringing good luck and successful harvests to curing diseases and preventing death. Clients who commission such krises do not wear them but keep them carefully as a valuable asset. Before starting work on a kris, the* empu *meditates, fasts and performs other spiritual deeds. So too must the client so that he receives a perfectly matched kris.*

become so attached to her husband that she will never leave him. If you make love on the sixteenth, do the same as on the first night and so on.

"As for the formula, it can be used as a substitute for what I have just told you and must be pronounced before or during the act of lovemaking. It goes as follows: *Allahumma janni binus saetan ma rajattana*. My dear, the best of all lovemaking is with your own wife. Before you start, read the *ta'awud* to ask for God's protection from Satan, then say the *bismillah* (the phrase, which means 'in the name of Allah') and end with the mantra *rabbana rabbini rabbi inni*. When orgasm is reached, blow on her forehead three times while holding your breath. Say this phrase in your heart: *Bismillahi rahmani rahim, macan putih ana ndhadha, umetu banyu uripe, ing urip sajroning toya, la ilaha illalah Muhammad rasulullah*. During the act, it is best that you don't talk."

Remembering his four lovely wives, Mas Cabolang enquired: "I ask one more thing, uncle. If a man has more than one wife, how does he maintain harmony and peace between them?" Ki Amongtrusto smiled and replied: "When you finish making love with one of them, don't wash yourself, but make love straight away with the other wives. Certainly they will live in harmony with each other." By then, dawn had broken and Mas Cabolang asked leave to return to Ki Amat Tengoro's home. He then went to the zoo and the market, where he bought a kris. He also visited Ki Empu Anom Mataram, the kris smith of Mataram, to enquire about Javanese weaponry. The subject matter was so complex that Mas Cabolang had to stay a few days with Ki Empu Anom to understand it all.

### 3) Ki Pujangkoro

With Mas Cabolang as his guest and the *mangunah* he possessed, Ki Amat Tengoro's wealth increased so much that he began to think of building a bigger house. One afternoon, he brought Mas Cabolang to visit his uncle, Ki Pujangkoro, to seek his advice on when to build the house. Ki Pujangkoro was an official of the court of Mataram and knew how to determine the most appropriate month and time for embarking on such projects. In fact, his job was to calculate the right time for the performance of functions and ceremonies at the court. Whenever the king wanted to promote his sons and daughters or enlarge the palace, he was the person who would be tasked with determining the appropriate time for doing it.

Entering Ki Pujangkoro's front yard and paying homage with folded hands, Ki

Amat Tengoro said: "Kyai, I want to introduce a son of Kyai Naradi of Cilacap to you. He and his *santris* are waiting outside." Kyai Pujangkoro said: "Well, my son Tengoro. Why are they waiting outside? Let them come in, I'll meet them in the *pendopo*."

When they were comfortably seated, Ki Pujangkoro asked: "My son Tengoro, is your visit here only to introduce Mas Cabolang or do you have other things in mind?" Ki Amat Tengoro replied: "In fact, yes, uncle. I would like to ask my reverend uncle advice for building a house, since the one I have is old and leaking." Ki Pujangkoro said: "That's a good idea. The next month of Dzulhijjah is ideal for that purpose, but it coincides with my plan to marry your sister Ni Mustari to Bagus Samsu, the son of Ki Ngabehi Mangunarjo from Pengasih, on the fourteenth of next month. In fact, you and Mas Cabolang must attend the wedding. You should postpone building your house and help me with the wedding preparations."

Mas Cabolang asked: "Are there auspicious times for building a house or holding a wedding ceremony, Kyai?" Replied Ki Pujangkoro: "Oh, yes! The appropriate time for building a house are in the months Rabi'ul Akhir, Sya'ban, Dzulka'idah and Dzulhijjah. The other eight months are not good for the purpose. There are also auspicious times for promotions or conferring positions on high-ranking officials, which is why the king has a special official like me to take care of such matters." As there was much to do for the upcoming wedding, Ki Amat Tengoro and Mas Cabolang were not allowed to return home.

4) **Preparations for the wedding**

Ki Pujangkoro recruited the help of several people for the wedding. One of them was Nyai Cundamunding, a meat seller, who gave advice on how to slaughter water buffalo or cows so as to get the most out of them. Another was Nyai Padmosastro, who advised on the decorations for the house and on the use of garments and ornaments for the bride and groom and their parents. She stressed particularly on the wearing of green, which is said to be the favourite colour of Nyai Loro Kidul, Queen of the South Ocean. Under no other circumstances whatsoever should green be worn. Then there was Nyai Sriyatno, who took care of matters concerning offerings for the gods and all kinds of spirits.

When the evening prayer was over, Ki Pujangkoro, Ki Amat Tengoro and Mas Cabolang met Pak Goniyah, who would conduct the ceremony for the wedding meal offerings. Although he had performed the pilgrimage to Mecca and was entitled to wear the title of 'haji', he was more popularly known as Pak Goniyah (Father Goniyah, after his daughter's name). While enjoying warm tea and snacks, they talked about everything related to the wedding ceremony, including the meal offerings and prayers. Pak Goniyah explained further: "The setting up of a *tarub* (additional structure for wedding guests) is in fact done to commemorate the marriage of Raden Lembupeteng, a son of the last king Brawijaya of Majapahit,

to Dewi Nawangsih, the daughter of Kyai Ageng Tarub and the angel, Dewi Nawangwulan. When Kyai Ageng Tarub died, Raden Lembupeteng took over his father-in-law's position as a religious teacher and took on his name as well." He would become the forefather of Kyai Ageng Selo, who would, in turn, be the ancestor of the kings of Mataram. The prayer to be recited for the setting up of the *tarub* is the supplication for the welfare of the whole family.

"Then there is the *midodareni* ceremony, which celebrates the visit of nymphs and fairies to the bride on the eve of the wedding. The word *midodareni* comes from the word *widodari*, which means both 'nymph' and 'fairy'. On the eve, a fairy or nymph would enter the bride's body. The bride is believed to look like a nymph if a nymph enters her body and like a fairy if a fairy enters her.[4] The prayer to be recited on this occasion is the supplication for the welfare of the prophet Muhammad and his family, his companions and all his followers. The prayer for the other wedding ceremonies, whether they are held on the fifth or thirty-fifth day after the wedding, is the same. The only difference is the mention of the occasion."

5) ***Lailatu'lqadr, mu'jijat, karomah, ma'unah* and *istiijrat***
At long last, the fourteenth day of the month of Dzulhijjah arrived. Proceedings for the wedding began in the morning and ended with the *temu* ceremony, where

above left: *An offering specially made for weddings. Javanese weddings are incomplete without the giving of offerings, the purpose of which is to ask for God's protection and to pray for the well-being of one's ancestors in the hope of getting their blessings.*
above right: *As part of the wedding preparations, the bride's father puts up a blaketepe on the roof of the house. It is a structure made from woven palm leaves attached to a bamboo frame.*

---

4 In the Javanese mind, fairies and nymphs are beautiful creatures.

the bride meets the groom, in the evening. Since morning, a never-ending stream of guests had been walking in. They exchanged greetings and sat together forming groups of their choice. They talked about everything, but most of all they were praising the decorations and the beauty of the bride. As time passed, the topics focused on more serious subjects, such as traditions and religious matters.

One group of very important guests comprised prominent dignitaries and high-ranking officials of the Mataram court. They were discussing the *lailatu'lqadr* of the month of Ramadhan (Night of Power in the Fasting Month): "If the first of the month of Ramadhan falls on a Sunday, the night of power would come on the twenty-seventh of the month. If it falls on a Monday, then the night of power would come on the twenty-ninth. If it falls on a Tuesday, then the prominent night would be the twenty-fifth. If the month of Ramadhan begins on a Wednesday, the night of power would be on the twenty-seventh, whilst if the first of Ramadhan falls on a Thursday, the night of power would come on the twenty-third. If the month of Ramadhan begins on a Friday, then we would have the night of power on the twenty-ninth. Finally, if the first day of Ramadhan falls on a Saturday, then we would have the night of power on the twenty-first. Keep all this in mind and perform good deeds on this particular night so that you may prosper."

A religious official by the name of Ki Candhana then asked about the meaning of the words *mu'jijat*, *karomah*, *ma'unah* and *istiijrat*. Another guest by the name of Ki Amat Kategan explained them as follows: "*Mu'jijat* is the magical power of a prophet. *Karomah* is the magical power of a learned religious guru. *Ma'unah* is the magical power of a devout Moslem. *Istiijrat* is the magical power of an infidel. Magical power from the first three are only used for good purposes, whilst the last is always applied for evil, which leads to sinful deeds."

6) **The script *Jamus Kalimosodo***

The guests talked not only about religious matters but also of legends and legendary figures. They talked of King Darmokusumo, the king of Amerta from the *Mahabharata* epic, who could not die because he could not read a holy script called the *Jamus Kalimosodo*. The story goes as follows:

❀ *King Darmokusumo was a lonely man. All his brothers and sisters, even his grandchildren, had passed on and he was looking for ways and means to end his life and leave the world, which he felt had become noisy with greedy people whose only preoccupations were worthless worldly pursuits. He made penance so severe that the Gods were afraid that he would destroy the whole universe just to end his life. God Guru descended to Earth one day and told the king that only a Moslem saint—one who was able to read and explain the contents of the holy script—could help him find his goal of having the perfect death. God Guru advised him to be an ascetic in the forest of Glagahwangi (Perfumed Savannah of Reeds) on the island of Java. Heeding the advice, he went to Java and found the forest near the city of Demak, which was not yet founded. For many long years, he made penance there to meet his goal.*

*One day, Sunan Giri ordered a Moslem saint by the name of Sunan Kalijogo to clear the forest of reeds. He wanted to build a mosque there and he wanted it to be the seat of the first mosque on the island of Java. Although Sunan Kalijogo brought hundreds of people to do the job, the reeds kept on growing. Not only that, they grew so fast that a cleared area would be filled with reeds overnight. Curious to find the cause behind it, he went deep into the forest and found an ascetic deep in meditation. He joined in the meditation to wake him up. When the man was fully awake, Sunan Kalijogo asked him who he was and why he was doing penance in such a horrible place. The king told him of his wish to die and that only a Moslem saint who could read and explain the meaning of a holy script called* Jamus Kalimosodo *could help him.*

*Sunan Kalijogo asked to see the scroll. When he opened it, he saw that it was written in the Arabic script. No wonder the king could not read it for he was a Hindu and only conversant with the Devanagari or Pallava scripts and the Sanskrit language. Sunan Kalijogo then explained to the king that he would become a Moslem just by reading the script, as the Kalimosodo text was in fact the* kalimah sahadah, *the Moslem creed. The king accepted the explanation. Sunan Kalijogo then recited the creed, followed by the king. When the king finished pronouncing it, he drew his last breath in peace but not before telling Sunan Kalijogo about the history of the Pandavas. Sunan Kalijogo's knowledge of this history is the reason why he is known as the inventor of the wayang (shadow puppet show) and the gamelan. The king was buried in the north-east corner of the garden of the mosque of Demak. Till today, we can still see his grave, marked under the name of King Yudhisthira.*

7) **The case of the diamond beads**

Ki Amat Setomo, an expert in the knowledge of the Holy Qur'an, then came forward with the story of King Amat Salekan, a powerful ruler of the kingdom of Istambul in the Middle East:

*King Amat Salekan was a just and generous king, who was very much loved and adored by his people. A religious and god fearing man, he always recited the Qur'an with perfect style and understanding. However, there was one verse which always perplexed him—watungiju man tasa'u, wa budi'lu man tasa'u, meaning 'God The Almighty could change good fortune into a bad one in a second and vice versa'. He thought deeply about it and said to himself: "Well, Almighty Lord! If it happened that my palace was burnt down to the ground,*

*I don't think I will fall into poverty in a second because I still have wealth and riches in other areas of my kingdom."*

*One day, after the morning prayer was over, he felt he was in the midst of a forest in the country of Syam,[5] approximately two months journey away from his capital city. He was dressed very simply and the only thing of value he had with him were his diamond beads. For days he wandered about the forest, looking unsuccessfully for food or even a drop of water. He thought to himself: "At this very moment, my palace in Istambul is not burnt down. I still have my wealth and power, but still I cannot find any food or drink. For days I have suffered as I have never suffered before." With this thought, he fell to the ground from hunger and exhaustion. By chance, a merchant came by and looked after the king until he came to. As an expression of his gratitude, the king offered the merchant his diamond beads and asked that he be allowed to travel with him to the city of Syam and later on back to Istambul. The merchant agreed.*

*At Syam, the merchant enjoyed good business. All his goods sold out very quickly and he was ready to make his return trip to Istambul. Only the thought about the diamond beads disturbed him. He felt it would be better for him to sell them off than keep them, but nobody could afford to pay the price. As a last resort, he offered the beads to the King of Syam. The king, however, became suspicious and put him in prison, promising to release him if he could bring the original owner to him. The merchant had no choice but to bring King Amat Salekan before the King of Syam. Looking at his dishevelled appearance and attire, the King of Syam did not believe he was the owner of the diamond beads. And so he ordered King Amat Salekan to be jailed. His feet and hands were shackled and he was in great agony. In this condition, he became aware of the truth of the verse* watungiju man tasa'u, *which originated from Qur'an, 3, 26. One second, he was a powerful and wealthy king and the next, he had lost all his power and wealth and was a prisoner in shackles. This newfound realisation made him repentant and strengthened his faith in God The Merciful and Compassionate (*innallaha ghafururrahim, Q, 3, 31*). Day and night, he did not cease to pray for forgiveness.*

*Now, the King of Syam had a very intelligent daughter. She was well versed in all kinds of knowledge and could recite the Qur'an, which she would diligently do every morning and evening. Every time she made a mistake, she heard someone correcting it and the voice would come from the direction of the jail. She thought: "It is impossible that someone with such expertise can be a criminal. How can one who knows the Qur'an so well be evil? He knows the law. It is inconceivable that he dares to break it." This conviction changed her*

---

5 Syam is an old name of Damsyik, which in the Western world is known as Damascus.

*admiration for the person into pure love. One day, she made an audience with her father to explain her views and request permission to marry the person. At first the king was outraged, but the princess stood her ground and even threatened to take her own life if refused. In the end, he admitted that he was a bit too hasty in handling the matter. He gave his permission and the wedding was performed in secrecy behind bars.*

*The princess did not return to her chambers but stayed with her husband to tend to his wounds. She cleaned them with a special oil that belonged to her father and as if by magic, the wounds healed instantly. His countenance also returned, so that when he appeared in front of the King of Syam with the princess, the king was overwhelmed and made a humble salutation. King Amat Salekan then disclosed his real identity to the delight of the princess and her father. A royal wedding was held followed by festivities that lasted forty days and nights, after which King Amat Salekan returned with his charming bride to Istambul. He perceived that all his sufferings were the result of his wavering mind towards the truth of the words of Allah and his return to glory was also the confirmation of it. His faith became more steadfast and brought him greater inner happiness and moral security."*

Thus ended Ki Amat Setomo's story. For a few moments, there was silence all around until it was broken by an explosion of handclaps.

### 8) Siti Dara Murtasiyah, the exemplary spouse

Let us now enter the inner room where the ladies were sitting around in small circles and discussing exemplary wives of the past. One of the ladies, Nyai Atikah, related the story of Siti Dara Murtasiyah:

*Seh Akbar came from the country of Ngatas-angin[6] (Windward Country) to the island of Java and made his abode near Wonosari Mountain. He had a wife, Siti Supiyah, and a 17-year-old daughter called Siti Dara Murtasiyah. A devout* Moslemah *(female devotee of Islam), she was known for her intelligence and beauty. Her name was always on the lips of would-be suitors. Because of their kindness and generosity, they were very much respected and people came to stay at Wonosari just to be near them. The village became so prosperous that it received the epithet of Wonoraharjo (Place of Peace and Prosperity).*

*Curious about the girl's reputation, a young religious teacher by the name of Seh Ngarip decided to investigate. One Friday, he disguised himself as a wanderer and visited the village where he joined in the communal prayer at*

---

[6] In Javanese stories, Ngatas-angin usually refers to India.

the mosque. On seeing him, Seh Akbar invited Seh Ngarip to lead the prayer and give the sermon, which he did clearly and eloquently much to the pleasure of the audience. Dara Murtasiyah was very impressed by his deep knowledge and simple yet attractive appearance. After the prayer, Seh Akbar invited Seh Ngarip for lunch and in the conversation that ensued, he asked his guest to assist him in teaching the religion. After some time, Seh Akbar gave his daughter to him in marriage. As was the custom, on the day of their wedding, the father of the bride gave some instruction to his daughter in the form of a story. It was the story of Prophet Sulaiman (Solomon) who wanted to test the love and devotion of a couple:

"Prophet Sulaiman summoned the husband to his chambers and told him that he would make him heir to the throne if he were prepared to kill his wife. He then gave the husband a sword to carry out the order. But the man could not do the job when he saw his wife and children sleeping peacefully and so he returned the sword to the prophet. The prophet then summoned the wife to his court and told her that he loved her very much but was hindered by the presence of her husband. If she were prepared to kill her husband, he would marry her and make her queen of his kingdom. The wife agreed to carry out the job and he gave her a shining sword to do the deed. When she arrived home, she found her husband sleeping with the children. Driven by the prospect of becoming queen, she attacked her husband. However, the sword broke into pieces as it was made of tin. Realising that she was tricked, she fell to her knees and begged her husband for forgiveness. The couple then went to the prophet to ask for an explanation as to why he gave those orders. Prophet Sulaiman was in conference with the dignitaries of the land but when he saw them, he said: 'Honourable members of the court. Look at the foolishness of the wife, whose example no wife should follow.' He sought forgiveness from the couple for testing them in such a manner and sent them home with presents."

Seh Akbar ended his story with this advice to his daughter: "Thus, my dear daughter, a wife should love and devote herself to her husband." With eyes brimming with tears, she fell on her knees and said: "My reverend father! Give me your blessings so that I will be able to follow your advice fully."

Seh Ngarip and Dara Murtasiyah were happy together. After a year of marriage, they were granted a daughter called Siti Warsiti. Unfortunately, a mishap struck when the baby was nine months old. Seh Ngarip was having dinner—his wife was sitting nearby with the child on her lap—when the lamp suddenly began to dim. Dara Murtasiyah panicked and quickly put the baby in the crib. To make the lamp brighter, she plucked three strands of hair from her own head and used them to replace the wick of the lamp. Seh Ngarip was surprised that his wife acted without first asking his permission. In his opinion, her action was a big mistake. He ordered her to leave the house, even though it *was pitch dark outside. And when she did not move quickly enough—because she did not have the heart to leave the baby—he beat her several times with a piece of wood and threw her outside the house where she lay unconscious on the ground.*

*When she regained consciousness, she realised that her behaviour was inappropriate in her husband's eyes and decided to return to her parents' home. Her father, however, shared the same opinion as her husband and forbade his wife to give anything to her, not even a drop of water. Dara Murtasiyah had no choice but to go to the forest in the dark of night where she thought she might find happiness… in death. Although it was almost dawn when she reached the wild forest, it was still very dark inside as the sun's rays had yet to penetrate the thickness of the woods. Out of exhaustion, she fell on a flat stone and lay there motionless. It was late in the afternoon when she began to stir. She wanted to pray and looked around for water to wash. But she could not find any and implored: "Well, my Lord! Look at your miserable slave. Even to find water to purify myself for worshipping You, I fail. Even if I succeed in finding water, my clothes are full of filth and unfit for prayer. How can I worship You?"*

*God sees everything, corporeal as well as incorporeal. As she was not guilty of anything and was loyal and devoted to her husband, He sent the angel Jibril (Gabriel) to provide her with all the necessities for prayer. When she finished praying, the angel said to her: "I am ordered to wipe your face and you are ordered to return to your husband." So the angel wiped her face, which became more beautiful and radiant than before. She returned to her husband, but he did not recognise her. She told him that she was his wife's friend and had a message for him, one that asked for his forgiveness. Seh Ngarip forgave her and at that moment, she revealed her true identity. They expressed their deepest gratitude to God The Merciful and Compassionate.*

That was the end of Nyi Atikah's story. Dawn arrived and the guests took their leave but not before being invited to a wayang performance that evening. Before he left, the shadow puppeteer Ki Panjangmas invited Mas Cabolang to visit him.

9) **Partodewo and Murwokolo**
That morning, Kyai Pujangkoro's residence was a hive of activity. People were making preparations for the puppet show, setting up the stage and arranging the gamelan instruments. The women and their assistants were busily preparing food for the feast and for the workers.

When the evening prayer was over, the gamelan players arrived and made final arrangements for the show. They began to play when the host signaled he was ready to receive guests. For the guests, the music was a sign that all was ready and they were welcome to visit. The *pendopo* was covered with mats of good quality.

# the pre-adulthood journey

below left: *A view from behind the screen of a wayang show, where the gamelan orchestra, singers and* dalang, *or puppeteer, are seated. The story being told is that of Partodewo and Murwokolo. The* dalang *can be seen at the front playing the antique Murwokolo puppet. He narrates the story, manipulates the figures, makes the voices and sound effects so as to bring the puppets to life.*

below right: *Holding the Partodewo puppet is the renowned* dalang, *Ki Manteb Sudharsono.*

Guests sat on the mats around low, round tables and helped themselves to snacks and sweetmeats. Soon the puppeteer would start the show. He would take his place near the puppet box, hit the box several times to get the audience's attention and then put some wayang figures on the screen for the first scene, all the while reciting mantras to ensure that the show would progress without any problems.

That evening, the story that was being performed was called Partodewo. The first scene showed King Duryudhono holding an audience at his court of Hastina. The Pandavas had left Amerta in a power vacuum and he wanted to annex the country to Hastina. However, a foreigner, King Partodewo, had occupied the throne. King Duryudhono then ordered his priest, Priest Drono, to drive away the foreign king, but he was not successful and they ended up with great losses.

Another part of the story tells of Priest Kesowo who lived with his younger sister, Endang Mardudari, at the hermitage of Wringin pitu. Endang Mardudari wanted to visit heaven and so they meditated until the gods permitted their souls to travel to heaven. There, she saw King Karithi—the third of the missing Pandava brothers—living lavishly amongst beautiful fairies. She whispered to her brother but in a voice loud enough for the king to hear: "Isn't it a shame that the king is enjoying himself whilst his brothers are missing and perhaps living in misery or even dead?" On hearing her words, the king became cross and wanted to kill her. She fled with her brother back to their hermitage. King Karithi was right behind them but found only Priest Kesowo. The king accused the priest of hiding the girl. They quarrelled and a terrible fight broke out. The result was that Priest Kesowo turned into King Kresna, King Karithi into Prince Arjuna and Endang Mardudari became Princess Subadra. With the return of Arjuna, the other Pandava brothers went back to Amerta to meet

the foreign king, King Partodewo, who was in fact Kamajaya, the God of Love.

The next story told was the story of Murwokolo. God Kala was a demon and the youngest son of God Guru. One day, he asked God Guru for food of human flesh and not his usual food of sandstone. Fearing that God Kala would destroy the abode of the gods if his request were refused, God Guru ordained that the demon would be permitted to devour only the *sukerto* type of human beings. These were, for example, children—either a pair or pairs of siblings of the same or opposite sex—in a family. The demon went on an eating spree much to the disdain of God Guru. God Guru then ordered the gods Narada, Vishnu and Brahma to protect human beings from the demon. They devised a special ceremony, which later became known as Murwokolo (Measures to Control the Demon Kala)."

Five days after the wedding, the bride and groom departed—the bride in a palanquin and the groom on horseback, accompanied by family members. They were going to the home of the groom's parents. Ki Pujangkoro gave his daughter last advice on how to behave properly towards her husband and also reminded the groom to protect and care for his wife.

## 10) The canons, Kyai Setomo and Nyai Setomi

After the departure of the bride and groom, Mas Cabolang, Ki Amat Tengoro and the *santris* took leave from Ki Pujangkoro. Since it was still early in the day, Mas Cabolang proposed to see the twenty canons that belonged to the sultan, all presents from the Europeans. According to the official on duty, Ki Norotoko, the Portuguese gave two canons called Kyai Setomo and Nyai Setomi. And as tribute to Sultan Agung of Mataram, the governor general of the V.O.C. Jan Pieterszoon

below left: *Carvings of Kalamakara can be seen on the gate of the Singosari temple. As an ornament, the Kalamakara motif is found over the entry gates to holy places to prevent demons and harmful spirits from entering.*

below right: *In a tradition that is still played out in Java today, a groom and his bride are about to be 'paraded' around the neighbourhood in a horse cart.*

Coen gave the canons called Kyai Gunturngeni and Kyai Swuhbrastho. Mas Cabolang asked Ki Norotoko whether the canons Kyai and Nyai Setomi were the transformations of the vizier of the kingdom of Pajajaran and his wife. Ki Norotoko confirmed the existence of the legend and said: "After the fall of the kingdom of Pajajaran, the canons Kyai Setomo and Nyai Setomi were brought to Mataram. Later on, Kyai Setomo was returned to Batavia [Jakarta] as it made scary noises at night and frightened the guards. That was what I heard from my ancestors about the story of Kyai and Nyai Setomi."

**11) The pauper**

On the way home, Mas Cabolang and Ki Amat Tengoro met Ki Cendaniraras, a security guard at the sultan's palace. When they came across a beautiful mansion, Ki Cendaniraras told the following story:

*That house belongs to Ki Bagus Hartawan, perhaps the wealthiest man in the city of Mataram. His father, however, was known as the poorest man, not only in Mataram but perhaps in the whole world. His name was Hardosangsoro, which means 'the most miserable man'. Whether it was his real name or a nickname, no one knew. What everyone knew was that he and his family never had enough to eat and were always clad in tatters. Misfortune, one after the other, always befell him and whatever he did would turn into disaster.*

*One day, when he was at his lowest point, he decided to seek the help of the spirits of Roban forest. While walking in the forest, he met an old man called Sorosedyo. The man claimed to know the master of the forest, Ki Wredo, and said all his problems would be solved if he could fulfill the master's wish. Ki Hardo said: "I'm already at the bottom of my lot and all that can happen is for me to die or for things to get better. I have nothing to lose." Ki Sorosedyo replied: "All right! Let's see Ki Wredo. My brother, when we meet him he surely will ask you to marry one of his daughters. When you have chosen one of them, you will be asked to return home to prepare your house to receive her. Do you think you can do it?" Said Ki Hardo: "What? If the test is only to marry, let alone one, two or three girls at once, I think I will have the energy for it. In the city where I come from, not even an old widow would cast a glance at me!" Ki Sorosedyo said: "Really? But I warn you, don't take it too lightly. There might be serious repercussions." Ki Hardo replied: "No worries, brother."*

*When they came to a big banyan tree, Ki Sorosedyo burnt some incense and suddenly the forest transformed into a mansion. In the front hall sat an old man, enjoying his tea. Ki Sorosedyo paid homage with folded hands, likewise Ki Hardo. Ki Sorosedyo said: "Master, I bring with me Ki Hardosangsoro. He wants your help to obtain wealth in abundance." Ki Wredo said: "Ki Sorosedyo, you know the requirement. If he is prepared to marry one of my daughters, I*

| mas cabolang |

will make him the wealthiest man in the world. Well, my son Hardosangsoro, will you marry one of my daughters?" Ki Hardo answered: "With pleasure, master!" Ki Wredo then called his daughters and they paraded in front of Ki Hardo, who could not believe his eyes or his luck as they were beautiful. Ki Wredo said: "Make your choice, my son! Later, you have to prepare your house for her arrival. When you are ready, come back to take your bride home. Only then will you receive sustenance from me." Even with his eyes closed, Ki Hardo was convinced he would make a good choice. So it was a quick affair and he was permitted to return home. The mansion changed back into a jungle.

Ki Sorosedyo then said: "My brother, so far the test seems very easy. But when you return to take your bride home, she will look far different from what you saw just now. She will look horrible and her body will be full of smelly wounds. That will be the real test." Ki Hardo did not realise the seriousness of the warning. With a light heart, he told his wife and children about the matter. They had no objections, since it gave them hope for a better life.

When a week had passed, Ki Hardo returned to the forest to take his bride home. Once again, he met Ki Sorosedyo who gave him another warning: "Be warned, my brother. Remember this when you have your bride safely home. If she asks you to make love to her, decline kindly because if you do so, you will be brought back to the forest and your family will never see you again." They then made their audience to the master of the forest, who asked his daughters to come forward. All of them looked horrible beyond imagination and smelled like a corpse. But Ki Hardo was prepared. He accepted his wife and brought her home. On the way back, she turned back into a beautiful girl.

Ki Hardo's wife and family were away when they arrived home. His new wife asked him to place bamboo tubes at the four corners of the house. That night

above left: *The canon Kyai Setomo. Also known as the Meriam (canon) Si Jagur, it is displayed in the Fatahillah Museum in Jakarta.*

above right: *The canon Nyai Setomi is kept inside this chamber in the palace of the Surakarta kingdom, Central Java.*

**top left:** *Roban forest.*
**top right:** *The hardy trunk of the bamboo tree can be made into useful receptacles.*
**above:** *A rebana band. The size of a band can vary from five to twenty players. Such bands are hired to play on special occasions such as weddings, circumcision rituals as well as religious and national holidays.*

*she asked her husband to make love to her but remembering Ki Sorosedyo's warnings, he refused kindly. The following morning, she went back to her father in the forest with the promise of returning the following week. On checking the bamboo tubes, Ki Hardo found them filled with diamonds, gold and all kinds of jewellery. That happened many times and Ki Hardo became very rich. His bride came every week, each time more beautiful and alluring than before. One night, Ki Hardo could not refuse her request and they made love. Ki Hardo died the next morning and disappeared with his new wife into the forest of Roban. His first wife and son, Bagus Hartawan, inherited all of his wealth and riches.*

### 12) But we are nearer to Him... (Qur'an 56, verse 85)

When Ki Amat Tengoro and Mas Cabolang arrived home, Ki Tengoro's mother reminded him that it was the night of remembrance for his father's death. There would be a celebration and he should make preparations for it. He proposed to Mas Cabolang that they hold a *rebana* recital for entertainment. Mas Cabolang and his *santris* agreed as the lyrics contained religious teachings and were most beneficial for the audience. After the evening prayer, Nurwitri prepared the drums. Then he handed them over to the most senior cleric, Ki Abdulgafur, with the request to start the recital. Ki Gafur delegated the job back to Mas Cabolang and Nuwitri.

After a song or two, Mas Cabolang explained the meaning of the lyrics. Questions concerning *Dalil*, *Hadith*, *Ijmak* and *Qiyas* came to the fore. Mas Cabolang interpreted the words as follows: "*Dalil* are the words of Allah in the holy Qur'an; *Hadith* is the collection of the traditions of Prophet Muhammad, peace and blessing be upon him; *Ijmak* is the agreement among Moslem clerics; and *Qiyas* are elucidations of examples of the life of prominent people in the past. The four of them form the basis of the Islamic law. The *Qiyas* should always agree with the *Ijmak*; the *Ijmak* cannot deviate from the *Hadith* and the *Hadith* should always conform with the Holy Qur'an as the most fundamental source of all." As an example, Mas Cabolang recited a *dalil* from the Qur'an, which reads *nahnu akrabu ilekum wa kinna latupsirana*. It was derived from Qur'an 56, verse 85: *wa nahnu aqrabu ilaihi minkum, walaki lla tubsirun* (but We are nearer to him than you are, though you don't see Me). The verse tells of the prophet sitting by the side of a person who was near death and Allah saying that God was nearer to him even though the prophet could not see Him.

The guests became more captivated and asked about the meaning of the words *ujub*, *riya'*, *kibir* and *sumengah*, to which Mas Cabolang explained: "*Ujub* is the state of having pride but one which is still in the mind. *Riya'* is the state of pride which people can see, for instance, in one's behaviour. *Kibir* is one step further, where one feels he is better than someone else. *Sumengah* (*sum'ah* in Arabic) is the state in which pride is already established in one's nature. We should be aware that pride is a great sin, one that is never tolerated by God."

## 13) The teaching of *sastra jendra hayuning rat* or *sastra cetha*

The next morning, Ki Amat Tengoro and Mas Cabolang visited Kyai Tumenggung Sujonopuro, a high-ranking official of the Mataram court. When they arrived, Ki Tumenggung ordered Ki Amat Tengoro to leave Mas Cabolang with him. It was clear that the *tumenggung* wished to be alone with the *santri*. He led him to the west wing of the *pendopo* and once they were seated comfortably, Ki Tumenggung handed Mas Cabolang the *Lokopolo-Kawi*[7] book and showed him the part he had to read for discussion. It was the section where Priest Wisrowo gave instruction to the demon king Sumali, which is also known as the s*astra jendra hayuning rat* or *sastra cetha*. Before Mas Cabolang departed, Ki Tumenggung gave him this message: "My son, Cabolang! You are a bright and good-looking young man. I advise you not

---

7 There are some peculiarities about this teaching. According to the findings of some students of Javanese literature, the book *Lokopolo-Kawi* (in which the *sastra cetha* was explained) was written by Kyai Yosodipuro II, a court poet of Surakarta. However, in *The Centhini Story*, it was stated that the deities who discussed the *sastra cetha* took their material from the *Jitabsara*, a book written by Raden Ngabehi Ronggowarsito, the last court poet of Surakarta and also the grandson of Kyai Yosodipuro II. Professor Dr Poerbatjaraka, a great scholar in the field of Javanese languages and literature, states in his book *Kapustakan Jawi* (p160) that the *Jitabsara* was written by Raden Ngabehi Ronggowarsito. Furthermore, he is of the view that Raden Ngabehi was not successful at all in his writing of the *Jitabsara*. In the *Kapustakan Jawi* (p158–63), he discusses two books of Raden Ngabehi, the *Paramayoga* and the *Jitabsara*. He is of the opinion that the material in both books was derived from the *Serat Kandha* and have been mixed with some ideas invented by Raden Ngabehi himself, for instance, that a certain Priest Palasara of the country of Amerta wrote the *Jitabsara*. However, Professor Dr Poerbatjaraka maintains that the *Jitabsara* written by Priest Palasara never existed. The other peculiarity was the fact that Raden Ngabehi was the grandson of Kyai Yosodipuro II. Why then was it stated in the *Lokopolo-Kawi* that the *sastra cetha*, written by the grandfather, was derived from the *Jitabsara*, written by his grandson? Perhaps a mistake was made by the original authors or copyists of *The Centhini Story*.

to stay too long in the city as doing so will hinder your spiritual growth." Mas Cabolang admitted that he had difficulty keeping clear of the amorous overtures of the women of Mataram and said he would leave the next day.

## 10 Ki Ajar Sutiksno of Kepurun

Mas Cabolang and his attendants left the capital city very early the next morning. Ki Amat Tengoro went with them as he wanted to visit an old friend of his father's, Ki Ajar Sutiksno, in the village of Kepurun. When the sun had almost reached its apogee, they had lunch in a hut alongside a road but did not rest for too long as it was still a long way to the village. Over at Kepurun, Ki Ajar was aware that they were coming to see him. He ordered his *endangs* to prepare food and drinks, then walked to the periphery of the village where he waited for them. When they arrived, he welcomed them warmly and took them to the hermitage.

Mas Cabolang caught sight of the pretty girls busily placing food and drinks on the table. Ki Ajar laughed: "You only see girls here because the boys are hard at work in the fields. The boys and girls staying here are the children of village chiefs and officials. They have been sent here to learn things that would help them when they grow up." Said Mas Cabolang: "Ki Ajar, forgive us if we are too demanding. Ki Tengoro and I are still single and also very concerned about our future. We would like to know how to find a good wife and build a secure and happy family." Ki Ajar said: "Let's see what I can do whilst you are here."

**1) The Javanese way of finding a good wife**

"The Javanese custom of choosing a wife is based on three principles, called *bobot*, *bebet* and *bibit*. *Bobot* refers to making a choice based on family background. A girl is thought to come from a good family if her parents are of the noble class; live simply; are religious, wise, knowledgeable and courageous; and last but not least, involved in agriculture. The principle *bebet* is tied to the father of the girl, who should be beneficent and wealthy but not tight-fisted. *Bibit* refers to a girl with beauty (in appearance and heart) as well as competence in all things important. There are twenty types of girls. But as there are too many to describe, here are some of them:

- *plongeh*—a girl of this type is always kind-hearted, friendly, faithful, well behaved and capable of achieving orgasm in sexual congress;
- *sumeh*—a girl of this type smiles readily and is calm and patient; her face always glows with intimacy;
- *manis*—such a girl is sweet in nature; all of her behaviour is a source of fascination and charm; and
- *mrakati*—a girl of this type is affectionate and filled with compassion and forbearance."

left: *A Javanese bride on the way to meet her husband, who is waiting in a horse cart. This part of the wedding ceremony takes place after the solemnisation, which usually takes place in the bride's parents' home. On this special day, the bride wears traditional Javanese make-up and her hair is adorned with jasmine, jewellery and ornaments.*

Added Ki Ajar: "Note that the descriptions are only approximate. This is because there are no rigid rules in matters of love. Even if a girl is not attractive, if two hearts find compatibility in each other, any shortcomings will not matter. People say what matters most in wedlock and partnership is harmony. If there is harmony between husband and wife, then a good marriage is very easy to achieve. Nothing is easier than this. On the other hand, if the marriage is difficult, there is nothing more complicated than that. There is a saying that harmony cannot be bought with wealth and riches. The first requirement is feelings. If both sides have nothing to disagree on, then affection would grow, leading to love and harmony. Use the description of the women I have given you to help you choose a wife. You need to make sure your feelings are compatible from the start, otherwise it would be too late and the result would be disastrous. For this reason, everything has to be meditated upon deeply."

2) **How to safeguard marriage**

Ki Ajar continued: "The first thing to remember is that when the wife is too young and has not begun to menstruate, the husband has to wait until she comes of age. If she is forced to have sex before then, she will become a nymphomaniac and can't have children. Secondly, a husband should be aware of five things that can affect his wife. They are *wirya* (position, status), *rahsa* (enjoyment, feeling), *guna* (skill, cleverness in earning a living), *dana* (wealth) and *warna* (good looks). You see, a wife can be tempted by another man whose social position is higher or better than her husband's. She can also be tempted by the desire to have sex with another man

if she is tired of her husband, or she can be tempted by a man who is more skilful in earning a living than her husband. It is also likely that a wife can be tempted by a man who is wealthier than her husband and finally, in many a case, a wife is tempted by a man who is better looking than her husband."

3) **The science of lovemaking**

When Mas Cabolang asked Ki Ajar to explain the real meaning of *ilmu asmaragama*, he replied: "The literary meaning of *ilmu* is science, *asmara* is love and *gama*, which comes from the word *sanggama*, means 'lovemaking'. Thus, the term means 'the science of sexual intercourse between a man and a woman in all its details'."

Amongst other things, Ki Ajar explained the meaning of *katitih asmara* (failure in lovemaking): "If the penis is not strong enough but forced to do the act, the result will be impotence in the man and dissatisfaction on the part of the woman, and she will lose respect for her partner. This impotency is usually caused by mental or physical deficiencies, such as *susah* (worry), *lara* (illness), *luwe* (hunger), *kapok* (aversion), *isin* (shame) and *cuwa* (dissatisfaction). These are some of the twenty causes that lead to impotence and failure in lovemaking." Mas Cabolang smiled as he remembered his own experiences with his former wives.

4) **How to have a decent sex relationship**

"To have a decent sex relationship, there must be good intentions between husband and wife as well as affection and attraction towards each other. The right body language as well as mental attitude can influence the vigour of the penis. There are many constraints and obstacles to be overcome. The exception is a man who approaches sex with the purpose of satisfying his desires, regardless of whether his partner is ugly or attractive, or smells good or bad. Keep in mind that any act that aims to satisfy unbridled passion, in most cases, leads to the man's undoing.

opposite: *Javanese girls waiting to participate in a ceremony.*

below: *Relief of male and female genitals on the floor of the Sukuh temple. This Hindu temple is located on the slopes of Lawu Mountain in Central Java. The elaborate and somewhat exaggerated genitalia symbolises fertility.*

"When the penis has reached its ultimate strength and tension, then the congress should be executed with care because lovemaking should not be one-sided. The man has to satisfy the woman. He should fully understand that there is something known as *wuri purana* ('something behind the screen', that is, the clitoris), which if touched by the penis will result in a sensation that spreads all over the body. Therefore, make attempts to touch it again and again so that the sensation fires the sexual desire, which can be observed in the movement of the partner. If the sensation reaches its apogee, she will release her secret weapon called *barunastra* (the arrow of the god of the sea), a liquid that makes the vagina very slippery. Her movements will influence the penis and an indescribable pleasure will come forth. But he must always keep his pace and be conscious

# the pre-adulthood journey

of her movements so as to help her reach ecstasy along with him. If he is not careful, he will be dragged away by his own enjoyment and will end before his partner is ready to come along. In this case, the husband will fail. *Katitih asmara*, people say, because he will not have any strength left to satisfy his partner.

"On the other hand, the wife can have many orgasms depending on her fitness and stamina. What can one do to prevent failure? The first is to be aware of the situation. When her body movements, along with her soft moans, increase and *barunastra* is discharged and the penis is on the verge of breaking down, stop everything to calm down. Then start again by touching the *wuri purana* with the penis until she seems to run into frenzy. This is the moment to finish all resistance with a great bang. If the penis is still strong enough and the husband wants to start again, he can whisper words of encouragement to his partner until she gradually comes back. Start slowly, touch the *wuri purana* in slow motion just to awaken the sensation, so that the battle can be set up again. If both sides have reached the climax, he must finish the contest with full zest.

5) **The conception**

"When the great bang takes place, the opportunity for conception opens up, marked by an aroma like that of Yasmine (the jasmine flower). With God's mercy, the wife will become pregnant. The pregnancy is described as follows: When the embryo is one month old, it is described as *kusuma anjrah ing angkasa* (flowers strewn in the air); a two-month-old embryo is described as *bremara ngajap angkasa* (bumblebees flying in the sky); at three months, it is known as *isinya wuluh wungwang* (the contents of an empty bamboo tube); at four months, it is known as *brama sakonang angasataken samodra* (a flame the size of a firefly, which is able to dry an ocean); at five months, it is known as *tapaking kuntul ngalayang* (traces

far left: *Jasmine and rose petals. The Javanese use the jasmine flower in ceremonies and special occasions such as weddings, births and death rituals. Its colour and sweet fragrance makes the flower a symbol of purity.*

middle: *Herons taking flight. At five months, the foetus in the womb is likened to* tapaking kuntul ngalayang, *or traces of a flying heron.*

left: *Relief from the Borobodur temple depicting a newborn baby in its mother's arms.*

of a flying heron); at six months, as *canthoka kinemulan elengnya* (a frog hidden in its hole); and at seven, eight and nine months as *jalma lumpuh angideri bawana* (a cripple exploring the world)."

6) **Determining the gender and character of a baby in the womb**
Continued Ki Ajar: "When at the moment of orgasm, the passion of the husband is greater than the wife's, the baby will be a female. If the passion of the wife is greater than the husband's at the time of climax, it will be a male. Should the passion of both be equal, then a twin boy and girl will be the result. Twin girls will be born if the male partner, at the beginning of coitus, wishes to have a daughter and his passion is greater than hers when they reach the climax. Twin boys will be born when the opposite happens.

"The couple's state of mind before, during and after conception can affect the baby's nature. Its character can also be affected by what his mother is going through. For example, if she so happens to witness an unpleasant event while pregnant, she is advised to pray for the well-being of the baby in her womb. Hopefully, doing this will free the child from whatever mishap its mother experienced."

They had been talking since evening. When the night turned to morning, Ki Ajar addressed Ki Amat Tengoro: "It is late, we need to rest. But you have to leave now because on Thursday, the sultan will make you *khatib* (mosque official). Let Mas Cabolang and his *santris* stay here for a few more days." The anticipation of being promoted made Ki Amat Tengoro happy. He embraced Mas Cabolang before taking leave and blessings from Ki Ajar.

During his stay at Kepurun, Mas Cabolang also discussed other topics, such as obtaining wealth or high position by seeking the help of *dukuns* (witch doctors) and by making offerings to statues and trees. Ki Ajar did not agree with such means to get riches or a high position, believing that hard honest work should be the way. Furthermore, supplications should only be directed to God The Almighty and not to created things. They also talked about the Islamisation of Java. Ki Ajar told Mas Cabolang that religious elements from the pre-Islamic age could be maintained along with Islam, the religion of the holy prophet.

Mas Cabolang promised to cherish all of Ki Ajar's teachings. When the time came for him to leave, Ki Ajar gave him a parting message—that his future wife would be Rancangkapti, the daughter of Sunan Giri Parapen, and that he should study with Panembahan Romo of Kajoran.

## 11 Prambanan and the story of Lorojonggrang

From Kepurun, Mas Cabolang and his *santris* proceeded towards the southeast. After walking a few hours, they stopped to rest by a pool with clear water. In it were fish of all sizes, swimming around as if confused to see strangers. Shortly after, a woman arrived to collect water in an earthen jar. She told Mas Cabolang that they were at Prambanan and Ki Harsono was the village chief. Ki Harsono himself had learnt of the strangers and met them at the pool. Before bringing them to his home, on Mas Cabolang's request, he took them on a tour of the Prambanan temple complex, beginning with the Sewu temple and then the Jonggrangan temple. At the Jonggrangan temple, Mas Cabolang asked about a stone statue[8] and enquired about its smoothness. Ki Harsono told him that the statue was actually made of bronze. Today, the Jonggrangan temple is called the Lorojonggrang temple.

They spent the night with Ki Harsono, talking about stories related to the temples of Prambanan. Ki Harsono told the story of Lorojonggrang temple, which concerns the kingdoms of Pengging and Prambanan. In *The Centhini Story*, the story of Lorojonggrang was very long and complicated with many twists and turns. Pengging was ruled by King Poncodriyo whilst Prambanan was ruled by a demon king and manslayer called King Karungkolo, who had a younger sister called Roro Jonggrang. The demon king had asked for the hand of Princess Rarasati, King Poncodriyo's daughter, but his request was turned down and so a long war ensued between the two kingdoms. Together with the help of Prince Damarmoyo, King Poncodriyo finally defeated the demon king. As a reward, he gave his daughter Princess Rarasati to the prince in marriage. Out of their union was a son called Prince Bandung Bondowoso. Princess Roro Jonggrang married Prince Boko. He became king of Prambanan when his wife's father, King Karungkolo, died. In time to come, King Boko killed Prince Damarmoyo. When Bandung Bondowoso came of age, he took revenge and attacked the kingdom of Prambanan. In the battle, Prince Bandung killed King Boko. And as

---

8 There is some confusion here. Mas Cabolang asked about the statue at the Lorojonggrang temple, which is made of stone. However, according to archaeological findings, the statue made of bronze is that of Brahma and was located in the main Sewu temple. Here, the confusion was made on the part of the writers of *The Centhini Story*.

left: *The Lorojonggrang temple. Also known as Prambanan temple, it is part of a group of Hindu temples located in Prambanan District. With some 224 temples, it is the biggest temple complex in Java.*

was the custom then, the king's wife Queen Roro Jonggrang became the property of the victor. The prince wanted to marry the queen, but she would only agree to it if he could build 1000 temples with statues in them in a single night. Prince Bandung could have succeeded in fulfilling the condition but did not because of a trick the Queen played and he lacked one statue. Out of anger, he cursed her and she turned into a statue of stone to make the required number.

*The Centhini Story* also tells of many cases of incest. Here is one example. King Salembi's daughter was married to his younger brother. The couple separated and the wife met her father, the king, again. They did not recognise each other and got married. Subsequently, she gave birth to a demon called Darmomoha, who was in fact the re-incarnation of King Karungkolo. Because the demon defeated the army of Pengging, Queen Roro Jonggrang agreed to marry King Karungkolo, who was her own brother.

Dawn broke, Mas Cabolang asked leave from Ki Harsono to continue his journey to Kajoran where he was to study with Panembahan Romo.

## 12 Panembahan Romo and the stages of knowledge

When they were at Kajoran, Nurwitri asked Panembahan Romo about the stages of knowledge. He explained it as such: "There are four stages of knowledge, the first stage is called *shariah*, which must be practised by the body. The second stage is called the *tariqah*, which should be practised by the heart (spirit); the third stage is called the *makrifah* and must be practised by the soul. As for the fourth stage, it is called the *haqiqah*, which is the part to be performed by means of God's consciousness. The first stage can be likened to the knowledge one has of a boat; the second stage to the

| the pre-adulthood journey |

*above left: Entrance to the Grand Mosque of Mataram in the Kota Gede Royal Cemetery complex, south of Yogyakarta. Behind the mosque lies the grave of Panembahan Senopati, founder of the Mataram Islam kingdom, and the graves of his family.*

*above right: A view of the roof from the porch of the Grand Mosque of Mataram.*

knowledge a sailor has; the third stage to the knowledge of the ocean depths where the precious pearl lies; and the fourth stage to the sum total of all that knowledge.

"For instance, there is no in point having a boat (first stage of the knowledge) and a sailor (the second stage of the knowledge) if we don't have all the information about the ocean—we still won't be able to find the pearl. The person who knows all four stages of knowledge is not an ordinary person, although he or she may be just above average in their knowledge. The one who is most knowledgeable is the one who has already reached the knowledge of a *wali* (saint). At present, such a person is Sultan Agung, the sultan of Mataram. If he wishes to acquire a pearl or go somewhere, he doesn't need to do anything or physically depart from wherever he may be. People who have performed the pilgrimage to Mecca have claimed to see him taking part in the congregational prayer at the holy mosque every Friday. Another example is that of Seh Lemah-abang when he was accused of leaving the *shariah* (Islamic law) and sentenced to death. His body disappeared after the execution, but then his voice was heard giving instruction to mankind to practise the esoteric science in its entirety with sincerity and pure heart. When the voice faded away, the air was filled with a sweet aroma."

Panembahan Romo continued: "But don't misunderstand the stories. I mean, don't abandon the teachings of the holy Prophet as they are the only way to return to God The Almighty. The meaning of the story of Seh Lemah-abang, according to experts in esoteric science, is as follows—for a person who practises the *shariah*, at his demise his body will be separated from his soul. For one who practises the *tariqah*, at his demise his body and soul will not separate but remain as it was in the mortal world. For one who practises the *haqiqah*, when he dies his body and his soul do not separate but complement each other in the realm of death. And finally, for one who practises the *makrifah* after his death his body and soul continue to exist without changing at all."

## 13 The *kalang* people

The next morning, when Mas Cabolang took leave from Panembahan Romo, he was given another message: "Your learning is not complete. You still have to go through much misfortune, including immorality. Please always be careful in whatever you do. May God always look after you! *Insya'A'llah!* (God willing!)" Mas Cabolang paid homage with folded hands and went his way. The *santris* walked down a footpath lined on both sides by paddy plants, swaying slowly as if wishing them a good farewell. Birds could be heard in the distance, their song alternating with the sound of water flowing from the upper terraces of the rice fields to lower ones. Not one of them talked, as if their thoughts were still in Kajoran.

When it was time for the evening prayer, they were still deep in the wilderness, an area with wild bushes and thick undergrowth. Nurwitri remarked: "It's useless to go further and best that we look for lodgings." Kartipolo mumbled: "There is not a single human being around, let alone a place to stay." Saloko suddenly said: "Not entirely true! I smell smoke." Mas Cabolang took the lead and walked against the direction of the wind and through the thorny undergrowth. After a while, they saw four campfires in a clearing, which raised their hopes that there were people around. In the middle was a tree, on which there was a hut. A ladder led to the entrance of the hut.

The owner of the tree house was Ki Wreksodikoro, chief of the *kalang* people (officials of the court of Mataram, whose duties were to look after the forest and serve as guides for people travelling through it). On hearing voices, he came out. He was extremely surprised to see five people standing under the tree and quickly climbed down. How happy he was to learn that one of them was Mas Cabolang. In the capital city of Mataram, he had heard much about this young man from his close friend Ki

left: *Located between the islands of Sumatra and Bali, Java is one of the word's most volcanic islands and is blessed with extremely fertile soils. About 35 percent of cultivated land consists of irrigated rice terraces. Other major commercial crops include rubber, tea, tobacco, timber and sugar. Java is also rich in coal, tin, gold and silver.*

## the pre-adulthood journey

Amat Tengoro and had wanted to meet him for a long time. He invited them to go up to the hut and without waiting for an answer, disappeared into the dark to get some food. He was accustomed to darkness and so could move fast; in a second, he was already beyond the reach of the campfire. Not long after, he returned with two deer, plenty of bananas and other fruit and called out from below the hut: "Well, my dear guests! Give me a hand!" All five of them came down and helped him. He quickly skinned the deer and hung the meat in a corner of the hut. Saloko made the fire and soon the hut was filled with the aroma of barbecued meat. Ki Wrekso said: "The smoke will drive away the mosquitoes." Without more ado, they partook of the meat and fruit and drank palm wine. After dinner, they made up their resting place, which consisted of a mat of plaited palm leaves and a wooden pillow. While lying down, they talked.

Ki Wrekso started the conversation by telling about himself: "I am the chief of the *kalangs*. Many people cut through the forest on their way to the city and back. In the past, people got lost or were robbed. It's much better now, though we can't say it is truly safe." Mas Cabolang replied: "Ki Wrekso, can you tell me about the history of the *kalang* people?"

Ki Wrekso replied: "By all means! In olden times, the Javanese house was built of stone, like the temples. But stone has its defects, for example, roofs made of stone leak when it rains. In the solar year 850 or lunar year 883, a capable high-ranking official by the name of Dipati Santan had the idea of replacing the stone roof of the ruling king's palace with a wooden one. The new roof was a success. And when King Widoyoko ruled over the Mendangkamulan kingdom, he built a big palace mostly out of wood. Because the *kalang* people were experts in cultivating trees, preparing timber for building materials and constructing homes, he appointed them as lower rank officials in his court. The chief of the *kalangs* received the position of a regent, called *kalangkobo*. He had four assistants, namely *kalangblandong* or *kalangkamplong*, *kalang kobo*, *kalangapek* and *kalangbret*. From then on, there existed many types of houses. There are, up till now, *kalang* people who do not acknowledge the authority of the king of Mataram. Those who do are called *kalang mendak*.

**below left:** *A teakwood house belonging to a* kalang *family. Even though the* kalang *people originally came from East Java and Bali, they are presumed to be the natives of Kotagede, which was once the capital city of Mataram kingdom. They moved to Kotagede when Mataram needed skilled labourers and builders. The people are also known for their skills in carving wood and gold.*

**below right:** *This house used to belong to a rich* kalang *family but now functions as a public hall.*

1) **Wood as building material**

"When one wants to build a house, one should know about dendrology and arboriculture, in this case, teakwood. There are many types of teakwood, depending on the place and soil the trees grow in. Teakwood that grows on red soil is hard and its fibre is fine, which makes it a very good material. On the other hand, teakwood growing on black soil is soft and its fibre isn't so fine, and so it is not good building material.

above: *A house under construction.*

"The Javanese believe that the type of wood used in building homes can have good and bad *angsar* (influence) on people. The *angsar* of the wood depends on the wood's colour and the shape of the tree, of which there are eleven varieties. Take, for example, the *uger-uger* (pillar, post). This teakwood tree, which has only two branches, is good for pillars or doorframes. Its influence is good; people living in a house built with posts or pillars from such wood are secure and live in harmony. Another example is the *traju mas*, a tree with three branches. Whoever lives in a house built from this type of tree will have good fortune; the wood is good material for the back hall and the upper parts of the house. An example of a wood with bad influence is the *tunjung*. This tree is the nesting place for big birds and a refuge for animals like monkeys. Whoever lives in a house built with this wood will have bad luck and experience failure in life. This kind of wood is only good for building stalls for cattle and other animals."

2) **Tree felling and wood processing**

Ki Wrekso added: "Before cutting a tree down, we first have to incise around the trunk, about three or four feet above ground level. The incision must be deep enough so as to reach the red inner core of the wood. Then the tree is left in this condition for one year, after which the wood will become dry and the tree is ready to be cut down.

"The spot where the tree will fall should also be considered. Trees should fall in the north or west direction, and not fall on or get caught among other trees. Otherwise, the wood from such trees will have a bad influence. This is how you determine the direction a tree will fall. In the morning or afternoon, when the height of the tree and the length of its shadow is the same, note where the north or west is and mark the length of the tree in one of those directions where no other trees stand in its way. Then make a first cut on the side where you want it to fall. Move to the other side and cut the trunk at a higher position than the first. The difference in height between the first and second cut depends on the size of the trunk; the bigger the trunk, the greater the distance but must not exceed one foot. This way, the tree will fall where it is intended.

| the pre-adulthood journey |

*Marmaningsun aneng donya, dhapur sira ngandikani, tansah ing raga winangwang, among winong sih-ngashi, tansah sih asinung sih, karsanira among kayun, jabeng jro jati suksma, welatung wijil Marapi, tingalira sirna dening tingalira.*
*Yan tan ana ananira, mangsa ana ing dumadi, solahingsun solahira, tan kena kari myang dhingin, tunggal sapati urip, punapa ta rupa nipun, lamun dera tilara, gununge wong Majapahit, kawruhingsun sirnane kawikana.*

**The reason I am alive is because you have ordered me, we are always protecting each other, always loving each other, always giving and receiving affection, your wish is my wish, body and soul are The Supreme Soul, oil coming from Marapi, my vision disappears in Yours.**
**Suppose You (God) don't exist, how could the world come into existence? My deeds are Your deeds, impossible to be in front or behind, whether we live or die. What will happen, if You left me, the mountain of Majapahit, if what I know vanishes, where should I look for it?**

The guests were so impressed with the opening performance that they wanted Mas Cabolang and his friends to stay for another month and perform again. But they declined as they had to leave for Ponorogo the next morning. The recital lasted the whole night. When dawn came, they departed with Kartipolo and Polokarti carrying the drums. The *kalangs* escorted them and when they reached the edge of the forest, one of them said: "If I may, can I give the name Ki Mangunarjo to the big drum and Ki Mangajapsih to the small one?" Mas Cabolang clapped his hands in agreement.

## 14 Tembayat

### 1) Ki Salahudin

Walking through villages and passing through highlands and lowlands, at length they arrived at Tembayat Mountain where they saw a small but beautiful mosque. Mas Cabolang and his attendants went straight to the mosque and met a religious official, Ki Salahudin by name. He told them that they were in Tembayat village, which was founded by Kyai Ageng Pandanarang, later known as Sunan Tembayat. Kyai Ageng was buried on Tembayat Mountain, while his companion, Seh Domba, was buried nearby at Cakaran Mountain. Mas Cabolang expressed his desire to visit their graves.

When they arrived at Kyai Ageng's grave, Mas Cabolang uttered the formula for greetings, to which he received a reply from the grave so clear it could be heard by all present. The same thing happened at Seh Domba's grave. Ki Salahudin was very impressed and when they were back at the mosque late that night, he asked about the greetings and the replies. Mas Cabolang answered that he was just lucky and it had nothing to do with his personality. He also added that both Kyai Ageng and Seh Domba were great ascetics for whom death did not mean extinction but a move from the corporeal to the incorporeal world.

Then Mas Cabolang explained the meaning of *salam* (greetings) in everyday life: "The word *salam* means 'peace', so that one who gives his greetings to another person is in fact giving away his peace to that person. That is why it is obligatory to reciprocate to such greetings in at least the same way, if not better, so that the person giving the greetings receives peace in return. In this way, nobody suffers any loss. Giving greetings of peace is a good deed, one that brings about double benefits—receiving greetings in return and also receiving the reward of God's mercy, which is at least ten times greater and perhaps even 700 times greater than the value of that one good deed. Therefore, Moslems should not think that giving back greetings is unimportant and should know that failing to return greetings exposes one to sin. The only exception is if the greetings are directed to a group of people, then the obligation rests with the group. If one person in the group returns the greetings, the whole group is free from sin, but God's mercy will be given to only that person who returned the greetings."

Ki Salahudin could not keep his eyes open. He mumbled goodnight almost inaudibly and dozed off.

## 2) The story of Kyai Ageng Pandanarang

At breakfast, Mas Cabolang asked Ki Salahudin: "Forgive me for asking another favour. Could you tell me the story of Kyai Ageng Pandanarang and why he was also known as Sunan Tembayat?" Ki Salahudin replied: "With pleasure. Almost everyone here in Tembayat knows the story. I heard it from my grandfather, who knew the *sunan* (king) personally." He proceeded to tell the story:

above: *Seh Domba's grave. Located in Paseban village in Tembayat, pilgrims visit the saint's grave to pay their respects and pray for his well-being. The stack of wood is called* kijing wilangan *and replaces the usual headstone. It consists of nine rectangular pieces of teakwood. The number 9 is symbolic; although Seh Domba is not one of the Wali Songo (Nine Saints of Java), he is as well respected as them.*

❧ *Now, Kyai Ageng Pandanarang was the regent of Semarang and a very rich man although a little tight-fisted. One day, he saw an old man selling bunches of tall grass at the market. Remembering that his stable needed a new roof, he approached the man and asked: "Well, old man! Is the grass for sale? How much are you asking for it?" The old man replied: "Yes, Kyai! The price is three cents!" Ki Ageng said: "All right, old man. Bring it to my house." The man quietly did as told. He received the money and as he was leaving, Ki Ageng told him to bring another load the next day. The man nodded and went away.*

*The next morning, Ki Ageng was having breakfast when the old man came.*

## the pre-adulthood journey

*He ordered the man to put the grass in the stable. When he returned, Ki Ageng asked: "Where do you live, Ki? It's still so early and you're here already." Said the old man: "Kyai, I live at Jabalkat." Ki Ageng asked: "But that's very far away. Do you have lodgings here in the city?" The old man answered: "No, Kyai! I left home this morning." Ki Ageng was surprised and thought: "Who is this man? Does he have special powers or is he a big liar?" He then threw three cents to the man, who had to pick them up from the ground.*

*As he stood up, the old man said: "Actually, I want to ask you a favour, Kyai." Without saying a word, Kyai Ageng threw another cent to him. The old man continued: "I don't want money, Kyai! If I want money, I do not need to sell tall grass." Ki Ageng remarked rather crossly: "What? You don't want money? Don't you know that cents are part of a guilder? If you don't want money, what do you want then?" The old man said calmly: "Kyai, money and gold will only distance you from heaven. This is because worldly riches make people forget their duties towards God and they forget to do good deeds. If I want money or gold, I can get it easily with just one stroke of the hoe. I can get more than enough gold for this lifetime." Kyai Ageng became really angry. He brought a hoe and said indignantly: "If you speak the truth, prove it!" The old man took the hoe and with one stroke on the ground, gold, diamonds and other riches came forth.*

*Kyai Ageng couldn't believe his eyes and realised that he was in the presence of a saint. He fell on his knees and begged for mercy: "Master, I beg your pardon a thousand times. The glitter of gold and the jingling of money have blinded me. I realise now how wrong I am. Forgive me and take me in as your student. Who are you, master?" The old man said: "I am Seh Malaya! If you want to*

below left: *The entrance to the tomb of Kyai Ageng Pandanarang. As a devoted follower of Sunan Kalijogo, he voluntarily resigned as regent of Semarang and settled on Jabalkat Mountain in Bayat subdistrict to spread Islam. He was later known as Sunan Tembayat.*
below right: *The grave of Kyai Ageng Pandanarang, located inside the tomb.*

*study with me, come to Jabalkat. But there are some things I want you to do before that. First, I want you to sound the drum [spread the Moslem faith] in Semarang. Second, leave all wealth behind. Finally, bring along with you* iman *(faith) and* taqwa *(obedience) to God The Almighty. That's all. I'll wait for you at Jabalkat." He stood up and walked away. Before Kyai Ageng could come to his senses, he had disappeared.*

3) **The bamboo stick**

*Kyai Ageng gathered all his family and told them of his intention to study with Seh Malaya. He made his younger brother the new regent of Semarang and asked him to establish Islam there so as to bring about the best in the people. He then ordered his wives and children to give away all his riches to the poor and needy. Finally, he donned himself in a white garb of coarse cotton.*

*His first wife then asked his permission to accompany him. Kyai Ageng did not stop her but gave a warning instead: 'Nyai, the master said that if we study with him, we must leave everything behind because material things will only bring about trouble and suffering. Can you do that?' She nodded in agreement and dressed herself like her husband. She carried their young baby on her back and appeared in front of her husband, holding a walking stick made of bamboo. Without making any comment, Kyai Ageng turned around and started to walk. Nyai Ageng followed him closely. Those left behind couldn't hold their tears.*

*Kyai Ageng walked and walked without resting even for a minute. At the start of the journey, Nyai Ageng could keep up with her husband, but as the day went on, she struggled to keep the distance. Her stick had become heavier and heavier and as it did, her strength waned and the burden became most unbearable with every step. She lagged so far behind that she couldn't even see her husband... for she had disregarded his warning and filled the stick with gold and money.*

*Then trouble came. Three men ambushed Kyai Ageng and demanded his belongings. Kyai Ageng said: "If you are in dire need, wait for a lady behind me. Take her stick, but do not harm her." From afar, Nyai Ageng could see the men and from their behaviour she knew that they had evil intentions. In her mind, she called out to her husband for help: "Kyai! Help! There are three men with evil intentions!" As she neared them, they snatched her stick and ran away. Nyai Ageng was too scared to stop. Without the stick and driven by fear, she ran very quickly. But she still couldn't catch up with her husband. He was too far ahead. She thought: "Baya lali Kyai Ageng karo aku (Perhaps my husband has forgotten me)." Just as that thought came to her, she could see Kyai Ageng waiting for her. She told him about the robbery with great agitation, but he calmly answered: "O God, forgive your sinful slave! And Nyai, be calm! Did*

# the pre-adulthood journey

*I not tell you to leave everything behind especially worldly riches as they only bring trouble? All is fine now; the stick is gone. From now on, the place where you met the evil-minded robbers will be known as Salah-tiga or Salatiga. And the place where you thought that I had forgotten you will be called Boyolali. Now walk ahead. I will stay behind and keep a lookout for likely dangers."*

### 4) The man with the goat head

*"Where is my share?" demanded Sambangdalan, the fourth robber. "You come too late. Everything has been split up," answered another. Another spoke: "We only robbed the wife. Perhaps you can get your share by robbing the husband. He must have a lot of things too. We didn't have time to take his stick." Without delay, Sambangdalan set off to look for the husband.*

*Strangely, Kyai Ageng seemed to know beforehand that another robber would come along and attack him. Not wanting his wife to witness the scene, he deliberately slowed down his pace to widen the distance between them. When Sambangdalan saw Kyai Ageng, he savagely snatched his stick. But it was a plain wooden stick and it was not hollow. Throwing the stick back at him, the robber demanded: "Well, old man, where did you hide your things? Quick, give them to me or I will beat you up black and blue." Kyai Ageng said: "I have nothing on me. Why do you shout like a bleating goat?" Unaware of the changes that were happening to him, the robber began to shout more loudly. But only the weak wavering cry of a goat came out of his mouth. And his head slowly changed into that of a goat's.*

**below**: *This white cement structure, which roughly resembles a goat, was made as a symbol for Seh Domba. It is located in Cakaran on the way to the saint's grave.*

*Kyai Ageng was shocked. Never did he expect his words would turn into a curse and with such terrible consequences. He tried to retract it but to no avail. Realising that only Seh Malaya would be able to undo the curse, he began to walk faster so as reach Jabalkat earlier. Sambangdalan continued to shout threats at Kyai Ageng, stopping only when he came to a brook that cut across the road. There, he felt very strange and became fearful of the water. Looking into the water, he saw not his face but the head of a goat. He then realised that the old man he tried to rob was a saint with the power to punish him very severely. With that discovery, he jumped from stone to stone to cross the brook, while begging for mercy. Again, all that was heard were bleating sounds.*

*It was almost evening when they arrived at the top of Jabalkat Mountain. They found a small mosque. Next to it was a big vat, but there was no water in it for ritual ablution. Kyai Ageng told Ki Sambangdalan: "Listen carefully. If you want to repent and be released from your sins, fill up the vat with water, but don't plug up the spout. When the vat remains full, it means that your sins are forgiven and you will return to your original form."*

*To Ki Sambangdalan, it was an impossible task. The vat was on top of the mountain, the water was in the valley below, and the path up and down was difficult and slippery. Whatever water he carried up the hill and poured into the vat would all be drained out before he could even reach the pool in the valley. He knew that he was being punished, not only for robbing Kyai Ageng but also for murdering and harming innocent people. Now he wanted to show his repentance and sincerity. Day and night, tirelessly and without resting a minute, he worked and worked, his mind focused only on The Almighty, The Merciful and Compassionate.*

*After some time, Seh Malaya appeared. He accepted Kyai Ageng and his wife as his pupils and changed Ki Sambangdalan back to his original form. The vat remained filled with water even though it was not plugged up. Seh Malaya, who was also known as Sunan Kalijogo, then bestowed the name Seh Dombo on Ki Sambangdalan. The master then shoved his walking stick into the ground. When he pulled it out, water gushed out and a spring was created; this spring has never since dried up.*

Added Ki Salahudin to Mas Cabolang: "The present *sunan* of Tembayat, Sunan Tembayat II, is the son of the legendary Kyai Ageng Pandanarang, who later on was known as Sunan Tembayat. The robber with the goat head later became a great religious teacher." He then told his guests that he would bring them to see Sunan Tembayat II.

5) **Sunan Tembayat II**

It was a Friday when Ki Salahudin brought Mas Cabolang to meet Sunan Tembayat II. When they arrived, Ki Salahudin went ahead to report their arrival while Mas Cabolang and his attendants waited outside. The king was sitting in the main hall with a guest from Mataram, Ki Empu Kinom. Ki Salahudin paid homage with folded hands and sat respectfully in front of the *sunan*, waiting to be addressed. Sunan Tembayat asked: "Salahudin, who was the person calling the prayer this morning? Do you have guests?" Ki Salahudin replied: "Yes, milord! They arrived last night before the evening prayer. They introduced themselves as *santris* from Kedu. One called himself Mas Cabolang. They wanted to visit the graves of your father and Seh Dombo and so I brought them there."

Said Ki Empu to the *sunan* (king): "I know this young man, my brother. He is the son of Seh Anggungrimang or Kyai Ageng Akadiyat of Sokoyoso." Sunan Tembayat then ordered Ki Salahudin to bring them in. When they finally met, Mas

# the pre-adulthood journey

above: *The Khaol ceremony with* rebana *devotional music is performed yearly to commemorate the death of Sunan Tembayat. Death is seen as the beginning of life in the immortal world and so, death for holy people like Sunan Tembayat is to be celebrated.*

Cabolang related all of his experiences to the *sunan*, who was so fascinated that he asked him to stay. For the next few days, Mas Cabolang was tasked with the job of recording all that Ki Empu Kinom said concerning the kris and other matters. It so happened, too, that the king would be celebrating his birthday in a few days. Mas Cabolang was ordered to give a performance of *rebana* music and magic.

The birthday celebration was a roaring success. Everyone, including the *sunan*, was captivated by Mas Cabolang's magical skills. For instance, he made a twig with small fruit grow rapidly and bear so much fruit that there was enough for everyone in the audience. Even Nurwitri cooked rice and chicken in a piece of cloth. The evening closed with songs of praise to the holy prophet. When all the people had gone home, Mas Cabolang asked the *sunan* about the meaning of the words *fasik, munafik, musyrik, majusi, maksiyat, gidib, lacut, murtat, kafir, kafir 'inda nas* and *kafir 'indallah*.

The king gave his explanation as follows: "A *fasik* is not really a believer, but he wants to perform the *shariah* (law, rule) of the holy prophet. A *munafik* is one who knows the rules and the meaning of *fardlu* (obligatory), *sunnah* (optional), *makruh* (things to be avoided), *batal* (void, invalid) and *haram* (forbidden), but he never observes them despite promising to do so and thus disregards God's commands. A *musyrik* is one who does not believe in the existence of God and so worships other created things. A *majusi* is an unbeliever who has promised to observe Islam but still does things contrary to its laws.

"*Maksiyat* are acts not in accordance with the laws of Islam. *Gidib* means false, untrue words, which are only sweet talk. *Lacut* means 'to break all bonds of decency'. *Murtat* is the act of leaving the fundamentals of Islam. *Kafir* means 'unwillingness to perform religion'. A *kafir 'inda nas* is an unbeliever, one who adheres to a religion that is not Islam. A *kafir 'indallah* is a person who performs the religious laws, but in his mind he does not believe in God."

Later, the *sunan* talked about the ceremonial rice offerings that are held on five different nights in the month of Ramadhan. The offerings—which commemorate the descent of the Qur'an and its revelation to Prophet Muhammad—are held on the twenty-first, twenty-third, twenty-fifth, twenty-seventh and twenty-ninth of the month. These are special nights because six chapters of the Qur'an were revealed on each of the nights. *Lailatu'lqadr* (Night of Power in the Fasting Month) is believed to be the night when the holy Book descended to Earth and on that night, God sent his angels and spirits to distribute wealth to men of his choice. The *sunan* then explained the important days in the month Dzulhijjah.

Dawn broke and the discussions came to an end. Nurwitri made the call to prayer. When prayers were over, Ki Empu Kinom departed for Mataram. Mas Cabolang and his companions proceeded with their journey to Ponorogo.

## 15 Ki Wonokarto

It was after the evening prayer. The moon was like a little sickle, not bright enough to discern the difference between a stone and a hole. Only few stars decorated the black sky above. Mas Cabolang was unsure as to which direction to take for they were in the midst of a vast plain and there was neither fire nor light to show the presence of people. He looked around and saw a light beam soaring into the sky and exclaimed: "Look! That lighted spot doesn't seem too far away. Let's go there." They walked on, but when they thought they had arrived at the spot, there was nothing to be seen. The *santris* were again trapped in gloomy darkness. They sat and waited for the light that might come to show the way.

Along came an old man. Introducing himself as Ki Wonokarto, he invited them to his home and told them about himself: "My son, I too originally came from Mataram. When I was young, I was a close friend of Kyai Pujangkoro. My wife and I learnt much from him. Many people came to us seeking our advice or for herbal medicine. We were so busy we didn't have time for ourselves. So we left Mataram for a quieter place."

After dinner, Mas Cabolang enquired about the kind of advice that people usually asked of him. Ki Wonokarto explained: "They are mostly about choosing a wife or daughter-in-law and how to have a good marriage by knowing the nature and character of the girl based on her date of birth." Nurwitri asked: "Kyai, you know that I'm single and, if you don't mind, I would like to know the way to see the character and nature of girls and boys. Later, when it is time for me to marry, hopefully I'll be able to make a good choice." Ki Wonokarto explained all that he knew. Finally he said: "That is all I know. But you should also realise that those are only assumptions. If it is determined that the girl is good, don't be too happy. Neither should you despair if the outcome is not good, because it is God's mercy, for which we should be thankful." Nurwitri made homage with folded hands to express his gratitude.

### 1) The luminous plain

Mas Cabolang continued: "Kyai! Forgive me a thousand times! When we were in confusion in the midst of pitch-black darkness, we saw a light not far from us. We let ourselves be guided by the light, but when we came near, the light disappeared. We were plunged into greater confusion until you found us. Can you perhaps explain this peculiarity?"

Ki Wonokarto answered in a low voice: "My dear son! When I was still in the capital city, I had a talk with Ki Pujangkoro about the future of the world in general and of Mataram in particular. He told me that the kingdom of Mataram would

*above left: A mix of herbs and spices commonly used for medicinal purposes in Java. Javanese traditional medicine is called* jamu. *Clockwise from top left: sesame seeds, coriander, candlenuts, coffee, rice, corn, cinnamon, keluak nuts, star anise, soy beans, mung beans, nutmeg. Centre: kidney beans*

*above right: Pare or bitter melon. The Javanese use this as a remedy for impotency.*

exist for only two more generations. I couldn't believe my ears because Mataram is a strong and powerful state. The ministers are very capable, the king is a *khalifah* (vicegerent) and a *waliyullah* (friend of God). How is it possible that the fall of such a kingdom is so near? But Ki Pujangkoro's opinion was based on the *Nitisastra* book, which said that there would be big wars in the *dupara* age. The signs can already be seen, such as land that radiate light to the sky. That place you refer to is located west of Pajang. But let's not talk anymore about things that are still a secret of God. I'm afraid the knowledge can be misused by irresponsible people." Mas Cabolang agreed, even though he longed for further information.

2) **Traditional medicine**

Meanwhile, Saloko helped Nyi Wonokarto in the kitchen. He used this opportunity to ask her about the traditional medicine that the people still rely upon. She gave him the prescription for several ailments:

- for fever—roast and then make a paste of wild ginger, turmeric and shallots. Rub the paste on the body. Or pound fennel, rice, wild ginger, pepper, cubeb, shallots, chillies, sugar and salt into powder; stir well in a cup of boiled water and drink.
- for intestinal worms—make a concoction by chewing *laos* (galingale), *dlingo* plant, *bengle* herb, *mungsi* herb, *bawang putih* (garlic), salt and charcoal of teak wood. Put the paste in a cloth and squeeze into the mouth of the patient.
- for deafness—mix together pepper, the root of the *merenggai* tree (Moringa Sp.) and gizzard of a black chicken with sesame oil. Apply the paste on the affected ear. While applying, recite the chapters An Naas [Mankind] (Q, 114) and Al Falak [The Daybreak] (Q, 113).
- for myopia—knead the leaves of the *kecipir* (four-sided bean) and apply the paste on the affected eye.

- for headache—mash up *pulasari* (anise), *kapulaga* (cardamom), *kemukus* (cubeb), garlic. Add water and drink.
- for toothache—mash up garlic and tamarind, and apply on the affected tooth."

Ki Saloko asked: "Is there a potion for impotency, Nyai?" Nyi Wonokarto answered: "Yes. Use leaves of the *pare*-vine (bitter melon or momordica), mash it up and apply it to the penis before intercourse. For lack of stamina, extract oil from the *brutu* (fleshy part of the tail) of a black chicken. Put the oil in a bottle and apply on the penis when needed. These medicines have more power if applied in the right manner and right time in accordance with the *wuku*."

## 16 Pajang

After staying and studying with Kyai and Nyai Wonokarto for three days, Mas Cabolang and his friends left their company and continued their journey. They passed through pasture where children were grazing their sheep and goats.

The children had seen Polokarti and Kartipolo carrying their drums and followed them. One child was so rude as to beat a drum with the handle of his whip. To stop him from further mischief, the *santris* began to beat the drums very loudly, which frightened the children and they ran away. But they did not stay away for long and came back soon enough, laughing and giggling. Ki Saloko pulled out a bunch of grass and scattered it around. The grass changed into coins, which jingled as they fell on the ground. The children scrambled for the coins but could not find any because Ki Saloko played another trick and turned the coins back into grass. By the time they came to their senses, the *santris* were already out of sight.

As they sat under a sapodilla tree, an old man carrying a sickle walked up to Mas Cabolang. He introduced himself as Ki Mastuti and offered some information about the place they were in: "This area is called the region of Pajang and where we are standing at present is the old site of the city of Pajang. Its history is rather different from that of Mataram although the genealogy of the house of Mataram and Pajang goes back to King Brawijaya of Majapahit.

"King Brawijaya had 101 sons and daughters from many wives who came from different places. His third daughter, Ratu Pembayun—who was born from Queen (An)dorowati from Campa—married the Regent of Pengging and had two sons. Her elder son, who did not convert to Islam, was Ki Kebokanigoro. Her younger son, Ki Kebokenongo, embraced Islam and was also known as Kyai Ageng Pengging. Now, Kyai Ageng Pengging had a son called Mas Karebet. When he and his wife passed away, Mas Karebet was brought to Tingkir and looked after by a woman called Nyai Ageng Tingkir, which is why he was known as Ki Jokotingkir, the young man of Tingkir.

From a young age, Ki Jokotingkir could be seen making penance in caves and forests. When he came of age, he joined the Royal Bodyguard Brigade in Demak. The

# the pre-adulthood journey

*above left: The photo shows* glagahwangi, *or aromatic reed (foreground). Also known as* rumput bambu, *it is a tall grass that grows to a height of 4 metres.*

*above right: Located behind the Demak Mosque are the graves of Raden Patah (brown headstone) and his family. Raden Patah settled in Demak and Demak kingdom became the first Islamic kingdom in Java. The kingdom reached the height of its power in the middle of the 16th century and ruled as far away as West Java.*

king of Demak, Sultan Trenggono, loved him very much and gave him a high position in Pajang. After the sultan's death, the *wahyu kedaton* (God's spiritual power bestowed on the one destined to become a king) moved from Demak to Pajang. Ki Jokotingkir became king of Pajang and took the name of King Adiwijoyo. When he died, the seat of government moved to Mataram but his son, Prince Banowo, remained as prince of Pajang. The prince had a daughter, Princess Banuwati, who married King Mangkurat Senopati of the Mataram kingdom. When the king died, he was known as Sultan Sedakrapyak (the king who died in Krapyak). King Mangkurat Senopati was the father of the present king of Mataram, the great grandson of King Adiwijoyo."

### 1) Sultan Syah Alam Akbar I

Ki Mastuti continued: "Among King Brawijaya's many children was Raden Patah, his thirteenth son. He was born to Su Ban Chi, a princess of Chinese origin. When she was three months pregnant with Raden Patah, King Brawijaya bestowed her to Aryo Damar, the regent of Palembang. With Aryo Damar, she had a son called Raden Kusen. When both her sons were older, they left home to serve with King Brawijaya. On the way to Majapahit, they stopped at Ngampeldento to study with the Sunan of Ngampeldento. Raden Patah decided to stay on in Ngampeldento while Raden Kusen continued his journey alone to Majapahit, where he was appointed Regent of Terung.

"Over in Ngampeldento, Raden Patah proved to be a brilliant student and was much loved by the *sunan*. The *sunan* made him his son-in-law by marrying him to his daughter, Dyah Juminten. After the wedding, Raden Patah was ordered to go to the west to look for a forest of aromatic reed (Glagahwangi). Together with his wife and several attendants, they travelled to the region of Bintoro and found the forest.

They settled in Bintoro and soon, many people came to stay. The community grew into the thousands after a few years.

"One day, Raden Kusen went to the forest to convey a royal order to his half-brother, Raden Patah. Their father, King Brawijaya, wished to see him. Raden Patah obliged. The king was happy to see his son again and appointed him as Regent of Bintoro. Not only that, he gave him several thousand people from Majapahit. The regency grew very fast and became the kingdom of Demak/Bintoro.

"When King Brawijaya died, Raden Patah was crowned king and took on the name of Sultan Syah Alam Akbar I. He was the first Moslem king of the first kingdom of Java. Raden Patah had six sons. The eldest was Prince Sabranglor, who became king when his father died and was called Sultan Syah Alam Akbar II. When he died, his younger brother Prince Trenggono ascended the throne in Demak and became known as Sultan Syah Alam Akbar III. It was he who took Raden Jokotingkir as son-in-law, when he arranged for his daughter Princess Dyah Banar to marry him."

2) **Sultan Agung**

Ki Mastuti explained further: "King Brawijaya of Majapahit once suffered from syphilis, an incurable disease. One night, when he was deep in meditation, he heard a voice say that he could be cured if he spent the night with a yellow-skinned *wandan* girl. He heeded the advice and was cured, but the girl became pregnant and gave birth to his fourteenth son, Raden Bondan Kejawan. The baby was sent away and looked after by a person called Buyut Masahar. When he came of age, he was sent to study under Kyai Ageng Tarub. Kyai Ageng had a daughter called Dewi Nawangsih with his wife, the angel Dewi Nawangwulan. When Kyai Ageng died, Raden Bondan Kejawan took over his position as guru and changed his name to Kyai Ageng Tarub II.

"Kyai Ageng Tarub II had three children—two boys and the youngest, a girl. His eldest son, Raden Dukuh, also known as Seh Ngabidullah, married a daughter of Sunan Majagung and lived in Wonosobo. His second son, Raden Depok, also known as Seh Ngabdullah, married another of the *sunan's* daughter. As he lived in Getaspandowo, he was known also as Kyai Ageng Getaspandowo. His daughter Roro Kasihan married Kyai Ageng Ngerang and was known as Nyai Ageng Ngerang.

"Now, Kyai Ageng Getaspandowo had twelve children. His second child was a boy called Raden Sogom, who was later known as Kyai Ageng Selo. Kyai Ageng Selo had fourteen children, one of whom was Bagus Enis. Bagus Enis went to Pajang to devote himself in the service of King Adiwijoyo as a bodyguard. The king loved him so much that he gave him land in the region of Nglawihan, free from tax. Bagus Enis lived and died in Nglawihan, which was why he was also known as Kyai Ageng Nglawihan.

| the pre-adulthood journey |

above: *The entrance to the graveyard complex that houses the grave of Kyai Ageng Nglawihan.*

"Kyai Ageng Nglawihan had two sons; the eldest was Bagus Kacung, later known as Kyai Ageng Pemanahan. Like his father had done before, he was a bodyguard to King Adiwijoyo of Pajang. The king was so pleased with his work that he gave him the lands of Mataram. As such, Kyai Ageng Pemanahan was also known as Kyai Ageng Mataram. When he died, he was buried at the grave behind the mosque at Kota Gede in Mataram. In his life, Kyai Ageng had thirty-three children, of whom his second was a son called Raden Sutowijoyo. This son was later on known as Ngabehi Loring Pasar (Nglawihan) because he lived north of the market of Nglawihan.

"When King Adiwijoyo died, Pajang remained a princedom as the throne had moved to Mataram and was ruled by Raden Sutowijoyo. Raden Sutowijoyo did not want to be called king and so was known by the title of Panembahan (One, worthy of worship) Senopati of Mataram. When he died, his son became king and took on the title of Mangkurat Senopati. He was the one who married Princess Banuwati, the daughter of Prince Banowo. King Mangkurat Senopati had a son who succeeded him after his death. This son is Sultan Agung, the present ruler of Mataram."

After hearing the stories of the famous and important figures in Java's history, Mas Cabolang expressed his desire to visit Kyai Ageng Nglawihan's grave. So Ki Mastuti brought him to see Ki Ngabdul Antyanto, the chief caretaker of the grave, who was also related to Sultan Agung. Ki Antyanto invited Mas Cabolang to stay the night with him and introduced him to his younger brother, Ki Ngabduljulur, an assistant village chief of Sala and therefore, he is also called Ki Sali.

| mas cabolang |

left: *Pilgrims visiting the Imogiri royal cemetery. Located on a hill south of Yogyakarta, it was built in 1645 by Sultan Agung of Mataram. Access to the cemetery is via 454 stone steps. Under Sultan Agung, Mataram reached the peak of its power which covered all of Java except Banten and Cirebon (both in West Java) and Batavia (Jakarta). His grave lies at the very top of the hill. Only his descendants, royal members of the Surakarta and Yogyakarta kingdoms, are allowed to visit his grave. The graves of the royal families from these kingdoms can also be found in the cemetery's many courtyards.*

They were knowledgeable people and so Mas Cabolang took every opportunity to get more information about the future of Mataram. Ki Sali related the prophecy of King Jayabaya about the future of Java, which he had heard from his teacher who, in turn, had relied on the *Book of Musarar*. According to the prophecy, the history of Java was divided into three ages [of past, present and future]—the age of Kalisworo, the age of Kaliyogo and the age of Kalisengoro. Java's history began with the arrival of people from Rome who came to populate the island and would end at the time of doomsday. Ki Sali's account lasted well past midnight.

3) **Sayid Markaban**
Ki Antyanto then told the story of the wise and caring King Abdulrahman, who ruled over the kingdom of Mesir (Egypt):

*Every night, King Abdulrahman would secretly inspect the city to see for himself the conditions of his people so that he could help those in need as quickly as possible. His people loved him for his benevolence and generosity.*

*Amongst his subjects, there was one whose behaviour was very unusual and puzzling, to say the least. His name was Sayid Markaban. Even though he did not have a regular job and income, he would hold a banquet every evening for anyone who cared to come. He had a strong and sturdy body and was gifted with many skills, so that earning money was not an issue. Every day he divided his earnings into two parts; he gave one part to his wife for family expenses and spent the other part on food and drinks for the feast. Curious to know more* about this man, the king disguised himself one day and attended the feast. When he arrived, Sayid Markaban welcomed him jovially: "Come in, brother! Don't worry about anything. Let's be happy." The king was amazed with the warm welcome and that no questions were asked. While having his meal, he asked: "Brother, where do you get the money to provide such good food every day?" Sayid replied: "Well, my brother! All these come from the generosity of our king and the blessings of God The Merciful. Every morning, I gather wood in the forest and sell it in the city. Whatever I earn, I give one part to my wife and the other to buy food for people who do not have anything to eat. Enough talk, let us eat and be happy!"

Back at the palace, King Abdulrahman instructed his vizier to forbid people from taking wood from the forest. So when Sayid Markaban went to the forest the next morning, he found it guarded by soldiers. He then went to the city and earned money by pounding rice, cutting hair and doing a bit of sewing. That day he earned $100. He gave $20 to his wife and spent the rest on the feast. When the king asked him where he got the money, he related what had happened and concluded: "My brother. I feel I'm really blessed by Allah through our beneficent king. Let's stop talking and start eating and be merry!"

Because of the king's determination to stop Sayid Markaban from earning money, he set new rules. From then on, the man earned very little. Yet, with whatever he earned, he would always set aside money for his wife and the feast. King Abdulrahman enquired one day: "Well, brother, what happens now? There is almost nothing to eat." Sayid Markaban replied: "Well, brother, fortunes come and go. I don't have much money today because the king has disallowed many things. But let's still be thankful to God and pray for the king's welfare. If you are thankful, God will increase your sustenance." The king shook his head in disbelief and said: "Brother, what has happened to you? Your king is a despot for preventing you from earning money. You must curse him. That will be most appropriate. Let's leave the country. It's no use staying with a king like that." He countered: "Don't say that, brother. It's not proper to say such harsh words about the king. He does not mean harm and I feel that all these regulations are for the good of the people. Furthermore, I was born here and have been living happily for a long time. For what reason should I leave country and king? And finally, how will you help me? You come here every night to have a meal. It would be best for you not to say anything anymore because if the king heard of it, you might get yourself into trouble."

The king was flabbergasted. The next morning, Sayid Markaban found all avenues of earning money closed. There was nothing he could do except to become a soldier, from which he received a salary of $150. He gave $50 to his wife and spent the rest on the feast. King Abdulrahman was most surprised to hear that Sayid Markaban had spent almost a whole month's salary on one night's feast and was curious as to what the man would do the next evening. Yet, a feast went on as usual. And when he learned that the man had pawned his service sword for money, he became furious. Back at the palace, he devised a plan to put Sayid Markaban on the spot.

The next morning, the king announced that he would sentence to death two ladies-in-waiting. Everybody was puzzled; no one could understand why their king had become so cold-hearted. The queen pleaded for the lives of her favourite attendants, but the king was adamant. When the time came to decapitate the women, the guards could not do the deed and offered their resignation. Only Sayid Markaban was left. He was in a dilemma. He couldn't resign as it would mean insubordination towards the king's order, which came with a most serious repercussion. He also had no sword, having pawned it to host the previous night's feast. He would certainly face the death sentence if the king knew what he had done. However, he had an inspiration at the very last minute. Paying homage to the king, he requested permission to speak. The king was surprised and allowed him to speak. Sayid Markaban said: "My Lord! The ladies are to die for unspecified reasons and I am supposed to carry out the king's decision without question. However, I feel that I, as a slave of the king, should protect his master from making the wrong decision. So I pray to Allah The Almighty and Merciful to replace my sword with a bamboo sword if He declares the two ladies free of blame." He drew his sword and to the amazement of all to see, it was indeed a bamboo sword. Sayid Markaban faced the king, fell on his knees and bowed his head low.

King Abdulrahman was most impressed by the man's wisdom. He stood up and spoke: "My ladies, all dignitaries of the court and all my subjects present today. At this moment, we witness the ultimate wisdom of Sayid Markaban. He protects me, his master, from conducting a grave mistake. Out of loyalty and devotion, he facilitates the release of the ladies from death. Last but not least, we come to know of his philanthropic life and devotion towards God The Merciful. I would like to have him in my service. From now on, the old vizier is released from his present duties and will become tutor to my beloved son. I order Sayid Markaban to take the position of vizier and assist me in ruling the kingdom. May God approve and witness my decisions."

When he had finished relating the story, Ki Antyanto told Mas Cabolang: "I would like you to stay for another day or two, but it is with regret that I have to say goodbye to you. You have to continue your journey and your search for more in life." Mas Cabolang was most impressed by his sagacity. It was as if he already knew what was in his mind. Thanking him profoundly for all his teachings, the *santris* asked leave and blessings. At daybreak, they were already on their way.

## 17 Majasto

### 1) Raden Joko Bodo

A few days later, the south mountain range appeared bigger, the forest became thinner and the grave of Majasto loomed in sight, glittering in the afternoon sun. Mas Cabolang and his friends stopped under a tamarind tree next to the Dengkeng River to rest. After a while, they washed and purified themselves in the river and made preparations to pray.

Their arrival was noticed by Kyai Joyomiloso, who had seen them from the front yard of his house, which was built on higher ground not far away from the grave. He ordered his wife to prepare food and drinks and then went to meet them under the tamarind tree. Ki Joyomiloso introduced himself: "I am Ki Joyomiloso, the caretaker of the grave of Majasto. If you don't mind, please stay with me tonight as it will become dark soon." Mas Cabolang replied: "Thank you for the invitation, Kyai. When we came, we were attracted to the grave and would like to visit it before heading for your home."

While walking to the grave, Ki Joyomiloso told them a little of its history: "When the Majapahit kingdom fell, Joko Bodo, one of King Brawijaya's sons, went

| mas cabolang |

to the region of Tembayat and became a devotee of Sunan Tembayat. He was given the name Sutowijoyo. When he completed his studies, he was sent to the region of Majasto to preach Islam. Eventually, Ki Sutowijoyo became known as Kyai Ageng Majasto. When he died, he was buried here. I am a great, great grandchild of Kyai Ageng and I've been tasked to take care of his grave. In return, I've been given land around here, free of taxes." Mas Cabolang said: "If that is so, then all the rice fields I see around here are yours, Kyai?" Ki Joyomiloso replied: "Yes, my child. You are right, but I take only what my family needs. The rest is for everybody living in this area as they help me cultivate the lands." Mas Cabolang said: "What an original idea! That is what I call true charity. Ah, Kyai! I'm dying to visit the grave."

When they arrived at the grave, Mas Cabolang pronounced the words of greeting. As if by magic, the gravestone moved as though to show its appreciation. Mas Cabolang repeated the words as he left and the gravestone moved again. Ki Joyomiloso just knew that his guest was not an ordinary *santri*.

opposite: *The entrance to the Astana Majasto graveyard complex, Sukoharjo Regency in Central Java. There is a mosque just inside the gate at the top of the steps. Behind the mosque is the graveyard where Joko Bodo's grave is located.*

2) **The raft and the crocodiles**
After dinner that night, Mas Cabolang asked his host: "Kyai, there is a peculiar dent around the trunk of the tamarind tree. Do you know how that happened?" Ki Joyomiloso answered: "Yes, there is a story behind it."

❖ *Kyai Ageng Majasto went to Banyubiru. He wanted to visit a friend, Kyai Ageng Banyubiru. While there, he met Ki Jokotingkir, the son of Ki Ageng Pengging, and another person by the name of Ki Wilo. Kyai Ageng Majasto learnt that Ki Jokotingkir had been expelled from the court of Demak for a grave misconduct—he had killed an aspirant young man called Ki Dadungawuk, who wanted to serve in the Royal Bodyguard Brigade and boasted to have spiritual power. Ki Jokotingkir challenged him to a trial, to which the young man agreed. He hit the man with a betel-leaf, which caused a wound and killed him. Sultan Trenggono was angry with Ki Jokotingkir. To him, a cadet should undergo certain tests but should not be killed over them and he summoned Ki Jokotingkir to Prawato Mountain to explain himself. Kyai Ageng Banyubiru, however, believed that the kingdom of Demak would become weaker should Ki Jokotingkir leave the sultan. To prevent that from happening, he took a handful of earth from Banyubiru and gave it to Ki Jokotingkir. The earth would later remind the king of his need for Ki Jokotingkir's services.*

*Four people left Banyubiru for Prawato Mountain—Ki Jokotingkir, Ki Wilo, Kyai Ageng Majasto and his son, Ki Mas Monco. They crossed the*

---

9 Ki Wilo is known in the *Babad Tanah Jawi* (*The Chronicles of Java*) as the younger brother of Kyai Ageng Majasto. Ki Wilo also looked after Ki Mas Monco, the son of Kyai Ageng Majasto.

| the pre-adulthood journey |

above: *The Dengkeng River. The river has its source in Merapi Mountain and empties into the Bengawan Solo River, Java's longest river.*

*Dengkeng River on a bamboo raft. When they reached Majasto, they tied the raft to the trunk of the tamarind tree. Kyai Ageng Majasto ordered the tree to stay put and not succumb to the force of the current in the river. That night, he gave the three youngsters advice concerning good behaviour as well as some mantras to recite. When they removed the rope to use the raft the next day, a dent had been formed in the tree trunk and has remained there since. Sailing down the river, they were attacked by man-eating crocodiles. But they could overpower the reptiles by using the tricks they had learnt from Kyai Ageng. As a token of surrender, the crocodiles agreed to carry the raft downriver to their destination. When they reached the landing place of Sultan Trenggono's palace, the men left the raft and entered the forest.*

*"In the forest, Ki Jokotingkir caught a wild buffalo and put the earth he received from Ki Ageng Banyubiru in its mouth. It made the buffalo mad and it began to attack everyone who stood in its way, even unnerving the ladies of the court. Many people were hurt trying to capture the beast. At first, the king was delighted as he had never before seen such a spectacle but grew concerned after a while. Then he saw Ki Jokotingkir and sent his valet to summon him.*

*Sultan Trenggono said: "The buffalo has been disturbing the peace for many days. The ladies of the court and your wife are frightened to death. Kill* the buffalo!" Ki Joko Tingkir couldn't believe his ears… that his beloved wife, Princess Dyah Banar, was here with her father, the sultan. He made homage with folded hands and immediately ran out to look for the animal. He was away for weeks and months, which made his wife angry with her father as she wanted to be with her husband. Sultan Trenggono said: "My dearest daughter! Do you want to see your husband? Look, he's in the front yard, fighting the buffalo."

The princess, shocked beyond imagination, cried out: "Father, how cruel you are! How could you order my husband to fight the wild animal?" She ran out to the verandah and there he was, being butted up into the air by the wild beast. She shouted his name and almost fainted. Ki Jokotingkir heard the cry, shouted back and waved his hand. That brought her back to her senses and she stood up and watched. Now Ki Jokotingkir, while feasting his eyes on her slender figure and beauty, decided to show off. He allowed the beast to butt him on all sides and trample over his body until the ladies cried out in fear. Then the sultan called out: "Enough, Joko! You are making the dust whirl around." On hearing the king's order, he performed his final stunt. He let the buffalo butt and throw him into the air. But in a sudden move, he swept across the sky and struck the beast on its head with his hands. The blow shattered its head, spewing blood and brain all around. All the women, including his wife, fainted. The show was over. Inside the palace, people were busy helping to revive the ladies. Outside, Ki Jokotingkir was humming a serenade of love as he proceeded to clean himself up."

3) **Kyai Ageng Banyubiru**

Mas Cabolang then asked Ki Joyomiloso: "Kyai! I ask your pardon a thousand times if I disturb you with questions that might distress you. I want to ask you about Kyai Banyubiru. He was so powerful and wise and gave Ki Jokotingkir special gifts that helped him become king. I would like to visit his grave to pay my respects and pray for his blessings." Ki Joyomiloso replied: "That is not so difficult to arrange. The caretaker of the grave is Ki Suhud, a relative of mine who is also from Majasto. I'll take you to the grave. Let me now tell you the story of Kyai Banyubiru's life.

"This story goes back to King Brawijaya of Majapahit kingdom. The king had more than 100 children and when the kingdom fell, his twenty-eighth son Raden Aryowongso made penance at Pilang. He then went away to study with Sunan Kalijogo. One day, Sunan Kalijogo told him: 'My son, go and preach Islam. But if you want to give instruction in the secret knowledge [*tasawwuf*, or mysticism], do that on Banyubiru Mountain near Gajahoyo Mountain. Change your name to Kyai Purwoko Sidik. After giving instruction in the secret knowledge, soak yourself in a pool with blue water.' Kyai Ageng did as told and lived in Banyubiru (blue water) village. So at Pilang where he made penance, he was known as Kyai Ageng Pilang;

# the pre-adulthood journey

at Banyubiru, he was known as Kyai Ageng Banyubiru. He founded another village north of Banyubiru, which he called Taruwongso. It is probable that he died at Banyubiru as he was buried there. One of his descendants, Ki Hercaranu, was also buried at Banyubiru and would sometimes make his presence known to Ki Suhud, the caretaker of his grave. That's all I can tell you at the moment. Ki Suhud and his brother, Ki Sahid, might be able to tell you more."

Together with Ki Suhud, the entire party visited the graves of Kyai Ageng Banyubiru and Kyai Hercaranu. Mas Cabolang prayed and pronounced the words for greetings, to which he received replies. At Kyai Hercaranu's grave, Mas Cabolang received this message—that although Mas Cabolang could not see him at present, they will meet at Wonontoko at a later stage of his life.

## 18 Girimarto

### 1) Kentol Endrasmoro

The next morning, Ki Suhud accompanied Mas Cabolang and his friends on their way to Ponorogo, whilst Ki Sahid returned to Taruwongso. The walk to the village of Teleng was pleasant as they passed through picturesque countryside. Ki Suhud left them at the village. Following closely Ki Suhud's directions, they eventually arrived at the region of Girimarto.

They stopped at Hermoyo pool and sat under a leafy tree. Mas Cabolang sat by the pool and submerged his feet in the water. Polokarti and Kartipolo, the *rebana* carriers, played the drums softly, while Saloko and Nurwitri sang in a low voice.

| mas cabolang |

far left: *Kyai Ageng Banyubiru's grave in Wonogiri Regency, Central Java. Pilgrims visit his grave to pay their respects.*
middle: *Banyubiru pool, Wonogiri. The local people are not familiar with the stories attached to the pool and it is probable that the story of Kyai Ageng Banyubiru was written only in* The Centhini Story. *These days, any pond that has 'blue' water is simply called* banyubiru.
left: *Pesantren Tremas. This old traditional religious school in Pacitan region is known for its expertise in Arabic grammar. Pesantrens have served as major centres of Islamic education in Java since the early 16th century. Their main objective is to preserve the teachings of Islam. Each school offers a specific area of study, such as Qur'anic literature, Islamic Law and Arabic language.*

Kartipolo and Polokarti became so sleepy that they covered their faces with the *rebana*. Their breath touched the drum skin, which vibrated rhythmically, making very soft, hardly audible sounds. Still, Nurwitri and Saloko did not notice the difference and continued singing. After a while, they too fell into slumber. Mas Cabolang was fascinated by the sight of big red carp swimming in the pool. One or two even dared to touch his feet. The sun was leaning low to the west and it was around this time of day when girls from the village would gather at the pool to collect water. They were surprised to see the young men there. As they came nearer, Mas Cabolang looked up. The girls were immediately overwhelmed by his good looks and their behaviour became awkward. One dropped her water vessel; another fell into the water with a resounding splash, waking up the *santris* with a start. Their sudden movements surprised the girls even more and they quickly ran away. The boys exploded into laughter.

Not long after, a well-dressed young man appeared and introduced himself as Kentol Endrasmoro, the son-in-law of the village chief. Mas Cabolang told him that he was a wandering *santri* and wanted to go to Ponorogo to study religion. Kentol Endrasmoro felt a sudden closeness to the *santri* and said: "My younger brother, Cabolang! I was once in the same situation as you. Several years ago, I was also on my way to Ponorogo. I stopped at this same spot with ten other *santris*. My father was a religious teacher and leader of the mosque of Winong in Mataram. He forced me to go to Ponorogo because I was naughty and didn't want to learn the religion. He believed that the school there would turn me into a god-fearing person. However, it seemed that God had already planned something else and other ways to achieve the same objective. I met a girl, a sweet little girl, with dimples in her cheeks. I was sitting at the exact spot as you are, red carp darting around my legs. Then she appeared. I looked up and I was so surprised that I stared at her and then I fell into the pond. The last thing I saw was her smile, which caused dimples to appear in her cheeks. If my companions didn't help me out of the water, I certainly would have drowned to death." Mas Cabolang responded: "You're kidding, my brother! You're so melodramatic." Ki Endrasmoro smiled and said: "So, you won't believe me? I'll show you." He took hold of Mas Cabolang's right hand and as if dragging him along, led him towards the village. The other *santris* had no choice but to follow them.

On the way, Ki Endrasmoro continued: "But, my brother, if you see her, you mustn't fall in love with her for she is now my wife." Again Mas Cabolang laughed heartily and voluntarily followed his newfound friend to his house who explained further: "You see, brother! When I came to my senses, I asked my companions to accompany me to see the village chief, Ki Nurgirindro. I told him about the girl I saw and described her to him. I had fallen head over heels in love with her and begged him to help me find her. He invited us to sit and gave me dry clothes to wear. While I was changing, Ki Nurgirindro interviewed my companions and came to know of my background and the reason why I was going to Ponorogo. When I returned, the chief said to me: "Well, young man. I heard from your companions that you are a bad boy and that your father wants you to study at Ponorogo. That's not a good start to find your dream girl. Her parents certainly will not allow you to marry her but I have a plan. If you promise to become my student and study hard and mend your ways, I give you my word that I'll help you find her. Do you want to do that? For a long while, I kept quiet. Then I said: 'Master, I can't promise you that. My companions are right. I am bad, through and through, but to find that girl, my God! If you help me, master, whatever and however hard your order, I will do it.' I turned to my companions and told them: 'Go to Ponorogo and come back later. If I succeed, you will find me here, but if I fail, tell my father that I am dead.' Then I prostrated at Ki Nurgirindro's feet and said: 'Master, my fate is in your hands.' My companions left the next day and returned after a few years to find me happily married."

Mas Cabolang asked: "Why do you stop so abruptly? Did you succeed in finding her? Who was she?" Ki Endrasmoro answered: "Questions, questions! My brother, think! If I don't succeed, if I don't marry the girl of my dreams, do you think I'd still be alive? Do you think I can live without her or with another girl?"

When they were in the *pendopo* of Ki Endrasmoro's house, Mas Cabolang asked: "Brother! You haven't told me who your dream girl was. Now, please tell me. Don't keep me in suspense!" Ki Endrasmoro said: "That girl, the girl with the dimples, proved to be my master's daughter. Yes, she is Indradi, the daughter of Kyai Nurgirindro. I found that out after a few days, but her father was very strict and stricter still in keeping me bound to my pledge. I studied and studied as a good student should, and worked and worked as a would-be son-in-law should." Mas Cabolang laughed but stopped abruptly as four beautiful ladies appeared with snacks and drinks.

Ki Endrasmoro said: "Well, my brother Cabolang! Let me introduce my wives. The first is Indradi, the second is Suresmi, the third is Suwadi and the fourth is Lulut." Mas Cabolang exclaimed: "Brother! You said you couldn't live without sister Indradi or with any other girl. Now you introduce me to four girls as your wives! What does this mean?" Ki Endrasmoro replied: "I said I can't live without Indradi. It's true... she is my first wife and always will be. However, I didn't say that Indradi would be my only wife. Now the number is complete! Four is still within the limits of the *shariah*." Mas Cabolang was flabbergasted and a bit confused. The ladies, on the other hand, were amused and smiling.

above: *A relief from the Borobodur temple depicting two lovers.*

After the evening prayer, Ki Endrasmoro joined his guests at the cottage that he had specially provided for them. He wanted to discuss *makrifah* in its relation to the *shariah* as an important matter in life. Mas Cabolang explained as follows: "In the book *Palakil kobra*, it is mentioned that the nature of man's existence—whether good or bad, lucky or unlucky—is already pre-ordained. Man does not need to do anything to change it. What man must do is follow Providence. There is no need to have an individual concept of life. In the *shariah*, man has to make special effort to better one's destiny. So the difference is whether to make the effort or not."

Ki Endrasmoro replied: "Frankly, I can't adhere to the *tasawwuf* (mysticism) entirely and wait for destiny to play its part. On the other hand, I'm not prepared to tire myself to make efforts. Brother, is there a middle way?" Mas Cabolang replied: "In my opinion, *tasawwuf* is related to the heart, the spirit or the soul, whatever you understand it to be. The *shariah* is related to the ordinary life, the physical life. Man should live in accordance with the law and leave the result to God." Ki Endrasmoro added: "If that is so, then having four wives is in accordance with the law. What I should be doing is to make them happy so that they do not fight among themselves. The result is destiny." Ki Endrasmoro was happy with his findings. However, Mas Cabolang said: "And how would you make four wives live happily with each other? If you have the answer for it, please tell me!"

## the pre-adulthood journey

**2) The secret of sex-play**

Later on, Mas Cabolang enquired: "Brother Endrasmoro, tell me about the secret of sex-play, as it will be very useful for me in the future. Don't hesitate and be assured that I will be most grateful."

Ki Endrasmoro replied: "All right! Because you have regarded me as your older brother, I'll tell you man to man. If you want to make love to your wife, sit facing her the way you would sitting at the first half of prayer. Hold her head with both hands, as though you are going to massage her forehead. Lower your right hand and place it on her right thigh and your left hand on her left thigh. Spread her thighs, so that they are squeezing your thighs. Then, still sitting and with her right leg in the same position, stretch out her left leg and put it on your right thigh. When both are comfortable, pronounce the *bismillah hirrahmanir rahim*, followed by the *ayat qursi* (Q, 2, 255). Then you can go into her. Begin by placing the penis just halfway into the vagina; then slowly and gradually go deeper and stronger. Watch her movements. You will know she is at the point of orgasm when you see her body hair standing on their ends and she is panting for breath. At that moment, you as husband should remember these points:

- If the woman is of the *bongoh* type (ample and firm body), the penis should enter the vagina like a wild snake into its hole but slowly.
- If she is of the *dhenok* type (soft and fleshy body), she should be positioned halfway upright and the penis should move lightly as though kissing a flower.[10]
- If she is of the *sengoh* type (broad shouldered), the penis begins its way from a point below the right side of the navel, then slides down until it reaches the vagina. The woman must lie on her back, her knees bent and a little apart.
- If she is of the *merakati* type (attractive), the penis first touches a point below the vagina and then slides up into the vagina, like a canoe into a cave. Once it is inside, it can move stronger. When the vagina is wet with viscous fluid, move faster.
- If she is of the *sumeh* type (friendly and affable), the penis begins at a point below the navel, then slides down into the vagina. When slimy fluid comes forth, move stronger.
- If she is of the *manis* type (dark skinned but sweet), begin by touching the penis below the navel, then move to the left of the navel and slide down and enter the vagina, like a bee entering a flower for honey. If the penis has been inside long enough and has touched the clitoris again and again and viscous fluid is abundant, the signs of orgasm on the part of the wife is visible. Finish intercourse with a bang.
- If she is of the *merak hati* (kind, sweet-natured) type, enter her gently as though caressing her forearm. The movements are cautious. When there is slimy fluid and uncontrollable gasping, reach orgasm together.

---

10 In the Javanese context, kissing is not kissing with the lips but with the nose. So 'kissing a flower' means to touch the flower with the nose and inhale its fragrance.

- If the woman is of the *jatmika* type (calm and patient), first touch the point below her navel with the penis, moving as one would breathe in the smell of perfume. Then using the penis, touch the vagina once and then again, just to tease a little and to fire up the desire. Once fluid flows freely, run for ecstasy. Don't hesitate.

"Brother! In addition to all these, there are still other things to note, such as her appearance, expression and physical features. If her skin is very tanned, the point of sensation is in her lips and navel. So if you make love, start by kissing her lips, take in her breath deeply and then kiss her navel. The time of orgasm begins at 2 o'clock in the morning. If her skin is yellowish, the time of arrival of orgasm is between midnight and 8 o'clock in the morning. If her skin is a deep brown, the point of sensation is on the left temple. The time of ecstasy starts from midnight till 4 o'clock in the morning. If her body is slim, the point of sensation is in her eyes. Start the foreplay with kisses on her eyes; the arrival of passion is from sunrise till later in the morning."

Ki Endrasmoro's discourse was interspersed with humour and jokes and there was much laughter, which attracted the attention of his father-in-law, Kyai Nurgirindro. After the usual introductions, he invited them to his house to attend the birthday celebration of the Prophet.

When the celebrations were over, Mas Cabolang discussed several subjects, including the *Asmau'l Husna* (Beautiful Names of God), of which there are ninety-nine. In addition, Ki Nurgirindro said: "Many people come to me for advice on how to get their wishes or desires fulfilled. I tell them to practise the *Asmau'l Husna*, but they do not do it the correct way and so they fail. And then they turn to witch doctors and shamans instead of finding out where they went wrong. They do not know that there are two ways to practise the *Asmau'l Husna*—the easy and hard way—and that both have to be done simultaneously. The easy way is as mentioned in Qur'an 7, 180 [saying the names of God repeatedly] and the hard way is saying God's names with total concentration of mind, faith and patience and abandoning any desire for worldly things. It is by practising the hard way that one will find what they want."

### 3) Nyai Puspomadu

In the village of Paricoro, there lived a rich widow of a village chief by the name of Nyai Puspomadu. People held her in high esteem because of her generous nature and devotion to God, as well as her faithfulness and loyalty towards her late husband, Ki Demang Paricoro. Though she was still young and beautiful and most wealthy, she did not want to re-marry. Every year, she would commemorate her husband's death by holding a ceremony during which the holy Qur'an would be recited. She would also give alms and ritual offerings, all for the benefit of her husband's soul. By chance she heard about the Kyai Nurgirindro's guests, the five *santris* from the region of Kedu. Upon learning that they were adept in *rebana* music, she invited Ki Nurgirindro to lead the *khaol* (ceremony for the dead) and extended the invitation to his guests.

On this occasion, Mas Cabolang came disguised as a woman as he wanted to mix with the lady guests and Nyi Puspomadu. He called himself Ni Suwadi. The ceremony proceeded solemnly and without mishap. Ki Nurgirindro asked Nurwitri to begin the *rebana* recital. After a while, Nurwitri invited Ni Suwadi [Mas Cabolang] to sing. First, he sang songs in Arabic. Even though the people could not understand the meaning of the words, the tunes and the singer's sweet voice delighted them. Then Ki Nurgirindro asked Ni Suwadi to sing in the local language so that the people could understand the meaning. He obliged and used lyrics with *wangsalans* to make the session more enjoyable.

*Panu biru munggeng jaja, puspita lesah ing gelung, sun-tohi layon wong ayu, gong alit ing pawayangan, sun-tedha bisa-a kumpul, karanjang pangubak nila, wus kaburan wartanipun.*

**Blue skin-fungus on the chest, withered flowers in the hair knot, <u>o, sweetheart,
I prefer to die, if we can't get together</u>, a basket filled with sticks
to beat the indigo, as the news of our engagement has spread wide and far.**

The meaning of the riddle is shown underlined. The riddle is as follows: *Panu biru munggeng jaja is toh*, found in the word *sun-tohi*. *Puspita lesah ing gelung is layon* (meaning 'death' or 'to die'), *gong alit ing pawayangan* is *kempul*, found in the word *kumpul*; *pangubak nila* is 'a stick to beat the indigo'; and beating the indigo *kebur* is found in the word *kaburan*. When Ni Suwadi had finished singing, the next performance was an *emprak* (magic) show featuring the Dewaruci story.

**4) The teachings of Dewaruci, the little deity**

The version of the Dewaruci story, as told in *The Centhini Story*, concerns the episode where Bima was in audience with the deity Dewaruci to get instruction in the unio mystica of man and his Creator. In it was told the journey of the soul searching for ways to return to its Origin, the Supreme Soul. This is a very old theme, one that is very much cherished by mystics in general and Moslem sufis in particular and the common people at large. Its story spread through word of mouth, written text and wayang. In Java alone, the story was written as a *kekawin* (poem) in the olden days; today, it is told in modern Javanese in handbooks for the wayang.

It was predicted in the Vedas that a war between the Kauravas and the Pandavas would take place in the future. The victor would obtain the kingdom of Hastina and the loser would be doomed. Therefore, it was not surprising that King Suyodana,

the eldest of the Kaurava brothers, always made attempts to kill the Pandava brothers even before the war became a reality.

Priest Dorna was the teacher of the Kauravas. It so happened that Bima, the second of the Pandava brothers, wanted to study under this same priest to find the *amreta* (elixir of life) so that he would not be touched by death. Taking advantage of the situation, King Suyodana asked the priest to mislead Bima to his death. The elixir of life was also called *tirta perwita suci*, from Old Javanese *tirtha pawitra*, meaning 'water of purity'. Priest Dorna told Bima that it was hidden inside a mountain cave guarded by two horrible ogres. Bima succeeded in killing the ogres and destroying the mountain, but the elixir of life was not there. Before they were killed, however, the ogres—who were in fact deities—advised Bima to return to his teacher for further instructions.

The second instruction brought Bima to the ocean depths. King Suyodana was certain that Bima would meet his death this time because no one had ever returned from there alive as the ocean was full of danger. True enough, a dragon attacked Bima. Bima killed it but was bitten and severely wounded in the fight. When he came to, he found himself on a small island watched over by a tiny deity called Dewaruci. Dewaruci ordered Bima, who was as big as a hill, to enter his body. Inside his body, Bima received the instruction concerning the perfect life and death. It was

above: *A painting on glass depicting Bima (left) and Dewaruci meeting in the middle of the ocean.*

above (all): A Reyog Dance parade in progress. This spectacular performance includes gamelan music, drama and magic shows. The central figure is the Singa Barong, the mythical half-man half-animal creature. The warok, as leader of the troupe, has to hold the Singa Barong's heavy mask in his jaw. He also has to carry a jathil on his shoulder and still dance with energetic movements. This is why the role is honoured for the strongest warok.

but people say they get it by having sexual relations with men, not with women." Mas Cabolang and his companions stopped eating, their mouths open in surprise. Finally, Mas Cabolang remarked: "May God save us from such absurdities!"

Ki Nursubadyo continued: "The act of having sexual relations with men is called *gemblak* (homosexuality) and a homosexual is called a *gemblak* or *warok*. The warok's partner is called *jathil*. After a few years, a *jathil* will lose his manly characteristics. His appearance and behaviour becomes feminine. If a young man happens to be good looking, many *waroks* will compete to get his favours. Sometimes, they are prepared to buy him or exchange him for two or three cows." The *santris* were amazed to hear of such things.

Mas Cabolang added: "My father once told me that in the Hindu era, there were many brahmins called *sukla brahmacari* (pure brahmin). They never married and they abstained from sex, even with men. The sperm they saved changed into pure energy and became a source of their supernatural powers. If *waroks* do not save their sperm, certainly it wouldn't change into energy and so their so-called supernatural power is in fact not real power." Ki Nursubadyo replied: "You are right, son. Their 'power' only gives rise to arrogance and conceit. The *jathil* is no exception. Very often, they are used to earn money by acting as *ronggengs* (dancers) or by taking part in circumcision processions for boys about to undergo the ritual. If you want to see a *warok* or *jathil*, stay here for a few days. It is market day tomorrow in Pucang, I'm sure you can see a *warok* or two there. I've also received an invitation from Kyai Tegalombo to attend the circumcision feast for his son. You can come along. But for now, it's best to rest." He gave Mas Cabolang and Nurwitri a room north of the *langgar* (small prayer house), while the other three companions stayed in rooms south of it.

## 2) The deal

On the way to their rooms, they met Ki Wredojogo, the gatekeeper. He was taking some women to see Ki Nursubadyo. They claimed to be saleswomen on their way to Ponorogo market and had asked to stay overnight with the village chief as it was getting dark. With the excuse of having to leave early the next day, they requested a place outside and were led to the north verandah, which was near Mas Cabolang's room. The women were actually the seven girls the *santris* had met at the river. Troubled by pangs of love, they had resolved to go after the two stealers of their hearts. Mas Cabolang and Nurwitri clearly remembered them.

The moment the gatekeeper left, the girls silently walked to Mas Cabolang and Nurwitri's room. And the moment the young men heard footsteps outside their door, they flung it open and pulled the first two girls inside. Only a thin bamboo wall separated the other five girls and the lovers inside the room. All the furniture in the room, too, was made of bamboo, so that even the slightest movement and the softest of sounds could be heard. There were groans and moans of enjoyment, then heavy breathing, like that of fish out of water, followed by explosions of short grunts. The girls outside were quickly drawn into passionate raptures and they broke out in sweat. No wonder then that when the first round was over and the girls came staggering out, the second group rushed in with vigour. The game was replayed with the same intensity and aggressiveness. It was the same with the third batch of girls. The last girl though suffered the most serious anguish, having had to wait alone and bear the cries of passion. When the door finally opened, she leapt up and ran into the room, almost colliding with her friends.

Whispering calming words, Mas Cabolang led her to the bamboo bed, laid her down on her back and meticulously took off her garments. His touch made her tremble all over. She was the youngest in the group and the sounds she heard through the bamboo wall were her first exposure to lovemaking. Mas Cabolang felt very fortunate to be able to lead her to the Garden of Eden. With unbelievable tenderness, he guided the virgin in all the stages of sexual intimacy. His calm and tender

below: *The spartan interior of a bedroom in a simple traditional house. The walls are made of bamboo and a wooden screen serves as the bedroom door.*

approach had a great impact on the girl, who eagerly followed all his instructions, so that in a very short time she could already understand and adjust herself to his touch. When dawn sent her flimsy light, the girl was spent and had to be carried away by her companions. Mas Cabolang got up to do his compulsory bath.

3) **The incident at the marketplace**

The market at Pucang was at its busiest when the five companions arrived there. They wandered around, observing the hustle and bustle of people selling and buying merchandise. Markets in remote places are different from those in country towns; the sellers are friendlier and conversations are tinged with humour and laughter.

Suddenly, there was a change in the mood of the crowd and people were hurriedly moving away from the main road. The *santris* saw a *warok* carrying his *jathil* on his shoulder, boisterously announcing his presence: "Here I am, the famous *warok* Kromoleyo. Pay your tribute." His followers collected money from the vendors and other things the *jathil* fancied. Another *warok*, Ngabdul Singonebah by name, appeared on the far side. He carried a stick, which he boasted was given to him by the legendary figure from the shadow play, Wrekodara: "With this stick, I can destroy a mountain with one stroke and dry up the ocean with one hit. Who wants to challenge me?" Kromoleyo became very angry. He picked up a big stone from the roadside and threw it at Singonebah, who easily broke it into pieces with the stick. Kromoleyo became angrier and attacked Singonebah. A fierce scuffle broke out between them and after a while, both collapsed to the ground exhausted. Nobody paid them any attention; they just walked away.

right: *A sunatan (circumcision) ceremony for a young boy. Such ceremonies hold deep symbolic meaning for the Javanese. During the Hindu period, circumcision was seen as an initiation rite marking a new phase in a young boy's life. When Islam came to Java, the role of circumcision shifted. Moslem boys between 7 and 10 years old are expected to pray. Circumcision ceremonies were held to mark this new responsibility for the child.*

## 4) The clash

The incident at the marketplace was a common enough occurrence in the region of Selawung that people were not interested to talk about it. Even the police simply ignored the antics of the *waroks*, unless they terrorised the public or disturbed the peace too much. In many instances, though, their fights and squabbles were confined to themselves. As long as they did not get too close to each other, nothing serious would happen. But it was not so this time.

It was the day of the circumcision ceremony at the residence of Ki Tegalombo. Two boys were to be circumcised. One was Ki Tegalombo's son, who was under the protection of *warok* Singonebah, while the other party from Tegalsumprit was under the care of *warok* Kromoleyo. It so happened that Singonebah had kidnapped a *jathil* from another *warok* and Kromoleyo wanted to lay his hands on the new acquisition. When the circumcisions were over, the parties went their own ways, each performing their own parade. At a certain point, however, Kromoleyo's group took a side route to ambush Singonebah's party. The clash escalated into a fierce battle. Singonebah's head was smashed, but before he fell, he speared Kromoleyo's stomach with his sword, tearing it apart. Both fell to the ground, not dead but badly wounded. Mas Cabolang cured them and advised them to return to the right path. Before they parted, the *waroks* admitted that they originally came from Selawung. They promised to return to Selawung and reform their ways.

## 5) An evening of culture at Selawung

Because Mas Cabolang had helped them realise the many mistakes they had made, the *waroks* asked their 'wives' to cook food for Ki Nursubadyo, the village chief, as a token of gratitude. There was so much food that Ki Nursubadyo proposed to hold an evening of dance and serve the food to the guests.

When evening came, Mas Cabolang and Nurwitri dressed up as *ronggengs*. They looked beautiful. They performed the opening *gambyong*[12] dance, their movements imitating the dance of the nymphs Suprobo and Wilutomo from the abode of God Indra. The men, especially the *waroks*, were so spellbound watching them that their sexual desires were aroused and they satisfied their lust on the women near them. And by wonder, the women they touched did not refuse their advances. On the contrary, they responded most receptively as they, too, were enchanted.

Under a tree, hidden by darkness, two young women sat talking to each other. The older one, let us call her A, said: "I'll give whatever it takes to have sex with those two. I hear they are very good. Mas Cabolang is very strong and adept in arousing passion to great heights. Nurwitri is a bit slow, but the sensations he brings can be

---

12 A *gambyong* dance is a dance show performed by several female dancers and is usually used as the opening dance to welcome guests. The dance is said to have been created by a Chinese called Gam Yong. He presented it to the prince of Surakarta, who was very pleased with it. The dance became known as the Gam Yong dance, later pronounced as *gambyong*.

felt from the tip of the toes, creeping upwards until the whole body is saturated." The younger one, whom we shall call B, replied: "Sister, is that true? Where did you hear that from?" A replied: "I heard it from the seven women from Pacitan, who disguised themselves as saleswomen and went after them for that very purpose. They said they got the most satisfactory treatment ever imagined that night." B came closer and whispered in her friend's ear: "Sister, if that is the case, I feel the same. My loins are wet just listening to your story. So whatever you do, I'm with you." A replied: "No, no, sister! That's not right. You are a married woman. You have a husband, while I am a widow. My husband died when our marriage was only a few months old. I'm free now." B countered: "Sister, please! My husband is a *jathil* now. He has lost his manhood and has given me permission to seek satisfaction with other men, as long as it is kept secret. So I'm virtually free, too. My husband won't be angry." A said: "Really? Alright then. Let's get ready and wait for them in their room. It's not locked!"

Meanwhile, the *gambyong* dance had come to an end and Mas Cabolang and Nurwitri went to a room to rest. Nyai Nursubadyo wanted to see a *bondan*[13] dance and asked if that was possible. Mas Cabolang was agreeable and also proposed to perform another round of the *gambyong*, this time with a fee imposed on any man who wanted to dance with them. The *bondan* dance made the public more insane and the *gambyong* with payment was so popular that a second show was needed. The performance ended very late that night.

Mas Cabolang and Nurwitri returned to their room, feeling a bit tired. To their surprise, they found a woman on each of their beds. One was sleeping on her side, which made the hollow between her breasts obvious. The other lay on her back, her cloth unfolded to expose her thighs. Their desires were aroused and they forgot about their weariness. Mas Cabolang ordered: "Take the one with the yellow skin, I'll take the other. We can switch girls later on." Nurwitri agreed and without waking the girls up, they began to touch them teasingly, putting into practice all that they had learnt from Ki Endrasmoro. The women kept their eyes closed, but they could not contain their passion and groaned in ecstasy.

### 6) The second night

The next day, Ki Nursubadyo said to Mas Cabolang: "Last night, the *waroks* asked me whether you and Nurwitri are willing to teach their *jathils* how to dress and put on make-up like the ladies in the city and, if possible, to dance the way you did last night." Thinking he would have the opportunity to play with the *jathils*, Mas Cabolang agreed to the request.

---

13 The *bondan* dance is performed by a female dancer portraying a girl playing with a doll and singing a lullaby. The most interesting thing is that the dancer performs on a *kendi*, an earthenware flask for drinking water. When the dance is over, the dancer smashes the flask into pieces to show that there was nothing in it to take her weight.

So just before noon, the *waroks* came one by one, bringing their *jathils* with all their clothing and jewellery. When they had taught them how to dress, put on make-up and dance, Mas Cabolang said: "Now that you have gained something from me, it's my turn to learn something from you. I would like to learn to play *jathil*." One of the *jathils* said: "Why worry about learning? If you like, we can practise what we do right away." Mas Cabolang and Nurwitri agreed. They locked the doors, drew the curtains and began with the play.

At first, it was just curiosity, but when they got the taste of it, they just could not stop. All the *jathils* got their turn with the *santris*. Mas Cabolang exclaimed: "Indeed it is different, perhaps better than sexual play with women. No wonder the *waroks* are addicted. Now I want to be the *jathil*. Please begin!" Said one of them: "I beg your pardon, master. Except for Sadilah, we have all lost our manhood." So Sadilah came forward and soon Mas Cabolang and Nurwitri obtained the satisfaction they desired. Time passed, the late afternoon prayer was over and all the preparations for a second evening of dance were made. The *waroks* came to collect their *jathils*; they will bring them back later after the evening prayer with a spectacular parade.

The evening opened with the *gambyong* dance. The *jathils* were all dressed as *ronggengs* and took part in the dance. They were then divided into groups, each tasked to perform a special dance. The night ended with the *gambyong* dance with payment. It was agreed that *waroks* whose *jathils* were dancing should not be allowed to take part. All the proceedings went smoothly as planned. The *waroks* were satisfied because they could see that their *jathils* had benefited from the guidance of Mas Cabolang and Nurwitri. Those feeling dissatisfaction were the women—they had no chance to see Mas Cabolang and Nurwitri dance because Mas Cabolang was occupied with the proceedings of the show and Nurwitri had joined the musicians as vocalist. When the evening closed, the proceeds were beyond expectation. There were three baskets full of money, which would go to the owner of the house and the performers.

7) **The realm of death and hell**
The *waroks* spent the next few days learning more from Mas Cabolang and Nurwitri and having sex with them. The day before they left Selawung, Mas Cabolang asked Ki Nursubadyo why the *waroks* abused the knowledge they had attained. Ki Nursubadyo admitted that he was to blame. As their guru, he had given them some magic powers to protect them from danger in distant places. However, they had no notion of life in the hereafter, especially punishment in hellfire for bad deeds, and so they abused those powers. Ki Nursubadyo mused: "If only they could understand the message contained in the story of the prophet 'Isa with the skull, perhaps they could return to the straight path." Mas Cabolang begged Ki Nursubadyo to tell him the story. He obliged and began thus:

## the pre-adulthood journey

❈ *One day, while on his regular journey around the world, Prophet 'Isa saw a skull on the side of a road. He was very emotional and prayed to God, asking God to give the skull the ability to speak so that it could relate all its experiences in this world and the next. Allah granted his supplication and the skull began to speak like a human being.*

*He told the prophet that he was once the wealthy and powerful king of Syam. Although he did not belong to any religion, he had lived righteously, giving away alms and helping people and other living beings. Because he did not believe in God, he was punished with a severe illness towards the end of his life and when he died, his soul was treated very harshly. A question was put to him: "Who is your God?" He could not answer the question. From that moment on, he was tortured relentlessly and unceasingly, so that not one part of his body was free from torment and agony. After that, he was brought to hell and received punishment after punishment, each more painful than the other. However, as he had done a lot of good deeds and since God is Love and Mercy, he received a little bit of mercy. His soul was placed in a skull, which was flung on the roadside for everybody to see and learn from.*

*That was how he drew the attention of the prophet 'Isa. He begged the prophet to pray to God The Merciful to return him to life so that he could repent to the fullest. The Prophet asked him who or what he worshipped and who the prophet was at that time. He replied that he had worshipped a statue of the golden calf and the prophet at that time was Prophet Elias. Then Prophet 'Isa asked: "If I pray to God to return you to life and He grants it, will you worship a created being again?" The skull replied: "Well, Holy Spirit! If I get the opportunity to return to life, I will only use it to perform good deeds and worship God The Merciful." So Prophet 'Isa prayed and a voice was heard: "Your prayer is granted. Order the skull to stand up." Relieved, the prophet looked at the skull and spoke: "Well, skull, arise. God The Merciful has granted my supplications and given you life."*

*The skull returned to its former form. The king fell on his knees to pay homage to the prophet and pronounced his belief that there is no god except Allah. Prophet 'Isa spoke: "Remember this! Don't think for a fraction of a moment that I can give life and death to God's creatures. No, not at all! Only God has that power. Also, I remind you again never to worship any other than God The Almighty." With that, Prophet 'Isa disappeared.*

*The king of Syam did not waste any time repenting but used every minute to worship The Almighty, whether it was in the form of prayer, almsgiving or helping other human beings live decently. He lived for 800 years and not one minute was lost due to neglect. In the end he died from a short illness. God was pleased with his soul and admitted it into paradise.*

Ki Nursubadyo said: "That's it, my son. Good deeds and generosity alone cannot wipe out sins caused by not believing in the existence of God. Only persistent repentance can bring about God's favour and mercy." Mas Cabolang and his companions understood that those words applied to them, too. Said Ki Nursubadyo: "My son! The time has come for you to proceed with your journey. The path of immorality has to be endured, but I advise you sincerely to go to Wilis Mountain and visit Seh Matyasto of Majenang." Mas Cabolang made homage with folded hands and said: "I beg your forgiveness and blessings. We ask leave to depart tomorrow."

After prayer the next morning, they left silently for fear of being held up by the *waroks* and *jathils*. By the time the people of Selawung realised that the *santris* were missing, they were already far away from the area. The *waroks* wanted Mas Cabolang to return to Selawung and they dispersed in all directions to find them. When they found him, he refused to return and so they decided to follow him wherever he went. But God decreed otherwise, for the *waroks* were besieged by heavy rains, gusty winds, thunder and lightning while in the midst of a forest. When the storm abated, they found themselves on a field in Karangtalun, in the vicinity of their village. They realised that it was God's will that the *santris* must leave them. So they went back home even though their hearts were still with them.

## 20 Majenang on the slopes of Wilis Mountain

### 1) Seh Matyasto

Mas Cabolang and his companions were walking near a field in a very miserable state. By chance, a woman passed by. She was Nyi Mawur, a young widow in the service of Seh Matyasto, who ran a hermitage at Majenang on the slopes of Wilis Mountain. She was on her way to the field to bring food for his disciples who were working there. But when she saw how tired Mas Cabolang and his friends were, she left them some of the food. She also promised to take them to Seh Matyasto but only the next morning as it was getting dark. When she returned from the field, she brought them to her home. While they were having dinner, she reported their arrival to the hermit. He ordered her to bring them to see him immediately.

The following days were filled with general discussions. Mas Cabolang learnt that Seh Matyasto originally came from Wirosobo, had lived in Mataram in his younger years and married a relative of the regent of Wirosobo when he returned home. At a meeting on the third day, Seh Matyasto asked Mas Cabolang about the *Sahadah Quraisy Mataram* and its difference with the *sahadah* (the common Islamic creed) that is known in the villages. Mas Cabolang explained: "According to the Khatib of Winong, the difference lies in the tune and tonal scale of the gamelan which accompanies the *sahadah*. There are also some differences in the creed but not much. The *sahadah* reads as follows: 'I bear witness that there is no god but Allah and I bear witness that Muhammad is the messenger of Allah.' In the *Sahadah Quraisy Mataram*, there is additional explanation—that Allah is the God of the Moslems, The Creator of the Universe; that His Existence is absolute; and that it is impossible that He does not exist. Concerning the prophet Muhammad, there is also a longer explanation. For example, it states that the Prophet was the child of Dewi Aminah and Sayid Abdullah; that he was born either on the eighth or twelfth of Rabiu'l Awal in the year Dal; that he moved to Medina at either the age of 23 years or 40; that he died at the age of 63 years on Monday, the twelfth of Rabi'ul Awal in the year Dal; and that he was buried at Medina."

2) **The three wishes**

Since the night was still young, Ki Matyasto told a story about a couple who could not live harmoniously with each other: "The wife never agreed to the wishes of her husband and the husband never listened to his wife. They quarrelled day in and day out. One day, the couple received an admonition from God in the form of three wishes he would grant them. Whatever they wished would come true. Fuelled by their scorn for each other, they wished angry things instead of good things that could better their lives together. And so they were worse off than before. Fortunately, they had not used up the final wish. For that, they had no choice but to ask to be returned to their original state."

Although everybody was amused by the story, no one could understand what it was trying to say. So Mas Cabolang asked: "Kyai, the story is funny, but what can we learn from it?" Ki Matyasto replied: "This is the moral of the story. A wife is a gift from God, but she shouldn't become a problem for her husband. If she becomes a problem, the result is always disastrous as it has been from the time of Adam till the present."

3) **Katim Tayi**

Mas Cabolang forwarded another question: "Kyai, we've heard about the place of a wife in a relationship. What is the truth about justice and generosity because I think a husband should be just and generous towards his wife."

Ki Matyasto explained patiently: "The subject of justice and generosity can be found in the *Tajjussalatin*. Concerning justice, it is told in the book that half of justice was granted to King Nusyirwan Adil and the other half was to be shared by the rest of the kings on earth. As for generosity, one half was given to a man called Katim Tayi and the other half was to be shared by the rest of the human race. There is a proverb—a generous person is the favourite of God, while a miser is scorned. The masters of religion say that a generous person spreads generosity to everyone around him and all will benefit, while a miser only spreads misfortune to everyone around him and so is scorned and not respected. In the book *Sitrul muluk*, King Bharam was well known as a great and powerful king. Before he died, he told his son to succeed him as king and advised him to look after the welfare of those subjects who believe their king to be righteous and generous. Such an undertaking would save the kingdom—the subject would praise the king and the king, in living up to his reputation, would not dare to make mistakes. In the book *Adabbussalin* [Adabussalatin], it is said that the reason why a kingdom is held in contempt is because the ruler is immoral and selfish. But if the ruler is righteous, God's mercy will always be present and all his plans will be brought to fruition, even if his people do not praise him." He then told the story of Katim Tayi:

*A long time ago, there lived an Arab called Katim Tayi. He was very generous and people say his generosity overshadowed that of kings. But his fame and all the praises that were heaped on him provoked the kings of Rum, Syam and Yahman. They could not comprehend how one man could be so charitable and benevolent, even exceeding the magnanimity and nobleness of kings. They deduced there must be something suspicious behind it all and set about to investigate.*

*One day, the king of Rum learnt that Katim Tayi had an excellent horse, which he cherished very much. The king sent three officials to buy the horse. They travelled for several days. When they arrived at Katim Tayi's house, heavy rain broke out accompanied by lightning and thunder. It so happened that earlier that same day, Katim Tayi had held a party and was short of food, especially meat and fish. He was deeply worried; his visitors had come from a foreign country, he wanted them to stay with him and dine at his house, but he had nothing worthwhile to offer them. At long last he decided to slaughter his horse. At breakfast the next morning, the officials gave him the king's letter. On reading it, his face turned pale and he was speechless. One of the officials asked: "Well, my brother, why do you turn so pale? What is the matter?" With a sigh Katim Tayi sadly replied: "My dear guests, the king asks to buy my horse. Let alone my horse, even my life, if he wants it, I will give it to him. But you are also to blame. Why did you not give me this letter when you arrived? As you know, it rained heavily yesterday and I had nothing to offer you for dinner. So I slaughtered the horse. Now, where can I look for another horse like that? I turned pale because I was thinking how disappointed the king would be." He slumped on a chair with tears in his eyes. The officials were overwhelmed by the man's reaction and tried to comfort him: "Well, brother, what's there to say? No use in crying over spilt milk. We will report everything to the king truthfully." When they arrived in Rum, they went straight to the king and described the whole episode. The king said: "Then the stories and praises about Katim Tayi are true. I am satisfied and I pay tribute to him."*

*Next to test Katim Tayi was the king of Syam. He demanded of the man 100 camels, all of which had to be well built and of the same colour and have*

# the pre-adulthood journey

black eyes. Katim Tayi said to the king's officials: "Such camels are rare and very difficult to find, but with God's grace and mercy on the king's part and my luck, they will be found." So he travelled far and wide and managed to secure 100 camels, which he sent to the king. The king was most impressed and said: "It proves that Katim Tayi is really favoured by God. Return the camels to him and load them with all kinds of riches." The king also regarded Katim Tayi as his personal friend. When the camels were returned to him, Katim Tayi did not accept them for himself but gave them away to his children and relatives.

Of the three kings, the king of Yahman was the most offended by Katim Tayi's reputation. He had heard that the man was a descendent of a shepherd and dismissed the news of his benevolence as a mere publicity stunt. How could he come to such riches and be so generous? To make matters worse, while he was giving audience to his subjects one day, he received a letter from the king of Maghribi asking information about Katim Tayi. He was enraged to learn that the man's fame was known even so far away as Maghribi. Certainly, Katim Tayi must be investigated and he should be punished if everything that was said about him was false.

The king of Yahman ordered his most faithful official to behead Katim Tayi and bring his head to him. After a long and exhausting journey, the official arrived at the man's house and rested by the gate. By chance Katim Tayi saw the official and said: "Uncle, I think it's better for you to come inside and rest and have a drink of water. Better still if you stay for dinner and spend the night here. You can leave tomorrow when you aren't tired any more." The messenger, a bedouin, was very happy to accept his invitation. Over dinner, Katim Tayi asked his guest to stay with him a week or so. Said the bedouin: "It's a pity I cannot do that as I've have been ordered to do something very important as soon as possible." Katim Tayi enquired: "Uncle, if you don't mind, tell me what it is you have to do. Perhaps I can help." The man replied: "Ah! My son, perhaps you could. I have to find a man by the name Katim Tayi. The king of Yahman wants him to be killed and his head brought before him. I've not met this man yet." Katim Tayi laughed: "If that's your job, I can help you. Katim Tayi lives in this village, too. He has a strange habit. Every morning, he goes to another village south of here. You will find him sleeping on a bench under a big banyan tree. So go there first thing tomorrow morning; don't wait for me as I might oversleep. Here, take this sword of mine."

The next morning, the bedouin had breakfast on his own and set off for the village. He found the banyan tree and, indeed, there was someone sleeping on the bench, covered in a thick blanket. He thought: "How correct is my host. That man is perhaps Katim Tayi." So he drew the sword that his host had lent him and was on the verge of cutting off the man's head when a thought entered his mind: "I'm a messenger of a king. Why should I act rashly without first *checking? I might kill the wrong person." And so he lifted the blanket. To his surprise, he found his host under it and remarked: "Well, my son! What is the meaning of this?" Katim Tayi replied: "Uncle, I am Katim Tayi, the man you're looking for. I'm the one your king wants to kill. I know how disappointed the king will be if you fail and perhaps you'll be punished severely. Uncle, enough talk now! Do your job, I am ready!"*

*But the messenger sat down beside Katim Tayi on the bench and said: "Yes, you are ready! But I'm not! My son, I will return to the king and tell him everything. Even if I will be cut to pieces in your place, I will be ready, very ready! Goodbye, my good fellow!" He jumped on the back of his horse and galloped away and in a few seconds, disappeared from sight in a cloud of dust. He reported everything to the king, stressing Katim Tayi's readiness to give his life to please the king. The king concluded: "Then all that is said about him is true. Don't kill him."*

Seh Matyasto then said: "It was mentioned in the book of *Jawahiru'l amaryati* that ten generations after Katim Tayi's death, his grave was destroyed by a flood. His body was found intact, a blessing of God; there was no trace of decay at all. His intact body was proof that a generous person is a good man and a miser is evil."

### 4) Thursday night at Majenang

On Thursday evening, the hermitage of Majenang was peaceful even though it was a hive of activity. Every one, students and *santris*, had taken their ablution and were clad in white. Nurwitri made the call for the evening prayer, while Kyai Matyasto led the prayer. In the kitchen, the offerings for a ceremonial meal were almost ready. Everything was done in an atmosphere of increasing quietude. All movements were carried out with utmost care so as not to make any noise and distract the people's attention. Finally, the meal offerings and all the side dishes including roast chicken were set out in the mosque.

Ki Matyasto then sat in front of the *mighrab* (niche in the wall facing the direction of Mecca). Facing him were Mas Cabolang and his friends; the other *santris* sat behind them in rows. The mosque was full. In a low voice, Ki Matyasto spoke: "I have just given you something that you already possess. Therefore accept it with a pure heart. Begin with the pronouncement of the *sahadah. Ashadu 'allah ilaha illalah, wa ashadu an*

below: *The pendopo of the Grand Mosque of Yogyakarta. It is the venue for the annual Sekaten ceremony which celebrates the birth of Prophet Muhammad. Qur'an recitation and Azan (call to prayer) contests are held on this day. As well, two special sets of gamelan instruments, called Kyai Gunturmadu and Kyai Nogowilogo, are taken out and played. People believe that listening to the music will bring them rewards and good health.*

*la muhammadan abduhu wa rasulluhu* (I bear witness, that there is no god except Allah and that Muhammad is the slave and messenger of Allah)." All the followers repeated the words in a low voice, too.

Without delay, Ki Matyasto began his sermon about the pillars of Islam, which became the foundation of the faith. He added: "We must keep in mind that there are four kinds of *kiblah* (orientation). They are:

- the orientation of the corporeal body, which means that the corporeal body must know how to perform all the movements and how to pronounce all the formulas of salutations used in prayer;
- the orientation of knowledge, that is, the awareness of being a soul. So all that is performed in the first stage, the *shariah*, is in fact utilised to awaken the awareness or consciousness of the soul;.
- the orientation of the soul, meaning that the act of worship is performed by the soul and not by the body. The body and movements of worship are only the tools of the soul, which can lead to the complete consciousness of the soul; and
- the orientation of the consciousness to the existence of the Supreme Soul or God's consciousness, with the consequence of the union of the consciousness of the soul and the consciousness of The Supreme Soul, leading to the union of the two."

The atmosphere in the mosque became intensely quiet, almost void. The absorbing quietness was broken a little when Ki Matyasto began to explain the four realms—*nasut*, *malakut*, *jabarut* and *lahud*—in its relationship with the *Martabat Tujuh* (Seven Stages of Creation). He closed the discourse with an explanation of the four realms, which constituted the main elements of creation. Then all present partook of the ceremonial meal offerings.

When the evening came to an end, Ki Matyasto said: "My son Cabolang. Pay tribute to God and the prophet Muhammad for your successes so far. But there is still one more stage to be passed. It will be very hard and perilous, but you will be alright as long as your remembrance of God is unrelenting." Mas Cabolang paid homage with folded hand and begged for the guru's blessings.

## 21 Wirosobo

### 1) Ki Jamali

The next morning, Mas Cabolang and his *santris* left Majenang for Wirosobo. He was advised to stay with Ki Jamali, the *pengulu* of Wirosobo, who would put him in touch with the regent, Ki Adipati. At the marketplace in Wirosobo, they attracted much attention, partly because they were strangers and partly because Mas Cabolang was good looking. Women and girls began to follow them wherever they went. They sensed trouble and made several detours to lose them. By chance,

above: *Markets such as these are found in villages throught Java where rural produce are sold by the locals. There is no fixed price and so bargaining is expected.*

they found a mosque and sat quietly on the verandah and waited for the situation to calm down. But there was one woman who did not lose them. She was the young wife of Ki Jamali. When she was certain that the strangers would be at the mosque for some time, she hastened home to inform her husband of their presence. He went to the mosque reluctantly, but all doubts vanished once he saw them and he invited them to his home. Ki Jamali then reported their arrival to Ki Adipati.

During their stay in Wirosobo, the *santris* lived on the income they earned from giving *emprak* shows and *rebana* recitals at wedding feasts and other festive occasions. From time to time, they were invited to perform for newlyweds whose relationship was still shaky; for the couple, they would usually became most compatible after the performance. Such positive outcomes only made the *santris* more popular and not one day passed without them having to perform at least one show. It so happened that the Ki Adipati's wife was in a very advanced stage of pregnancy; in fact, she was a few months overdue. His subordinates suggested that he holds a *rebana* recital to help correct the time of birth. The regent promised to hold both a *rebana* recital and a magic show, and not long after, his wife gave birth to a child with ease. He decided to hold another rebana recital on the night of the next full moon.

2) **The *rebana* and *emprak* show on the night of the full moon**
A full moon was shining brightly on the night of the *rebana* recital and *emprak* show. Ki Adipati sat facing east, surrounded by his concubines. Everything was ready and the performers were waiting for the regent's order to begin. Then he gave the signal. Mas Cabolang sat with his drum on his lap and sang the opening song. All chatter and laughter among the audience ceased. They became quiet, their emotions whisked away by the melody.

above: *An* emprak, or magic show. The magicians, always in a trance, show off their powers performing gruesome acts such as chewing glass, breaking solid steel bars or stabbing themselves with knives. The group on the left is helping a magician who is just recovering from his trance, while the man standing on the right is still in a trance. Such travelling shows were common in the past.

Suddenly, the little drum barked aloud; starting off slowly and steadily, the rhythm gradually gained speed till it reached a vast rumble. The spectators awoke with a start, their emotions stirring. They moved in rythym to their instincts and impulses and did strange things. Pickpockets and sexually inclined people were in their element. Hands roamed everywhere, touching bodies and taking anything that was of value. No one seemed to mind. Women screamed and cursed. In dark corners, young girls and boys were adjusting themselves to the situation around. The sound and melody of the *rebana* pushed and pulled, pressed and caressed, and once the booming of the drums muted into a murmur, the energy too dissipated. Only gasps and moans were left. Ki Adipati turned to Mas Cabolang, gave the sign to pause and said: "Drink and eat for a while to restore energy and spirit. Afterwards, you better put on the magic show." Meanwhile the spectators, especially the women, were taking account of their condition. Their clothes were torn and in disarray. They tidied themselves up, grimacing a little from bruises caused by frenzied hands.

After a short rest, Mas Cabolang was ready to start again, this time with a magic show. He prepared four cones of ceremonial rice offerings and covered each of them with a chicken cage enveloped in white cloth. Then he burnt incense on the four corners on the show arena, so that the smoke could be smelled everywhere. He danced around for a while. Then he took the cage off and to the surprise of the audience, the cones had changed into four different types of plants. There was a chilli plant with red fruit, looking very hot to the taste; a watermelon plant, its fruit large like footballs; a gourd, also with big fruit; and another plant, indescribable in shape and colour. Mas Cabolang announced that all the fruit could be picked. Ki Adipati ordered his concubines to collect the fruit and put them into three baskets. Then Mas Cabolang asked for two wooden blocks for pounding rice and a pair of pounders. While he chanted a mantra, the pounders began to attack each other so fiercely that Mas Cabolang had to separate them. Then he ordered them to make music. Immediately, they began to jump all over the pounding blocks, making music the way village girls would when one of them was going to get married. Many other tricks were performed that night.

To round up the evening, Ki Adipati decided to *udhik-udhik* (distribute money) by way of throwing coins on the ground, which the people would clamour to pick. Mas Cabolang was asked to do the job. The first group, the regent's concubines, crowded around him and he lost his balance. The coins fell over his body and the girls jumped on him. There was nothing he could do to free himself from their soft, full bodies. By the time the show closed, dawn had broken. Ki Adipati gave Mas Cabolang thirty-five gilders as his fee and ordered him to stay with Ki Jamali for the time being. He had other plans for Nurwitri; he wanted Nurwitri to train a *ronggeng* band, which he would form shortly.

3) **Sexual indulgence**
Ki Adipati was sitting with Nurwitri in the rear hall of his residence. The regent was half drunk and Nurwitri looked more beautiful to him. An unusual feeling of love began to stir within him and he said: "I'm sleepy. Give my leg a massage and sing for me, my sweet." Nurwitri was thrilled that Ki Adipati called him his sweetheart. In his heart, he believed the regent had fallen in love with him. It did not take long before Ki Adipati's hands were reaching for Nurwitri's neck and he was kissing the *santri* over and over again. Remembering his experiences with the *waroks* of Selawung, Nurwitri was able to guide Ki Adipati in his new sexual escapade. The regent, having forgotten his wife and concubines, kept Nurwitri in the room for two days and two nights.

Meanwhile, Mas Cabolang could do as he wished. There were many women—girls, widows, even married women—who had fallen in love with him and he was able to satisfy them all. Even the regent's concubines, especially Jahe Manis, and Ki Jamali's young wife did not escape his spell for he possessed a special knowledge. He knew the *pangontong-ontong* spell, which allowed him to change the size of his manhood to fit his partner for the best result and satisfaction. Moreover, he liked to give them presents and money, and not only to those from outside the regent's residence but his concubines as well.

On the third day, Ki Adipati summoned Mas Cabolang and told him that he wanted to hold another bigger and more spectacular *rebana* recital on the night of the next full moon. But that was only a pretext; his real purpose in sending for Mas Cabolang was to fulfill his sexual desires with the handsome *santri*.

After sending Nurwitri to rest in another room, Ki Adipati said: "Tell me, Cabolang! So far you have always played the female role. I wonder whether it feels different, I mean, in terms of the sexual enjoyment. Whose enjoyment is greater, a man's or a woman's?" Mas Cabolang replied: "To be honest, milord! The woman's enjoyment is greater and more fulfilling. That's why many boys choose to become *jathil*." Ki Adipati said: "If that is so, give me that experience." Mas Cabolang could not refuse because he, too, wanted to experience what it was like to wield power over the most influential man in the territory. Preparations were quickly made.

When they were ready, Mas Cabolang entered the regent from the rear. He then pronounced the *pangontong-ontong* spell, which casued Ki Adipati unbearable agony. He grunted and groaned and bled profusely when Mas Cabolang withdrew. He fell on the floor, writhing like a worm and totally humiliated. Nurwitri brought some herbal ointment, which helped ease the pain a little. The painful experience, however, brought the regent to his senses and reminded him of the love and care that he gets from his wife and concubines. He dismissed Nurwitri and Cabolang.

Mas Cabolang's escapades with the women of Wirosobo caused much hostility and made brothers, husbands and fathers revengeful and vindictive. When Ki Adipati heard of the young man's impudence with the ladies, he became angry and ordered his arrest. But God still protected Mas Cabolang. Ki Jamali's wife tipped the wayfarers of the impending arrest. That evening, the regent's subjects came to arrest them but the birds had flown.

### 4) Priest Donodarmo

Mas Cabolang realised that all his adventures and escapades, which culminated in Ki Adipati's humiliation, had only brought him up the wrong path. He admitted to his companions that he had sinned in two matters—towards his parents by not heeding their good advice and towards God The Creator. He wanted to repent to the fullest to God and return to his parents to ask for their forgiveness. Saloko, the eldest *santri* among them, advised him to study with Ki Buyut Donodarmo, a priest who resides in a cave in Semeru Mountain, before returning to Sokoyoso. Priest Donodarmo was already of the incorporeal world. His cave was visible only to those who wanted to meet him; otherwise, it was nowhere to be found.

Dewdrops glittered in the sun, but the wayfarers did not notice them at all. Their eyes were focused on the footpath, which was only a foot wide. To one side loomed the mountain wall; the other opened to a deep ravine, so deep that it was still covered in fog. It was also very cold up there on Semeru and the clothes they were wearing were only suitable for places like Wirosobo.

They stopped under a *kesambi* tree, their eyes searching around for a cave which people said was located near it. Mas Cabolang felt sad at the thought that he might not be welcomed there. Kartipolo said: "My father and his friends once looked for the same cave but failed. And they heard that Ki Buyut Donodarmo had moved to the cave of Sigolo." Mas Cabolang hoped he would find the cave and thought to himself: "If I fail, I won't go home but die on the mountain."

The *santris* stayed on that slope and performed *pati geni* (asceticism by eating uncooked food) and prayers and concentrated on God The Almighty. They did only that for seven days and nights. On the final night, Mas Cabolang saw the opening of the cave. He also saw Ki Buyut sitting in meditation in front of the cave. The priest beckoned Mas Cabolang to approach him. Mas Cabolang went forward, making homage with folded hands. Ki Buyut said: "Cabolang, you are the son of a great cleric. You are handsome. So why do you like to indulge in immorality? But the fact that you can meet me means that God has mercy on you. Do you repent to the full?" Mas Cabolang replied softly: "I beg your full pardon, reverend priest. I have seen the light of repentance and I am humbled by regret." Said the priest: "You must know that your father and I were very good friends and we studied with Seh Kadir Jaelani of Karang. We were inseparable. When I saw you, I had the feeling your father did not teach you about the *salat da'im* (constant remembrance

left: *Semeru Mountain. Also called* Mahameru *or 'Great Mountain' and at 3,676 metres, it is the highest in Java. It is located in the Bromo-Tengger-Semeru National Park, which covers over 50,000 hectares of mountainous highland and fertile valley.*

of God)." Mas Cabolang replied: "I totally surrender myself to you, master." The priest continued: "It is best for you to break your fast first, to restore energy. Afterwards give the rest of the meal to your companions for them to break their fast. Tell them that they cannot see me. Only you can see me and only for one night. Tomorrow morning, you must leave."

Though a bit disappointed that they would not be able to see the priest, the companions were most happy for their master. From him, Mas Cabolang received instruction about *roh ilapi*, which formed the source of all matter. It was explained using the metaphor of a vessel filled with water, reflecting the full moon. The vessel was the corporeal body; the reflection of the moon was the soul. The vessel could be reached by the five senses, but the reflection of the moon was incorporeal. Though able to be sensed by the senses, if the moon disappeared, the senses would not be able to reach it. Then Mas Cabolang asked about the perfect faith in Islam. Ki Buyut Donodarmo answered: "The perfect faith relates to the heart of the perfect Moslem, meaning one who never stops keeping God in his mind."

It was daybreak when the priest gave the final message: "The night is almost over, get ready to return to your parents. You must know that they have adopted two children of Sunan Giri Parapen, called Jayengsari and Rancangkapti. I bid you farewell, my son." Mas Cabolang paid homage and expressed his heartfelt gratitude. When he got out of the cave, the sky was already shining red. His four companions were also ready. So while reciting a verse from the Qur'an (Q, 2, 255), they went downhill. Mind and body moved in unison in one direction.... to Sokoyoso, back to his mother and father.

## 22 Sokoyoso—the return of the prodigal son

It was late afternoon. Seh Akadiyat was sitting in the mosque giving instructions to Ki Jayengsari about a most favoured topic—life in death and death in life. It was most interesting for people who yearned for *khusnu'l khatimah* (the perfect death). Suddenly Rogotruno, one of Seh Akadiyat's disciples, appeared. He was panting and almost out of breath. Seh Akadiyat asked: "What is the matter with you, Rogotruno? Calm down!" Rogotruno fell to his knees and said: "Guru, the young master is back. He's in the field now, waiting for your order." Seh Akadiyat replied quickly: "Aha! Cabolang is back! No wonder you were in such a hurry. Rogotruno, bring him here. Don't make him wait any longer."

After a while, he came back with Mas Cabolang and the four companions. Mas Cabolang quickly prostrated on his father's lap. Kyai Akadiyat responded by caressing his son's head. Raden Jayengsari was very much moved; in his heart he wondered when would he get the opportunity to prostrate on the lap of his father or his brother. His eyes were brimming with tears, stopped only when he heard Ki Akadiyat addressing him: "My son, Jayengsari. This is your brother, Cabolang. And you, Cabolang, pay homage

# mas cabolang

to your brother." Mas Cabolang made a bow and extended his hands: "Brother, accept my homage." Ki Jayengsari replied: "Thank you, my brother. Welcome home." Seh Akadiyat then ordered Rogotruno to bring his wife to them.

Nyai Wuryan came in haste, followed by Rancangkapti on her heels. She saw a visitor but could not make out who he was. But when Mas Cabolang fell at her feet, a sudden recognition flashed into her mind. She embraced her son, crying out: "My son, my son! How cruel you are to leave your old mother behind in sorrow." Rancangkapti also cried, not knowing whether it was from joy or sorrow. At length, Ki Akadiyat spoke: "Nyai, calm down. Your son is back. There is nothing to be sad about anymore. It is better that you thank God." Turning to Rancangkapti, he said: "My daughter Rancangkapti, this is your brother, Cabolang. Welcome him!" She folded her hands and said: "Welcome home, brother." Cabolang: "Thank you, sister!"

The months passed peacefully. Mas Cabolang and Ki Jayengsari became very close studying together under the same teacher. Mas Cabolang and Rancangkapti became more and more intimate, so that Ki Akadiyat and Ki Jayengsari agreed that they should be married. A few months later, Kyai and Nyai Akadiyat passed away peacefully.

A month later, as Ki Jayengsari, Mas Cabolang and Rancangkapti were sitting in the mosque discussing religious knowledge, Saloko appeared before them with some news: "Masters and mistress, I beg your pardon a thousand times. There is something you have to know. My friend in the village tells me that several days ago, a certain tradesman from Surabaya was making inquiries about master Jayengsari and mistress Rancangkapti. He is a spy of Pangeran Pekik, who is ordered to look for the master and mistress. What do you want to do?" After discussing the matter thoroughly, they decided to leave Sokoyoso. Mas Cabolang gave these instructions: "Saloko! It is better that we leave Sokoyoso. Run the hermitage as best as possible. Later on, I will give you a message as to where the *santris* can join us." Saloko replied: "All right, master! It is better that you send brother Buras later. I don't think we can all join you together at the same time but one by one and in secret."

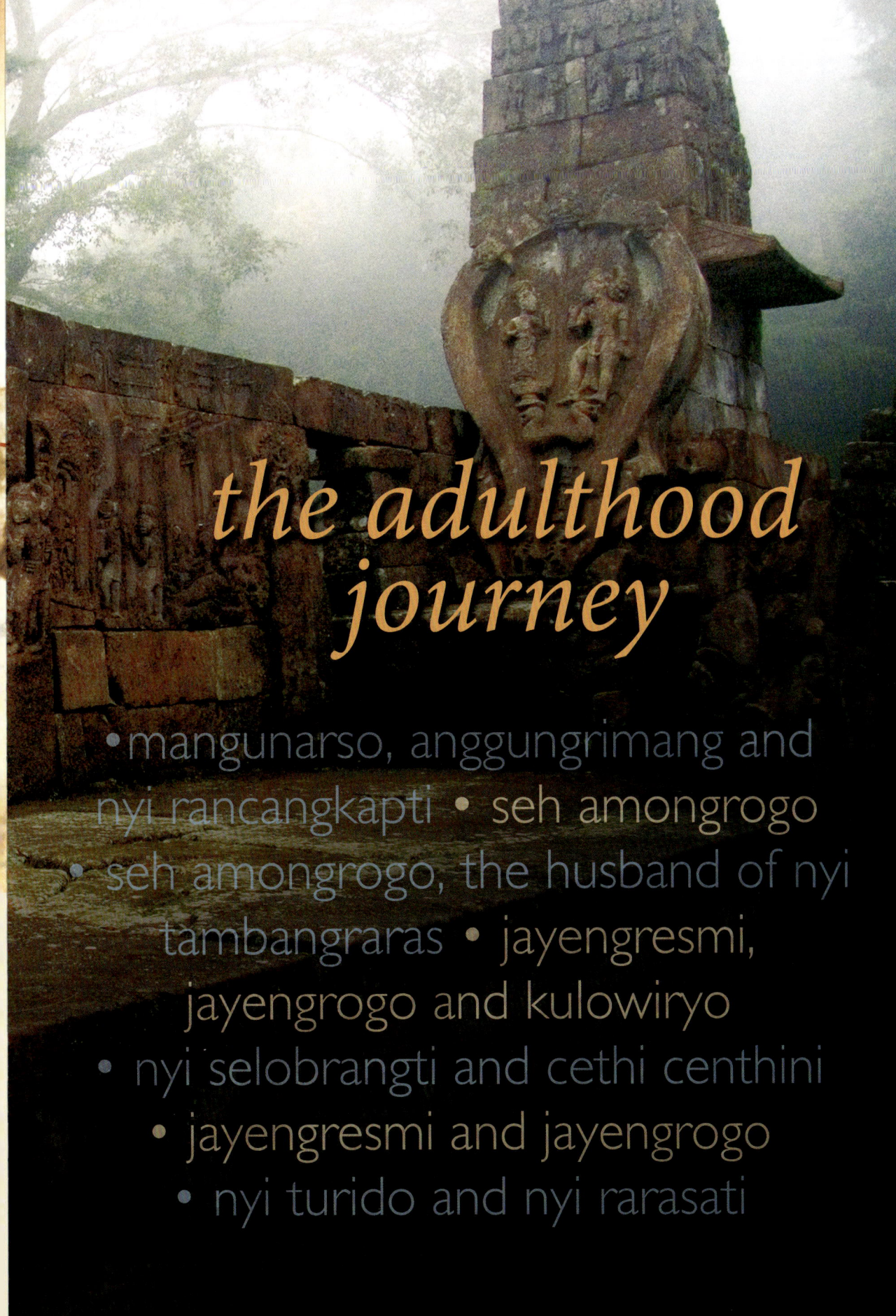

# the adulthood journey

- mangunarso, anggungrimang and nyi rancangkapti
- seh amongrogo
- seh amongrogo, the husband of nyi tambangraras
- jayengresmi, jayengrogo and kulowiryo
- nyi selobrangti and cethi centhini
- jayengresmi and jayengrogo
- nyi turido and nyi rarasati

## Mangunarso, Anggungrimang and Nyi Rancangkapti
### FROM SOKOYOSO TO WONONTOKO

### 1 Ki Seh Hercaranu

Four people left Sokoyoso. Buras was the vanguard as well as the pathfinder. Behind him and in single file were Ki Jayengsari, Nyi Rancangkapti and Mas Cabolang in the rear. Their journey through highlands and along the beaches westward was most difficult. They had travelled for three days, only stopping to rest when it was dark. As they were exhausted, they stopped under a *wuni* tree (Chinese laurel) at the foot of a mountain.

Looking around and up the slope, they saw a very old hermit sitting cross-legged under a banyan tree. Ki Jayengsari immediately stood up, followed by the others. Their minds were not at ease. How could such an old man climb up a mountain so high? But when they saw him beckoning them to approach, all doubts quickly vanished for it was the ascetic, Seh Hercaranu.

They heard his voice. It was very weak but most distinct: "Well, my grandchildren, come here. I've been waiting for you for a long time." One by one, they paid homage solemnly. In turn, he embraced them and kissed their foreheads. Seh Hercaranu continued: "My grandchildren, how hard your sufferings must have been. But you must accept them with forbearance because your hardships will lighten the sins of your father. He is receiving God's wrath for throwing away his sainthood and hankering for worldly power. Remember that always!"

Ki Jayengsari said to the hermit: "I do not wish to oppose the king. For now, all I want is to live peacefully, thank God for His mercy and meet my older brother." Seh Hercaranu advised: "Don't worry about your brother! He is fine and now studying

opposite: *Bima temple. For the locals who adopt Javanese mysticism, this is the most sacred of all the Hindu temples on Dieng plateau in Wonosobo Regency, Central Java. It is part of a large group of 7th-century temples (the first to be built in Java) scattered around the caldera of a collapsed volcano and is the only temple in the complex that has the famous and rare* kudu *statues which depict a woman's face wearing a crown. Out of 24 statues, only a few remain, the rest having been looted by thieves.*

| the adulthood journey |

with Kyai Ageng Karang of Banten. He has already received the mercy of God. You will meet him later when you have successfully dealt with some more obstacles and drawbacks that will come your way. Increase your devotion to the Merciful and you will surely find your dreams. I will help you to attain your other goals, live in peace and devote yourself to God. Now hold on to my robe and close your eyes. Do not open them until I ask you to. I'll take you to Wonontoko, a serene valley surrounded by hills and mountains. Nobody will disturb you there."

## 2 Wonontoko

They followed the ascetic's advice and in a very short time, arrived at Wonontoko. Seh Hercaranu told them to open their eyes and when they did so, they saw in front of them a valley of incredible beauty. It came complete with all necessities, from a house and mosque to rice fields and vegetable gardens. They remained at Wonontoko for two

months, receiving instructions from the hermit on how to live in peace and harmony, while securing the grace of God.

When all had been taught, Seh Hercaranu said: "It is now time for me to leave. But before I go, it is best for you, Jayengsari, to change your name to Seh Mangunarso and for Cabolang to be called Seh Anggungrimang, after his father. My granddaughter Rancangkapti doesn't need to change her name. Buras should change his name to Santri Montel." Everyone agreed to make the changes.

"One more thing," added Ki Hercaranu to Seh Mangunarso, "it is best that Anggungrimang and Rancangkapti live apart from you so that you will not disturb each other in your devotion to God. Mangunarso, I will bring them to another place called Gunungsari. It is not far from here." The next moment, the priest disappeared into thin air. He did not stay long at Gunungsari as everything that was needed was there and nothing was lacking. Santri Montel was sent back to Sokoyoso to arrange the move of the other *santris* privately and in secrecy.

below: *Rice fields are very much a common sight in the countryside of Java. Families cultivate rice for their own consumption and that of the village they live in.*

## Seh Amongrogo

#### FROM KARANG TO WONOMARTO

## 1 Back on the road

At the hermitage of Karang in the region of Banten, Kyai Ageng Karang was sitting with Ki Jayengresmi on the verandah of the mosque. Gathak and Gathuk were also present, which was a bit unusual, too. Noticing the gloom on Jayengresmi's face, Ki Ageng said: "My son, the expression on your face tells me there is something serious you want to say. You have my permission to speak." Ki Jayengresmi made homage solemnly, then spoke: "Kyai Ageng, I would like to express my heartfelt gratitude to you for having accepted me as your son and disciple. I hope I will not disappoint you."

Said Ki Ageng: "My son, the pleasure is mine. You know, my own son has gone away and you fill up the emptiness in my heart. I thank God for that. You are now my son and the heir to my knowledge. I have the greatest and sincerest hope that you will be able to convey that knowledge to other people." Ki Jayengresmi continued: "Kyai! Father! That is what makes it so difficult for me. As you know, I've been trying to look for my younger brother and sister. I've lived with you for a few years now and I still haven't heard any news about them. It worries me a great deal. Ah, father, I would like to ask your leave to continue my search for them."

Replied Ki Ageng: "I don't blame you for wanting to do that, my son, because you are their elder brother. You feel the responsibility to protect them. But you don't need to worry about them. With God's mercy, they are well and safe and their knowledge has almost reached the level of yours. I can't tell you where they are at present but I can tell you this. If you want to look for them, go to the hermitage of Wonomarto. There you will find a big religious school under the leadership of Kyai Bayi Panurto. He has

opposite: *This is* Tuwuhan, *a wedding day decoration of plants and leaves placed at the entrance to the bride's family home. Every* Tuwuhan *must have ripe bananas (to signify the couple's ability to adjust to married life) and young green and yellow coconuts (to signify the couple's undying love for each other). Additional items have been placed for this* Tuwuhan. *The peanuts, sweet potatoes, vegetable marrow, bitter melons, aubergines and breadfruit all symbolise wishes for wealth and fertility.*

replied: "I never married. I found my daughter in a bush. You can say this child was a godsend."

It was soon time for the evening prayer. Seh Amongrogo was asked to lead it and everything went smoothly. In their hearts, Ki Suksmo and Pamegatsih marvelled at the extent of his knowledge. Still, Ki Suksmo wanted to test how much he knew. And so, when the prayer was over, they held a discussion about religion. He began by asking about the first thing that God created. Seh Amongrogo said that it was *Dzatullah* (Essence of Allah) and explained the matter in detail. Roro Pamegatsih then asked: "We know there are four *nafsu* (passion). Which one leads to evil and which one leads to goodness?" He answered: "The passion leading to goodness is the *mutmainah*. The other three passions—*amarah*, *lawammah* and *sufiah*—lead to evil."

All their questions were answered to satisfaction. Ki Suksmo then told Seh Amongrogo of the vow his daughter had made. Since it was clear that he could match her in terms of knowledge, the priest wished him to marry her. However, Seh Amongrogo declined saying he was on a quest to look for his brother and sister but promised to come back after he had found them. Dawn broke, the guests took leave and were soon on their way again.

## 3 Ki Nuripin

On the road, Jamal met a cowherd and asked: "Uncle! I beg your pardon! Be so kind as to tell me the way to the village of Wonomarto?" The cowherd replied: "This is the road to Wonomarto. There is only one road. In fact, you can see the village from here. By the way, where do you come from and why do you want to go there?" Said Ki Amongrogo: "Brother, we are *santris* from Karang in the region of Banten. I have heard about the master of Wonomarto, Kyai Bayi Panurto, who is famous all over Java. I want to study with him." Nuripin, for that was the cowherd's name, replied: "That's true! Here, in the eastern part of Java, no one can be compared with Ki Bayi. Many regents and wealthy merchants have studied with him. As it is almost dark, I think it would be better for you to stay with me tonight. I live very near Wonomarto, in Pagutan village. I'll take you to Wonomarto tomorrow. In fact, I'm also a *santri* of Wonomarto and know exactly the procedure for visiting or leaving the hermitage. I also know people who can help me arrange a meeting with Ki Bayi." Ki Amongrogo agreed to stay with Nuripin that night.

They continued their conversation about Ki Bayi after the evening prayer. Ki Nuripin explained: "Ki Bayi has five brothers and three children. The eldest child is a daughter called Ni Ken Tambangraras. She's very intelligent and extremely beautiful. Her only flaw is her refusal to marry. She has refused hundreds of marriage proposals. His other children are sons, Ki Jayengwesthi and Ki Jayengrogo, the youngest. Both are married but do not have any children yet. People who want to study with Ki Bayi must meet one of the sons first and discuss religious matters with them. He will only agree to teach those whose knowledge is ranked higher than that of his sons. Otherwise, either Ki Jayengrogo or Ki Jayengwesthi will take care of them." Ki Amongrogo commented: "Perhaps she is looking for a highly intelligent cleric, as she is intelligent herself. Perhaps people will think that I will ask her to marry me!" Said Ki Nuripin: "That's unlikely. There have not been any marriage proposals for several months. You better rest now, master. We'll leave early tomorrow."

## 4 In Wonomarto with Ki Jayengwesthi and Ki Jayengrogo

Ki Amongrogo, his companions and Nuripin walked leisurely to Wonomarto, enjoying the sights along the way. The road itself was wide and straight, and the fields were ripe with rice. The region looked very prosperous. Nuripin was talking all the way; the visitors merely added a word or two as if encouraging him to go on with his stories about the people, their hobbies and their professions. It was almost midday when they reached the village. The farmers had just got home and while waiting for the midday meal to be ready, were either repairing tools on the verandah or playing the drum or just singing a song. Everything seemed so peaceful and serene. As they neared the village centre where shops were located, they saw people busy buying things or just looking around. The atmosphere had changed; it was not one of a village anymore but that of a small town. No wonder people called the village of Wonomarto a *kerajaan* (city). The visitors were very impressed.

below: *At the foot of Anjasmara Mountain lies the village of Wonomarto. This prosperous, peaceful place is located in Wonosalam District, Jombang Regency, East Java. The regency is known as a 'santri (disciple) city', for its* pesantren *or traditional religious schools. Many of the founders of such schools across Java would have studied here in Jombang Regency.*

| the adulthood journey |

right top: *This is the kind of 'gate' that Nuripin hid behind. Called* regol, *it is the main gateway that leads to big* joglo *houses. Regol is more than just a main gate. With a roof on it, it served as a resting place for wayfarers in the olden days; there would also be an earthenware pot filled with water for them to drink. It is rare to find* regol *these days. This photograph of an old* regol *was taken in Tegalsari village in Ponorogo Regency, East Java.*

right bottom: *The* pendopo, *or front hall, of a traditional* joglo *house in Tegalsari village. The steep roof is supported by four main pillars, as can be seen in this photograph.*

On the main road, Ki Amongrogo saw a man being carried in a sedan chair by four people. Everybody on the street greeted him respectfully; even those who were busy working stopped whatever they were doing and resumed only when he passed by. Ki Amongrogo enquired about the man and Nuripin replied: "He is Ki Kulowiryo, the youngest brother of Ki Bayi. He has a great sense of humour, but he can also be very strict and will punish bad people very severely. He likes to make fun of me, though.

| seh amongrogo |

left: *A view of the imposing roof of a joglo house. Houses like the one shown here, with their large gardens, would usually belong to high-ranking officials and the rich.* Joglo *houses are typically built with three main sections. The front hall with its steep roof is the* pendopo *and is used for receiving guests. The middle part, called the* pringgitan, *is often a narrow passage that links the front hall with the* ndalem, *or the private back area.*

Let's hide behind the gate until he passes us." When Ki Kulowiryo had passed them, Nuripin said: "Master, it would be better for you to wait for me here. I will go ahead and look for Santri Luci. He will help us meet Ki Bayi Panurto."

On finding Santri Luci, they both went to see the master's sons first. On that particular day, Ki Jayengwesthi was visiting his younger brother, Ki Jayengrogo, who was copying a religious manuscript. They listened to Nuripin's report attentively and then asked him to bring the visitor to them. Ki Jayengrogo ordered his servants to tidy up the *pendopo*. When Seh Amongrogo was seated comfortably, Ki Jayengwesthi said: "Welcome to Wonomarto, brother! Please tell me your name and why you are here?" Seh Amongrogo replied: "My name is Seh Amongrogo and I come from Karang in the region of Banten. I wish to study with Kyai Bayi Panurto, as his fame is known far and wide." Said Ki Jayengrogo: "If the intention is only to study, my father will usually leave that task to me or my brother." Ki Jayengwesthi offered: "I think it's best that brother Amongrogo rests first. Let's discuss the matter again tonight and then inform our father about your arrival."

Evening came. With the excuse of honouring a guest, they asked Seh Amongrogo to lead the sunset prayer. From the way he conducted himself, Ki Jayengwesthi concluded that Seh Amongrogo had no intention of studying at Wonomarto as he was already very learned. But he wanted to be sure and so at the evening prayer, he asked the *santri* to lead the prayer again, this time with the excuse that he, Amongrogo, was very good and could influence the congregation to perform better. He obliged and began to recite the chapters Al-Jumu'ah [The Assembly Prayer] (Q, 62) and Al-Munafiqun [The Hypocrites] (Q, 63). Ki Jayengwesthi was all the more convinced that Seh Amongrogo was an outstanding cleric. In his heart, he felt something extraordinary. It was not the feeling of competition but that of an intimate friendship, even though he had known him for less than half a day. The congregation felt the same.

When the prayer was over, Ki Jayengwesthi said to his wife: "Turido, serve whatever you have cooked today. Get your sister and Jayengrogo's concubines to help." She replied: "All right, dear." While preparing the meal, Nyi Turido expressed her view to Nyi Rarasati, Ki Jayengrogo's wife: "My sister, I have a strange feeling this guest of ours isn't an ordinary cleric. When he led the prayer, the congregation performed in a more serene and solemn manner." Nyi Rarasati replied: "I agree, sister! Looking at the way the discussion went tonight, I think my husband has no chance of winning." Said Nyi Turido: "Let alone your husband, even mine is not better off. Moreover, I have this feeling that our guest would make a good husband for our sister Tambangraras." Nyi Rarasati replied: "Strange, sister! I feel the same and pray that it will happen."

At the mosque, Ki Amongrogo started the conversation by asking: "My dear brothers! Now is the time to say whatever we feel in our mind." Ki Jayengwesthi said: "My brother, thank you. I'm very convinced that you are an exceptional cleric. I feel tonight's discussion cannot be called a discussion anymore but would be better described as both of us begging you to wipe out the impurities in our heart." Added Ki Jayengrogo: "I feel the same way and because I'm the youngest and the most foolish, permit me to ask the first question. Brother, this is a question to which I have no answer. What is the knowledge that has no space and is also not written down? All the clerics I meet give me this problem, but none has been able to solve it."

Seh Amongrogo answered: "My brother, the perfect knowledge is that which fits with the rhythm of the soul. If the knowledge deviates from the soul, the knowledge will get lost. The knowledge that does not need space and isn't written down is in fact the Qur'an and the *Sunnah* (traditions of the holy prophet) and other religious books. All the knowledge contained in those books should be learnt by heart and practised so that its totality is reduced to memory. Only the mind is the perfect place and, just like the ocean, it is never dry. So space and writing are not needed. A person who doesn't understand this only deifies himself. He will consider himself as the perfect man, an attitude that only serves to complicate matters. In the end, he himself will plunge into total loss." Ki Jayengrogo recognised the truth of the explanations and said: "I never realised that the disappearance of the knowledge from space and writing was because it has moved into the soul or heart. I remember when a certain Kyai Tatasjati visited us, he claimed to be God, as mentioned by brother Amongrogo. Now I'm convinced that he was mistaken."

Ki Jayengwesthi then said: "My turn now, brother! I would like to know where Allah was at the time of Void and what He created first and thereafter." Ki Amongrogo explained: "At the time of Void, what actually existed was *la takyun kun*, meaning 'the time of the existence of non-existence'. The meaning of *la takyun* is 'non-existence' and *kun* is 'existence'. It is also said that any existence is false (*la takyun*) and what exists (*kun*) is new but cannot be ascertained. It is also explained that *la takyun kun* means 'not yet exist'. Another explanation mentions that it is the *nokat wilayat ga'ib*, *ga'ibul uwiyah* or the three *ga'ibul uwiyah*, which is the *ga'ibul guyub*, the most subtle intelligence. *Nokat wilayat ga'ib* is explained as 'the most subtle unseen things', which exist without cause. *Ga'ibul guyub*—the most unseen of the unseen—certainly exists, but it cannot be seen as it is covered by the thickest darkness. *Ga'ibul uwiyah* is a step further—the existence is certain, but it is not covered by darkness; yet it is unseen. That is the explanation of what was created first and what was created next. If mention is made about the world and the sky at that time, it is the unseen world and sky. So it can be concluded that at the time of Void, God already existed, but the existence is non-existence because cause and reason are non-existent." The brothers told Seh Amongrogo: "We have nothing more to ask, brother." In their mind, they hoped that one day he would become their brother-in-law.

Seh Amongrogo then whispered a message in their ears because what he had to say was not to be heard by others: "My brothers, you should do nothing but meditate and be silent for seven, or better still, for nine months. In the stillness, you should concentrate only on one thing… the growth of the seed of consciousness, that "I am the Perfection of Life". The seed has to be implanted there within seven months and in the next 100 days, the seed of *nurbuah waliyullah* (sainthood) should already grow. Continue your efforts for another two months until there is the consciousness of "I am Life"—'I' meaning 'nobody else, not two or three' and 'Life' meaning 'free from death'. My brothers, this is The Perfect Reality or The Real Life. Void or Emptiness and Knowledge that does not need space or writ stops here into perfection." The brothers were silenced by the knowledge that was whispered into their ears and tears began to flow. They expressed their gratitude to Seh Amongrogo. Meanwhile, night had turned into dawn.

When they reached home, Ki Jayengwesthi told his brother that he felt different. Ki Jayengrogo replied that he too felt different. Ki Jayengwesthi then added: "My brother, I think it will be very good if our guest marries sister Tambangraras." Ki Jayengrogo nodded in agreement and prayed it would happen. Said Ki Jayengwesthi to his wife and sister-in-law: "Turido and Rarasati, talk to sister Tambangraras about our guest. Praise him a little to attract her attention. I will also speak with our father should he not come up with the same idea."

## 5 Ki Bayi Panurto

After breakfast the next morning, Ki Jayengwesthi asked Ki Amongrogo: "My brother! Do you think you should meet our father as soon as possible? If your knowledge was not higher than ours, I would have asked you to stay here. But that is not the case and now my brother and I are your disciples. If your knowledge is higher than my father's, then there is much more he has to learn." Ki Amongrogo replied humbly: "Oh, brother! When I came here, I did not expect a contest of knowledge. What I truly want is only to bring our knowledge into line."

Ki Bayi Panurto was in the small mosque which he uses to teach the reading of the Qur'an. With him were his wife, Nyai Malarsih, and their daughter, Ni Ken Tambangraras. Not only had Ni Ken completed studying the big books of exegesis, such as the *Bahwi-Barlawi* and *Jaelani*, she had also mastered many religious books and was even better than her brothers where religious matters were concerned. Ki Bayi was a little surprised to see his sons come in a hurry. When they were seated, he asked: "What is it, my sons, that makes you come here in haste?" Ki Jayengwesthi said: "Forgive us, father. We have a guest who claims to come from the hermitage of Karang." Ki Bayi asked: "Have you tested his knowledge?" Replied Ki Jayengwesthi: "Yes, and we were totally defeated. When he asked a question about the seat of The Creator and what goes to heaven, we couldn't answer it as you haven't taught us that yet." Ki Bayi smiled: "Perhaps that is his special knowledge. All right, bring him here!" Ni Ken then asked: "Brother, is the intention of your guest merely to boast about his knowledge? Which *santri* on earth wants to debate religious knowledge with our father? Has he not heard of our father's fame?" Ki Jayengwesthi replied: "Ah, sister! In the past, I could always defeat clerics who claimed to be highly knowledgeable, but this time I had to surrender totally and unconditionally." Ni Ken was interested to meet the guest as soon as possible to see whether he was really a scholar or an impostor.

When Ki Amongrogo arrived, Ki Bayi went down the steps to meet him. Ki Amongrogo wanted to kiss his feet, but Ki Bayi quickly grabbed his guest's hands, brought him to stand up and shook his hands. In his heart, he said: "It looks like this person is a great scholar, but he doesn't want to show it. All his behaviour shows he is a man of noble origin." Ki Bayi said: "I heard that my son comes from Karang. Is it Karang the village or Karang the hermitage?" Ki Amongrogo replied: "Karang the hermitage, Kyai, but I'm only a humble *santri*. I studied there for many long years, but

right: *This is an example of a typical meal served in Javanese households. Surrounding a cone of steamed white rice are* tempe goreng *(deep fried soy bean cake),* serundeng *(a relish of grated coconut and spices) and mixed blanched vegetables. The pink item on the right are crackers.*

because of my low intellect I haven't been able to further my knowledge. That is why I have come to study with Kyai." Ki Bayi replied: "My son, the hermitage of Karang is the house of prominent scholars of Islam. If they can't help you, how can I? I think it's better that we just try to help each other."

Not long afterwards, Nyi Malarsih came to serve drinks and snacks. Ki Bayi made the introductions and she and Ki Amongrogo exchanged greetings. Though the encounter was brief, she felt affection creeping into her heart. Ni Ken, who was peeping from behind the bamboo screen, could see everything very clearly. She thought: "The guest is very good looking. All his behaviour is simple, yet he seems to have a great influence on people. Ah, if my father wants us to marry, I will thank God for that." Time passed slowly, as if playing with the emotions of the people involved. Suddenly, Ki Bayi ordered lunch to be served. Lunch was over by the time the call for the midday prayer was announced and they went to the mosque together. Ki Bayi led the prayer. After that, there was a discussion concerning types of conduct, such as *batal* (cancelled, null and void, disqualification), *haram* (forbidden), *riba* (usury), *sunnah* (preferable) and *fardlu* (compulsory). The discussion carried on until it was time for the late afternoon prayer. Ki Bayi then excused himself to have a bath and make preparations for the evening prayer. He took the opportunity to talk privately with his wife and daughter about Ki Amongrogo. Both of them had only positive things to say about him.

The discussion continued after the evening prayer. Ki Bayi asked: "Well, my son Amongrogo! Now say what is troubling you. Is it concerning the kris entering the sheath (*curiga manjing warangka*), the sheath entering the kris (*warangka manjing curiga*) or the soul entering the body (*suksma manjing ing badan*) and the body entering the soul (*badan manjing ing suksma*)?"

Ki Amongrogo bowed and answered: "I beg your pardon, Kyai. I'm not looking for that kind of knowledge, which is based on the *Dalil* (words of God), *Hadith* (collection of the traditions of the prophet), *Ijmak* (agreement of the religious leaders) and *Qiyas* (findings based on comparison). All of them are still considered knowledge.

*above left:* This kris making workshop, which belonged to Ki Empu Djeno, was destroyed in an earthquake that struck Central Java on 26 May 2006. Ki Empu died a few days before the disaster.

*above middle:* A kris blade being shaped by a kris smith. Each blade is made from layers of certain mixtures of iron, nickel and steel. While some blades can be made in a relatively short time, 'spiritually powerful' krises take years to make.

*above right:* The photograph shows the upper part of kris sheaths. Known as wrangka, they are often made from wood, with some made from ivory or even gold. Some sheaths are elaborately decorated with designs and carvings.

| the adulthood journey |

Ki Bayi spoke further: "Listen to my words, my precious! There are six things you should always do. First, respect your husband and never dispute his words. Second, love him no matter what may happen. Like all the things he likes and dislike all the things he doesn't like. Third, be understanding and agree with whatever he wants to do. Fourth, trust him; always remember his advice and guidance and never break the rules he has set. Fifth, be observant and carry out whatever he wishes. And finally, be loyal to him, even if it means you have to suffer." Ni Ken's mind became calm.

## 7 The wedding at Wonomarto

### 1) The preparations

Ki Bayi went to see his sons to discuss the wedding arrangements, which had to be as simple as possible. It was finally agreed that it would be held in the village and that government officials would not be invited. Still, the wedding would see about 1000 people and with only three days to go, he divided the workload among his relatives and friends. Since Ki Amongrogo's father was held captive, Ki Jayengwesthi would stand in as Ni Ken's father-in-law. Ki Jayengrogo would be in charge of the catering and seeing to the venue for the various ceremonies. Nyi Malarsih was to be responsible for the bride and guests. Assisting her would be Nyi Doyo, who was once the favourite concubine of the regent of Wirosobo. She knew everything concerning preparations for the bride and so was responsible for putting on the bride's make-up. Centhini would assist her. Then there was Nyi Sembaling, Nyi Malarsih's *cethi*, who would help with the shopping for ingredients for the feast and offerings, ordering the spices, supervising the slaughtering of the animals and the cooking. Not surprisingly, she had the most helpers.

right: *A Javanese bride getting ready for her wedding. A* pemaes *(traditional make-up lady) is applying the finishing touches on her. As well as learning make-up techniques in beauty schools, many* pemaes *take on an apprenticeship with professional and well-known* pemaes *to gain experience and special knowledge. Before the wedding day, many* pemaes *also fast and pray for guidance in 'transforming' the bride into a beautiful vision. Traditional bridal make-up includes* cengkorongan, *special designs drawn in prescribed shapes and designs on the forehead. A chignon is attached to the bride's hair, which is elaborately adorned with golden accessories and jasmine.*

### 2) *Midodareni* night, the night the fairies visit

Everybody was most busy on *midodareni* night, the night that fairies come to visit the bride. It is believed that on this night, fairies visit the bride to give their blessings and one fairy will possess the bride to make her look as beautiful as the fairy. That night, Ni Ken was confined to her room and watched by the elderly ladies who were giving her last minute advice.

Meanwhile, Ki Jayengwesthi was sitting with Ki Amongrogo when his brother and three of his uncles came from the mosque to join the night vigil. Nuripin, Jamal and Jamil were also present to serve them. Ki Amongrogo said: "My brothers and uncles! Be aware that the *Kadariyah* and the *Jabariyah tariqahs* (mystic's order) are very complicated. Many religious scholars have studied them, but still they are very difficult to practise. If you adhere to the *Kadariyah*, you are in danger of becoming *kafir 'inda'llah* (one who performs the religious law, but in his mind does not believe in God) and if you adhere to the *Jabariyah*, you are in danger of becoming *kafir 'inda nas* (an unbeliever, one who adheres to a religion that is not Islam). If you follow only one of them, for sure you are an infidel. If you follow both of them, you are still regarded as an infidel, unless you are a strict follower of the *sunni* sect without flaw and blemish. In life, we have to possess strong will and intention for it is only in that condition that the body will obey as it should. It is indeed easy to study the Qur'an or perform the *salat* (obligatory prayer), but it is not easy to have strong resolution and intention to do them. Resolution and intention will become the criterion for determining whether a person is good or not. Resolution has its source in the heart (soul). The best is when both resolution and intention unite."

While that was going on, Ki Bayi was in the *pendopo* meeting the guests. Amongst the older ones were Ki Sembagi and Ki Jumeno, who were absorbed in

below left: *On* midodareni *night, the bride has to stay in her room, which is also the bridal room for the couple after the wedding. Close female friends and relatives will visit to keep her company. Later on in the night, another ritual will take place in the room—her parents will feed her for the last time, as from then on, she would come under the care of her husband.*

below right: *An important ritual called* siraman *(holy bathing) is performed on the day of* midodareni *night for both the bride and groom. In their respective homes, spring water infused with flowers is poured on their head, hands and feet to symbolically clean the body and soul as they enter a new phase in their life. The photograph shows a bride being 'bathed' by a relative.*

conversation. Ki Bayi said: "Well, uncle Sembagi! What are you talking about with Ki Jumeno? Must be very interesting." Ki Sembagi replied: "We were just talking about the possibilities of predicting one's fortune in marriage based on the value of the Javanese alphabet." Ki Bayi then asked: "If that is the case, calculate the fortune of the marriage of your granddaughter Ni Ken with Ki Amongrogo." Ki Sembagi said: "But I remind you Kyai, that all this is based on *budo* (pre-Islamic) knowledge." Ki Bayi replied that it did not matter as the knowledge of Allah was unlimited. After a while, Ki Sembagi said: "According to our calculation, theirs will be a happy marriage." Ki Bayi then asked about their destiny. Ki Sembagi said: "The groom's destiny is good in the first part of his life, but there will be a lot of grief when he is separated from his parents." Hearing those words reminded Ki Bayi about what Ki Amongrogo had told him.

In another group, two of Ki Bayi's younger brothers, Ki Panamar and Ki Kulowiryo, were playing chess. Many people were gathered around them; one group sided with Ki Panamar and another with Ki Wiryo. In the end, Ki Wiryo won a goat as the prize. While handing it over, Ki Panamar grumbled: "Indeed, gambling is bad. Fortunately our religion forbids gambling. It is only the miserable who don't want to obey." Meanwhile, Ki Bayi was asking about the appropriate time to hold the wedding ceremony. It was decided that it would take place after the late afternoon prayer and would be followed by the *temu* ceremony, where the bride would meet the groom. Ki Bayi asked for a *rebana* and started to play.

**3) The dragon of Wirosobo**

Nyi Malarsih was flitting from one place to another. One moment she was inspecting the bridal room and another she was in the kitchen supervising the cooking. She just wanted to keep herself busy and make sure nothing would go wrong. In a corner sat a group of elderly ladies talking about everything just to keep awake on this night that the fairies would visit. Among them were Nyi Parti, a saleswoman who used to travel to distant places, Nyi Doyo and Nyi Sumbaling, who was also a well-known dancer in her younger years. It could be imagined that between them they had a lot of experiences to share. That night, however, their attention was focused on their sexual experiences.

Nyi Sumbaling asked Nyi Doyo: "Nyi, how many times did you marry?" Nyi Doyo replied: "Only twice. The regent of Wirosobo abducted me when I was married for only six months to the young man of my choice. We loved each other very much and spent every night making love to satisfaction. One day, the regent saw me and took me away by force to his residence. I was given food and clothes but never allowed to see my husband. What was the use of nice clothes and delicious food when I was separated from my lover whom I missed so much? The other concubines, even the regent's wife, advised me to accept him, but I was stubborn. Day in, day out, I cried and cried."

above: *Women seeing to the final preparations of a wedding meal in a large kitchen area at the back of a house. In small village homes, makeshift kitchens will be specially built for occasions where space is needed to prepare for large feasts, such as weddings. The materials used are often simple, such as woven bamboo for the wall and bamboo for the roof.*

Nyi Doyo's sad story made the other ladies miserable. Asked Nyi Sumbaling: "But how did you finally become the favourite of the regent?" Nyi Doyo explained: "That, my dear, happened on a fateful afternoon. Nature was in uproar. There was pouring rain, thunder and heavy winds. I was sitting with the other concubines—we were very cold—when the regent appeared suddenly. My friends quickly ran to their rooms, but he caught me and carried me to his room. We both fell heavily on the mattress. Then what had to happen happened." Nyi Sumbaling enquired excitedly: "Nyi, what happened? Tell us, Nyi! Explain as clearly as possible. Let us be satisfied!"

Nyi Doyo continued: "All right! The regent behaved as though he was possessed by the devil himself. His eyes were red, his hands moved like that of a magician. In the wink of an eye, my *jarit* (cloth) was lost, my *kebaya* in rags. I was naked like Eve in paradise with Adam because at that very second, the regent had taken off his clothes and was stark naked, like Adam. I don't know how well endowed Adam was, but what I do know is the size of the regent's member, which looked menacing and horrible. In size, my husband's was nothing." The ladies were breathing heavily; some were even swallowing their saliva. Almost shouting, they urged Nyi Doyo to tell them more.

Nyi Doyo continued: "When I looked at the regent's weapon moving menacingly, I became terrified. Suddenly, he pounced on me like a tiger. He kissed my lips and

right: *Traditional attire of Javanese women. Jarit is a long cloth of batik, 2 metres long by 1 metre wide, wrapped around to cover the lower part of the body. It is secured with a large waist band called* stagen.

his hands caressed my breasts. I fought back and pushed his hands away. But like lightning, his hands were already on my thighs. He parted them and slipped his body in between. It was as though an all-seeing dragon was between his loins as he penetrated me. Even though I was a little too small for him, the wild dragon had no consideration and pushed through forcefully. I felt myself shudder from the thrust and I cried out with the cry of a virgin wounded by a dragon. But the regent had no mercy at all. He continued to penetrate with a perpetual thrusting movement, creating both pleasure and pain. The rain continued to fall heavily and after a long battle, he relented. I noticed my breasts were full of bites, but I didn't care. The regent was very concerned and began to caress them, which aroused him again. At the same time, I inspected his powerful weapon, which could make me fly to the seventh heaven. It wasn't powerful any more but still had a presence. I touched and pinched it until it came to life again. Now, no battle ensued but the art of sexual play, which shook heaven and earth and was accompanied by the soft sounds of drizzle. The world didn't count any more and thoughts of my husband vanished. Thus we moved together until we were out of energy, like clouds were out of rain."

Nyi Doyo stopped talking. The ladies were breathing very heavily. At length, she broke the spell: "Now it is my turn to ask. What about you Nyi, or mBok Tengah? How many times did you marry?" Nyi Pengulu replied: "Only three times. The first marriage was one between a boy and a girl because we were both not yet eighteen and had no experience whatsoever. Too many mishaps happened and we were divorced after two years. I lived as a widow for six months and then married Amat Badar, one of Ki Pengulu's younger brothers. I loved him very much. He was very well endowed. Nyi Doyo is right… a well-endowed man can satisfy. Mas Badar didn't initiate playful sex very often, but once he started, he didn't want to stop. We spent whole long nights in each other's arms. I can tell you that the way to a man's heart isn't only through his stomach but primarily through his loins. Very often he wouldn't eat, but if he did, he would eat very quickly just to have more time in bed. Sometimes, he would order me to stay in bed and wait for him. As a good wife, I obeyed. But we lived happily for only a short time. We didn't even have a child when he died. Four months later, Ki Pengulu took me as his second wife. Sex with Ki Pengulu isn't as satisfactory as with his brother because he is small and doesn't fit me adequately. You can say that if I yawn, it will come out." The ladies laughed, though with some restrain.

Then Nyi Pengulu asked Nyi Parti, the lady-merchant, to tell her story. Nyi Parti moved a little closer and with a smile, she said: "I married only once, but as far as sexual indulgence goes, perhaps I beat all of you. Because I am a saleswoman by profession, I have to be friendly with all my customers, both men and women. At first it was only sharing a joke or two with the men but then those casual sessions slowly became more intimate. We started to touch each other, teasingly at first, but later on more seriously until we finally ended up in bed. Once, I had a very good looking and well-endowed partner and thereafter I became addicted every time I saw a handsome face. After a while, the face didn't count too much, but the dragon between his loins became more important because we made love, not in a lighted room, but under the cover of darkness. The darker the place, the more secure the feeling and the action became most breathtaking. It was literally breathtaking because we would be gasping by the time we finished. Business wise, it was also profitable. Some clients never ask the price and would just pay up. No questions were asked. I even went with men of this village, including Ki Kulowiryo and Ki Pengulu. Ki Kulowiryo is good. Ki Pengulu, as you say, isn't very good to say the least." Again, restrained laughter was heard.

By chance, Nyi Malarsih passed by and remarked: "What is the cause of all this merriment?" The women replied in unison: "Ah, nothing really. Just talk to keep from falling asleep!" Nyi Malarsih added: "If that is the case, ask Sumbaling! She was a well-known dancer when she was young and was very much in demand." The ladies pointed their fingers at her, saying: "Now the secret is out. Speak out, Nyi!"

Nyi Sumbaling smiled and said: "There is no secrecy at all. If it is a secret, then it is a public secret. Everyone knows! Indeed, I was already a well-known *pesinden* (female singer in a gamelan orchestra) before I turned seventeen and as Nyai has said, I was very much in demand. Though I was expensive, many men were crazy over me. They were of all nationalities—Chinese, Indian, Javanese—and none was refused. Once I had an Indian called Subede. His body was solid and

# the adulthood journey

above: Pesinden *is a female singer in a gamelan orchestra. Always dressed in* kebaya *and* jarit*, she is one who has mastered the patterns and variations that are appropriate to the different sections of melody in Javanese songs. Well-known* pesindens *earn a good income and can afford to perform on a fulltime basis. The man in the background is a gamelan player.*

his dragon formidable, bigger and longer than what you mentioned before, but it was too big for the hole. Because I was afraid its head would damage the walls, I tied a handkerchief around its neck to prevent it from entering fully. But I was consumed by the sensation and couldn't control myself. I pushed the dragon inside. It got pinched and struggled with all its might, moving back and forth, turning from side to side. Finally, it spewed out its venom like a flood, causing me to shudder and tremble until I lost all my strength and fell in a swoon. But the dragon wasn't better off. It was choked to death and became flaccid. The athletic body of Subede fell lifeless beside me. Until today, when I recall the battle of the dragon in the hole of ecstasy, I still feel the poison creeping all over my body. It's a wonder that the poison seemed to have the effect of the elixir of life, as I felt fresh and relaxed afterwards, though the body had not fully recovered."

Near the ladies was a young widow drying dishes with a cloth. Although her hands were busy working, her ears were glued to the women's stories. She ran to the bathroom, moaning and grumbling to herself: "Really, they have no consideration at all. But what a story!" She hit her rigid buttocks again and again.

## 4) The wedding
### 4i) *the ijab-kabul ceremony*

Said Ki Bayi to his wife: "Nyai, the wedding ceremony will take place when the late afternoon prayer is over. Dress and make up your daughter as best as possible but not too extravagantly. This is the wish of your future son-in-law. It's best we comply with his wishes, since he is indeed greatly worried about his brother and sister." Ki Bayi was then kept busy attending to guests who had arrived with donations and contributions for him and his wife. The regent of Wirosobo had contributed bags of rice and animals including cows, buffaloes, sheep and chickens that would go towards the wedding feast. To Nyi Malarsih, the regent's wife sent a special messenger bringing a donation of 250 guilders.

Then there was Ki Wonohito from Pucangan village. He was a close relative of Ki Bayi, a great-grand uncle in fact, and very much revered by the people. He had heard about the wedding and set out to attend the ceremony with his grandchildren. Along the way, people stood on the side of the road as a mark of respect. Ki Bayi was surprised to see the old man and got up to welcome him: "Well, great grand-uncle, why do you tire yourself to come here. Your great granddaughter and her husband will visit you after the wedding to beg your blessings." Ki Wonohito replied: "My grandson, I can't wait for Ni Ken to come. I fear I will be gone before then." When he was seated, Ki Bayi asked: "Great grand-uncle is already so old. We were just worried that something might happen to you on the way. How old are you now?" Ki Wonohito said: "I was born at the beginning of the Pajang kingdom era. I could be 126 years old." All present were more respectful towards the old man, who still looked full of vigour.

When it was late afternoon, Ki Bayi ordered the call to prayer and walked to the mosque. All the guests followed him. He led the prayer himself. The *ijab-kabul* ceremony would take place soon after in front of the *mighrab*. When everyone was seated in their respective places, Ki Bayi asked the *pengulu* to perform the ceremony: "Kyai Pengulu Basarodin! I ask your assistance to perform the wedding ceremony of my daughter Ni Ken Tambangraras with Seh Amongrogo. The dowry is a copy of the holy book Al Qur'an." After saying a prayer, the *pengulu* pronounced the *ijab* (offering of marriage) as follows: "I declare the marriage of Ni Ken Tambangraras with Seh Amongrogo is in progress. Seh Amongrogo, do you accept the *ijab*?" Seh Amongrogo pronounced the *kabul* (acceptance of marriage) as follows: "I accept Ni Ken Tambangraras as my lawful wife, with the dowry in the form of the holy book Al Qur'an. Furthermore, I promise to pass on to her the knowledge of religion from the beginning to the end, from this world to the hereafter."

BELOW: A Tuwuhan *(special decoration of plants and leaves) being set up for a village wedding. In addition to bananas and coconuts, this* Tuwuhan *consists of leaves from the banyan tree (to symbolise the couple protecting each other) and a variety of leaves with medicinal value (to signify the couple's ability to ward off misfortunes such as sickness and bad spirits).*

## seh amongrogo

Ki Pengulu added: "May God The Merciful bless both of you with all happiness in this life and the hereafter." Then the witness, Ki Talabodin, came forward to proclaim the *janji dalem* (king's order): "Seh Amongrogo, if you leave your wife for three years abroad or six months in this country without giving any sustenance to her, divorce proceedings will be carried out." Ki Amongrogo accepted the conditions. Ki Nursukidin then read the prayer of marriage to close the ceremony.

Ki Amongrogo shook hands with Ki Bayi and asked Ki Wonohito for his blessings. He responded with the prayer, *Rabbana atina fi ddunya khasanah, wa fi'l akhirati khasanah, wa qina adzaban nar* (Our Lord, give us all the good things of this world and the good things of the hereafter, and save us from the torments of the fire). The ceremonial proceedings closed with Ki Amongrogo shaking hands with Ki Pengulu, witnesses, uncles, brothers and other members of the family. Then everybody left the mosque and proceeded to Ki Bayi's house for the *temu* ceremony, where the couple would meet each other formally for the first time.

### 4ii) the temu ceremony

Even before the *ijab-kabul* ceremony was held, the bride was ready for the *temu* ceremony, which was to take place in the *pendopo*. When they heard that the *ijab-kabul* was over, Nyi Malarsih said to Nyi Doyo: "Auntie, if Ni Ken is ready, I will take her to the centre door to wait for the groom." Nyi Doyo handed over the bride to her mother, who took her to the centre door. To Ni Ken's right was her mother; to her left was Centhini. Behind her were her sisters-in-law, followed by other women in the family. They waited for the groom behind the door.

*opposite: The* ijab-kabul *is the most important requirement for legalising marriage. Here, the groom is pronouncing the* kabul, *or acceptance of marriage. He is holding the bride's father's hand. The wedding celebrant (not shown) is seated to the father's right. On the chair next to the groom is the dowry, in this case, it is money arranged in a fan-like shape.*

*below (both): The bride is on her way to meet the groom. Clutched tightly in her left hand are rolled betel leaves, which she will throw at him as a symbol of her love and affection.*

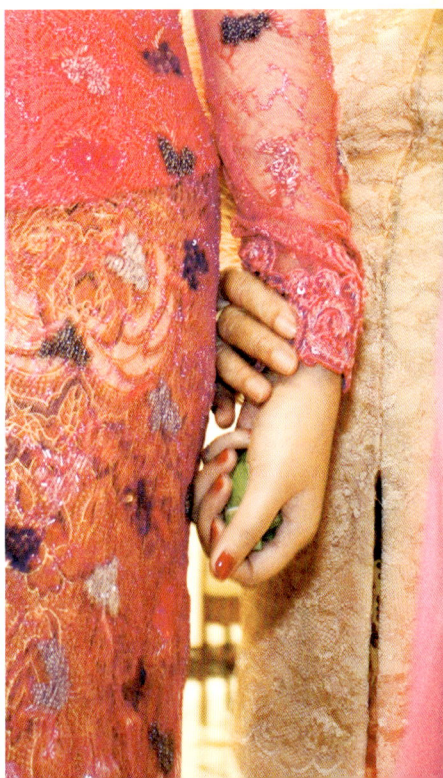

things in mind—*gemi*, *wedi*, *gemati*. Take care of the sustenance that your husband gives you (*gemi*). You must comply with whatever your husband wishes; don't disagree or argue (*wedi*) with him. And you have to attend to your husband as well as possible (*gemati*). Whatever food or clothes your husband likes, you should like them, too. Also keep in mind the three things that can make your marriage fail—*wani* (disagreeing with your husband), *angugemi* (following your own desires, without any consideration to your husband) and *sanggarunggi* (not having faith in your husband). If you commit these three misbehaviours, your marriage will be doomed to fail and end up in divorce. For a girl, divorce is the most shameful thing that can happen. Remember always this message of your mother, my child." Nyi Tambrangraras prostrated on her mother's lap and asked her blessings that she may be able to carry out the message.

## 8 The metaphor of the proa and the sea

Meanwhile, in the *pendopo*, Ki Bayi asked his son-in-law to make a discourse of something from the *Book of Ilhar*, written by Ibn Kajar. Ki Amongrogo chose to talk about the metaphor of a proa entering the sea and the sea entering the proa. It was mentioned in the book that no matter how many boats there were or how much rubbish was thrown into the sea, the sea would never be full. The metaphor should be related to the *shariah* (Islamic law, the common knowledge for Moslems) and the *haqiqah* (the ultimate truth in mysticism).

Since no one had the slightest idea what the metaphor meant, Ki Amongrogo explained it this way: "The proa and rubbish can be likened to human beings and the sea to the knowledge of Allah. The proa, no matter how many there are, cannot fill up the sea. In verse Q, 31, 27 of the holy Qur'an, it is mentioned that if the sea was ink and the timber of all forests in the world was made into pens, they wouldn't be enough to write down all of Allah's knowledge. Concerning the sea entering the proa, it can be understood as follows: If there is a man who is so knowledgeable that he has mastered the *shariah*, the *haqiqah* as well as the *tawhid* (faith), then it can be assumed that the sea has entered the proa. In this case, the true believer already has the consciousness of a soul and can be regarded as a light in a spiritual building. The light can never be turned off because the light and the flame have the same source, which is the *sahadah* (*La ilaha illa'llah, Muhammadar rasulullah*). The light can also be regarded as the light of The *Dzat* (Essence) and its flame, Its characteristics. This is usually termed as two in One or the Union of Creator with creature. Such a man isn't afraid of death; he is happy to welcome death. In fact, it is not correct to call it death but only moving to another place."

opposite: *A young mother waits for her husband to come home from fishing. On the beach are proas, typical Javanese fishing boats with sail and outrigger.*
below: *This is a naturally occurring fire and the biggest in Asia. Located in Bojonegoro, East Java, it is fuelled by gases coming from under the ground. The fire has never extinguished, not even when it rains. This place is called Kayangan Api (The Fire of Paradise). It is believed to be the site where a famous kris smith from the Majapahit kingdom made a powerful kris for the king to use against rebels.*

| the adulthood journey |

above: *At weddings,* rebana *bands sing the Salawat, a compilation of songs in praise of Allah and Prophet Muhammad, especially the Asmau'l Husna (The Beautiful Names of Allah). Singing songs of praise is akin to sending prayers to God asking for blessings.*

Arundoyo. He and eight friends played the *rebana*; their band was well known and they were always invited to perform at weddings. With a *rebana* on his lap, he began to tell his story: "Every member of the band was very good except for one called Si Bawuk. Bawuk never learnt to play the *rebana* well or sing the songs of praise." The audience called out: "Who was Bawuk, Kyai?" Ki Bayi bowed like a good performer, smiled widely and said: "Bawuk is now the *pengulu* of Wonomarto, Kyai Basarodin by name!" Laughter broke out when the name was revealed. Ki Basarodin then stood up and offered some stories about Ki Bayi: "Yes! Kyai is right. I was a good-for-nothing in the *rebana* band. I took the same medication as him and practised long hours, yet I think it is my destiny not to master the instrument. On the other hand, Kyai became better and better. Not only that, his voice was so good that it made the girls crazy. In his time, Kyai was the hero of the band and the hero amongst the girls."

This time, there was more laughter and loud applause. Ki Bayi then struck the *rebana* loudly and began to sing. Even in his old age, he could still enthral the people. At length, the celebration came to an end. Ki Bayi and Nyi Malarsih went home. Ki Amongrogo and his wife withdrew to the little mosque, followed by Centhini, their loyal maidservant.

## 12 Centhini, the co-learner

Said Ki Amongrogo to Nyi Tambangraras: "My dear wife, in life a Moslem has to take care in the way he performs the *salat*. It is not enough to just pray but one should strive to improve on the prayer until perfection is reached. The time for prayer should be always right, not too early and not too late. Make the effort to keep the body, speech and the heart/mind clean and pure when praying. This means saying the words as perfectly as possible and restricting the movements of the body to only those that are needed in the prayer. The purity of these three will lead to purity of the soul." Nyi Tambangraras replied: "Thank you, dear husband! Give me your blessings so that I will be able to carry out all your teachings as best as possible."

Ki Amongrogo continued: "My dearest, now I will tell you about social intercourse. A Moslem should love another Moslem. If he does not, even if it is only one person, it is equal to hating the prophet. If a Moslem hates the prophet, it is equal to resisting God The Almighty. This was stated in the traditions of the prophet. On the other hand, a person who loves God will be very strong in his faith and will be rewarded with heaven. Loving another Moslem, even though it may only be one person, is equal to loving oneself. And hating another Moslem is equal to hating oneself. That is why every Moslem is always told to love one another and maintain *silaturahmi* (the bond of love). Now I want to tell you about the *salat da'im*, which is the performance of *zikrullah* (constant worship and remembrance of God). This should be done all the time and ceaselessly. Pronounce the word *hu* while breathing out and the word *Allah* when inhaling." After a short pause, Ki Amongrogo said: "My dearest! You are a very intelligent and knowledgeable woman. You should also be careful not to fall into self-conceit." Nyi Tambangraras respected her husband even more for leading her from darkness to the light.

Ki Amongrogo spoke again: "My dearest! This maid of yours, Centhini, has spent the entire evening listening to my teachings. I don't think she has missed anything." Nyi Tambangraras answered: "My dear husband! Indeed, she has been reading the Qur'an and other religious books for a long time. The only thing she doesn't have enough knowledge in is exegesis." Ki Amongrogo said: "If that is the case, let her listen to my discourses from now on. It is the same as you teaching her yourself and you will still be rewarded by God." She replied: "All right, my dear! Centhini, do you hear that? You are permitted to join me and listen in to his teachings." Centhini said: "Thank you very much, master. I can't thank you enough!" In the background, the sound of drums and the cheers of the crowd welcoming the magic show could be heard.

## 13 Another wedding celebration at Ki Jayengrogo's house

Although the newlyweds were expected to arrive when the late afternoon prayer was over, Ki Jayengrogo had been busy with preparations to receive them since early in the morning. Among other things, he was seeing to the *rebana* and gamelan orchestra and making sure the gamelan players and puppeteers had been invited.

*below left:* A vendor selling leather puppets for wayang shows. The process of making the puppets takes several weeks. The outline of each puppet is first transfered from a master model on to leather or parchment. The figures are then smoothened, usually with a glass bottle. Small details for the mouth and eyes are cut out and then painstakingly coloured in. Finally, the movable upper and lower arms are mounted to the body with a stick.

*below right:* A wayang show telling the story of Murwokolo. The puppets depict the characters of Bima and Batara Kala.

Widiguno and Cremosono were ordered to move the gamelan set called Kyai Alun Jaladri (the Sea Waves) to a special corner in the front hall. Kyai Alun Jaladri was an old and revered heritage. According to legend, its first owner was the very first regent of Wirosobo. The story goes that the gamelan could arouse sexual desires in men and women when played, but if it were played at wedding feasts, there would be fewer guests and the couple would divorce or die. For this feast celebrating the union of Ki Amongrogo and Nyi Tambangraras, Ki Jayengrogro assured his father and brother that the gamlean would only be played during the day and will stop when the couple arrives. And contrary to the caution in the legend, many people attended the feast, bringing with them donations and contributions for Ki Jayengrogo and his wife.

When it was time for the late afternoon prayer, the reception group of ladies, followed by throngs of men, was ready to collect the couple from Ki Jayengwesthi's house. The couple's new quarters was near a mosque and the ceremony proceeded in exactly the same way as in Ki Jayengwesthi's house. After the evening prayer, Ki Bayi and his wife visited the newlyweds and asked whether they wanted to watch the magic and *bagor* (mask dance) performances. Ki Amongrogo declined, saying: "Excuse us a thousand times, father. We prefer to listen from here." When they left, Ki Amongrogo, his wife and Centhini then went to the mosque to meditate. They were meditating so seriously that they reached the state of *luyut* (unison between Creator and creature) and fell stretched out on the floor, unconscious of their surroundings.

**1) The mystery of God**

When Ki Amongrogo came to, he saw them sobbing uncontrollably. It was a sign of success and he felt a deep sense of satisfaction. He waited for a while, then said to his wife: "My dear, you and Centhini have been successful in your meditation. Express your gratitude to God The Almighty and ask for His forgiveness. From now on, meditate regularly so that you'll not experience difficulties in attaining the state of *luyut*." She replied: "Forgive me, my dear husband. Only your assistance can help me overcome any difficulties." And so with a little guidance, they managed to control their breathing.

He continued: "My dear wife! Remember further the mystery of God, which consists of four things—perfection of *af'al* (action), perfection of *asma* (name), perfection of *sifat* (nature, characteristics) and perfection of *Dzatullah* (God's Essence). The four perfections are so subtle that they are most unimaginable. Only a *mukmin* (a believer who surrenders totally to the Godhead) who is a Moslem can tell of the secrets of the four perfections. Such a person is said to have attained the state of 'two in One'; the creature has united with The Creator because they have the consciousness of being one. The *Dzat* (Essence), *Sifat* (Nature), *Asma* (Name) and *Af'al* (Action) of The Creator are no different from the *ujud* (form), *ilmu* (knowledge), *nur* (light) and *suhud* (abnegation) of the creature. In fact, they are the same."

Ni Ken asked: "My dear husband! I beg your pardon. If you don't mind, please explain the similarities and differences between *Dzat*, *Sifat*, *Asma* and *Af'al* with *ujud*, *ilmu*, *nur* and *zuhud*. My heart is like soil, which is thoroughly cracked from the heat of the dry spell. Now it is as though rain has cooled it down, but the cracks are still there." Replied Ki Amongrogo: "My dearest, listen carefully! The truth about *Dzat* is only one it cannot be two. The truth about *Sifat* is miracle or wonder; there is no equivalent. The truth about *Asma* is eternity; it cannot be disputed. The truth about *Af'al* is certainty; it cannot be invalidated. As for our form, it is in fact the essence of God. Our knowledge is the nature of God. Our light or the truth of our life is in fact the name of God. Our Destiny or death is in fact the action of God. My dear, that is the mystery of God. This condition is in fact impossible because it is not possible to have unison between creature and Creator. The idea that there is no creature if there is no God or there is no God if there is no creature is also impossible. The existence of a creature with God's characteristics or the existence of God with the creature's characteristics is also impossible. This is the mystery of the two in One, not united, yet not separated either, not two but also not one. Nothing is difficult, but nothing is also easy. The two are united, the difficult one is also the easy one or difficult is easy. Our existence is God's Existence. Our perfect state is God's existence. That is absurd. The unison of Creator and creature in the sphere of Void is an absurdity.

"My beloved, be aware of the truth about Void. If you can understand it with the true or real consciousness, then you can understand the real or the true reward, the true absurdity. It cannot die, it cannot be damaged, it is never wrong in speech. It is Life without dimension. That is Truth. My beloved wife, if that is already stabilised in your heart, conceal it as best as possible so that no one can see it. Conceal it in your love and fear towards God The Almighty who rewards and tortures. Those receiving His reward are those who worship Him faithfully; those tortured are those who refuse to have faith in His Existence. My beloved, you have to be careful in what you reveal and all that you conceal. Do not be arrogant. You are knowledgeable but all rewards will become torture if you are haughty or boastful. Be constant in your devotion, love and trust in God. Pray and praise always."

Nyi Tambangraras was pleased for the deep understanding had penetrated into her consciousness. She said: "My dear husband! I beg your blessings and I'll follow your words to the letter." The roosters were crowing, marking an end to the *emprak* and *bagor* show, and then the call for the morning prayer was heard.

## 2) Sang Hyang Sedyo Suksmo, The eternal Soul

Breakfast was over by 10 o'clock. Kyai and Nyai Bayi and all the guests had gone home. Only the newlyweds and Centhini remained. After a while, they moved to the mosque because Ki Amongrogo wanted to talk about something important. They were soon joined by Ki Jayengrogo and his wife, Nyi Rarasati.

| the adulthood journey |

above: *This photo of masks was taken after a mask dance performance in Kediri, East Java. The black mask represents a wild boar. Mask dances are usually held during special events such as national holidays.*

Ki Amongrogo said: "Indeed I'm going to tell your sister about the most powerful Sang Hyang Sedyo Suksmo, The eternal Soul. All of its conduct doesn't differ from the conduct of human beings. Its relationship is just like the relationship of the body and the soul, and all its conducts are the same. The relationship between Sang Hyang Sedyo Suksmo and human beings can be compared with a maskdancer. The movements the dancer makes are the same as the movements of the figure he is representing. Think of a flower floating on water. The flower moves in the same direction as the current. You can say the same happens with the elephant and its rider. The rider goes wherever the elephant is heading to. Going back to the example of the mask-dancer—the dancer's movements in his stage role are different from those in his daily life. Likewise, the desires of the elephant are not the desires of the rider, although the elephant acts in accordance with the wishes of its rider. It is this difference that you have to know—which is the same and which is not? Which is 'yes' and which is 'no'? Thus also is The Almighty. He gives guidance to people, but they don't know that it is He who has given the guidance and so they don't respond. For those who respond and can receive the guidance that has been revealed, the reward is invaluable.

"My dear brother and sister and wife, if you can understand the teachings of Sang Hyang Sedyo Suksmo, you can see the Truth. Then cover the Truth with the *shariah, tariqah, haqiqah* and *makrifah*." At this point Ki Jayengwesthi and his wife, Nyi Turido, appeared at the mosque. Ki Amongrogo continued the discourse, this time on the subject of the true *shariah, tariqah, haqiqah* and *makrifah*."

## 14 The other wedding celebrations

After the celebration at Ki Jayengrogo's house, more celebrations took place in other people's homes, namely those of Ki Bayi's younger brothers and that of Ki Basarodin, the *pengulu* of Wonomarto. The programme was almost the same in all the homes. There was the *emprak* show for guests and while that was going on, Ki Amongrogo would be discussing religious matters, usually about Sufism, with his wife and Centhini. If Ki Amongrogo were asked to speak to the people, he would usually talk about the *shariah*, with occasional references to Sufism. The final celebration was held at Ki Basarodin's house. After that, the couple returned to stay with Ki Jayengwenthi. Then the plan to build a house for the newlyweds began in earnest. Ki Bayi felt deep gratitude towards Ki Nuripin for bringing Ki Amongrogo to the hermitage of Wonomarto. He therefore promoted Nuripin to be the chief of fifteen hamlets.

## 15 The house for the couple

When Ki Bayi suggested that the house for his daughter and son-in-law be built and made ready for occupation within forty days, all his brothers and sons gave their assurance that it could be done. And true enough! It was completed as planned. Everybody was amazed that the construction had gone so smoothly. While many people were of the opinion that it was due to Ki Bayi's spiritual power, others believed it was because Allah was pleased with Ki Amongrogo's conduct. What impressed them most were the trees and plants, which did not show any traces of being newly transplanted. All grew luxuriantly and were either blooming or fruiting. So on the advice of Ki Sembagi, Ki Bayi decided that the couple would move into their new home the following Friday. Nyi Malarsih was delighted with the news. She asked Nyi Doyo to pack all the furniture that was in the bridal room and include everything that was familiar to her daughter so as to encourage consummation. She was a little concerned as they had been married for over a month. But Nyi Doyo advised her to be patient, feeling that Ki Amongrogo was waiting for the most appropriate time.

A few days later, as Ki Bayi sat in the *pendopo* of the new house he announced: "My son Amongrogo, the house is ready for occupation. You will move in this coming Friday, after the *Jum'ah* prayer. Now that we are resting, let's talk about something useful. My son, can you tell us what makes life a success or a failure?" Ki Amongrogo bowed respectfully and said: "There are ten points to be considered:

- The basis of all is the *kalimah sahadah* (the Islamic creed)—the cause of failure in life is the failure to understand and practise the teachings contained in the Islamic creed. It means not following the religion of the holy prophet;
- To perform good deeds—the cause of failure is dislike in doing good things;
- To know the purpose of life—the cause of failure is not following the guidance of the guru;
- Having strong faith in God—the cause of failure is dishonesty, that is, doubting the existence of God while calling oneself a Moslem (follower of Islam);
- Sincerity in doing things—the cause of failure is rash behaviour without proper considerations and proper knowledge;

below: *The process of building a house is not complete without a special offering often placed when the roof is newly completed. The intention is to make 'peace' with the guardian spirit(s) of the area to help ensure protection from evil forces. This tradition is rooted from the pre-Islamic period when the people embraced animism and Hinduism. The red cloth symbolises courage, while the white symbolises purity. Wrapped inside is rice, which symbolises a wish for a prosperous life.*

- Persistent intent—the cause of failure is the absence of intent;
- Prayer or supplications to God and for God's sake only—the cause of failure is disturbances in the mind and heart;
- To desire to go to heaven—this means having a strong conviction in the *syari'at*, the Qur'an and traditions of the holy prophet. The cause of failure is disbelief in these matters;
- Not believing in the existence of hell; and
- Denying the teachings of the holy prophet."

Kyai Bayi nodded approvingly and said to all present: "Be attentive to what Ki Amongrogo has said, for he has given us a prosperous and happy life. Tonight keep watch at the new house. On Friday night when he and his wife have moved in, we will have a night of remembrance for the holy prophet."

Everything went smoothly as planned on that special night. The proceedings were led by Ki Amongrogo himself and the celebration closed with the recitation of the chapter Al-Ikhlas [The Purity] (Q, 112) three times by all present. It was late when everything came to an end. Ki Bayi and Nyi Malarsih retired, the guests dispersed and Ki Amongrogo went straight to the mosque to find his wife waiting outside for him, again accompanied by the faithful Centhini.

## 16 The origin of man

After taking ablution, Ki Amongrogo led his wife by the hand to enter the mosque. Ni Centhini was right on her heels. The three of them sat on the floor calmly, Ki Amongrogo facing his wife and Centhini behind her. He said: "My dear wife, man should know his origin if he wants security and felicity in life." He then proceeded to talk about the origin of man: "The holy prophet said, 'Whoever knows himself, knows his Godhead'. Man's existence is the will of God. He created man from water originating from the last rib and the breastbone. The moment of creation occurs at the time of the meeting of the passions of man and woman. Initially, *Dzat* (Essence) is independent and motionless, but with passions aroused during consummation, it creates a will to produce. At that moment, *akadiyat* (the first stage of Martabat Tujuh, the Seven Stages of Creation) meets *takyun* (nothingness). There is no space, colour or smell yet, but the meeting of the passions surely exists.

"During the first 40 days the *nukat ga'ib*—the union of *akadiyat* and *takyun*—is called the *gaibu'l guyub* (the most mysterious amongst the mysteries). My beloved, the realm they [*akadiyat* and *takyun*] are in is called the realm of *lahut*; it is very dark, as dark as the darkness of the heart in grief. During the next 40 days, the *gaibu'l guyub* is called the *gaibu'l uwiyah*; the realm they are in is called the realm of *malakut* and it is not so dark any more, but neither is it so clear. During the third 40 days, the *akadiyat* and the *takyun* become a clot of blood, still staying in the centre of *gaibu'l uwiyah*—the realm is called the realm of *nasut* and it is already clear and bright. During the fourth 40 days, the clot of blood changes into a lump of flesh, staying in the realm of *jabarut* in the centre of *gaibus sububun*.

"Then that lump of flesh descends to the four realms, amongst them the realm of *arwah* which forms the borderline between the three immaterial or incorporeal realms and the corporeal worlds. During the fifth 40 days, it descends to the realm of *ajesam*. It has a form or shape but one that is not definite yet. During the sixth 40 days, it stays in the realm of *mithal*. By now, it has a definite form and its gender is also visible. During the seventh 40 days, it stays in the realm of *insan kamil*; the form of man is already clear or definite. The stage of the creation of man is over. The entire duration of the creation is 288 days or 9 months and 10 days.

"Then its lifespan is determined, followed by its destiny. All this happens while the baby is in the womb. After 9 months and 10 days, the baby comes into being. Some people say that 1,993 angels guard each human being; others say man has only one guardian angel each. At the same time, there are many other things bestowed on man that helps him face life on Earth, such as intelligence. That was why the holy prophet urged man to express gratitude and humbleness to God The Merciful and The Compassionate. Other creatures like cattle, horses and monkeys do not receive as many gifts as man. Despite this, many people do not feel privileged. And if one is pre-ordained to be bad, then he will not have any intention to change to improve the condition of his life.

"Therefore, my dear, we have to try all the time to follow the guidance of the holy prophet. If we don't try to do our best to follow the good path, it is possible that we will lose our prominent status, the same way that heat turns into cold and wetness is defeated by dryness. And so, my beloved, when we have the fortune to meet in love and passion later on, look for the way of goodness. Never forget God."

Nyi Tambangraras' heart felt as though it had been hit by a club. Prostrating on her husband's lap, she said: "May my dear husband give his blessings so that I can follow all his guidance fruitfully." Meanwhile, roosters were starting to crow and darkness was slowly giving way to the light of dawn. He reached for his wife's hand and said: "Come on, my love! Let's take ablution and prepare for the worship of God The Merciful." The call to prayer soon vibrated in the air.

## 17 Cethi Centhini

It was Friday, the day Ki Amongrogo and his wife would move into their new house. That morning, the couple was sitting with Nyi Malarsih and Ki Bayi when all the other relatives joined them and discussed the move. The men would deal with the furniture and heavy things, while the women would pack all the bride's belongings. Commented Nyi Malarsih to her husband: "Centhini will receive the furniture and personal belongings and take care of everything, as Ni Ken trusts her totally."

above: *Worshippers of all ages listen intently to a sermon before the start of the* Jum'ah *(Friday) congregational prayer. The sermon is given by the imam, who will later lead the prayer. Attending the Friday prayer is obligatory for all men but not for women, although women can attend if they wish.*

This statement raised questions and Nyi Turido and Nyi Rarasati asked: "Who is Centhini really? We know her only as the handmaid of sister Tambangraras. How can she trust her so?" Nyi Malarsih replied: "I don't really know! But she is Ki Bayi's relative. When she was little, my God, she was very troublesome and would beat her sister many times. But she was never at odds with Ni Ken and have been friends the moment they met." Ki Bayi explained: "Indeed she is related to me! Her grandfather, Ki Sampur, was my grandfather's brother. So in fact I have to call her sister. She is Ni Ken's aunt, even though she is of the same age as Ni Ken, perhaps a little younger." It was only then that all present realised the relationship between Nyi Tambangraras and Centhini. Although she was younger than Nyi Tambangraras, in terms of family relationships, she was her aunt. That explained the protective attitude of Centhini towards her mistress.

When the time for the Friday congregational prayer drew near, they left for the mosque. Ki Amongrogo and his wife were dressed in white. The women carried umbrellas of all colours to protect themselves from the sun. The congregation knew that the couple would be moving into their new house that day. *Boyongan* or 'moving', the Javanese would say. At the mosque, Ki Bayi's brothers stood up together and called the prayer. Ki Amongrogo led the prayer and gave the sermon. After that, they returned to the new house where the offering meal was held. After the people had left and only the elders remained, Ki Bayi said: "I thank you all very much. Now my duty as a father has ended. My only daughter, who was always reluctant to marry, now has an excellent husband. I ask your support to pray for their welfare in marriage." In the rear hall, Nyi Malarsih asked her daughter, yet again, whether her marriage had been consummated. She shook her head. Nyi Doyo told Nyi Malarsih to have more patience.

| seh amongrogo |

## 18 The perfect knowledge

While enjoying the offering meal, Ki Bayi asked Ki Amongrogo: "My son, could you explain what is meant by the perfect knowledge?" Ki Amongrogo explained calmly: "As far as I can remember, the holy prophet was once quoted in the book *Tanbihul afilin* as follows: 'The perfect knowledge is the knowledge about the perfect *iman* (faith), *tawhid* (the oneness of God), *makrifah* (mysticism) and *Islam* (the religion, law).

"Imam Smarakandi explained it this way in his books *Durat* and *Bayan Tasdik*. A Moslem should totally believe in *salat* (as in the *shariah*, law) and *tawhid* (faith in the Oneness of God). There should be no doubt whatsoever about the Oneness of God. There is only One God. *Shariah* and *makrifah* should be combined. A Moslem who has the true knowledge about God (*makrifah*) should still adhere to the *shariah*, which regards God as the Perfect Purity, for it is this Perfect Purity that purifies those performing the worship. In the meeting of the two comes unification. It is a unity or union that cannot create dissimilarity or contrast. It is the unity of creature and Creator, between slave and The Lord, so that both become small or great. The Creator and the creature are different, distinct to each other but at the same time, are not different. If one cannot understand that that difference is the same as 'not different', he fails. Because if the understanding is only that The Creator is not different from the creature, then both are understood to be The Creator—the creature doesn't exist, both are Great and Eternal. On the other hand, if the understanding is only that the creature is not different from the Creator, then only the creature exists—both are small and experience trouble and mishap. The difference between The Creator and creature is that The Creator is limitless. His Greatness cannot be fathomed and his smallness cannot be discerned. The creature, on the other hand, is definite and destructible.

"Concerning Islam, it is already described in twelve books which originate from the same source, the Al Qur'an. They are *Sitin*, *Semarakandi*, *Bayan Tasdik*, *Sa'il*, *Sujak*, *Ilah*, *Mukarar*, *Juwahir*, *Kidayatun*, *Sukbah*, *Mustahal* and *Adkiya*. Moslems must follow the orders mentioned in these books. *Dalil* is the command of Allah. *Madlul* is the transfer of the commands of Allah in the *hadith*. *Hadith* is amongst others, the words or commands of the holy prophet. *Hadith Qudsi* is a *hadith* that was directly received by the prophet but not transmitted to his companions. *Ijmak* is knowledge upon which all four imams agreed. Whoever does not want to follow any of the four imams is regarded as *kafir*, an unbeliever."

Ki Bayi nodded in agreement, then turned to his guests: "Please think about what Ki Amongrogo has said because we are followers of the law, brought down by the holy prophet. All of you must be tired. Let us close the discourse and return home." Ki Amongrogo and his wife accompanied their parents to the gate.

below: *Another offering meal. Tumpeng Nasi Kuning consists of yellow rice,* perkedel *(potato croquette),* serundeng *(relish of grated coconut and spices),* kering tempe empal *(spicy cubes of fried beef,* emping *(fried chips from Melinjo fruit),* kerupuk *(crackers),* rempeyek *(crackers made of fried peanut with rice flour).*

# the adulthood journey

Ki Amongrogo broached the idea of giving his brother-in-law, Ki Jayengwesthi, a new name: "Father, if father doesn't mind and my brother Jayengwesthi is agreeable, I would like to give to him the name that I received from my parents." Ki Bayi was delighted to hear the proposal. Ki Jayengwesthi had no objection and said: "My brother, I thank you from the deepest of my heart beforehand. I hope it will give me the impetus to study more diligently." Ki Bayi asked: "I think all present here will welcome your idea, my son. What is the name?" Ki Amongrogo said: "The name my parents gave me is Jayengresmi." Ki Bayi replied: "What a wonderful name! I think Jayengwesthi will be most happy to accept your present. Let's celebrate this glorious event. Santri Luci, give the order to prepare porridge for the celebration of my son's change in name." He conveyed the order to the attendants in the kitchen and soon, the porridge offering was served to all present. And so it was official that from that day on, Ki Jayengwesthi was to be called Ki Jayengresmi.

## 22 The perfect end

In bed one night, Ni Ken addressed her husband: "My dear husband, if you don't mind, please explain to me what the perfect death (*khusnu'l khatimah*) is and the way to achieve it. Ki Amongrogo replied patiently: "My love, if you want to know the path to the perfect death, learn to die while you are still alive. That is the path to life while we are dead. What is called death is in fact the worship of The Omniscient, disregarding all living beings, good as well as bad. One's soul or spirit should have eyes only for The One, The Supreme Soul. In other words, death is the realisation of one's identity. One who knows his true Self will know who and what he is. Then he will see the path, which is nothing else but good deeds. This stage can be likened to arriving in the capital city but not yet meeting the king. Only good deeds can lead one to the king. There

**below:** *Another view of Wonomarto village in Jombang Regency, East Java. Cloves, coffee, cacao and fruits are cultivated on this hilly plain.*

is no other way. One who knows the noble path will arrive at the perfect death. Every living being consists of the body and the soul. The body and the soul are already united with The Omniscient and are in the realm of Tranquillity. Try to keep that unison of body and soul, together with everlasting purity, free from impurities in the form of desire to return to the world of sound. The ambitions of man should correspond with the commandments of Allah. The metaphor is that of a man looking in the mirror; he sees only his own reflection. The worship he performs is the worship towards his own self, which is already united with The Supreme Self, united in *ajal* and *abad*. *Ajal* is the beginning of existence without cause and *abad* is the end of that existence, with nothing after that. So his existence is actually The Existence of God. His sight and ability is God's Sight and Potentiality. My beloved, understand that God's Essence, Nature and Actions are your existence, knowledge and life."

above: *A traditional Javanese porridge offering is* bubur merah putih *(literally, red and white porridge). The white porridge, which symbolises purity, is made from white rice and coconut milk and has a sour taste. The 'red' porridge, actually a mixture of brown rice and palm sugar, is sweet and symbolises courage. Here, the porridge is put into bowl-shaped banana leaves.*

Ni Ken asked: "My husband, what is the truth of all these?" Ki Amongrogo replied: "The truth about social behaviour in the world, my dear Ni Ken, consists of four things—having kind words, nothing coarse or vulgar; practising the religion by both men and women; having a profound fear of God, The Most Pure; and performing good deeds to fellow living beings and praising God. Fasting or abnegation of the self also consists of four things—fasting for the benefit of the physical body by not indulging in idle talk, not being boastful, not humiliating others, and having moderation in eating, drinking and sleeping; fasting for the benefit of the soul by banishing evil thoughts; fasting for the benefit of the spirit by refraining from lust and evil conduct; and fasting for the benefit of god consciousness by not looking at undesirable objects and avoiding polytheistic practices."

Since Ni Ken was able to absorb all the teachings, Ki Amongrogo continued: "Now I will talk about the four causes of failure in all good conducts. The first is arrogance, snobbery and self-esteem, thinking of oneself as worthwhile. The second is not believing in the Qur'an and the *Hadith*. The third is breaking the prohibitions mentioned in the Qur'an, *Hadith*, *Ijmak* and *Qiyas*.[3] And finally, dishonesty such as telling lies, breaking promises and deviating from truth. Keep all these in mind, my beloved!"

When the teachings were over, Ki Amongrogo and Ni Ken made love again. All the while, Ki Amongrogo whispered to his wife the knowledge of lovemaking. Thus was the transfer of knowledge concerning sexual activity between lovers, delivered simultaneously with the practice of it.

---

3 These are the four fundamentals of Islamic law, which is common knowledge for Moslems. The Qur'an is the primary source containing all the fundamental directives and instructions of Allah. The *Hadith* is the collection of the teachings of Prophet Muhammad, which explain the instructions in the Qur'an. *Ijmak* (consensus) is the agreement of opinion among Moslem scholars. *Qiyas* (analogy) are laws derived through analogical deduction when there is no specific provision in the Qur'an or the *Hadith*.

## Seh Amongrogo, the husband of Nyi Tambangraras
FROM WONOMARTO TO TUNJUNGBANG

### 1 The three letters

Beneath the happiness Ki Amongrogo had found with Nyi Tambangraras and her family in Wonomarto, there was something that disturbed him deeply. It concerned his brother and sister. All that he had heard from prominent clerics was that his siblings were still alive and well. But whether they were as secure and prosperous as he was, he did not know. Every guru he met advised him to continue to be patient and strengthen his faith towards The Almighty, but such advice did not lessen his anxiety and worry. Instead, it gave him the impression that his brother and sister were in dangerous circumstances, though perhaps not as dangerous as he imagined. Thoughts about their welfare had been troubling him for some time.

He had been at Wonomarto for three months. For forty days, he lived very comfortably with his beautiful wife and her supportive family. But for the last eight days, he had been considering this situation and finally made the decision to look for his brother and sister, even if meant going to the capital city, Mataram. So on the eighth day after the evening prayer, Ki Amongrogo shared his thoughts with his wife: "My dear, I ask your pardon if I have neglected you. Remember that behind all this happiness, I am troubled by thoughts of my brother and sister. Therefore, my love, give me your leave to look for them. I will come back to you the moment I find them, but if I am unfortunate enough to fail in this endeavour, I give you permission to remarry. Look for a good and knowledgeable husband."

On hearing those words, Nyi Tambangraras felt as if her she had been hit with a hammer. She fell on her knees, clung to her husband's feet and said in a broken voice:

opposite: *A procession for the* larungan *ceremony on Kelud Mountain. The local people hold this ceremony every year on the 1st of Suro (the Javanese New Year) to thank the spirits of the mountain for good harvests and also to ask for blessings for a good harvest in the coming year. The people are carrying rice, fruit and vegetables, mainly harvested from the area. The umbrella is an accessory used as a sign of respect.*

# the adulthood journey

above: *A kampung house in Wonomarto village. Such houses are built mainly from wood and are cleverly put together without nails. Clay tiles make up the roof. In villages where there is no piped water, all cleaning and washing is done in nearby rivers, ponds or springs. Water for cooking is also drawn from these sources.*

"My dear husband! The thought of remarrying has never entered my mind. If you have to go, bring me with you. I don't mind suffering a lot or even finding death. I'm happy as long as we are not separated from each other." Ki Amongrogo was touched by her devotion. He took her to bed and comforted her with reassuring words. Eventually, he made love to her. And when he saw that she was fast asleep, he wrote three letters—one for his wife, another for his parents-in-law and the last for his brothers-in-law, Ki Jayengresmi and Ki Jayengrogo. He put the letters under some pillows and slipped out of the house through the rear door where Jamal and Jamil were already waiting for him. One after the other, they left the village of Wonomarto quietly.

But their departure did not go unnoticed by the animals of the night, which made quite unusual sounds as if to show their disapproval of Ki Amongrogo abandoning his beloved wife. The birds, awakened from their slumber, responded to their call. They had intended to welcome the sun on a new day with new stories of life, but the departure of the three wayfarers changed the sound of their mood into one of anguish, for they feared that mishap and disaster would fall on Wonomarto. Once in a while, Ki Amongrogo looked back at the outline of the village with a broken heart. Jamal and Jamil, too, could feel the emptiness in their master's heart.

Nyi Tambangraras woke up with a start. She turned to her left, but her husband was not there. Centhini was also not in sight. Believing he was at the mosque, she called for her: "Aunt Centhini, why didn't you wake me up? And where is my husband?" Centhini replied: "Forgive me, mistress! When I woke up, Master Amongrogo wasn't here any more. I looked for him in the bathroom and the mosque, but he's nowhere to be seen." Remembering his intention to look for his brother and sister, she fainted and fell to the floor. In no time, all her family members were gathered around her. She was on her mother's lap when she came to and quietly told them about the conversation they had. Ki Bayi recalled very clearly how he had urged him to marry her first before starting on his search. Indeed, Ki Amongrogo was carrying out his plan. Meanwhile, Centhini had found the letters, which explained everything very clearly. Ki Bayi said: "Calm down all of you! Think what can be done. Ni Ken, stop crying! Let us pray to God that Ki Amongrogo succeeds in finding his brother and sister and that those left behind find solace. Return to your homes and as I say, ponder about what we can do. Your mother and I will stay with Ni Ken for the time being."

## 2 Sirupan cave

Ki Amongrogo and his companions walked until they reached a spring in the region of Pasuruhan. Ki Amongrogo noticed a menacing-looking cave nearby, known locally as Sirupan cave. People avoided the cave as it was believed to be inhabited by ghosts and spirits known to be hostile to human beings. But the story did not bother Ki Amongrogo and instead, it made him want to explore it.

Inside the cave was a stone flat and big enough for people who dared to enter to sit or sleep on. By chance, it was time for the evening prayer. Jamal made the call to prayer and soon the three of them were absorbed in prayer. Ki Amongrogo was pleased by the quietness of the cave. He found peace there and decided to stay for a few days. But he did not know what was to come for in the deep of night, the stillness changed into turmoil. From the depths came the sound of lions roaring, jackals barking, monkeys screeching, all mixed with the cries and clamour of unknown animals, perhaps even that of ghosts and spirits. They could also see images of grimacing heads with sharp and pointed fangs, muscular arms and hands with sharp nails, as if ready to pounce on them. Ki Amongrogo wasn't afraid; he murmured some mantras and the clamour turned into shrieks of pain and gradually disappeared. Peace and quiet returned. Ki Amongrogo stayed for seven days and nights in that cave, fasting all the while.

As they left the cave on the morning of the eighth day, Ki Amongrogo saw a bird. It was making shrill noises as if beckoning them to follow it. They followed the bird and were brought to a field rich with tuber, sweet potato and other crops. The owner of the field, Ki Nitipolo, was very surprised to see three men coming from the direction of the cave and walked over to meet them. He introduced himself as the caretaker of the cave. Ki Amongrogo introduced himself and his attendants as *santris* from Wonomarto and said that they had come to do asceticism in the Sirupan cave. While they were resting, Ki Nitipolo went home. He returned shortly after with boiled tuber, corn and drinks for them to break their fast. When they had eaten, they took leave and continued their journey in the northwest direction.

They walked day and night, climbing mountains and stopped when they reached Gending Mountain in the region of Probolinggo. They stayed there for forty days

# the adulthood journey

**above left:** *A view of Grojogan beach, looking towards Grojogan forest in the far southeastern tip of Java. There are many caves inside the forest, some of which are used for meditation. In the forest is a temple called Pura Agung. It is the site of the Hindu Pagerwesi ceremony, which celebrates an ancient battle between good and evil.*

**above right:** *This hilly limestone outcrop is Nusobarong island. Situated 5 kilometres off the southeast coast of East Java, it is inhabited only by water birds, small mammals, snakes and the green sea turtles that nest there.*

she was able to draw strength from her husband's teachings and surrender herself to God The Merciful. Her faith towards The Almighty motivated her to worship and pray more. She fasted on Mondays and Thursdays and gave alms. Reading the holy book became her daily occupation. Her father conferred with his sons, brothers and village leaders as to how they could find Ki Amongrogo. There was some news that he had been seen in the region of Panarukan, walking to the east, probably towards the region of Blambangan. They also talked about going after him, but in the end it was agreed that they would wait for him to return.

Back on Nusobarong island, Ki Amongrogo fasted and, by chance, the last day of the fast fell on a Friday, the tenth of Muharram. The night before, he performed the Tahajjud and Tasbih prayers, twelve units of prayer each, followed by *zikr* (remembrance of God) until he reached the state of *luyut* (unison with God). He fell on the temple floor and lay there for some time. When he came to, he pronounced *Alhamdulillah* and closed with the prayer *iyyaka na'budu wa iyyaka nasta'in* (only You I worship and only to You I beg for protection). Then he plunged again into solitude.

The sound of rolling waves breaking up on the rocks brought him out his quietude. For the first time on the island, he heard the song of birds welcoming the morning sun. They seemed to wake him up, to tell him that the world was still rotating on its axis. The birds seemed to call out: "Master, it's time to continue your journey. Don't be too occupied by the stillness of the place. Later, the sea at Tunjungbang Bay will tell the story of the delivery of sorrow and grief." Another bird continued: "That's right! That will be later, at the end of the dry season and the beginning of the blooming season." The barbet nodded while saying: "Yes! At that time the liberation will come."

Jamal made the call to prayer and soon they were occupied with praying and praising The Merciful on that glorious morning. After the worship, Ki Amongrogo took a stroll

above (both): *The 1st of Suro celebrations in Surakarta kingdom. The month of Muharram in the Islamic calendar coincides with the month of Suro in the Javanese calendar. On this holy day, people all over Java visit places deemed sacred, such as mountains, lakes, rivers and springs. They would also fast and meditate. In the photo on the left, a special heirloom—a kris—is being paraded around the palace square as a symbol to protect the kingdom from any misfortune. Leading the procession is a member of the royal family.*

along the beach. The sun was just rising out of the sea; its yellow golden rays were mixed with the rippling water, which moved like liquid gold and emitted a brilliant blinding glare. Then he saw coconuts and other fruit fall from the trees into the water and he saw the fruit change into fish swimming here and there. He went to the seashore to take a closer look and it was true… the fruit had become fish! He called out to his companions: "Hey, you two, come here! Something strange has happened." They looked and their eyes bulged in amazement. After some time, Ki Amongrogo understood the meaning of the strange sight. It was telling him something—that a change in his life would occur soon and it would happen at the end of the dry season and the beginning of the rainy season. He, too, will fall into the sea and find a better existence. He said: "Jamal and Jamil. Make the raft ready! We return to the mainland!"

They floated with the current and landed safely on the island of Java. Without delay, Ki Amongrogo set out north, crossing the river Kiting and heading towards the mountain of Pigang, which formed the border of the region of Jember and Lumajang. They climbed the mountain and found a cave on its slope. It was the Mirong cave. It was so large that several small hills fitted inside it. They spent four days there and then pushed forth towards Kilang Mountain, still on the border of Jember in the east and Lumajang in the west.

## 6 Kilang Mountain

At the foot of Kilang Mountain, they came across yet another cave called Gua Dalem. It was very dark inside and they lit a torch, which revealed four tunnels that branched out to different directions. Ki Amongrogo stayed in the cave for two days to prepare himself for the difficult climb to the top of the mountain.

| the adulthood journey |

Despite much hardship climbing the mountain, they managed to reach the top. It was quiet at first, but suddenly they heard noises like those in a busy crowded market. They heard the voices of people hawking their wares and bargaining. The sounds were loud yet indistinct to make out. It was a terrifying experience. Ki Amongrogo pronounced the *istighfar* (plea for forgiveness) and the noises stopped instantly. The wayfarers stayed at the top for a few days and explored every inch of the place. They found traces of offerings and evidence of incense, and concluded that it was a place where sacrifices were made. Ki Amongrogo then saw a lone hill, believed to be inhabited by savage demons that would kill anyone who dared to disturb their dwelling. As they neared the hill, Jamal and Jamil fainted. Ki Amongrogo knew that they had been attacked by the demons. So great was their fear that when they came to, they begged their master to leave the place. Ki Amongrogo said reassuringly: "Don't worry! Strengthen your faith in The Almighty. Now, let's go to the top."

The top of the hill was flat, like a plateau. In the middle was a hole filled with bird feathers as well as human and animal bones. There was even a whole skeleton. But Ki Amongrogo was not afraid and sat down to meditate. Black clouds reared overhead, plunging the world into unparalleled darkness, lightning clapped and rain fell in torrents. It seemed as though the Earth was quaking in tremendous fear. Ki Amongrogo did not move a muscle but kept on meditating and pronouncing the *istighfar*. Then, as suddenly as it started, the uproar stopped. The sky brightened and all the feathers and bones were no longer to be seen. Ki Amongrogo then saw another sign—that of a big river flowing into the ocean and from the surface of the water a lotus appeared. He understood the message, pronounced the *istighfar* and the sign vanished. They descended back to the cave, where they stayed for the night.

right: *Lamongan Mountain. Located high above sea level are the mountain's three lakes, which used to be volcanic craters and are connected to each other. Pigeon racing is a popular hobby taken up by the local men. The mountain is situated between the massive Bromo-Tengger-Semeru and Argopuro mountains in East Java.*

The next morning, they continued their journey northeast towards Cempaka Mountain in the region of Lamongan. They stayed on the mountaintop for fifteen days. During that time, they were confronted by constant sightings of beautiful ladies who would reveal themselves for a moment, then vanish into thin air, only to reappear again. It was believed that whoever was affected by the sightings would meet with misfortune. They then proceeded to Lawang Mountain, where they rested for ten days. Their journey thereafter followed the foot of the Kendeng range towards Maya Dwarawati Mountain on the border of the region of Lumajang and Ngantang. They passed through the mountains of Tunjung Sumbito and Prunggu and finally arrived at Indrokilo Mountain, where they found the Sangupati cave.

## 7 Indrokilo (Drekilo) Mountain

Their journey to Indrokilo Mountain took six weeks. They climbed the mountain in the morning and rested when they reached a pond that was naturally bordered by stones. Next to it was a *teja* tree, which gave much welcomed shade to travellers; its sweet-smelling flowers were gently falling into the water like rain. Ki Amongrogo was so taken in by the sight that he decided to stay for three days. During that time, he noticed the presence of a beautiful woman but suspecting she was a spirit who wanted to trouble him, he ignored it.

When they had rested enough, they headed straight for Sangupati cave on the mountaintop. According to legend, the cave was where Raden Dananjoyo, the third brother of the Pandavas, made asceticism and prayed for the safety of all his brothers and victory over the Kauravas in the Baratayuda. It was for this same reason that Ki

**below:** *The sacred Indrokilo Mountain in Trenggalek, East Java. In the famous Javanese adaptation of a heroic Hindu tale called Arjuna Wiwaha, the mountain is where Arjuna meditated in a cave and prayed for the safety of his brothers. As the mountain is not located on any map, people have always thought that it was fiction.*

| **the adulthood journey** |

Amongrogo wanted to go to the cave—he wanted to pray for the safety of his parents, brother and sister. Along the way up, the weather suddenly turned icy cold and affected Jamal and Jamil. They trembled as though attacked by fever. Ki Amongrogo prayed for the cold to go away and it did. He then found the cave and upon entering it, he noticed a flat stone in the centre. There was a dent on it, a print of someone's seat. He thought to himself: "How powerful Raden Dananjoyo was, to be able to endure asceticism so terrible that he obtained all that he prayed for from the gods." Ki Amongrogo wanted to do the same—to save his parents, his brother and his sister.

Exploring the cave, Ki Amongrogo came across another flat stone, which was big enough to sleep on. In another section, he found yet another big stone from which water flowed; it was where Raden Dananjoyo obtained holy water. Ki Amongrogo praised God for all that he had seen. He then noticed another flat stone in the northwest corner. He sat on it, found it very comfortable and decided to use it as a seat for meditation. He stayed in the cave for 100 days and then left the mountain. Travelling along the foot of the Kendeng range, they headed first for the Sempora and Rajegwesi Mountains where they stayed for two days. Then they pushed forth to the south for the Perunggu and Pegat Mountains. Finally, they turned southwest in the direction of Kelud Mountain in the region of Kediri.

## 8 Kelud Mountain

Kelud Mountain was the most dangerous mountain in the region of Kediri, being the dwelling place of demons and devils hostile to human beings. Ki Amongrogo and his companions found that out soon enough. The Earth shook as if there was

## seh amongrogo, the husband of nyi tambangraras

an earthquake and thunder exploded, making the place sound like a battleground. It started to rain ashes, which darkened the sky and caused shortness of breath. Ki Amongrogo, Jamal and Jamil found refuge in a cave, which was filled in no time with animals great and small. Little by little, the turbulence of nature abated, the sky cleared up and the animals dispersed. The three *santris* of Giri spent the rest of the night in the cave. The next morning, they climbed to the top to see what caused the sky to rain ashes. They found the crater of the mountain and stones piled up like steps inside it. They climbed down and stayed in there for three days. The next stop on their journey was Mendong Mountain, where they found a comfortable resting place with fruit trees and clear water. It was where Ki Amongrogo spent fifty days doing asceticism.

Meanwhile, over in Wonomarto, Ki Kulowiryo reported to Ki Bayi and his family that an old *santri* had seen Ki Amongrogo and his companions in the vicinity of Kelud Mountain, but he could not find them and there was no further news about them. Because of rumours that people who go to the mountain never return, Ki Wiryo reassured them that Ki Amongrogo was a knowledgeable cleric and would be able to handle even the most difficult of situations. On hearing her uncle's report, Nyi Tambangraras asked leave to go after her husband. Ki Bayi shed tears, whilst his wife embraced their sobbing daughter. Wonomarto was in great sorrow.

## 9 Wajak Watu-urip pool

From Mendong Mountain, they passed through the woods of Lodoyo where they heard tigers roaring during the night. After three days of walking, they arrived in the region of Gunung Sakethi (the 'ten thousand mountains' range), which stretched

below left: *Kelud Mountain in Kediri, East Java. This is one of Java's most dangerous volcanoes. Thousands of lives have been lost to its deadly eruptions recorded since AD1000.*

below right: *Kelud Mountain is the venue for the all important and holy* larungan *ceremony. Held on the 1st of Suro, the people give offerings to thank the spirits of the mountain for good harvests and also to ask for a good harvest in the new year. Offerings comprise harvests from the area. These are kept in bamboo containers and thrown into the mountain's crater lake.*

above: *A view of the Sewu/Sakethi mountain range. Stretching some 85 kilometres from Central to East Java, the range was once below sea level. Thousands of years of erosion has led to the creation of hundreds of conical hillocks and thousands of caves. Until today, geologists continue to discover new caves. Although* sewu *means 'thousand' and* sakethi *means 'ten thousand', the names do not reflect the actual number of hills but are simply used to mean 'many'.*

from Lumajang (East Java) to Imogiri (Central Java). When they reached the foot of Selondoko Mountain, they climbed it and stayed at the top for three days. There they saw people from Bantal Padhomasan and Wajak Watu-urip hunting wild animals. They kept away from the hunters to avoid being recognised. Even so, the hunters did not pay much attention to them, thinking they were just doing asceticism at Dieng Pakareman, another home to demons and ghosts. Up there on the mountain, they also found two stones. Clear water trickled out from one of them and flowed down to the village of Watu-urip where it formed a pool, called the pool of Wajak. The water in it was believed to have magical powers. On Tuesdays and Fridays, the water would appear oily. People would go there to collect the water and drink it. After staying at the pool for three days, the *santris* went to a cave above the pool, called the Merak cave.

People believed that the Wajak pool, the village of Watu-urip and the Merak cave were holy places. They also believed that one could obtain magic powers for life from the deities just by drinking water from the pool. A sign that one had been given such powers—which would also protect the person from harm—was physical disability of some form, such as being bald from the forehead up to the crown or having a stiff neck or even becoming deaf. With Allah's Grace, Jamal developed a stiff neck and Jamil became bald. Ki Amongrogo explained to them what the problems meant. They pronounced *Alhamdulillah* but most inaudibly because in their hearts, they still could not accept God's Grace. But there was no time to worry about it; they had to proceed further to the west and stop by several mountains in the region of Ponorogo.

## 10 The lake of Ngebel

When they reached Wilis Mountain, they climbed to the top and stayed near the lake of Ngebel for twenty-one days. Ki Amongrogo was very much impressed by its size, which was almost as big as a small sea. There they met a man meditating alone. He asked the man: "What is your name and what are you doing here? You aren't young any more. What is your worry?" The man answered: "Master, I'm from this region,

from the village of Sobo and my name is Ki Anggonolo. I'm in great sorrow because I'm always unlucky. Every time my crops are ready for harvest, pests would destroy it and I cannot support my family. I came here to pray for it not to happen again."

Ki Amongrogo pitied him and asked Jamal to help him. Jamal said: "Brother Anggonolo, listen to my word. When you get home, catch some grasshoppers and pierce them on bamboo skewers. Put the skewers on all four corners of the field. As you do that, say this mantra: 'Well, pest, if you don't go, I will pierce you with a bamboo skewer like this until you are finished.' Say it while walking around the field. Only your crops will be spared. If your neighbours ask you for help, teach them the mantra. They will thank you and you will become a prominent man amongst them." He paused and then said: "Can I ask you a favour, brother? Please tell us about this place." Ki Anggonolo thanked Jamal for the advice and agreed to tell them about this place.

As they walked around, Ki Anggonolo explained: "There are seventeen mountains surrounding the lake of Ngebel. Water from the lake flows out to four streams. Three of the streams can be found on the western side of the lake in the villages of Calam agung, Ebun-legi and Tambak. The stream on the eastern side flows to Kabuyutan, a very dangerous place because it is the dwelling place of demons and ghosts. No one dares go there. A little downstream from Kabuyutan, there are six pools called Sendang Selopati. Further down, there are six more pools called Sendang Pemandian and below them another six called Sendang Upas. According to legend, the condition of the water in the lake depends on the state of the water in Sendang Selopati. If the water there is in agitation, then the water in the lake will also be agitated, which in turn influences the water in the other pools. If the water in the Selopati pool is red, then the water in the lake will also be red, likewise that in the other pools." Ki Amongrogo said: "Let's take a look!"

They walked down a very narrow and difficult path, which made Jamal and Jamil complain: "Why is the path so narrow, Ki Anggonolo? Why hasn't it been widened a bit?" Ki Anggonolo quickly replied: "Sshh, not so loud and don't complain. This place is haunted. Don't talk about anything here and don't talk too loudly. How can you

above: *Ngebel Lake, with its 6-kilometre circumference, is located at the foot of Wilis Mountain and surrounded by thick hilly forest. Offerings are thrown into the middle of the lake on the 1st of Suro. The ceremony is held as a token of gratitude to God for all of His blessings. It begins with a procession of the offerings around the lake. The offerings comprise the* gunungan, *a mountain-shaped arrangement of glutinous rice decorated with fruit, and* uba rampe, *which constitutes all the other paraphernalia connected with the offerings, such as flowers, brown rice and incense.*

talk about widening the path? Not many people dare to come here, let alone widen the path. Do you want to be devoured by demons?" Jamal and Jamil were silenced at the warning. When they arrived at Sendang Selopati, Ki Amongrogo was very impressed with what he saw. The pool was fairly big; water flowed over a series of stones, making sounds of different tones as it flowed over them. He stayed there for three days. Then Ki Anggonolo brought them to Sendang Pemandian (the 'bathing place' pool), which according to legend was formerly the bathing place of fairies. Apparently, too many fairies bathe on the eastern side and so the pool slants to the east, but strangely the water does not flow over even when it rains heavily. They stayed at the Pemandian pool for three days.

Next, they went to the village of Lemah-abang (red earth) to see Sendang Upas ('poisonous' pool), which consisted of six pools. The earth there was red and so the water that came out of the ground was red. But not all the water in the six pools were red; the water in each of the other pools were white, blue, green, yellow and clear. Ki Amongrogo stayed one night there and then returned to Ngebel lake. This time he stayed on the eastern side. When he arrived at the lake, the water immediately became agitated. Thick black clouds loomed overhead and the mountains seemed to tremble. Within minutes, rain fell in torrents. Ki Anggonolo was scared and cried out mantras. Even Jamal and Jamil joined in. Only Ki Amongrogo kept his composure, pronouncing *astaghfirullah* (I ask Allah forgiveness) again and again. The turmoil abated, which was a sign that they were permitted to carry out their plans. The fact was that Ki Amongrogo had wanted to measure the depth of the lake so as to know its shape. To do this, Jamal and Jamil made a raft while Ki Anggonolo made ropes from bamboo. From their findings, Ki Amongrogo concluded that the lake was shaped like a large metal vessel for cooking rice.

Satisfied with their findings, Ki Amongrogo asked Jamal and Jamil to give Ki Anggonolo some rice seeds that would give him better crops. They then parted ways. The wayfarers followed the foot of Seribu Mountain until they arrived at the Kabarehan forest in the region of Pacitan. They stopped to rest at the foot of Mount Arga Liman.

## 11 Srobojo cave

The tide was low and while they were resting, Ki Amongrogo saw a cave. He saw steps leading down from the opening of the cave to the water and wondered how he could get to the cave. He observed the surroundings for a long time. He noticed the roots of trees trailing down to the water; they were intertwined with each other and in all probability, were strong enough to carry the weight of a man. Calculating the time of the rise and fall of the tide, he found that it was possible to climb down the roots and quickly enter the cave when the water subsided at low tide. He explained all this to Jamal and Jamil and asked them to watch him, so they could do the same. They moved fast and in a short while were inside the cave.

They explored the cave and found three rooms. In the first room near the opening, they found a spring of clear fresh water. In the second room, they saw a flat stone the size of a bed. The third room was very dark and when they entered it, thousands of swallows flew out. Ki Amongrogo meditated in the cave for ten days and saw a sign on the last night. He saw a lotus rising from the ocean and hovering in the air for a minute or two. Then he saw lightning flashing over and over again. He noticed the flashes were in the likeness of Arabic letters, which made out the words of the chapter Al-Ikhlas [The Purity] (Q, 112). With that realisation, he decided to leave the cave.

While resting under a tree, for they were feeling a little weak after that eventful stay in the cave, an elderly man in simple clothing approached them. After the usual salutations, he introduced himself as Ki Arisboyo. He said he had seen them when they arrived but presumed they were dead as he could not find them later. According to him, people who entered the cave would be killed by demons. Believing that their safety proved they were outstanding persons, he added: "I've never met a person who dared to enter the cave, let alone come back safely. You must be absolutely protected by The Almighty. I'm greatly surprised." Ki Amongrogo replied: "Thank you very much for your attention, Ki. Don't make a big deal of it. Just tell me the name of the cave and why it is believed to be so dangerous."

| the adulthood journey |

Ki Arisboyo said: "Master, the cave is called Srobojo cave. The word *Srobojo* is short for *Sosrobojo*, another of King Arjuno Sosrobahu's names (Arjuno, the thousand armed). According to legend, King Arjuno came to Java from India with a big army and many of his wives, said to be 800 in number. First, he went to Kedaton Mountain and then moved south to Sampar Paliyan. The words *sampar paliyan* means 'to stop and select'. In fact, he went there for the purpose of selecting women for his harem. From Sampar Paliyan, he moved to Penggung Mountain. His legacy there is the forest of Jati Cancangan. He moved again, this time to this region where he founded a kingdom called Kabarehan. He died here. His legacies are the cave of Srobojo and Mount Karanggajah, a mountain that looks like an elephant with its legs submerged in water. Srobojo cave is believed to be his kingdom in the realm of Nirvana."

## 12 Kabarehan, the city of ghosts and demons

Ki Amongrogo asked the old man: "Ki, please show me the way to the centre of the capital city of Kabarehan." Ki Arisboyo nodded respectfully and led the way. They went north and soon enough arrived at what was once the city centre of the Kabarehan kingdom.[5] Called Rowo Pakuwon, the place was presently a swamp. As they neared the swamp, they heard many unusual sounds and noises, such as that of wild beasts fighting amongst themselves and with demons. They also heard thunderclaps, heavy rain and sounds that would normally be heard in jungles. Ki Amongrogo murmured a mantra and in the wink of an eye, all the sounds and noises disappeared.

Amidst all the din, he saw in the middle of the swamp a tower surrounded by trees and a pond. Red and blue lotuses floated on water so calm it was as clear as glass. They stayed in the area for four days even though they were troubled every night by the noise of demons and wild beasts fighting each other. They also saw strange things, such as mosquitoes as big as camels swarming in a group and buzzing very loudly. When Jamal and Jamil asked about them, Ki Arisboyo put his index finger on his lips and warned: "Don't talk too loudly. This place is the centre of a city of ghosts and demons. Here, spirits can take whatever form they like. If they notice our presence, they might harm us. Fortunately, your master is a spiritually powerful man. If he wasn't, we would have been devoured by the demons." Not surprisingly, Jamal and Jamil were very frightened and began to tremble all over. Ki Amongrogo was also disturbed by the presence of beautiful ladies who tried to seduce him, but he was not tempted at all. Realising they had little impact on Ki Amongrogo, the ghosts and spirits returned to the tower.

Finally, it was time for Ki Amongrogo to continue with his journey. He and his companions took leave from Ki Arisboyo at Selokarung Mountain.

---

5 There are three stages in the history of the fictional Kabarehan. First was the Kabarehan kingdom, founded by King Arjuno Sosrobahu—a character in the Javanese wayang stories, which have their origins in the *Mahabharata* story. When the king attained moksa and returned to heaven, the kingdom changed into a swamp surrounded by trees and inhabited by wild animals. It was later known as the Kabarehan forest.

## 13 Probodalem cave

They walked for days, passing through mountains and lowlands, and stopped when they entered Kalak cave in Kalak Mountain. It was a large cave, about 100 steps long and seventy steps wide, and its entrance in the middle faced east. On the walls were reliefs depicting a house and a wedding feast with decorations, and food and drinks all laid out on a table. All these were carved on white stone.

There were three rooms inside the cave. There was a flower garden in the room on the left. The room on the right was arranged as a bedroom for a princess; this room was also called Song Putri (Princess' Quarters). The middle room, a kind of sitting room, was called *probo dalem* (inner room). It is from this room that the Kalak cave gets its other name—Probodalem. Ki Amongrogo noticed a basin filled with clear water behind this middle room. He took a bath and even though there was no trace of water wetting his body, he felt refreshed. Jamal and Jamil also had their baths there, but they did not feel refreshed even though water dripped from their heads. Instead, they felt more unpleasant. After their baths, they explored the room on the left.

At length, they left Probodalem cave and walked west towards a place called Pasanggaran. They had to cross a river to get there. At Pasanggaran, they found a mosque-like structure; on either side was a pond bordered by wild flowers. Ki Amongrogo stayed there for eight days. When they were about to leave the mosque, they heard bell-like sounds and found that the sounds were the result of water falling on stones.

While walking around, Ki Amongrogo noticed a pillar about five feet tall leaning on the south wall of Kalak Mountain. There was a cave above the pillar. He climbed the pillar to get to the cave, but it was not high enough for him to reach the entrance. He then noticed a dent about two feet above the pillar and a stone at the base of the opening. He understood what they were for and put his feet in the dent, reached for

below (both): *Located on a cliff some 25 metres high above Song Putri lake in Wonogiri Regency, Central Java, lies a cave the locals call Song Putri. About 100 metres wide, it stands alone and there is little to indicate at the present moment that it is connected to the Kalak (Probodalem) cave. The photo on the left shows the exterior of the Song Putri cave.*

the stone with both hands and lifted himself into the cave. The cave was arranged as a bedroom and there was a small basin filled with clear water flowing from above. Ki Amongrogo was very pleased and stayed there alone for twenty-one days in deep meditation. Jamal and Jamil could not get into the cave and so they spent their time collecting tuber and fruit for themselves and their master. One night, Ki Amongrogo again saw a sign like the one he saw previously… that of a lotus flower growing in the air. After taking a bath, he left the cave.

They went north and along the way met a middle-aged man called Ki Lokosroyo. He told them that there were four holy places on Kalak Mountain where people go to if they wanted to know about their future. The four places were the Song Putri room, the water basin behind the *probo dalem* room, the Pasanggaran ponds and the cave above the leaning pillar. Ki Lokosroyo then gave them directions to Salumbat Mountain. From there they could follow the foot of the Seribu mountain range to get to Senggami Mountain. The lake at the top of this mountain, called Madirdo Lake, was said to be the drinking place of a winged horse. According to legend, Senggami Mountain was also the place where King Arjuno used to do asceticism in his hermitage of Andong-bang at the top of Ratawu hill. It was here, at this same place, where Ki Amongrogo meditated for four days.

## 14 Dlepih Mountain

From Senggami Mountain, the wayfarers went to the village of Wiroko. Jamal and Jamil approached a man working on the field: "Uncle, can you tell us where Dlepih Mountain is?" The man answered: "Young man, don't make a joke about it. Don't you know that the mountain is the kingdom of ghosts and demons?" Jamal said: "I beg your pardon, uncle, but we are serious. We want to go there." The man pointed towards the southeast and said: "All right, it is over there. Be careful. You are still young. It will be a pity if you get into trouble."

They left the farmer to return to his work and walked steadily towards the mountain. They finally reached the Grunggung pool at the foot; it was where the headwaters of a river originated. They walked on until they reached Tireban forest and following the course of the river, they saw the Dlepih pool ahead. But there were tigers, elephants and other big animals blocking their path. The trees, too, were full of monkeys, orangutans and apes. The animals did not mingle together but stayed in throngs among their own species. Ki Amongrogo was not afraid and crossed the water to a stone in the middle of the pool, with Jamal and Jamil right on his heels. They sat on the stone and faced southwest. In a second, the Earth began to shudder, thunder clapped three times and scary cries, like the shrieks of the goddess Durga, screamed in the air. All the animals plunged into the water as if intent on wanting to crush them. But Ki Amongrogo was not intimidated. Holding his breath, he stroked his shoulders and moved his hands as if warding off the harassment. All the animals and disturbances disappeared in an instant. Ki Amongrogo sat on the stone for two days and one night, and then he saw a sign: a lotus, vaguely visible, in the middle of a pool.

Jamal and Jamil liked to watch the clear water of the Dlepih pool. Through it, they could see colourful stones at the bottom and fish with silver and gold scales darting around. Jamil wanted to take some of the stones, but every time he was about to grab some, the stones jumped away as if they were alive. Jamil cried out in astonishment: "How strange! The stones seem to be alive." Jamal warned: "Enough, Jamil! Stop it. The pebbles will catch you. Remember the farmer from Wiroko?" Ki Amongrogo smiled as he watched them and then said: "Let's go!"

They crossed the water to get to the side of the pool and then headed for the valley. They entered the forest of Pilang putih where colourful, sweet smelling flowers grew. There were many trees ripe with fruit, as if presenting themselves to Ki Amongrogo, but he did not pay attention to them, wanting only to worship The Almighty. Jamal and Jamil, however, were up and down the trees in an instant, collecting fruit and eating them heartily. Their appetites seemed insatiable and the more they ate, the hungrier they felt. When they had enough, they continued on their journey and stopped only when their master saw a cave on the southwest side of the mountain.

The cave looked like the mouth of the demon Kumbakarna when he fell down after being killed by the arrows of Rama and Laksmana, with the top of the mountain as the demon's crown. The locals knew the cave as the Jata cave. According to legend, it was the palace of Queen Widononggo, who ruled over the highlands of Dlepih. She was also the daughter of Queen Nyai Ratu Kidul, who reigned over the South Ocean and had her palace at Tunjungbang. Both queens were married to Sultan Agung of Mataram. Ki Amongrogo meditated in the Jata cave for six nights after which he headed for the village of Gondosuli in the region of Pancot on the slopes of Lawu Mountain.

below: *Kayangan Dlepih in Wonogiri Regency, Central Java. This is a sacred place for the Javanese. According to legend, this was where the young Raden Sutowijoyo (the name that Panembahan Senopati, the first king of Mataram, was known when he was young) meditated and met Nyai Loro Kidul (Queen of the South Sea) and obtained divine revelation to rule over the powerful Mataram kingdom. An offering ceremony is performed here every eight Javanese calendar years to commemorate the long and sacred relationship between Javanese kings and Nyai Loro Kidul.*

## 15 Lawu Mountain

below: *Lawu Mountain. On the slopes of this sacred mountain (also an active volcano) can be found the Sukuh and Cetho temples, which date back to the Majapahit Hindu kingdom. Other places on the mountain, such as Argo Dumilah (said to be the abode of the spirits of the mountain) and Argo Tiling (said to be the abode of The Supreme God Pramesti Guru) are significant for the Javanese.*

At Gondosuli village, there was a pool called the Pringgodani pool. From there on, the path was very steep. Jamal and Jamil found it difficult to walk and complained high and low. Passing through Cemoro-wayang, Bukur Pangarip-arip, Pangariboyo, Marcukundo, they stopped to rest at a place called Pakelengan.

Their troubles began as they got ready to climb Lawu Mountain further. Heavy winds slammed into them. Black clouds covered the sun, which was shining brightly just minutes earlier. Rain poured down from the sky, causing the weather to turn icy cold. Boulders began to roll down the slopes, which added to the deafening sounds of rain and thunder. From the depths of blackness, lightning appeared, crisscrossing and slamming into each other, as if fighting for hegemony of the sky. Wild animals fled to escape the horrible spectacle, crying and shrieking out of fear and pain. Jamal and Jamil trembled from cold and fright and lost all hope of coming out alive. Ki Amongrogo understood fully the danger that he and his companions were in. He observed a brief silence and prayed to God The Almighty to keep them safe. He uttered the words *La haula wa la quwwatta illa billahi* in earnest and with sincerity. Gradually, the uproar and noises died down, leaving only a gentle wind. The sun returned to drive away the chill. Jamal and Jamil stopped trembling; even their clothes did not show any sign of wear from the turmoil they had just experienced.

They then went to Argo Dalem, where Ki Amongrogo stayed for three nights. Thereafter, he stayed at Argo Dumilah for two nights and then began the descent to the Condrodimuko crater. A white and yellow starling was waiting for them and gave them signs to follow it. Ki Amongrogo understood and followed it wherever it went. It was clear the bird was showing them the easiest way to get to the crater, the place of torture for sinful creatures.

## 16 The Condrodimuko crater

Ki Amongrogo sat near the crater on a large flat stone called the stone of Mondrogini. He then threw a stone into the crater. What happened next made Jamal and Jamil frightened; the crater became agitated and the stone was reduced to dust in no time. One could imagine what would happen if a beast or a human being were to fall into it. Ki Amongrogo meditated on the Mondrogini stone for three nights.

The bird then led them to Taman Bidadari (Angel's Garden) on Mayang Mountain. All the flowers and grasses there smelled fresh and sweet. The last place they explored in the garden was an area called Cokrokembang. According to the wayang stories of old, Cokrokembang was the abode of Kamajaya, the God of Love, and his wife Ratih, the Goddess of Love. The *santris* continued their journey to the mountains of Petopraloyo and Tinjomoyo, and then returned to Cemorosewu. From Cemorosewu, they went straight to Selobanteng and from Gondosuli to Cemorolawang. Turning to the west, they followed a footpath that bordered a deep ravine and came across some tigers busily eating sandstones. When the animals saw Ki Amongrogo, they stopped eating and roared. Ki Amongrogo did not show any fear but calmly walked pass them. Strangely, the tigers merely bared their fangs. Slightly higher up, they found the Segolo-golo cave where Ki Amongrogo stayed for seven days. On their way back to Argo Dalem through the same footpath, they found seven tigers there. The tigers fled on seeing the men.

When Ki Amongrogo arrived back at Argo Dalem, he immediately sat on a round flat stone and rested. He looked very weak but felt refreshed after eating some fruit and began to walk towards Argo Tiling, a place said to be the abode of The Supreme God Pramesti Guru. Ki Amongrogo meditated at Argo Tiling for six days and received a sign that he and his wife, Nyi Tambangraras, would live at Terate-bang. Descending

**left top:** *Argo Dalem. This is the place where people from Yogyakarta and Surakarta kingdoms still place offerings for King Brawijaya, the last king of the Majapahit kingdom. As the king's direct descendants, the people believe he lived as a hermit on the mountain before attaining moksa and living in eternity. They give offerings to the king every year in a ceremony called* Labuhan.

**left bottom:** *Argo Dumilah is a hilly plain on the highest peak of Lawu Mountain. Pilgrims visit every year during the 1st of Suro celebrations to appease the spirits that are believed to reside there. This sacred place is usually covered by clouds, which gives an ancient feel to the place. The mound of stones not only signifies the highest point on the mountain, it indicates the border between the provinces of Central Java and East Java.*

again, it was that of a lotus rising from the sea, which then moved in a flash into the sky. Its emergence from the water and into the sky meant victory over death. He left the mountain the next morning and by the time he reached the bottom, he was so exhausted he collapsed under a tree to rest.

Not long after, a peasant by the name of Ki Sutogati appeared. He saw Ki Amongrogo's weary look and quickly returned home to bring some food and drink for him. Sitting respectfully in front of Ki Amongrogo, he made homage with folded hands and offered the food. Ki Amongrogo was very pleased. After drinking some coconut water, he asked: "Well, uncle! I'm very grateful, but who are you?" Ki Sutogati replied: "Master, my name is Sutogati. I'm the village chief of Lemah-abang. My gurus are Jamal and Jamil and I hear you are their master. They have been spreading the Islamic faith and I'm one of their converts." Ki Amongrogo said: "If that is the case, please be so kind as to inform them that I have left the mountain." Ki Sutogati nodded, made homage with folded hands and taking the leftovers of the food, went away to inform his gurus of their master's return.

When Jamal, Jamil and Wregojati were reunited with Ki Amongrogo, he asked them to build a mosque in the village within a week so he could stay in the *mighrab*. They agreed because they knew they had enough help. On their return to Lemah-abang, they ordered the new converts to build the mosque. Ki Sutogati also ordered his subjects, many of them non-converts, to help. The interaction between non-converts and converts resulted in many new people converting to Islam. And so, from about an original 200 people who were tasked to build the mosque, the number more than doubled with help coming from neighbouring villages. The mosque was ready on time. People believed it was mostly due to the spiritual power of Ki Amongrogo. Those who were not directly involved even believed that Ki Amongrogo built it on his own in one night.

With Ki Amongrogo around, more people visited the mosque and attended prayers. Many also wanted to become *santris*. Every time they reached ecstasy when praying, they would see Ki Amongrogo sitting on a golden throne in heaven, surrounded and served by angels and fairies. That vision reassured them that the teachings of Jamal and Jamil were true, that whoever did good deeds would live in heaven as their reward; and those who did evil deeds and did not want to amend their ways would be thrown in hell to be tortured there forever. They also distributed charms and amulets and performed more frightening stunts in their *emprak* shows to influence more people to convert. After some time, they began to call Ki Amongrogo as their great guru or Kyai Ageng or Ki Ageng Amongrogo. More people wanted to become students of the

*opposite: An* emprak *show in progress. When in a trance, people who obtain mystical powers are able to perform unusual acts, such as eating pebbles and stones, as can be seen in this photograph.*

*below: This entire space is the* mighrab, *or niche, in the Grand Mosque of Yogyakarta. The elaborate teak structure is the stepped pulpit where the preacher sits to deliver his sermon during the Friday congregational prayer. The size of* mighrab *varies among mosques. Where space is a constraint, the recessed area may be indicated through the use of tiles, a motif or simple calligraphy.*

and by early the next morning, they arrived at Sambiroto Mountain. They rested there. By this time, they had 1130 followers. From Sambiroto on, they walked only during the day as it was easier for the female *santris*.

The next stop was to be Sampar paliyan, but when they arrived there Kyai Ageng learnt that it was still too far away from the beach. He wanted to be near the beach as all the various signs he had been receiving indicated that any changes in his condition would take place at sea. Ki Jiwoyudo, a new convert from Sampar paliyan, then suggested Kanigoro village in the region of Giring. Even though there were many very dangerous caves there—such as Mawanti, Celor and Songputri—the village was located close to the beach. Kyai Ageng then asked Ki Jiwoyudo about the distance between Kanigoro and Mataram. Ki Jiwoyudo explained: "About halfway from Kanigoro to Mataram, there is a mountain called Mogoro. The road from Kanigoro to Mogoro is easier than that from Mataram to Mogoro." Kyai Ageng accepted the advice and ordered his followers to build a mosque at Mogoro. He also changed Ki Jiwoyudo's name to Gorojati and appointed him as the caretaker of the new mosque. Jamal and Jamil also had to change the names of all their followers. Later, Ki Gorojati and Kyai Ageng explored the caves together.

**2i) Celor and Manganti caves**

Ki Ageng Amongrogo ordered Jamal and Jamil to also set up camp at Jokotuwo Mountain near Kanigoro village, while he, Ki Gorajati and Ki Wregojati explored the caves. First they examined Celor cave, staying there for a day and a night. Then they went to Manganti cave, which was located on the banks of the Oyo River.

The opening of the Manganti cave was hidden behind a big stone. Beneath the opening, the current of the river churned and twirled fast. The path leading towards the entrance was very difficult and dangerous. When he got there, Kyi Ageng did not hesitate to enter the cave, which he found suitable as a place of recluse. Ki Wregojati and Gorojati noticed a scent in the air and surmising that spirits inhabited the cave, they became apprehensive. As they walked around, they noticed a big stone covering an opening. The opening led to another room, which was extremely dark. They entered the room and once their eyes were accustomed to the dark, they saw water trickling from the ceiling into a hole in the southeast corner. In the west corner was a flat stone, about two arm lengths long and one arm length wide. Kyai Ageng then noticed traces of chewed betel-nut and said: "Someone was here before us, a very powerful man." Ki Gorojati whispered: "People say this cave is the hermitage of the Sultan of Mataram. This is why no one is allowed to stay here." Kyai Ageng replied: "Well, that makes me want to do asceticism here." And he stayed in the cave for two days and two nights with the purpose of achieving the perfection of life. He did not move during that time; all his attention was focused on The Almighty. In the morning of the last day in the cave, his companions heard him say *salam* (goodbye).

## 2ii) The place of worship at Maladan

Crossing the Oyo River and turning to the northwest, they arrived at Maladan village. They saw a big tree, its massive roots intertwined very tightly. Two stones as big as water vessels were caught in this entanglement of roots. There was an opening among the roots, which made the entire mass look like a cave. Inside was a flat stone. Kyai Ageng climbed in and stayed there for a day and night.

The next morning, an old man from the village of Parumpung appeared. His name was Ki Baulopo and claiming to be the caretaker of that place of recluse, he said that the 'cave' was used by Sultan Agung of Mataram as a place of meditation. When Kyai Ageng took leave from Ki Baulopo, the old man asked permission to become his follower. He consented and Ki Baulopo became the main guide for the rest of the journey. They pushed forth, heading for the upper course of the river to get to the Drekaki pool and thereafter, the Songpati cave. At those two places, Kyai Ageng Amongrogo again missed Sultan Agung. He then returned to Celor Mountain where Jamal and Jamil were waiting for him.

below: *The entangled roots of an ancient banyan tree. Banyan trees can grow to as high as 40 metres. They produce aerial roots that hang down from horizontal branches and take root wherever they happen to touch the ground. These vertical roots can virtually create a forest of their own. An offering has been placed on the ground.*

## Jayengresmi, Jayengrogo and Kulowiryo

### FROM WONOMARTO TO LEMBUASTO AND BACK TO WONOMARTO

One Friday afternoon when the Friday congregational prayer at the mosque in Wonomarto was over, Ki Bayi Panurto did not return home but remained there with his brothers and sons, Ki Jayengresmi and Ki Jayengrogo. He wanted further news about his son-in-law, Ki Amongrogo, but no one could give a definite answer of his whereabouts. The information they gave even contradicted each other. Ki Bayi was very sad, as it had been fourteen months since he left them. He then spoke about a dream he had in which he lost three of his teeth, when in fact six teeth were missing.[6] Nobody could explain what the dream meant, but all agreed that it could be a bad omen. Again, that did not help Ki Bayi at all. So he suggested that they be patient and ask God for guidance. He then walked to his daughter's house while the others went to their respective homes.

Ki Bayi found Centhini, assisted by several maids, preparing the offering meal for the evening. His daughter Nyi Tambangraras rose from her seat and paid homage to him with folded hands. He looked at her, clad in white, her face still showing deep sorrow. She bowed and brought her father to his seat, then sat on the floor nearby to listen to him. Meanwhile, as Ki Jayengresmi walked home with his brother and uncle, Ki Kulowiryo, he brought up the idea of looking for Ki Amongrogo. Both of them agreed to the idea and they decided to depart that very night without asking leave from Ki Bayi. Ki Wiryo simply left a message to his wife that the three of them were leaving

opposite: *Worshippers leaving the Friday congregational prayer at the Grand Mosque of Demak. Friday prayers are mostly attended by men. If women attend, they will listen to the sermon and perform the prayer in a separate area in the mosque.*

---

6 To dream of missing teeth is considered a bad sign in the Javanese culture. It is taken to be a sign of losing something or often, the death of a family member. Ki Bayi's missing three teeth correspond to the loss of his son-in-law and the later loss of his two sons. The other three missing teeth refer to his daughter and daughters-in-law, who went away too.

# the adulthood journey

on a religious pilgrimage. They stopped by Nuripin's house and ordered him to go along with them.

## 1 The Kepleng adventure

above left: Tumpeng Megono. *This offering meal consists of a rice cone, spring chicken, fried soya beans, crackers (wrapped in plastic) and a condiment comprising shallots, sliced cucumber, red chillies and cabbage.*

above right: *A vendor selling* getuk, *a popular snack of steamed pounded cassava (on big plate on the left). Small portions are served on a banana leaf and topped with grated desiccated coconut and sweet dark sauce made of palm sugar.*

They made their first stop at the village of Kepleng. The village chief, Ki Surodigdoyo, seemed to have done a good job because the village looked prosperous. With the exception of a forlorn-looking mosque, all the other buildings were well cared for. The neglected state of the mosque indicated that the villagers did not pay much attention to religion and instead were immersed in worldly extravagance. On meeting Ki Jayengresmi and his party, Ki Surodigdoyo concluded that they were prominent people and invited them to his home.

Shortly after they arrived, his wife Nyi Surodigdoyo served them snacks and tea. With her was their young daughter Enduk Watiyah, three of her husband's concubines and his niece, who had been a widow for some years. Ki Jayengrogo looked at Enduk Watiyah and remarked to his uncle that she might be ready for sexual relations in about two years time. Ki Wiryo countered that it might be sooner than that and said in a parable: "But for now, the flower might already emit a beautiful smell." Ki Jayengrogo replied: "My uncle! For now, I will be satisfied if I can be near it." Ki Wiryo said: "Pray to God, I will be able to do a trick and bring the two of you together." Ki Jayengresmi did not like what he was hearing and looked sternly at his brother, who was silenced by the stare. His uncle, too, could feel the disapproval behind it. They then talked about conditions in the village. Ki Jayengresmi advised Ki Suro to pay more attention to religious matters. Ki Suro admitted that the villagers preferred *ronggeng* (dancing) and smoking opium to religion and promised to heed the advice. Ki Jayengresmi then asked leave to retire to the mosque, saying he was not feeling well.

Once his brother was out of sight, Ki Jayengrogo whispered to Ki Suro: "Is it true,

# jayengresmi, jayengrogo and kulowiryo

*above (both):* Ronggeng dancers. *Ronggeng* is also the name of a graceful yet dynamic social dance that moves to the rhythm of music provided by a small gamelan band of about four instruments. The dancers are often hired to perform on special occasions such as weddings and local festivals. These days, there are dancers who perform casually on the street in return for money. They travel from village to village together with the band. Previously danced only to traditional Javanese songs, the music now includes modern and popular songs.

my brother, that the villagers are more interested in culture than religion? If that's the case, can we organise a gamelan recital?" Ki Suro replied: "Oh, yes! That can be easily arranged. I'll invite Nyai Gendro's band. She is the most famous *ronggeng* in this area." When Ki Jayengresmi heard about the plan, he felt that his uncle and brother had forgotten the purpose of their journey, which was to look for Ki Amongrogo.

Ki Wiryo asked: "My brother! Why is the dancer nicknamed *gendro* (uproar)?" Replied Ki Suro: "Well, Nyi Gendro is the most popular of *ronggengs* in this region. Her body and face is so bewitching they arouse desire in everyone who sees her. Every time she dances, people forget themselves and do silly things. Men have given away their clothes and even fought just to get a chance to dance with her. And the fighting happens even amongst the elderly!" Ki Jayengrogo said: "If what my brother says is true, tonight will be a night to remember. What do you think, uncle?" Ki Wiryo smiled and said: "Oh, I can't wait to see a *ronggeng* who can arouse men's desires so wildly."

Soon, Nyi Gendro and Ki Citroguno, the leader of the gamelan players, arrived. Nyi Gendro took her place just under the shade of the centre light of the *pendopo*. Ki Suro announced her arrival: "Distinguished guests, I present to you the famous Nyai Dewi Taragnyono, also known as Nyai Gendro." Ki Wiryo remarked: "Well, well! Even her name is impressive. But come forward a little bit." Ki Suro looked at Nyi Gendro and said: "Yes, come forward! Don't sit under the shade of the lamp. It will make the youngsters crazy and cause trouble." Now, Nyi Gendro was not of the shy type, not at all. In fact, she was the opposite—showy and brazen. She stood up, took a few steps forward and then sat down a few feet away from the guests. The light shone on her face, bringing about a pent up cough of delight from Ki Wiryo: "Well, well. You really match your name, Dewi Taragnyono. In the wayang, the princess of that name made Prince Sombo lose his head, literally and figuratively. Brother Surodigdoyo! I think she will be a sensation if she has a little bit of make-up on." Ki Suro said: "You are right, brother!" To Nyi Gendro he said: "Go inside and ask my wife for make-up." She did

# the adulthood journey

**above left:** *A* rebab *player.* Rebab *is a two-string wooden fiddle covered with a thin layer of skin taken from the intestine or bladder of a buffalo or cow. Believed to have originated from the Middle East, the* rebab *was brought to Java with the expansion of Islam. This soft sounding instrument is often played by a senior musician.*

**above right:** *Providing the tempo and leading the music is the* kendhang, *a barrel shaped two-sided drum played with the palm and/or fingers.*

not say a word but stood up slowly, as if to show all the curves of her body, and all the while throwing coquettish side glances at the three men. They laughed heartily.

While waiting for the *ronggeng* to put on her make-up, Ki Wiryo remarked to his host: "Brother, I see the gamelan they brought is not really fitting for Nyi Gendro and also not complete. There are more players than instruments." Ki Suro replied: "Don't worry! I have a gamelan orchestra of my own, though it's not of the best quality. Citroguno, bring out my gamelan." Ki Wiryo said: "So, my brother is also a patron of the arts. I won't be surprised if you say that you can play the instrument, too." Ki Suro replied: "With all humbleness, my brother, you are correct! I can play the *rebab* and I also used to lead gamelan and puppet shows but only at the village level."

Nyi Gendro then appeared in front of them and began to make a seductive 360-degree turn. Ki Wiryo's mouth was agape, Ki Suro beat his thighs in delight and Ki Jayengrogo shook his head in amazement. Ki Jayengrogo was the first to come out from under the spell and said: "Now that all is ready, Citroguno, let the show begin!" Ki Wiryo closed his mouth and Ki Suro repeated the order: "Yes, Citroguno, let the show begin! Give me the *rebab*!" Ki Wiryo did not utter a word for his eyes were still transfixed on Nyi Gendro. They started with the opening tune, which served as an invitation for the villagers to leave their homes and attend the show. Nyi Gendro sang with a high-key note. Ki Suro played fairly well but Citroguno was a little out of rhythm with the *kendhang*. Ki Suro commented: "The orchestra is all right but Citroguno played the drum too fast. I think Ki Wiryo should play the drum to keep the rhythm." Ki Wiryo said: "Excellent! But I think Ki Suro should dance with Nyi Gendro. I want to see her dancing." Ki Suro asked: "But who will play the *rebab* if I dance?" To which Ki Wiryo replied: "Don't worry! Jayengrogo can do it." Ki Suro, who had been waiting for the chance to dance with the beautiful *ronggeng*, said: "Yes, and one more thing… I'll need a drink before I dance. That will make it perfect." Without waiting for a response, he asked for a bottle of rice wine and immediately drank from it. Nyi Suro asked her daughter Enduk Watiyah to bring more wine. She did as told and came back with her father's widowed niece, who had been flaunting herself at Ki Jayengrogo. But he had no eyes for her as his eyes were locked on the little flower of Kepleng.

That night, the village of Kepleng became the hunting ground of Kamajaya, the God of Love, who was shooting his arrows of sexual desire to everyone in sight. Ki Wiryo's heart was set on fire just watching Ki Suro dance with the *ronggeng*. Kama's arrows were torturing the young widow, too, for Ki Jayengrogo had shaken her heart so wildly and aroused her desires, which had been suppressed since her husband's death years ago. Kama was so busy that he finally used his favourite bow, the *naracaballa*, which could shoot arrows continuously. His work was visible in the acts of unfaithful hands which touched and groped writhing bodies lost in ecstasy and swaying to the rhythm of the dance shared by Nyi Gendro and Ki Suro. The village chief, already under the influence of alcohol, moved forcefully. He embraced Nyi Gendro tightly, lifted her up until her breasts were level with his lips. Ki Wiryo, beating the drum ever so loudly under the influence of their lustful movements, whispered to Ki Jayengrogo: "My son, Nyi Gendro is really something. She must be mine tonight, whatever it may take. What about you, my son?" Ki Jayengrogo said: "Uncle, my heart goes only to Enduk Watiyah." Just then, the dance came to an end. The dancers and the gamelan players rested to regain their strength. But in the bushes and under the cover of darkness, the action did not cease. Kama released more arrows, relentlessly and mercilessly. Those hit by them moaned and sighed, crying 'I'm dying, I'm dying' but not before ending with 'my love'.

With all his eloquence and sly tactics, Ki Wiryo easily convinced Ki Suro to allow his daughter to wait upon Ki Jayengrogo in his bedroom. Ki Jayengrogo was, after all, her 'foster father', having already expressed his wish to adopt her as his daughter and so it was not wrong for them to sleep in the same room. And Ki Suro, half drunk from the wine, gave his permission while Nyi Suro, as his dutiful wife, did not argue. She brought her young daughter to her 'foster father', who received her with open arms. Nyi Suro then closed the door behind her.

## 2 The collapse of the womanisers

Si Enduk Watiyah was comparable to a flower bud beginning to spread its fragrance, foretelling the blooming of a flower. The bumblebee, which tried to beguile the flower, found its efforts halted against a brick wall. Let us follow the actions of Ki Jayengrogo—womaniser or lady-killer, call him as you like—who was trying to know his 'foster daughter'. As was the case with village girls in general, Si Enduk, in her tender age, did not know anything about the game that boys and girls played, no matter how he

# the adulthood journey

explained it to her. Embraces, cuddles and flattery did not elicit the expected gasps of desire and heavy breathing but only filled her heart with fear. His weapon, impressive in all ways, could not break through her defence, which was like the wall of China. Moreover, he did not dare step too far for fear that her screams of pain would catch her father's attention. So to put her at ease, Ki Jayengrogo gave her a bagful of coins, which she put in the light. Absorbed in their glitter, she let him touch and stroke her. She felt a sensation never experienced before and said: "It feels good, uncle. Keep on!" Feeling encouraged, he spread her legs apart, positioned his weapon in front of the tightly closed flower bud and gave a sudden thrust. Si Enduk was startled. She moved backward and both fell on the floor. He quickly helped her back to the bed. She chided him: "Uncle! That's not nice! Don't do it again. It's painful!" He flattered her tenderly; she calmed down and they lay down side by side. Believing he had the upper hand again, he stroked her body gently and she closed her eyes.

Meanwhile, the young widow was waiting in suspense for Ki Jayengrogo. She had gone in and out of the house, to the kitchen and the bathroom, hoping to see him. By chance, she met Ki Wiryo. Now, since the evening began, Ki Wiryo had wanted so much to be with Nyi Gendro who had aroused his desires to the hilt. And so when he met the widow, he could not contain himself and grabbed her tightly. She pretended to push him away but actually moved her body closer to his. Ki Wiryo carried her to a dark place near the rice barn. Without delay, they held their cloths up and he penetrated her with ease, all the while moving as if in rhythm with the fast and exciting beat of a *jula-juli* song. But their tryst was interrupted when they heard someone approaching. The widow ran to the bathroom and Ki Wiryo hid in the barn.

right: *A ronggeng dancer getting ready for a show in a makeshift changing room. On the stage can be seen the wayang screen and flat wooden puppets called wayang* klitik.

## jayengresmi, jayengrogo and kulowiryo

In the bedroom, Si Enduk was almost asleep when she felt Jayengrogo's manhood touching her again. Instinctively, she closed her thighs tightly, which pinched him so hard that ejaculation could not be prevented. She was startled; she thought he had urinated on her and ran to the bathroom. Feeling dejected, Ki Jayengrogo went to the *gandok* (side room) and to his surprise, ran into the widow. Without uttering a word, he grabbed her. She did not protest. She, having found no satisfaction with Ki Wiryo, and Ki Jayengrogo, unhappy with his failure with Si Enduk, had some unfinished business to attend to. They played the game on equal terms and intent. Strength met strength with equal measure, gentleness was replied by sighs of comfort, and shortness of breath and gasps were echoed by sobs and sighs. But everything has its limits and the drum calling the morning prayer was struck, which coincided with the last drop of sperm from Jayengrogo's loins. He got up and walked to the river to bathe, leaving the young widow half-naked and dazed. But she regained awareness soon after, tidied herself and went to the *pendopo* hoping to see Nyi Gendro dance. However, she was too late as Ki Wiryo had already dragged the *ronggeng* to a secluded place where he was undressing her with haste. Nyi Gendro prayed for patience but received only the hasty reply: "It's almost time for the morning prayer. Let's be quick."

Now, Nyi Gendro, who was an expert in sex, acted quickly. While Ki Wiryo wrestled with desire, she groped into his pockets and retrieved everything inside. Ejaculation came quickly and when it was over, he hurriedly ran to the river, afraid to be late for prayer. There he met Ki Jayengrogo, sitting on a flat stone on the riverbank. Ki Wiryo asked: "Have you bathed? Were you successful?" Without waiting for an answer, he dived into the river and plunged his head repeatedly into the water. Ki Jayengrogo remarked mockingly: "It seems that uncle was also successful. How was Dewi Taragnyono?" Ki Wiryo replied: "Don't make fun of me. I was in a hurry, no time to enjoy. And she took everything from me! It's just bad luck. I'm really flayed to the bone. From here on, I have to rely on you." Ki Jayengrogo said: "Uncle, you sound pathetic." Ki Wiryo: "Do you think we should we complain to Ki Suro?" Ki Jayengrogo said: "No way, uncle. If Enduk complains to her father, I'm finished." Ki Wiryo asked: "What happened?" Ki Jayengrogo replied: "Uncle, the flower bud is truly as strong as the wall of China, impenetrable by any weapon whatsoever. I couldn't force her as I was afraid of creating further problems. Perhaps it isn't the time yet, as you said." Ki Wiryo shook his head with a groan: "This situation is absurd. Two lady-killers killed in the village of Kepleng! It's utterly preposterous!" They sat together in complete dejection.

At the village, Nuripin said to Ki Jayengresmi: "Let's go to the river, master. I'm sure Ki Wiryo is there. He has to bathe." After taking leave of the village chief who was having a hangover, he too was certain that his brother and uncle would be at the river. Nuripin was correct; he found both of them sitting on a flat stone by the river. Ki Jayengresmi spoke: "Well, uncle and brother! Let's go! Or perhaps my brother still wants to stay. It's all right with me. I'll pick you up later on the way back." Ki Jayengrogo replied: "No, brother! I'm ready!" Ki Jayengresmi then asked Ki Wiryo: "What about you, uncle? Do you want to go or stay?" Nuripin coughed and Ki Wiryo looked at him indignantly. Nuripin smirked and gave a restrained giggle. Ki Wiryo became flustered and barked: "Nuripin, you are rude. How dare you mock me!" Nuripin innocently said: "Who mocks you, master?" Ki Wiryo replied: "You! You look at me disdainfully. You cough and smirk at me. Is that not mocking me?" Nuripin simply said: "No, master. Is there any law against people who just look and laugh? It doesn't hurt and it doesn't lead to financial loss, such as stealing money or pinching a silver tobacco-case." Ki Wiryo became furious. He made a move to hit Nuripin, but the youngster was quicker and ran away. Ki Wiryo shouted at him: "Be on guard all the time because sooner or later, I'll get you!" Nuripin merely responded with mocking laughter.

## 3 Reward, punishment, blessings and disaster

They strode forth quickly. The clouds on the eastern horizon were golden-red in colour, reflecting the rays of the morning sun. The birds were singing praises to God The Creator. They never forgot the message of their ancestors—to praise God in the morning and evening to accompany the harp of David, the noble prophet. When Ki Wiryo had crossed the Konto River, he threw a stone backwards at Nuripin. It fell with a big splash and drenched his clothes. On seeing the success of his attack, he threw more stones in succession, making Nuripin beg for mercy. Ki Wiryo mumbled: "Now take that!" And they walked on, all the while following the course of the river.

At midday, they rested under a tree. Ki Jayengresmi addressed his uncle: "Uncle, instead of sitting idle, let's discuss knowledge. I'll put a question to uncle. What are the ways that bring *ni'mat* (reward), *kifarat* (punishment), *rahmat* (blessings, mercy) and *musibah* (disaster, danger)?" After thinking very hard, Ki Wiryo could not find the answer and gave up. Ki Jayengresmi then asked his brother who said: "I beg your pardon, my brother, but I can't think of the answer either. Please explain it to us."

Ki Jayengresmi proceeded to explain: "Well, uncle, and you, my brother! The path that leads to *kifarat* is by disregarding the religious law and paying attention to evil deeds. The path that leads to *ni'mat*[7] is by refraining from eating, drinking and sex. It's best if one can forgo them entirely. Avoiding food and drink as far as possible is beneficial to health; not only that, it will taste good when finally consumed. The path that leads to *musibah* is by breaking the religious law and doing things that are forbidden and which can taint the body and mind. The path that leads to *rahmat* are mercy and love, refraining from sleeping during the day and not sleeping in excess at night, so that one never dreams, let alone dream while awake."

He added: "These matters belong to the four inclinations, namely the inclination towards sleep, towards sex, towards complete worship till one surrenders totally to God

---

[7] We must differentiate between the meaning of *ni'mat* in Arabic and *nikmat* in Bahasa Indonesia. The meaning of *ni'mat* is 'reward', whilst the word *nikmat* means 'enjoyment' or 'to obtain or enjoy the benefit of something'.

| jayengresmi, jayengrogo and kulowiryo |

and finally, the inclination towards death, which is to understand the signs of death and not wait for fate to come or disregard time. We also have to be aware of the inclination towards sex. It is not permitted to have sexual congress at any time and place. We must also be very careful about the things we eat and drink, and not consume pork or alcoholic drinks as they bring more harm than good." Aware of their mistakes, Ki Wiryo and Ki Jayengrogo remained silent and bowed their heads low. Again, Nuripin found a way to take revenge. He coughed and Ki Wiryo felt the mockery against him. Feeling agitated, he took out the tobacco he was chewing and threw it at Nuripin's face. It struck him in the eye and Nuripin screamed as if he had been hit by a bullet.

After a good rest, they continued their journey west through the Selambur forest, which was inhabited by wild animals. The tigers and snakes kept away from the wayfarers but roared and slithered in all directions to make their presence known. The monkeys, orangutans and birds were different; their cries and song seemed to welcome the *santris*. When it was time for the midday prayer, Nuripin was ordered to look for water to clean themselves, but he was too afraid to do so. So Ki Wiryo looked around and found water and the prayer was performed. Afraid they would not be able to find water again, they stayed put until after the late afternoon prayer. Only then did they push on with their journey in the southwest direction.

They passed Palemahan village and crossed Kendorog River. Ki Jayengresmi then decided to stop at a flat, sandy place next to a waterhole called Kedung Bayangan. It was inhabited by crocodiles. Nuripin made a fire to drive away mosquitoes and animals that might venture too close and then sat down near Ki Wiryo. Ki Wiryo became suspicious and asked: "What's the matter? Why are you sitting so close to me?" Nuripin replied: "Nothing, Kyai. I'm afraid of the crocodiles and I feel safe next to Kyai. They know that Kyai is a good fighter and very powerful. But there are some really bad crocodiles that

below left: *A muezzin pronouncing the Azan, or the call to prayer. An official of the mosque, his role is to summon the call to prayer.*

below right: *Before praying, worshippers purify themselves by doing ablution with clean running water. This involves washing the face, feet, hands, ears, arms and nose. There is usually a place set aside in the mosque compound to do this. Men and women do their ablution in separate areas.*

don't even fear Kyai. See that one on the sandbank? It looks horrible and frightening. The croc said to his mate that he would capture Kyai. That's also why I sit near Kyai, to watch him and to warn him." Ki Wiryo replied sarcastically: "Thank you very much, my good fellow, but I don't need your watchful eye because those eyes of yours like to close when on the watch. Also, I don't think that horrible brute wants to eat me as I am old and my flesh is tough. You're different! You are young and your meat is still tender. I think it prefers you a lot more to me. So it's you who are in danger, not me." Nuripin said: "True, I'm younger, but I'm not an important person. I hope the crocodile will be prouder to get you than me." Ki Wiryo angrily replied: "Nuripin, you are a scoundrel! Are you trying to scare me?" He wanted to hit Nuripin on the head but did not upon hearing Ki Jayengresmi's remark: "Uncle, there is a proverb—a wise man is never afraid of danger or crocodiles because he knows that danger will lead to success. Anyone who is afraid of danger will live with worry, but one who dares to face it will be free of worry because he relies on God's mercy."

It was time for the evening prayer and Nuripin made the call. Ki Jayengresmi led the prayer. After that, he began a discussion about several religious matters with his uncle and brother, so that they did not get the chance to sleep. Only Nuripin slept soundly, seemingly unconcerned with the situation he was in. He snored. Ki Wiryo wanted to wake him up but was stopped by Ki Jayengresmi.

## 4 The prominence of man

Ki Jayengresmi said: "Uncle, how much one sleeps is a sign of one's prominence. A person decreed to be of low rank usually likes to sleep. If such a person wants to refrain from say, fasting, he will only be able to stop eating and drinking, but he will not be able to keep away from sleep. Not only that, day and night he will be preoccupied with thoughts of indulging himself in sex. On the other hand, one who is of high prominence usually looks for ways and means to reduce the need for food, drink and sleep, during the day as well as at night. Such a person performs everything with care." Ki Wiryo agreed with all that his nephew had said. Ki Jayengrogo then enquired: "Uncle, who has higher prominence—one who likes to eat and drink but refrains from sleep or one who refrains from food and drink but is very good at staying awake?" Ki Wiryo replied: "I don't know. I think both are the same."

Ki Jayengresmi continued: "My brother! One has to live in accordance with one's own capability, as long as one does not lie. 'Not lying' means not lying during the daytime, not lying at night, not lying to oneself and not lying to others. Let me explain. Not lying during the daytime means that one doesn't sleep during the day. Not lying during the night means that one doesn't eat. Not lying to oneself means that one always carries out all good intentions. And not lying to others means that one always fulfils one's promises. Or it can also be explained as the four kinds of honesty. Honesty during the day means eating in the day but not sleeping. Honesty during the night means sleeping at night but not eating. Honesty towards oneself means always having good intentions. And honesty towards others means fulfilling all that has been promised or said. All are very difficult to observe. If possible, one should try to practise them all together. If not, try to practise at least one. A person of low prominence will never be able to do them. However, if such a person manages to do all four of them, then he will be able to reach high prominence." Ki Wiryo commented: "It is indeed true, but not everyone can do all four of them. Only one who has prominence, like your brother Seh Amongrogo, will be able to do them all." With that, the conversation ceased and the *santris* dozed off, only to be disturbed by cries of fear from Nuripin.

They ran to where Nuripin was sleeping and woke him up. He then told them of a bad dream he had in which he was bitten by a crocodile and cried for help, but nobody came to his aid. Ki Wiryo was annoyed and began to hit Nuripin. Grumbled Nuripin: "Kyai is unfair. I was dreaming and did not disturb your sleep on purpose. I wasn't conscious of my acts." Ki Wiryo retorted: "It isn't your dream that makes me cross but the fact that I've lost my chance to have some rest." Ki Jayengresmi interfered: "Nuripin, don't grumble! It's best that you make a fire to warm us up. We don't need to sleep." But Nuripin did not get up and began to doze off again. Ki Wiryo, who was still angry, shouted: "Nuripin! You have been ordered to make a fire!" He woke up with a start and immediately went about gathering some dry grass. A fire was up in seconds, driving away the cold air. The warmth though made Nuripin sleepy again.

Not wanting him to fall asleep, Ki Wiryo ordered Nuripin to tell them a story. Nuripin replied: "A story? Kyai, you know I don't know of any stories to tell." Ki Wiryo said: "I know that and because it's difficult for you, you won't fall asleep again. You can make a choice. Either tell us a story or make your dream come true." Nuripin was puzzled and asked: "How can I make my dream come true? It's impossible!" Ki Wiryo countered: "It's very easy, really. I throw you into the water and the crocodiles will have you for breakfast. And we will not help you at all. That was your dream, wasn't it?" Nuripin said: "That's not a choice at all! It's like eating the *malakama* fruit—if you eat it, your father dies; if you don't eat it, your mother will die." Ki Wiryo retorted triumphantly: "It's entirely up to you. You pretend to know nothing, but you know about the fruit, which proves you are lying." Nuripin said dejectedly: "It's only a proverb, Kyai! All right, but don't blame me if it isn't a good story." Ki Wiryo said: "If it isn't good, you just have to make it up with another good story." Nuripin walked to a flat stone nearby, all the while grumbling: "That is cruelty without limit." He sat on the stone facing his masters, cleared his throat and spoke rather stiffly:

❧ *"Once upon a time, there was an old widow and widower. As they sat on a bench outside a barn, the widow said: "Kyai, let's play a game. I have a riddle for you to solve. I have a small purse, but no matter what you fill it with and how many times you fill it, it never becomes full. What is it?" The widower asked: "How big is your purse? I must see it and measure it." The widow replied: "It's small,*

# the adulthood journey

*I'll show you." They went into the barn and she showed him her purse. He took his stick and put it in the purse to measure its depth. He pushed the stick inside and drew it out, but could not see the mark yet. So he pushed it inside again and drew it out again. He did this many times until he lost count. He moved it right, he moved it left, and he became so preoccupied with the task that he did not realise that his silver tobacco case and money had gone missing."*

At this point, Ki Wiryo was aware that he was the widower in the story. He threw a flaming twig at Nuripin, which just about missed him. Nuripin grumbled: "His antics never change, whether in the city or in the wilderness. What a cruel bully!"

## 5 The cave of Selomangleng

By then, dawn had arrived and they took ablution and prayed. Without any breakfast, the wayfarers continued their journey to Selomangleng cave. From Kedung Bayangan, they walked south and followed the road till they reached Paingan market in the village of Mamenang, where they turned towards the plains. Nuripin complained about the heat, hoping they would stay in the village where they could buy food. But Ki Wiryo said: "Nuripin! There are four of us and you are the only one complaining about the heat. Only you will experience the heat of hell in the hereafter. Your whole body will be burnt; you will be neither dead nor alive. Your skin will burn until it peels, then new skin will grow, only to burn and peel and grow again and again." Nuripin asked

# jayengresmi, jayengrogo and kulowiryo

incredulously: "Is that the punishment for dreaming of being bitten by a crocodile? Is it so great a sin that I have to be tortured so severely? If I'm the only sinful one, so be it. But I think I prefer to be tormented on my own than be in the presence of a sinful one who hides himself in the cattle stalls." Again, Ki Wiryo felt the mockery and wanted to beat Nuripin, but he was already out of reach. After a long walk, they arrived at the village of Pakudon and met the village chief. He told them that the Selomangleng cave was located on the slopes of Klotok Mountain.

## 1) Ki Wonotowo

Following the directions given by the village chief, they arrived at Pakuncen village. They met Ki Wonotowo, assistant chief of the village. Ki Jayengresmi asked Ki Wonotowo to bring him to the cave. He was ready to help, as it was his job to take people to the cave and back. After a long and difficult walk, they arrived at the eerie cave said to be the hermitage of the lady-hermit Kilisuci (holy lady hermit). There were three chambers in the cave—one was called 'the sitting room', the other 'the bedchamber' and the last 'the flower garden' because it smelled good. The walls of the cave were decorated with fine engravings worthy of a princess.

The wayfarers sat together in the sitting room and later explored the other rooms. When the time for prayer came and Nuripin could not find water for ablution, Ki Wonotowo brought them to a place called *pambejen* outside the cave. The word *pambejen* comes from *beji* (water vessel, pool). The *pambejen* was, in fact, a stone water vessel, which formed part of a pool with retaining walls of stone. As the sun

*opposite:* A Pon *livestock market* There are five Pasaran *(market) days in a Javanese week. They are* Kliwon, Legi, Paing, Pon *and* Wage. *If market day falls on every* Pon, *it is called* Pon *market; if it falls on every* Paing, *it is called* Paingan *market. The Javanese use this system together with the Gregorian calendar system to remember important events, such as birthdays and deaths. Sultan Agung of Mataram kingdom, for instance, was born and died on Friday Legi.*

left middle: *The interior of Selomangleng cave. Scenes from everyday life, including a feast, have been carved on the wall of the main room. The statue on the left depicts a person meditating, but it is not known if it is that of the lady hermit, Dewi Kilisuci. Offerings of flowers have been placed on the ledge. The cave is located at the foot of Klotok Mountain in Kediri, East Java.*

left top: *The exterior of Selomangleng cave, The entrance to the main room is on the left; to its right is the entrance to the 'bedchamber'. Many remains, believed to be from the Kediri kingdom era, have been found in the vicinity of the cave.*

left bottom: *Interior of the cave. This photograph was taken from the cave's main entrance. The first chamber is presumably the bedroom. Another rectangular doorway within leads to a smaller room.*

| **the adulthood journey** |

above: *The dragon head in Selomangleng cave. It is found near the entrance to the main room.*

was almost setting, they quickly took ablution and performed the late afternoon prayer. They then returned to the cave and were surprised to see that the opening of the south room was decorated with a statue of a dragon creeping down (*manglung*) like a snake coming out of its hole. Perhaps that was why the cave was named *guha nada sela manglung* (the cave of the stone dragon creeping down).

After performing the evening prayer and as they sat around a fire in one of the rooms, Ki Jayengresmi asked Ki Wonotowo: "Kyai, have you ever met three *santris* who wanted to visit this cave?" Ki Wonotowo shook his head and said: "I don't think anyone has come here in the past few months. Those who do will seek my help as the cave is known to be haunted." On the morning of the second day, Ki Jayengresmi put another question to Ki Wonotowo: "Ki, is there a hermit or ascetic living around here who can tell me the whereabouts of the *santris*?" He replied: "Indeed, there is one hermit. His name is Seh Rogoyuni and he lives at the top of Klotok Mountain." Ki Jayengresmi asked if he could bring them to see him. Ki Wonotowo agreed but warned: "Not many people are able to see him. Even if a person can see him, he may not wish to speak. The person's mouth would feel as though it was clamped shut and he won't be able to speak. We must leave now while it's still early, as the path is narrow and difficult."

## 2) Seh Rogoyuni

The path was indeed difficult and steep and they could only move forward very slowly. As they reached the top of the Kalenglengan peak, the path became even more difficult to traverse because the stones on the ground were smooth and slippery. Shortly before midday, they arrived at a small plateau. There they saw a hut-like structure in the shape of a mosque. Its walls were bamboo and the thatch roof was made from the fibre of the sugar-palm tree. It was totally covered with creepers, which made it seem unlikely that any human being would live in it.

Ki Jayengresmi called out his greetings, which was answered from inside. It was a good sign. He entered first and made homage with folded hands. Seh Rogoyuni was sitting on the floor on a seat made from the stem of a palm leaf. To his left and right were stacks of books. He shook hands with the visitors and invited them to sit on a mat. Much to their amazement, he then offered them a variety of food. After they had eaten, Ki Jayengresmi spoke: "We beg your pardon, reverend guru, for disturbing your serenity. The purpose of our visit is to ask about our brother, Seh Amongrogo. We would like to know whether he has come here, and if so, perhaps our reverend guru will be so kind as to tell us where he is now. Secondly, we come to ask you for some guidance about life." The hermit answered: "All right, my son! Perhaps I can give you some information about your brother. I met him at the Realm of Silence. We are good friends. I think he doesn't want to return home. He is now at a location southwest from here and has almost found his destination. You can't find him yet because it is still a secret of God and he is still undergoing a test. In the future, his wife will meet him at the *alam walikan* (Realm of Reverse)."

Ki Jayengresmi asked about the Realm of Reverse. Seh Rogoyuni replied: "The *alam walikan* is called the *ardu'l 'ibadah* in the language of the holy prophet. It is the realm of the *wali* (friends of God) and the jinns. This is the reason why people cannot see or meet Seh Amongrogo unless he wants it to happen. The name of the location is Wonontoko, the Realm of the Dead. You will meet him there later. This is all that can be revealed. But you do not need to worry about him. Let's enjoy the food again." The visitors ate but not the hermit who only played with a mangosteen. The time for prayer came. Ki Rogoyuni brought them to the Prawati pool to take ablution. It was a short distance below the peak and was protected by a big boulder. Water flowed from the pool into the valley below. Ki Rogoyuni led the prayer. When it was over, Ki Jayengresmi resumed the conversation: "My reverend guru has fully answered the first part of my question. Now I want my reverend guru to give us some guidance about life."

### 3) The unity of seed or seedling with the land

Ki Rogoyuni answered with a smile: "My son, suppose you want to plant something. You will have to consider whether the seed or seedling is compatible with the land on which it will be planted. When the land has been cultivated as best as possible and the seed or seedling chosen carefully, then what is needed is the careful nurturing of it." Keen to learn more about the unity or suitability of seed with land, Ki Jayengrogo asked further: "I beg your pardon, master. If you don't mind, could you elaborate about the unity or union or unison of seed and land?"

Ki Rogoyuni answered: "I can't find the exact word for this mixture of seed and land or what is called the suitability of the two of them. It is a kind of blending between union (combination), unity (state of becoming one, harmony) and unison (concord or like in music, the sameness in pitch of two musical sounds). Perhaps it is the process from union to unity and finally to unison, in the sense that in the beginning there are two things that are suitable for each other, then the uniting process of the two to become one, and what comes last is the sameness of the two in form and action. It is just like a container and its contents. If the container is perfect in shape, the contents will be good, but if the container is imperfect, the contents will be also in bad shape. To be more exact, if a person is good, the knowledge he has will be good and will be used in the proper way for good purposes. But if he is bad, he will abuse the good knowledge for bad purposes. For instance, religious

Said Ki Jayengrogo: "Uncle, it's amazing that you get knowledge in a dream, even though it is confusing. How can it be that the Realm of the Living is equal to the Realm of the Dead?" Ki Wiryo replied: "Yes, that's why it's called a dream. What I'm most amazed of is Ki Rogoyuni. He is almost equal to your brother Amongrogo in terms of knowledge, perhaps even a little better." Joining in, Ki Jayengresmi said: "Uncle, there is a difference between them. Ki Rogoyuni is a true scholar while brother Amongrogo is a scholar-to-be. For sure, the true one is better than the would-be one."

Thus was the conversation between the three of them in the hut. The twigs that were hanging down the door looked like a fringe covering the forehead of a young princess; the fog covering the mountaintop was like a breast band; the white clouds overhead was like a scarf draped loosely over the shoulder of a beautiful lady. Dewdrops everywhere, on leaves and twigs, were like twinkling stars blinding the eyes of Hyang Aruna, the charioteer of the Sun God. With his powerful beams, he dispersed the fog and clouds; the dark valleys became brighter and the cold air warmed up. Before they parted, Ki Jayengresmi asked Ki Wonotowo to show them the way to the forest of Gagelang. He told them to head to the east and follow the foot of Selobale Mountain.

## 6 Pulung

They walked all day long, with Nuripin leading the way. While in a forest in the Pulung region, they stopped to perform the late afternoon prayer. And then they heard the faint tones of the gamelan. Ki Jayengrogo said to Ki Wiryo: "Uncle, it seems we are near a village. I hear the gamelan." Ki Wiryo replied: "When I hear the gamelan, all hunger and fatigue vanish in the blink of an eye. The empty stomach seems full already." Added Ki Nuripin: "If an empty tummy can be filled with the sound of gamelan music, I think you will get a tummy ache." Ki Wiryo snapped angrily: "Only tummies of fools, you hear!" Nuripin quickly ran away. Led by the sound of the gamelan music, they soon arrived at the village of Pulung. Nuripin walked ahead asking passers-by for the house of the village *pengulu*.

Ki Jabalodin, was delighted to hear that *santris* from Wonomarto had come to visit him. He prepared the drinks while his wife and daughter handled the food. By the time they arrived, everything was ready and all difficulties seemed to end… at least for Nuripin, whose eyes were locked on the food. And then they heard the music again. Ki Jayengrogo asked: "Ki *pengulu*, I hear gamelan music. Who is holding a celebration feast? He must be the village chief." Ki Jabalodin answered: "No, it is the rich widow, Nyai Sembodo. Gamelan players work in teams to provide the music day and night for her. She helps people who need money but charges high interest. That's how she becomes wealthy. She is also powerful. This is because people are afraid of refusing her demands for fear of losing her support should they need her help."

## jayengresmi, jayengrogo and kulowiryo

Ki Wiryo and Ki Jayengrogo signalled to each other with their eyes and in the next instant, took leave to attend to the call of nature. Ki Jayengresmi was certain they would be attending the gamelan show that night. The *pengulu* asked: "Master, who are they?" Ki Jayengresmi replied: "The older man is my uncle, the youngest brother of my father, Ki Bayi Panurto. The other is my youngest brother. Both of them like gamelan music. I think they will not return tonight." They then talked about religious matters, such as what to do with money that the *pengulu* receives for religious services rendered. Ki Jayengresmi explained the matter in detail, much to the satisfaction of the host. It was time to retire and Ki Jayengresmi chose to retreat to the mosque.

left: *Stalls in a market in Pulung village, located in Ponorogo Regency, East Java. The huge decorative structure of a peacock spreading its tail feathers is called* Topeng Dadap Merak (Peacock Shielded Mask). *It represents the Singa Barong, the mythical half-man half-animal character and central figure in the Reyog Dance performance. The mask, which comprises a tiger's head surrounded by peacock feathers, has become the symbol of the regency.*

# the adulthood journey

Ki Wiryo eagerly followed the maid and asked where Nyi Sembodo was. She replied: "She is waiting impatiently, master." When they reached her room, she led him to the bed. He drew aside the mosquito net and was quickly pulled in. The widow was naked, ready for the game. Her hands moved very quickly, disrobing Ki Wiryo and soon he too had nothing on. Ki Wiryo was defenceless. His manhood was aroused and the widow's warm welcome made him lose his senses. He was quickly dragged into the sexual game with the lovelorn widow.

Meanwhile, Nyi Kacer had left the room to bring mats for Ki Jayengrogo to sleep on. She found him in the *pringgitan* sitting behind some bamboo blinds. With the pretence of wanting to massage him, she kneeled beside him and began to caress his legs and thighs. Aware of the opportunity given to him, he rubbed his big toe on her breast and remarked: "By the way, doesn't Nyi Sembodo need you?" She replied: "Master, I think not. She was already wrestling in earnest with Ki Wiryo when I left them." The movements of his toe encouraged her to go further and she slid her hands up to his hips, where they brushed against his well-endowed manhood. Amazed with its size, she swallowed her saliva loudly and grasped it. With her other hand, she undid her waistband so that his toe could move further down. She began to kiss his manhood, which filled him with a strange but exciting sensation. He began to thrust it in her mouth until he felt his passion escalate and could no longer control himself.

Just then, she heard her mistress calling for her. Dragging her cloth behind her, she rushed to her room. Nyi Sembodo instructed her to wake Ki Wiryo up. Nyi Kacer asked: "How many times, Nyai?" To which Ki Wiryo answered: "Twice!" Nyi Sembodo added: "Only twice, but the night is young and there is still time for two or more games." Ki Wiryo complained: "Who could hold that far, Nyai?" But Nyi Kacer was already working on him. She applied her experience with Ki Jayengrogo on him. It worked and he could finish once more in Nyi Sembodo. Nyi Kacer tried to arouse him again and it was during this second time that an accident happened.

It happened this way. When Ki Wiryo failed to rise again, Nyi Kacer inserted his limp organ into her. He felt the difference clearly—she was in better shape and condition than Nyi Sembodo—and his desires were aroused. At the same time, Nyi Kacer caressed her mistress, an arrangement that worked perfectly for the three of them. It was at that moment that the accident happened and Ki Wiryo released himself in the young maid. Together with the last drop of his sperm, the drum calling for prayer was being beaten

below: *A headless statue with large phallus in the Sukuh temple, located in Sukuh village on the slopes of Lawu Mountain. This Hindu temple was built in the last period of the Majapahit kingdom.*

intermittently. By the time the last drumbeat was sounded, both women were spent and overcome by fatigue.

Gathering the last ounce of strength, Ki Wiryo grabbed his clothes and ran to the pool to take a bath. He found Ki Jayengrogo doing the same and wondered whom he was with since both women were with him till dawn had broken. Ki Jayengrogo did not say much but instead inquired about his uncle's condition. Ki Wiryo said in a half whisper: "I think the two women are nymphos. Nyi Sembodo still wants more and she also wants us to stay a few more days and attend a *tayuban* (*ronggeng* dance show), which she will organise in our honour. I think it's a good idea as it will let us recoup our energy and obtain some provisions as well." Ki Jayengrogo looked at his uncle and said: "For your sake, I will talk to my brother but only for one more night. After the *tayuban*, we must leave." Ki Wiryo agreed. They went out of the water and dressed themselves. Just then, the two widows appeared. They had come with the intention of snaring Ki Wiryo again but were stopped in their tracks at the sight of Ki Jayengrogo.

1) **The *tayuban* (*ronggeng* dance show)**

After the morning prayer, Ki Wiryo met Ki Duljoyo, head of the mosque at Pulung. Despite his position, he had neglected his duties many times attending to Nyi Sembodo's insatiable sexual appetite in return for some money. With strong words, Ki Wiryo reminded Ki Duljoyo of his duties. Ki Duljoyo asked to be pardoned humbly, but he was not sincere about it. On the other hand, Ki Wiryo could not blame Ki Duljoyo for doing what he did as he had a family to support. After all, didn't he, Kyai Wiryo, just do the same?

In the meantime, Nyi Sembodo was discussing the previous night's events with her maid. Nyi Kacer described Ki Jayengrogo's manhood: "Oh, Nyai, it was horrible but at the same time terrific." Nyi Sembodo replied in an envious tone: "You're lucky to be able to serve a handsome man with such a possession." But Nyi Kacer exclaimed with regret in her voice: "Oh, Nyai! It isn't as Nyai imagines. In fact, I was the unluckiest woman on Earth. I wasn't careful enough and he ejaculated on my face, causing terrible pain in my eyes." Nyi Sembodo tried to comfort her, saying: "Kacer, never mind. Man can only do his best, but in the end it is God who decides what happens." Nyi Kacer answered: "Oh, Nyai! You talk like a religious teacher… even talking about God's decree." Nyi Sembodo responded: "Well, my clients include many religious teachers, even if they are only of village standard. Don't despair. I hope Nyi Madu, the *ronggeng* from Bakungan, can whet the appetite of our man." With these words, she left her maid to prepare the food and drinks for the night's festivities. She then ordered Ki Duljoyo to invite Nyi Madu as well as important people of Pulung and its surroundings.

Nyi Kacer had invited the *santris* to breakfast and when they arrived, new clothes had already been prepared for them. Ki Jayengrogo refused to accept his, saying he had no need for them. For Nuripin, Nyi Sembodo gave a pair of bright red trousers and sarong with colourful floral designs. Ki Wiryo's clothes were placed in another room because Nyi Sembodo wanted to help him dress up. While assisting Ki Wiryo, she asked about Ki Jayengrogo. Ki Wiryo said: "His main interest is in dance and music. He has no interest in women even though he has women servants at home. So, tonight, if the *ronggeng* is really good, he might be willing to dance. If not, he might only join the gamelan players." The widow confessed: "Kyai! Frankly speaking, I'm crazy about him. Please talk to him. Tell him that he can have whatever he likes." Ki Wiryo asked: "What will you promise me to make me talk to him, even though there's no guarantee of success?" Nyi Sembodo replied: "Whatever you ask for, Kyai." Ki Wiryo said: "If that's the case, I will go now and talk to him." She replied in a seductive voice: "No need to hurry, Kyai! Let us sleep for a while." Said Ki Wiryo: "It's too early, Nyai. Better we do it later, after the midday prayer." But Nyi Sembodo was adamant and said: "Never mind, Kyai. We do it again after midday. Now, it is too difficult to refrain." She drew Ki Wiryo to bed and they wrestled with each other, each after their own liking.

Ki Jayengrogo was waiting impatiently outside. He had nothing to do but drink more coffee and eat more snacks. By chance, Nuripin came and he ordered his attendant to look for his uncle. Nuripin called out Ki Wiryo's name in the way one would call for a child. On hearing his voice, Ki Wiryo and Nyi Sembodo quickened their pace and in a few moments they reached the peak of their passion. Meanwhile, Ki Jayengrogo had succeeded in gathering some gamelan players together. When

right: *A ronggeng dance show in progress. The music is provided by a gamelan orchestra. In these village events, men are invited on stage to dance with the ronggengs.*

# jayengresmi, jayengrogo and kulowiryo

his uncle finally showed himself, the band was almost complete and they started to play. Nyi Kuwer came out from the kitchen to join them for a while. After a few tunes, she returned to the kitchen to supervise the cooking. Enjoying the music, too, were her assistants in the kitchen. But there was one person who did not enjoy herself, it was Nyi Sembodo. She was not happy that her play with Ki Wiryo was interrupted. Feeling dissatisfied, she summoned Ki Duljoyo to her room. Their tryst was over very quickly and before he left, he reported that he had already requested for Nyi Madu and had sent out invitations for the *ronggeng* dance show. Nyi Sembodo's hopes were revived on hearing the dancer's name. She began to feel hopeful that she would be able to snare Ki Jayengrogo, the most illusive fish she had known so far.

## 2) The night of sin

If World War II ended because of D-Day (Decision Day, the invasion of Europe), then Hari-H in Bahasa Indonesia was coined to replace D-Day. The only difference was that Hari–H had no meaning at all, only because the word *Hari* (day) begins with the letter H. Therefore, perhaps Nyi Sembodo was also justified in calling the night for the *ronggeng* dance show as Malam-M. The only difference with Hari-H is that the letter M has a meaning for her. Malam-M is an abbreviation for *Malam Maksiat*, or the Night of Sin. Tonight would be the night to snare the illusive fish, which she desires but has never yet tasted. Just as the illusive red pimpernel in

the history of the French was an English nobleman, the illusive Ki Jayengrogo was also a nobleman and a prominent devotee from the renowned religious school of Wonomarto, very famous in the olden days of legendary Java.

*Malam Maksiat* is difficult to describe. The following sentences will certainly not describe wholly of the events to come. They might only give a faint account of it. The original author or authors of *The Centhini Story* had the right of honour to put the theme of the night so clearly and vividly, so much so that readers even of this present time and age cannot identify the parts more important than this 'night of sin'. Until today, if one hears the name of Centhini, one's thoughts go back to the wealthy widow of Pulung and her night of sin. The significance of the whole story becomes blurred because the attention of the reader is focused only on those parts. In addition, key words containing important information are hidden by humour or behind deceitful passions for sexual desire.

### 2i) *Ni Sangidah*

After receiving his clothes, Nuripin returned to Ki Jabalodin's house to see whether Ki Jayengresmi needed his services. For sure, his master was attracted to his bright red trousers, which prompted Nuripin to relate the events of the previous night. Both Ki Jayengresmi and Ki Jabalodin shook their head in disbelief. Ki Jabalodin said: "Master, that is the life at Pulung. Nyai Sembodo seems to get *pulung* (the mercy of fortune) from God. All her business brings about gold and money, worldly influence and power. Her wishes come true and no one dares to oppose her. Therefore, do you think I should attend the show? Also, what should I use to guide me in my position as the *pengulu* of this village?"

Ki Jayengresmi replied: "Well, Ki! The fortune bestowed on Nyi Sembodo isn't a *ni'mat* (mercy) of God but more correctly an *istijrat* (curse), which will bring sin and punishment in the hereafter. To guide you in this sinful environment, you must have strong faith. One might say not a strong faith but a perfect faith. But a perfect faith in the midst of such conditions is certainly impossible. Therefore, try to strengthen your faith all the time by doing good deeds with increasing devotion. The basis for this is three-fold—purity of the body, purity in speech and purity of the mind or spirit. By taking ablution, we make the body pure; by praying and being honest, we purify the speech; and by intensifying the performance of obligatory and meritorious worship while avoiding the forbidden and shameful deeds, we purify the heart. With God's mercy, we will obtain guidance and help from God. There is a verse in the Qur'an (Q, 10, 9) which reads, 'If one does really try to walk in the path of Allah, God Himself will give guidance to him'." Ki Jabalodin was very much touched by Ki Jayengresmi's teachings and his faith became more grounded.

Their conversation was interrupted by the midday prayer and lunch, which was served by Nyai Jabalodin and her virgin daughter, Ni Sangidah. On seeing the handsome Ki Jayengresmi, Ni Sangidah became nervous and made mistakes,

| **jayengresmi, jayengrogo and kulowiryo** |

left: *In the quiet of the Sunan Ampel Grand Mosque in Surabaya, this man reads the Qur'an. Moslems believe the Qur'an to be the word of God, delivered to Prophet Muhammad through the angel Jibril (Gabriel) over 23 years. Comprising 114 chapters and 6236 verses, it is written in the early form of Arabic. Although the Qur'an has been translated into many different languages, Moslems are required to read and understand it in its original form.*

which caused much laughter and merriment. But having fallen in love with him, her heart was in uproar, smashed to pieces and blown by the storm of erotic desires. Meanwhile, Nuripin was so hungry he attacked the food with astonishing speed. Ki Jabalodin warned him to slow down, but the words fell on deaf ears. And then the accident he anticipated happened—Nuripin began to choke on his food. An alarmed Ki Jabalodin hit Nuripin on the nape of his neck but with so much force that the food was expelled through the mouth and the rear. Now it was Ni Sangidah's turn to laugh. By the grace of God, Nuripin was safe, but he had to clean the mess he created as well as wash his new clothes. Later, after putting on clean clothes provided by Nyi Jabalodin, he went to see his other two masters. He was still hungry, but this time he ate more cautiously. Nevertheless, Ki Wiryo remarked: "Well, Nuripin, you have new clothes. Where are your bright red trousers?" Nuripin did not reply but pointed his finger at his full mouth and continued to eat. Ki Wiryo cursed him in a low voice.

Returning to the topic of that night's dance show, Ki Jayengresmi advised Ki Jabalodin to be cautious because every evil had its sway in such an atmosphere. The devils were roaming everywhere. After the evening prayer, Ki Jabalodin took leave to attend the event. The gamelan had been playing since sunset and the atmosphere was festive. Guests were quickly filling up Nyi Sembodo's house.

# the adulthood journey

- After five shots, one is described as *panca sura panggah*, which means 'one feels very brave and dares to fight to the death';
- After six shots, the description is *sad guna wiweka*, meaning 'one's hearing becomes very sharp, so that when someone talks about him, he will hear all but misunderstand everything';
- After seven shots, the description is *sapta kukila warsa*, meaning 'one will look like a bird drenched by rain';
- After eight shots, one is described as *asta kacara-cara*, meaning 'one's behaviour and speech is indistinguishable';
- After nine shots, one is described as *nawa wraga lapa*, meaning 'one is like a lifeless snake due to hunger'; and
- After ten shots, the description is *dasa buta mati*, meaning 'one's behaviour is like that of a demon; although very scary, one cannot do anything but sleep as if dead.'

With the tenth description, Ki Duljoyo stopped. While rice wine was being served to those invited to dance, the *ronggeng* danced around as if trying to choose her partner. That night, she offered her shawl and hence the first dance to Ki Wiryo,

right: *These photographs, taken in two villages in Nganjuk Regency in East Java, show a rarely seen* tayuban. *Such shows started as a village tradition to celebrate weddings, circumcision rites and local festivals. Female dancers were hired and men in the audience were invited to dance with them. In these village shows, alcohol is served and* suwelan *is accepted. This is a practice where men slip money into the dancer's blouse to signal his wish to dance with her on stage. Such shows are still performed in villages but very discretely. Over the years, the* tayuban *has changed to become officially sanctioned performances conducted by professionally trained dancers (see photograph on page 331).*

top row (left and middle): Ronggeng *dancers getting ready for a show. They put on their make-up and get dressed at home, with assistance from family members. When they are ready, a male member of the family escorts them to the venue.*

top row (right): *The evening is opened by a* pramugari, *the master of ceremonies, who carries a tray holding a sash. The sash will be given to the host before the party begins as a token of appreciation. The* pramugari *also announces the rules for the night, such as how much money the men can give the dancers and how long they can dance with them. Each dancer wears a sash and will give it to the men in the audience as an invitation for them to dance with her.*

# jayengresmi, jayengrogo and kulowiryo

who had been chosen beforehand by Ki Duljoyo. But Ki Wiryo declined and gave his turn to Ki Wirodikrowoh. Thereafter, other people had their turn and when the shawl fell on Ki Jayengrogo's lap, many women were captivated with the way he danced. Then Ki Wiryo got his turn again and he danced with Nyi Sembodo, who was wearing a man's costume. Thus, there were four dancers on the stage—Nyi Madu, Nyi Gendam, Ki Wiryo and Ni Sembodo.

### 2iv) Nyi Tarijah

Amongst the many women in the audience, there was one who attracted Ki Jayengrogo's attention. Since early in the evening, he had the feeling that the girl—a beauty by village standards—was trying to steal his interest. She was sitting next to a younger girl. They were talking and seemed to be enjoying themselves. Sensing he was the topic of their conversation, Ki Jayengrogo asked Nuripin about them. Nuripin explained: "The younger girl is Sangidah, the *pengulu's* daughter. She tried to sleep with Master Jayengresmi, but he didn't want her. That is why she's here watching the show." Then he kept quiet, which infuriated Ki Jayengrogo as he was interested to hear about the other girl. So he hit Nuripin on the head, saying:

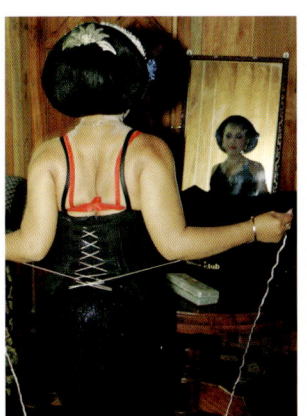

bottom row (left to right): *Dancers and guests mingle. In the middle photo, a male guest can be seen slipping money into a dancer's blouse, a sign that he wishes to dance with her on stage. In the photo on the right, a dancer has signalled her intention to dance with a man by placing a sash around his shoulders.*

# the adulthood journey

above: *Susur is a quid of tobacco mixed with betel-nut and other ingredients. Chewing* susur *is an old habit in Java. The lady sitting on the bamboo platform is mixing the* susur *ingredients for a customer.*

"You are mad, Nuripin. You know it's not her I'm asking about but the other one." Nuripin answered: "Ahh, you like her, don't you, master?" That question cost him another blow. Nuripin said: "Calm down, master! That woman is not a virgin but a young widow. Her husband died several years ago. She is rich and has a big and beautiful house. Her name is Nyi Tarijah and Sangidah is her niece." Ki Jayengrogo said: "If that is the case, arrange a meeting at her home. Don't fail because she has been looking at me for some time. For sure she has something to say. If she agrees, ask for a sign, a quid or something. Ask her to go home first. I will meet her there." When Nuripin saw that Nyi Tarijah was alone, he quickly set up a meeting and by the time Ni Sangidah returned to her seat, Nyi Tarijah had left. Ki Jayengrogo stood up to leave just as the attention of the spectators were on the actions of Ki Wiryo and his three partners. Nuripin led the way.

Nyi Tarijah's door was not locked and so he entered straightaway. She was already waiting. He took off his jacket and lay down on the bed. As she eagerly caressed his body, he undid her breast band and exclaimed: "Oh, your breasts are still firm yet soft. They seem to have never been touched." Nyi Tarijah responded: "Master, no one has ever touched me. I was only married for a short time when my husband died and our marriage was not yet consummated." She was surprised to find him extremely well endowed when her hands brushed against his manhood. Ki Jayengrogo said: "What do you think. Isn't it big?" Nyi Tarijah replied: "Don't ask! My cloth is already wet and you've only been working on my top!" She then placed her body on top of him and expertly pushed his manhood into her. Nyi Tarijah moaned softly, followed by sounds only related to intense sexual play.

The sounds attracted the attention of a young man who was crouching next to the bamboo wall. He was Ki Jenawang, Nyi Tarijah's boyfriend. They had agreed to meet that night. Angry to find someone else there, he burst in, took hold of Ki Jayengrogo's leg and pulled it with all his strength, so that he fell on the floor. But

## jayengresmi, jayengrogo and kulowiryo

Ki Jayengrogo was equally fast. With a step in the style of a heron kicking mud, he kicked the man with his other leg with a devastating result. Ki Jenawang flew out of the house, through the open door and onto the yard. Certain he was facing a formidable opponent, he hurriedly got on his feet and called a challenge: "Come out if you're a man! Let's finish it, man to man!" But then he ran away and disappeared into the dark. Ki Jayengrogo ran outside, but his opponent was nowhere in sight.

**2v) *The farewell***

When he got back to her house, Ki Jayengrogo spoke with sarcasm in his voice: "You claimed never to have been touched by a man. Now it is proven that you have men hidden away. How many? Tell me or I'll torture you!" Nyi Tarijah replied: "Master, I beg your pardon. Only three." Ki Jayengrogo retorted: "Only three? I think thirty will be more likely. You cause me bad luck." But in his mind, he told himself: "No wonder you're so good in the sexual play. You've had plenty of practice." Cursing and swearing, he left the house and headed for the river. He only became aware that he had left his jacket at her home when he began to shiver from the cold night air. He was just like a big monkey, trembling in the cold rain.

There was also a farewell in Nyi Sembodo's house, but it was of a different nature. While Ki Wiryo was claiming his dues, she was begging and imploring him to stay: "Please Kyai, consent to my last request, for sweet memories sake!" Ki Wiryo said: "Nyai promised to give provisions for the journey. Where are they?" Nyi Sembodo opened a cupboard filled with clothes and jewellery, and then another where she kept several kris, tobacco boxes and other things, and said: "They are all ready. Please, Kyai, have your pick, but I beg you to take your clothes off. Please, take off everything. I'm ready to serve you." Ki Wiryo selected what he wanted and put them in a heap in a corner of the room. Then he took off his clothes. Nyi Sembodo was quick to give a hand. Without any hesitation, he ripped away her cloth and *kebaya*. With one move called 'the step of the monkey reaching for the sky and lightning cleaving the earth', Nyi Sembodo was naked like a baby. The next second, she threw herself on the bed with the movement of a writhing caterpillar, followed by Ki Wiryo in the step of a bumblebee sucking out the honey of a flower. A wrestling contest ensued, which in the eyes of the inattentive looked like random movements but for Ki Wiryo and Nyi Sembodo, they were like the sounds of a battle song at the end of a wayang show.

Carrying several sets of clothing and accessories, as well as money, Ki Wiryo stepped out of the widow's house in triumph. Nuripin was not far behind. They met Ki Jayengrogo sitting on a flat stone by the side of the river. There, he revealed his misfortune at the hands of the young widow of Pulung. Ki Wiryo offered him some of the clothes but he wanted only his uncle's old robe. On his own initiative, Nuripin went back to Nyi Tarijah's house to retrieve his master's jacket, but the bird had flown away. Reporting the news, he concluded: "Masters! Keep in mind that man's fortune is like the wagon wheel. One second it's up and the next, it's under. Who lost out in Kepleng has won in Pulung and whoever won in Kepleng lost in Pulung." But before he could utter another word, Ki Wiryo snapped: "Nuripin, you are a fool. Even if you are a star, you are the comet without a tail, like a tail-less cur. Don't say another word! Go and fetch master Jayengresmi. Tell him we are waiting here." Soon after, four persons left the gate of the still sleeping village of Pulung, like shadows in the obscurity of dawn, leaving the sun still blanketed by dew.

## 8 The enchanted banyan tree

They walked for hours at a stretch, as though wanting to be far, far away from the place of so much vile and smirch as fast as possible. But when the sun was at its peak and it was swelteringly hot, they sought refuge in the shade of a leafy tree. Ki Jayengresmi noticed that his younger brother seemed quiet while his uncle looked fresh and wore new clothes. Without attempting to hide anything, Ki Jayengrogo told about his mishap with the young widow of Pulung. Ki Wiryo then spoke of his fortune from Nyi Sembodo. Not wanting to be left out, Nuripin said: "Master, indeed the fortune of men is like a wagon wheel, once up and once down." Ki Wiryo retorted: "There you go again. Gentlemen, I present to you Nuripin, the wagon wheel philosopher. What do you really want to say?" Nuripin replied: "I beg your pardon, masters. What I want to say is that the cards have changed. The one who found fortune at Kepleng found misfortune at Pulung, and the one unfortunate at

Kepleng found luck at Pulung, Ki Wiryo and Ki Jayengrogo are proof of this." His three masters kept quiet as if admitting to the truth of Nuripin's words.

Finally, Ki Jayengresmi said: "Well, my uncle and brother! Indeed, our conduct now in this world is an indication of the kind of life we will have in the hereafter. For this reason, regardless of the result in the hereafter, we must make the best effort to avoid bad conduct and promote good deeds. If our deeds are righteous, we will be in heaven. If our conduct is evil, hell will be our place." Ki Wiryo added: "You are correct. From this moment on, we have to make a promise to ourselves to improve our conduct." Ki Jayengrogo only smiled, as he was not convinced that he could avoid the temptation of women. Then Nuripin, imitating the puppeteer, said: "O, ye people! Let us forget the past and let us talk about those who have promised to better their lives …" He could not finish his story because Ki Wiryo threw a stone at him and to avoid it, he flung himself to the left with a move that is called 'the swallow swept down to catch the froth'. Ki Jayengresmi laughed aloud and said: "Indeed, Nuripin has many good sides. Often he can be very funny in times of restlessness." Replied Ki Wiryo: "You are correct, but at times he's also very annoying."

After a while, they continued their journey in a westerly direction. When they reached the market in Tajug village, Nuripin bought fruit and other provisions. By late afternoon, they were in the Padali cave and had a meal. Ki Wiryo and Nuripin were tired and fell asleep, but Ki Jayengresmi and his brother could not rest. They walked around and were amazed to see a banyan tree bearing jackfruit. Further away, they saw other trees bearing jackfruit, too. They picked a fruit. It was seedless and very sweet.

By the time they returned to the cave, the sun had left them, driven away by dark. Nuripin made a fire to repel mosquitoes and keep wild beasts away. After prayers, they settled down to sleep. The next morning, Ki Jayengresmi decided to stay in the 'enchanted' cave for another day or two. That morning, they were visited by a man who claimed to be the caretaker of the Padali cave.

## 1) Ki Sindurogo

The man's name was Ki Sindurogo and he lived at Tajug village, a few hours walk from the cave. Not wanting to reveal the truth, Ki Jayengresmi introduced himself and his companions as *santris* from Kabulangkir who were looking for their brother who had left home suddenly. He then expressed surprise that Ki Sindurogo knew of their presence at the cave especially since he lived so far away. Ki Sindurogo replied that he had learnt about them from some birds: "Yesterday, around the time of the late afternoon prayer, I saw four birds flying around my house. From this, I knew there were visitors at the cave. Usually, people who want to do asceticism or worship at the cave will come to me first because they are afraid to go there by themselves." Ki Kulowiryo asked: "Kyai, is the number of birds always equal to

opposite left: This is Waringin Sepuh, a sacred banyan tree in the square of the Mataram Royal Cemetery. It is believed to be the oldest tree in Java. Banyan trees, as the tree of the Gods, symbolise the trees that grow in heaven. People leave offerings and meditate under this tree as a form of 'wishing to connect' to the gods.

opposite right: A village market scene. The lady is selling *dawet*, a cold, refreshing and sweet beverage made from a mix of colourful rice flour beads, coconut milk and palm sugar.

### 3) Ki Sidolaku

The next morning, one of Ki Sindurogo's *santris* by the name of Ki Wonolelo accompanied the wayfarers to see Ki Sidolaku at the hermitage of Padangeyan. From Tajug, they went downhill and walked east till they reached the Seladakon plateau, where they saw many statues from olden times. By midday, they arrived at Pakuncen village, the burial place of Batara Katong. From there, the road went downhill and apart from a small accident in which Nuripin fell into a mud-hole, nothing much else happened on the journey. They stopped at a river north of the village of Gogo-kalang for Nuripin to wash his clothes as well as for them to perform the late afternoon prayer.

It was almost evening when the footpath leading to Ki Sidolaku's hermitage began to ascend. They arrived at the gate and Ki Wonolelo entered the compound

right: *This is the entrance gate that leads to Batara Katong's grave in Pakuncen village, Ponorogo Regency. It is the starting point for the 1st of Suro (Javanese New Year) ritual parade in the area. People continue to visit the grave.*

alone. Welcoming him were two attendants, Ki Pakujiwo and Ki Pakurogo. Soon, the visitors were invited to enter to meet the host. Ki Jayengresmi introduced himself and his brother as the sons of Mas Arundoyo, also known as Ki Bayi Panurto, who was now the guru of the religious school at Wonomarto, and Ki Kulowiryo as his uncle. Ki Sidolaku confirmed that he was indeed in Mas Arundoyo's close-knit group of friends. The other two members in the group whom Ki Sindurogo did not mention were Ki Ekawardi and Datuk Danumoyo.

As the time for the performance of the sunset prayer was coming to an end, they quickly took ablution and prayed. After dinner, Ki Jayengresmi told his host

above: *A view of Tunjungbang (Red Lotus) Bay, located near Gunung Kidul Regency on the southern coast of Central Java.*

the reasons for his journey—to look for his brother-in-law and to do asceticism. On hearing Seh Amongrogo's name, Ki Sidolaku was most emotional and advised them that knowledge based on Arabic and Javanese teachings should be treated as equal, which was what Seh Amongrogo had done. He added that Seh Amongrogo and Sultan Agung of Mataram were almost equal in terms of their knowledge and were only waiting for the resolution at the bay of Tunjungbang (Red Lotus). They were inseparable, like sugar and its sweetness, like the moon and stars, but as of that day the case was still covered by secrecy. The three *santris* of Wonomarto kept their silence, all the while trying to understand his words.

## 4) The Sentor cave

It was late evening when Ki Sidolaku took them to see the caves in Padangeyan Mountain. As they entered the Sentor cave, Ki Pakujiwo handed them some torches so they could see the inside clearly. Ki Sidolaku explained that the cave was formerly the hermitage of the lady hermit, Dewi Kilisuci. Her place of meditation was on the mountaintop. Because of her power, the cave later on became the place of worship and meditation for the ruling class of the kingdoms of East Java. For example, Klono Joyokusumo and his army leaders made asceticism in the cave when they wanted to invade the kingdoms in Bali. His soldiers did the same but in other caves, of which there were about seventy, located on the peak of the mountain. With the mercy of the deities, they succeeded in their mission. So, too, did Dipati Asmorobangun, the prince of Jenggala, who did not rely solely on his divine power and courage but sought the blessings of the gods by doing asceticism in the Sentor cave.

The examples prompted Ki Jayengresmi to ask about the atonement of the Islamic faith with that of the other pre-Islamic beliefs. Ki Sidolaku replied that

| the adulthood journey |

above: *Flower offerings such as the one shown here are often found in places meant for meditation. This offering consists of ylang-ylang, red and white roses, shredded pandanus leaves and some turmeric powder.*

men are divided into two groups—people in the lower group who strive for the weal of life while on Earth and those in the higher group who work for a happy life in the hereafter. So in the Islamic faith, people in the lower group live in accordance with the *shariah*, while those in the higher group strive to improve their God consciousness. In the other faiths, people in the lower group make offerings while those in the higher group spend time in meditation or remembrance of the Supreme Deity. From this discourse, Ki Jayengresmi, Ki Jayengrogo and Ki Wiryo could see that Ki Sidolaku indeed was an expert in all kinds of knowledge.

Back at the hermitage, Ki Wiryo asked about the knowledge taught in the *Panitisastro* and was given this reply: "The *Panitisastro* contains knowledge that can be used to recognise good from bad. If one cannot perceive good from bad, one could be called a fool. That person can be described as one bathing in rubbish; there is no way he would become clean or pure for he enjoys doing bad and evil things. Take, for example, poison! A dirty mind is like poison for one who strives to worship Allah The Merciful. Lust and perversion have corrupted his entire life and not one single prayer or worship will be accepted. His faith will vanish and he will be regarded as a puppet of rags to scare birds away." At this point, Nuripin began to cough repeatedly. Ki Jayengrogo enjoyed the discourse very much. Ki Wiryo, on the other hand, was irritated with Nuripin as he felt he was being ridiculed. Ki Sidolaku continued: "Grey hair is like poison to a maiden; it means she is still not married. She has shamed herself and her parents. On the other hand, an old man is also like a poison for a beautiful young maiden. His behaviour, flattery and flirtation cause only resentment." This time, Nuripin spoke up: "*Panitisastro* is 100 percent correct!" Ki Wiryo looked at him angrily.

Ki Jayengresmi asked: "Kyai, give us something good as an example, so that we can use it to guide us." Ki Sidolaku said: "The signs for a good man are as follows. All his behaviour is pleasing to others; he never insults people with strong words or inappropriate body language; his countenance is always bright and clear, never sullen; he speaks sweetly and never hurts other people. All these are difficult to practise, but the result is terrific if done. He will be respected, well-liked and nobody will dare to ridicule him." Ki Jayengresmi, Ki Jayengrogo and Ki Wiryo could understand the truth of the knowledge contained in the book of the *Panitisastro* and concluded: "Truly, the teachings of the *Panitisastro* can be used as guidance for life." Ki Sidolaku added: "My son, indeed the teachings of the *Panitisastro* does not contradict the Holy Book of Islam and the traditions of the prophet, which give teachings and guidelines to attain a happy life from this world to the hereafter." So engrossed were they in their discussions that they forgot about the time. It was as if dawn had come too quickly. Meanwhile, Ki Pakujiwo had prepared breakfast and some provisions for the journey because he too would be accompanying them as their guide.

## 5) Bajangkaki Mountain

From Padangeyan, the road went downhill to the south. They crossed the Denti River and arrived at the village of Mojopilang. It was there that Ki Jayengresmi ordered Ki Wonolelo to return to Tajug. They then took a southwest direction and arrived at the village of Patik at midday, where they rested and drank the juice from young coconuts. While praying along the banks of a river, they saw a strange looking mountain whose peak looked like that of an old man bowing low. Ki Pakujiwo told them that it was Bajangkaki Mountain. Although not very high, it was the most feared in the region of Sawo. Ki Wiryo and Nuripin pointed at the mountain and said mockingly: "The mountain looks like an old hunchback wearing a hat." Ki Pakujiwo was not amused: "Don't mock it, brother Nuripin." But Nuripin did not heed the warning and Ki Wiryo added more insults: "Yes, you are right Nuripin. It looks like a hunchback, coughing and covering itself with a cloth."

When they reached the village of Marantyan on the slope of the mountain, the path began to go uphill. Suddenly, misfortune struck. The sky became dark, lightning flashed, thunder rumbled and it began to rain heavily. The path became very slippery. A sudden gust of heavy wind blew the wayfarers off their feet, dispersing them in all directions. The most unfortunate was Nuripin, who was blown into a

below: *Bajangkaki Mountain, Ponorogo Regency, East Java. Its irregular shape can be seen on the right of the photograph just behind the first range of mountains. The* word kaki *in its name comes from* kakek, *which means 'old man' or 'grandfather'. In the foreground, farmers are erecting trellises for creeping vegetables such as string beans.*

thicket of bamboo and became stuck between two bamboo stems. He could barely breathe. Fortunately, Ki Jayengresmi and Ki Jayengrogo remembered to pray for safety and pronounced the *istighfar* (plea for forgiveness) repeatedly. The calamity slowly abated and the sun returned. The wayfarers inspected themselves and found their clothes filthy with mud and dirt. Looking around, they realised that Nuripin was not amongst them. It was Ki Pakujiwo who found him in that precarious condition. While cutting the bamboo stems to free Nuripin, he reprimanded: "Now you know, brother Nuripin. Because you mock the mountain, you have to pay for it." Nuripin replied: "You are right, brother Pakujiwo! I beg forgiveness from the mountain and from you, and to Allah I offer my most humble repentance." The others said *amin* (amen).

Then suddenly, as if from nowhere, an old man appeared in their midst and said: "Who are you? You look terrible. Come to my house to wash and have a little rest." Without waiting for an answer, he walked ahead. The *santris* had no choice but follow the stranger to the village of Pranten.

### 6) Ki Datuk Danumoyo

At the man's home, the *santris* had a bath, washed their clothes and put on the fresh clothes that he had provided for them. As the time for performing the late afternoon prayer was almost coming to an end, they quickly took ablution and prayed. After that, food and drinks were served. Their host did not eat but drank only *seruni* tea. When the opportunity presented itself, he asked: "Forgive me, my son! If you don't mind, I would like to know who you are and what your intentions are." Ki Jayengresmi answered: "My name is Jayengresmi. This is my younger brother Jayengrogo. And this is my uncle Ki Kulowiryo, the younger brother of my father Ki Bayi Panurto or Mas Arundoyo, as he was known in his younger years. My father is the guru of the religious school of Wonomarto."

Ki Datuk replied: "God be praised! My son, your father belongs to my gang of nine *santris* when we were young. Your father was the most liked in the group. My name is Danumoyo. At present, all nine *santris* are scattered, each having followed their own lot. Now tell me what you are after in coming to this isolated place." Ki Jayengresmi said: "Ki Datuk, I offer the utmost gratitude to Allah The Most Merciful! We have come to this place for two purposes—at my father's order to look for my brother-in-law, Seh Amongrogo, and secondly, to do asceticism for the benefit of our life." Ki Datuk asked: "Well, what do you want to do now? Do you want to rest or go straightaway to the peak to meditate?" Ki Jayengresmi replied: "Since it's not raining anymore, I prefer to meditate straightaway." Ki Datuk said: "If that is what you want, we have to go now because the sun has almost set and it will become dark very soon. We can continue our discussion up there."

So in a single file, they climbed the mountain and stopped at the cave of Sangsangan to take ablution. From there, they climbed a bamboo ladder to get to other caves higher up but just under the peak. They then looked for a suitable place to meditate. It was time for the sunset prayer. Nuripin made the call while Ki Jayengresmi led the prayer. In his heart, Ki Datuk praised Ki Jayengresmi for his deep knowledge. Darkness started to cover the mountain peak and fortunately they had brought some food and drinks. While they ate, Ki Datuk said: "My son. Concerning your brother-in-law, up to this minute, he is safe. However, his whereabouts is still held in secrecy by God. But like a river, he is almost flowing into the sea. Concerning your wish to do asceticism, since what you are looking for is the perfection of faith, it must be done with strong and focused intent and must not be sidetracked by worldly objects. Worldly objects can only be permitted if they serve as a pre-requisite for the final goal, the life in the hereafter. That is the path of the worldly oriented man. Those interested only in the life in the hereafter never deviates from that goal. One of the things that could lead to failure is *takabur* (arrogance), a feeling of superiority over other people because of the feeling of arrival at the destination. This feeling of arrogance can cause failure."

Ki Jayengresmi and Ki Jayengrogo could feel the truth of Ki Datuk's teachings, but Ki Wiryo wanted more clarification. He asked: "Ki Datuk, does it mean that our search for Seh Amongrogo will be fruitless? And how do worldly matters lead us to hell and jeopardise our goal for a happy life in the hereafter?" Ki Datuk replied: "My brother, I didn't say that your search for Ki Amongrogo will be fruitless. What I said was that his whreabouts is still a secret of God. So it is up to Him. If God wants you to meet him, it will happen. If He doesn't want you to meet him, your journey will be fruitless, as you say. As for your second question, it is indeed an easy question but answering it is most complicated. Why? Because the questioner and the respondent have yet to experience death! Any answer I give would only be tentative. It's like one walking with too a wide step, such that one falls on his behind." This clever and humorous reply made everybody burst into loud laughter.

When the laughter had subsided, Ki Datuk said: "My younger brother! It is like a wealthy man who has plenty of everything, yet for his everyday life he still looks for someone to give him a loan. There is a metaphor of a learned man who still wanders everywhere looking for a guru and he finds everywhere a guru who claims to have the perfect knowledge of Heaven and Hell. Every guru tells him his perfect knowledge, which proves to be not perfect at all. My dear brother, such a guru is in fact the manifestation of Satan who is after your money." Ki Wiryo asked how one could avoid those manifestations of Satan. Ki Datuk answered: "My dear brother! What I have told you is still only knowledge, not the real thing. Only after we experience death will we see the real thing. We will see which one is true and which is false."

Dawn broke and the *santris* performed the morning prayer. After breakfast, they took their leave from Ki Datuk, who once again advised them to be steadfast and patient as there were still troubles to overcome, troubles from criminals and women. In response to Ki Wiryo's request for a guide, Ki Datuk answered: "No need for that because the road is straightforward. Moreover, wandering ascetics should not avoid difficulties as doing so would reduce God's Blessings."

**7) The brigands**

The path from Bajangkaki Mountain to the village of Dringo went downhill all the way in a southeast direction. From Dringo on, the road was wide but not really easy to walk on... at least for Nuripin, as it was full of gravel and he was getting sores on his feet. At Blimbing village, Ki Pakujiwo was ordered to return and the wayfarers headed for the village of Bubuk. Along the way, Ki Wiryo caught a big millipede and threw it at Nuripin. The *santri* fainted from shock and when he came to, Ki Wiryo said: "Nuripin, you are incredible! Why are you so afraid of a millipede? It can't do anything to hurt you." Nuripin replied: "Ah, Kyai, fear has nothing to do with reason. You yourself are scared of baby mice. What can they do to you? They can hardly move!" Ki Wiryo replied in an irritated tone: "I don't like their colour, so bright red and shiny." Although Nuripin was often made the laughing stock, he had always been able to counter any attacks and make Ki Wiryo more irritated.

They continued their journey slowly and by sunset were at Tegaren village, where they obtained lodgings in the house of Ki Condrogeni. He was the village chief, who later on proved to be the head of a group of brigands. After performing the sunset prayer, followed by the *wabin* and the evening prayers, Ki Jayengresmi warned his brother and uncle to always be alert and prepared to face some robbers. When they returned to the *pendopo*, they saw that many people were already seated. They were there at the invitation of Ki Condrogeni, who pretended he was meeting them for the first time. All of them brought along opium pipes; some were busy smoking and paid no attention to the *santris*. Some of them had frightful names like Brojolamatan, Merakjamprong, Condrokolik, Gagaksetro, Barongkecer and Brojogambyar. To the *santris*, their behaviour was puzzling as they continued smoking even after Ki Condrogeni made the introductions.

Pretending not to know anything about them, Ki Condrogeni asked the people about their business. They responded by boasting about their activities, which included robbing, and describing the brutal way they would treat their victims. He also encouraged them to tell as much as possible, perhaps it was to intimidate Ki Jayengresmi and his party. Nuripin was affected by the stories and became fearful. Ki Wiryo, on the other hand, did not think they were so skilful that they could not be overcome. In Wonomarto and its surrounding villages, he was indeed known as the most dangerous martial arts expert around. Now he carried out his strategy. He offered money to Ki Condrogeni to buy some more opium for the brigands. Thinking the drug would make his men more courageous and daring, Ki Condrogeni welcomed the offer. Ki Wiryo thought otherwise—that they would lose control of reason and be easily defeated.

# jayengresmi, jayengrogo and kulowiryo

left: *An antique opium pipe. Opium was first brought to Java by traders and used as a painkiller and cough suppressant. In the 17th century, the Dutch began to source for opium in Bengal, India, and marketed it to Java and other regions in Southeast Asia. Opium gradually became the favoured method of payment for Europeans sourcing for Javanese coffee, sugar and other crops. Soon, people from all walks of life began to use opium as a pleasure-seeking drug. The drug would be mixed with* urang-aring *leaves and smoked in copper pipes.*

Finally, Ki Condrogeni said loudly: "I have the last bit of my opium, so I suggest you make up your mind whether to stay here or return home." His words were a signal for the robbers to get ready to rob the *santris*. So with the last inhalation of the opium and the resulting 'explosion' from the pipe, the lights went off and the robbers drew out their weapons. Ki Wiryo immediately stood up, recited the *condromowo* (black cat) formula, which gave him the ability to see in the dark. His hands and feet moved quickly. He snatched the robbers' weapons from their hands and hit them on the head with the handle of a lance. At the same time, his legs kicked right and left much to everyone's surprise. In the darkness and confusion that followed, none of the robbers could recognise who was friend or foe and they came to blows with each other. On seeing this, Ki Wiryo pronounced the *gelap ngampar* (thunderous thunderbolt) formula and laughed. The power of the formula made the sound of his laughter most thunderous and intimidating, increasing fear and confusion amongst the robbers. In no time, not one of them was left in the house. As dawn was breaking, Ki Jayengresmi decided to leave the place of disaster and look for somewhere better to perform the morning prayer.

## 8) Ki Nurbayin

It was almost midday. They had been walking through a forest and the sun was shining brightly, making the wayfarers thirsty and exhausted. After resting under a tree for a while, they pushed forth, hoping to see a village. Soon they came to the edge of the forest and in the distance, saw fields ripe with golden rice stalks. Their hope to meet peaceful peasants rose and gave them the strength to walk more briskly. When they saw an old man working in the field, Nuripin went forward to enquire about meeting the village *pengulu*. The man answered: "We don't have a *pengulu* here at the village of Longsor, only a *modin* (assistant religious official) called Ki Nurbayin. He is very much respected by the people. I will direct you to his house."

Upon meeting Ki Nurbayin, Nuripin told him that his masters were the sons and a brother of Ki Bayi Panurto, guru of the religious school at Wonomarto, and that they were looking for lodgings for one night. Ki Nurbayin had heard about Ki Bayi Panurto and so felt very honoured to have his family visiting him. As Nuripin

## the adulthood journey

and even though she did not appeal to him, he did not refuse and simply said: "You want it, you do it." Banem asked: "How do you do it?" He said: "I will not tell you. Do as you wish." She took off his clothes and started to visualise her mother sitting on her father, making love to him. She did the same to Ki Jayengrogo, but she could not get his manhood into her as it was lifeless. She was confused; it didn't happen with her father! She asked: "Brother, why is it so weak? What should I do?" Ki Jayengrogo answered curtly: "I don't know. It's your idea. Do as you think fit." Banem understood it as permission to do what she wanted. She did the same and this time his manhood responded, for he had put aside his dislike of her looks. He put his hands on her hips and pulled her down, forcing himself into her. Banem felt an incredible pain and wanted to withdraw, but his grip prevented her from doing so. Then recalling her mother's next movements, she did the same and began to enjoy the sensations. After a while, her body tensed and seized in spasm and she fell alongside Ki Jayengrogo with a loud groan.

Banikem and Baniyah, who were watching the game, became agitated by the thud of Banem's body on the floor and they burst into the room without any feeling of shame. Banikem saw her sister out of energy and breath, just like their mother. She looked at Ki Jayengrogo and seeing that he was still erect, lifted her cloth to her hips and sat astride him. She said to Baniyah: "Baniyah, help sister Banem. I'll take revenge." Banem said angrily: "Niyah, I'm all right. Nikem, get down at once! I'm not defeated yet." Banikem, however, did not take any notice and began to push him into her, but she failed to do so. Banem got up to draw her back, but Ki Jayengrogo said: "Hey you, Banem! You had your turn. Don't be greedy. Now let Nikem have hers." Banem did not dare to oppose him. She held her sister's hips and pushed Nikem down, the way Jayengrogo did with her before. Nikem felt a piercing pain and screamed a little: "Sister, it's awfully painful. I don't want it anymore!" She wanted to get off, but Banem tightened her grip and pushed her down again. Banem, feeling more experienced, said: "Hold a second. It will be good." The pain vanished and was replaced by an unbelievable sense of enjoyment. She moved more purposefully and said: "You can let me go now, sister. I can manage!" Hitting her playfully on the head, Banem laughed and said: "Good, isn't it?"

Baniyah was confused with the seemingly conflicting reactions of her sisters. She saw Nikem groaning in pain, yet Banem said it would be good and enjoyable. It made no sense. Banikem seemed to enjoy it, but why was she groaning as if in pain? She then looked at Banem, her face tense, mouth open, saliva dripping unnoticed from her mouth. And when she saw Nikem fall, her body in convulsion as if she was facing death, she did not know what to do. Banem held her hand and mumbled: "Now it is your turn." Baniyah was nervous but felt a curious mix of desire and fear. Ki Jayengrogo laughed silently just watching the sisters' behaviour. But then he touched her and when he felt her smoothness, he did not care about them. Instead, he remembered his failure at Kepleng, when his formidable weapon failed to penetrate the wall of China. Now he had another chance. With a wave of his hand, Banem and Nikem quickly pushed Niyah's bottom with force. But they did not realise how strong the push was and their combined force was too much for Niyah to endure. When the pole burst into the door with a double force, the pain also doubled. So unprepared was Niyah for the shock that she screamed and flung her hands outwards, hitting Banem and Banikem so that they fell on the floor. Sitting astride Ki Jayengrogo, she suddenly sprung up and was propelled backward. Fortunately, the wall behind prevented her from falling on the floor. She then ran out of the room.

Three bodies were left, two on the floor and one on the bed. Ki Jayengrogo was the first to recover, but the sisters were still a little confused. They moved to the bed and lay down beside Ki Jayengrogo. Banem spoke: "Master, what can I do to repay the loss caused by the foolish Niyah?" Ki Jayengrogo looked at their scantily clad bodies and demanded: "Take off all your clothes." On hearing those words, Banem and Banikem seemed to come to life and did as told. They wanted pardon, now they were going to get what they wanted. Without wasting any more time, he started with Banem. Banikem whispered urgently: "My turn, my turn." And so, he penetrated the girls alternately. Finally, he wanted to ejaculate into Banem, but just as he was on the verge of doing so, Banikem pulled his weapon out of Banem's loins. Without mercy, his sperm spurted out on the girls' thighs. Ki Jayengrogo fell weakly to one side, completely spent. The two sisters began to quarrel and blame one another for the fiasco. Again, Ki Jayengrogo felt failure. He stood up slowly and walked to the pond.

## 10) The Bagong waterhole

After bathing, Ki Jayengrogo sat on the side of the pond and meditated. He did not move a muscle even when he heard the call to prayer and only walked to the village gate to wait for his brother, uncle and Ki Rogomenggolo. The morning was not too cold. The sun was shining behind the mountain on the eastern horizon, framing the mountain in gold. The wayfarers walked towards the southeast, passing a spot where fights often broke out between the people of two villages. That morning, they came across some shepherds quarelling. Ki Rogomenggolo told the wayfarers not to interfere because the whole affair would take a few hours to resolve.

They reached the village of Wonosari in time to pray and have their lunch. Ki Jayengresmi asked Ki Rogomenggolo whether Lembuasto was still far away. Ki Rogomenggolo answered: "If we head straight for Lembuasto and not stop along the way, we can reach it before the evening." Ki Jayengresmi then asked: "Is there anything worthwhile to see around here?" Ki Rogomenggolo replied: "I think you must see Kedung Bagong (the Bagong waterhole). There are many fish in there but people don't catch the fish as they are seen to be holy. The place is held to be sacred." Nuripin interrupted: "My hobby is fishing. If possible, I would like to try

# the adulthood journey

my luck." Ki Rogomenggolo said: "I advise you not to because legend says the fish are the humble servants of Prince Menak Sopal. There was a man who fished there once; later on he and some family members died without reason. Those who did not die became crazy or suffered from an incurable sickness. Since then, no one has dared to fish there. Instead, people would feed the fish and ask for blessings."

Ki Wiryo said to Nuripin: "Nuripin, if you dare to fish there, you will be taken by the spirits and be made a servant of the fish." Nuripin replied mockingly: "If I become a servant of the fish, I will ask the spirits to take Kyai Wiryo, too, and make you their head servant, an important position indeed." Ki Wiryo grumbled: "Nuripin, you talk nonsense." They continued their journey and before the late afternoon prayer, arrived at the Bagong waterhole in the Kelampih River in the region of Trenggalekwulan. Ki Rogomenggolo mentioned that he had informed Ki Wijokerti, the village chief of Trenggalekwulan, that he would be at the Bagong waterhole that day. Not long afterwards Ki Wijokerti appeared, accompanied by servants carrying food and drinks for the wayfarers and also for the holy fish.

Ki Jayengresmi asked Ki Wijokerti about the fish. He explained: "In olden times, the waterhole was a lake called Telaga Sasi (Moon Lake). It was the amusement park for the royal family from the time of Prince Haryo Banyak Wulan of Singosari right down to a descendant called Haryo Menak Sopal. According to legend, Prince Menak Sopal made penance at the lake and in return, The Supreme Deity granted him anything that he wished for. He prayed for the lake to be the spring of rivers flowing through the kingdom of Kediri, viz the Ujang and Kelampih rivers. He continued his penance until he finally disappeared without a trace. People believe

below left and middle:
*The Bagong waterhole in Trenggalek, East Java. The local people believe in the legend surrounding the waterhole and regard the place as holy. Not much fishing is done here as it is shallow and most of the water evaporates in the hot months.*

he obtained his salvation in the lake he loved so much. Every night, people would hear gamelan music coming from the lake and sometimes the sounds of one having a feast." Ki Wijokerti stopped for a while to take a deep breath.

Ki Jayengresmi asked further: "Why was the name Telaga Sasi changed to Kedung Bagong?" Ki Wijokerti explained: "The story becomes more interesting. Because of the sound of the gamelan music, someone got the idea of borrowing Menak Sopal's gamelan for certain festivities. That person made offerings and prayed to borrow the gamelan. His prayer was granted and the gamelan appeared on the same spot as the offerings. The same would be done should there be a need for something else. When the festivities were over, everything that was loaned had to be returned to the same place. Another word for gamelan is gong and a holy gamelan is called Kyai Gong or mBah Gong. Slowly, mBah Gong became Bagong. Nowadays, no one can borrow anything from Menak Sopal and it's all because of one man's greediness. He borrowed some things from the prince but ran away with them instead of returning them. After a few days, he and everyone in his family died. Since then, nobody has been allowed to borrow anything."

Ki Jayengresmi said: "Greed has never brought prosperity from olden times till the present. But Ki Wijokerti, would you know if anyone has been permitted to fish here?" Ki Wijokerti replied: "My parents have said that permission to fish would be granted once in a while. If so, the person would be able to catch the fish very easily and it would be a sign, too, that he would have all his wishes fulfilled." Ki Jayengresmi then said: "If that is the case, I will pray. Start to give food to the fish." Ki Wijokerti and his followers began to sprinkle rice into the water. Fish of

below: *This is the grave said to be that of Prince Menak Sopal. It is located near the Bagong waterhole.*

above: *A* kempul *player in a gamelan orchestra.* Kempul *is a set of pitched medium sized gongs made of bronze suspended vertically on a wooden frame.* Kempuls *are played at regular intervals to punctuate the music.*

It is God's destiny that we don't have a son." To Ki Jayengresmi and Ki Jayengrogo, he said: "My sons, your aunt is emotional because if we had a son, he would be as old as you now. We have only a daughter, but she is very unusual. She stays in the forest and wild animals are her friends. She is known as Retno Ginubah. It is not the name we gave her. We don't know where she got that name from."

Food and drinks were served and the topic of conversation changed to art and culture. On learning that Ki Wiryo and Ki Jayengrogo liked gamelan music, Ki Demang ordered one of his brothers to call for the players and Nyi Grepet, the lady vocalist. They arrived shortly, arranged the instruments called Kyai Bermanis and started to play. While listening to the gamelan, the conversation turned to music and knowledge, which was very similar to the contents of the *Sastra-Gendhing*, a treatise on knowledge and music by Sultan Agung of Mataram.

Ki Demang continued: "What we are looking for in this world is goodness. If our life is based on goodness, we will find goodness in the hereafter." Ki Wiryo put a question: "My brother Demang! Please explain what you mean by goodness." Ki Demang replied: "In this life, it is enough to strive for two kinds of goodness—goodness at the tip of the *zakar* (penis) and goodness at the tip of the *zikir* (tongue). It sounds very vulgar, but in fact they contain hidden knowledge. The word *zakar* can mean *urat* (*aurat* in Arabic). In the Javanese language, *urat* means 'root', which in this case means 'root of all knowledge' because from the *zakar* comes the *zuriat*, or offspring. A good offspring—one who upholds the name of his or her parents—will bring about good family history, which can lead them to heaven.

"The Javanese also understand the word *zakar* to be *kalam*, which means 'word'. This is the point where *kalam*, in the sense of *zakar* (penis), meets *kalam*, in the sense of 'word', which originates from *zikir*, the tip of the tongue, which also means 'the remembrance of God'. This is the meeting point of *zakar* and *zikir*. *Zakar* in everyday life means to 'live in harmony with the wife'. *Zikir* means 'to meet all the needs of the tip of the tongue', namely having food and drink within the framework of remembering God. It means that whatever we eat and drink, we should remember the rules set out by God, namely to consume that which is permitted by the religion (*halalan tayyiban*). If we can successfully merge *zakar* and *zikir*, our life will be successful. On the other hand, life is full of obstacles, which also come from *zakar* and *zikir*, the tip of the penis and the tip of the tongue. Fulfilling sexual desires without limit will invite disaster; so too will indulgence in eating and drinking. In the hereafter, hellfire will consume us."

The conversation was halted by the late afternoon prayer but not before Ki Demang asked his brothers to prepare a *bagor* (mask dance) performance in honour of the guests.

## 2) The *bagor* show

Ki Demang then explained more about the *bagor* show: "In this region, the mask dance is the people's favoured and most treasured form of art. There are two sides to the dance—the physical and the spiritual. The physical side can be seen in the expertise of the dancer and the humorous scenes created by the jokers. The spiritual side is incorporated in the mask itself, because the mask is the disguise of the Soul to personify the world. The dancer puts on a mask and personifies its character, which can be good in the case of Sekartaji or Panji, or bad in the case of Klana. Any praise or criticism from the audience is directed at the character, not the dancer. When the show is over, the mask is taken off. It turns back into an object made of wood and is not worth a cent."

below: Jaranan thik. *This is a traditional village performance involving trance possession, mask dances and dancing with a kuda kepang (legless puppet horse made of woven bamboo). The main performer wears a dragon mask that claps its jaw and makes a ticking sound in the process, hence the word* thik *in its name.*

| the adulthood journey |

The *bagor* troupe arrived led by Ki Noyokenti, the show-master. They were given their costumes and soon were busy getting ready. In the *pendopo*, Ki Demang sat with his counterpart from Trenggalekwulan, Ki Demang Prawirancono, who had come with his brothers, wife and daughter, a beautiful young lady by the name of Roro Widuri. They brought presents for the host. The story that was to be told that night at the mask show was the *Panji Norowongso*, which revolved around the kingdom of Jenggolo. Ki Demang asked Ki Wiryo to dance the role of King Joyokusumo, ruler of the kingdom, and Ki Jayengrogo to play the king's son, Panji Inu Kertopati.

Just then, their conversation was interrupted by the arrival of Ki Demang's daughter, the well-known lady hunter Retno Ginubah. With her were two deer and a buffalo. She jumped off her horse and threw the reins to her uncle Wirobojro, who brought the horse to the back of the house. As she stepped inside the *pendopo*, she called out: "Mother, Father! Retno is home." Ki Demang and Nyi Widaryati embraced her. Ki Demang said: "I'm glad you came, Retno. We have guests, two brothers of yours. They are the sons of your uncle, Ki Bayi Panurto of Wonomarto. The other one is his younger brother." Retno replied: "Oh! So this is why the house is decorated." Ki Demang: "Yes, in honour of them. Let me introduce you to them."

They sat and Ki Demang introduced the guests to his daughter. Retno Ginubah said: "Welcome, brothers and uncle. If you don't mind, can you tell me why you have come this far?" Ki Jayengresmi explained that they were looking for Ki Amongrogo, their sister's husband. Retno offered: "Oh, him! Is his figure…? He's not very tall, but he's not small either. He always wears white clothes and his two *santris* always wear black. Is he the one?" Ki Jayengresmi said hopefully: "You could be right! Did you meet him recently? Do you know where he is now?" Retno replied: "I haven't met him, but I know of him. At present, he is in the care of the queen of Tunjungbang. Nobody knows where he is, but don't you worry! He's in good hands. You have to be patient."

Then she saw the costumes for the mask dance and asked whom they belonged to. Ki Demang replied that they were for Ki Jayengrogo and Ki Wiryo. Retno commented: "Oh! A little entertainment to forget the strain for a while will be good. Brother Prawirancono! Permit me to borrow your daughter Widuri to help brother Jayengrogo with his costume? Grepet can help uncle Kulowiryo." It was strange that nobody dared to oppose her. She herself put on Ki Jayengrogo and Ki Wiryo's headdress and mask. Not long afterwards, everybody was ready. Retno did not want to watch the show and got up to return to the forest. Ki Jayengresmi wanted her to stay, but she simply said: "I don't like this kind of thing, but I'll be back." She disappeared into the dark, followed by her hunting dog.

Everything was ready. Ki Noyokenti hit the [puppet] box and started to tell the story of *Panji Norowongso* and the kingdom of Jenggolo. Ki Kudonowarso, the vizier of the court of Jenggolo, was in audience. Then Panji Inu Kertopati—

# jayengresmi, jayengrogo and kulowiryo

played by Ki Jayengrogo—appeared. In the story, Prince Inu's wife, Dewi Sekartaji, disappeared in the night. Tormented by longing and passion for her, the prince became crazy. His father, King Joyokusumo—played by Ki Wiryo—entered to comfort his son. Ki Jayengrogo danced so well that the spectators were most impressed and the womenfolk became emotional and wept. His performance also sealed the attraction of Roro Widuri, who had fallen in love with him the moment she helped him dress up. Nuripin and Ki Asrodento acted as jokers and succeeded in enlivening the show with laughter, but not for long. The appearance of two other characters—Panji Norowongso, actually Dewi Sekartaji disguised as a man, and Dewi Onengan, Prince Inu's younger sister who was also disguised as a man—were most interesting. Without knowing the real identity of Panji Norowongso, Prince Inu fell in love with him and tried to seduce him. The spectators were saddened; they wept and called for him to come to his senses. Roro Widuri, too, whose heart was filled with unbridled love and compassion for Ki Jayengrogo, was influenced by the act. When she noticed that he was getting much attention and praise from the ladies, she became even more agitated. Afraid the other women would snatch Ki Jayengrogo away from her and unable to restrain her emotions any longer, she ran into the arena, wrapped her arms tightly around his legs and wept. The *pendopo* quickly became a web of confusion.

Ki Demang Prawirancono sensed trouble brewing and stood up. Surrounding him were his brothers, all prepared for any trouble that might occur from Widuri's unbecoming actions. On seeing the consternation on his face, Ki Demang Wirocopo tried to calm everybody down but to no avail. Suddenly, they heard the rattling crack of a horsewhip and Retno Ginubah appeared. Her voice, loud and sharp, ordered calm and a civil discussion of the situation. Ki Demang Wirocopo took a deep breath, relieved to know that his daughter would be able to resolve the matter. People began to return to their seats, except for Ki Demang Prawirancono and his group. Retno approached him and said sternly: "Brother Prawirancono, did you not hear me? Or are you waiting for the spirits of the forest to break your neck? Sit down and let's discuss the problem of Widuri and brother Jayengrogo." Ki Demang Prawirancono, his brothers and followers immediately obeyed. When Retno was the only one left standing, she said: "I knew this would happen. That is why I promised brother Jayengresmi that I would be back. Brother Prawirancono, give brother Jayengrogo permission to marry your daughter. I will marry them right away. Do you agree?" Once again, Ki Prawirancono could not oppose her and he agreed to the marriage.

The show was stopped for the wedding ceremony to take place. To the surprise of everyone present, it went smoothly. When it was over, the newlyweds were asked to retire and the show started anew. As Retno Ginubah turned to go back to the forest, Ki Jayengresmi once again tried to dissuade her from leaving, but she replied: "Brother! I told you that I don't like these events as they always lead to trouble. Now that the confusion is over, I'm not needed any more. But remember this. I will protect you later when you return to Wonomarto. Don't you worry."

In the bridal room with his new wife, Ki Jayengrogo faced the wall of China for the third time, but this time he had the key in his pocket, so that when the show outside was replaying the war between the forces of Ngurawan and Jenggolo against the invading army of Klono Sewandono, inside there was also a battle no less bustling and hustling. And this time, there was little resistance—only the sweet melody of love, just like the rhythm of the *semar pagulingan* tune.

### 3) Nyi Asem-sore, the *gender* player

The story would not be complete without relating the adventures of Ki Kulowiryo in his quest to satisfy his sexual desires. This time the object of his hunt for ecstasy was the *gender* player, Nyi Asem-sore. It is true that the position of a *gender* player in a gamelan ensemble was an important one. When the opportunity arose, he ordered Nuripin to invite her to his resting quarters. Without a single word of introduction, an agreement to play the tune of passion was signed. They met but at the peak of ecstasy, Ki Wiryo felt a sharp stab in his manhood. And when Nyi Asem-sore returned to her village, he was in such pain that he could only lie stretched out on the bed. Putting aside his fondness for disturbing his master with cynical remarks, Nuripin tried to comfort him. Ki Jayengrogo suggested to his uncle that he rubs a concoction of herbs on the sore to relieve the pain. When the pain subsided a little, Ki Jayengrogo returned to his wife. Ki Wiryo was left on his own.

right: *The photograph shows the* gender *instrument (pronounced as gen-dare). It is a type of metallophone with thin bronze keys. It produces elaborate forms of melodies in the gamelan orchestra. Each key is suspended by string over individual resonators held in a wooden frame. The keys are struck with two disc-shaped hammers.*

## 4) Peril in the jaws of a crocodile

People, especially women, praised Ki Jayengrogro for his good looks. It was not surprising then that Roro Widuri, a beautiful girl of noble and wealthy parentage, was crazy about him. She led a privileged life in which all her desires and needs were fulfilled. It was only in the matter of love that her father, Raden Ngabei Prawirancono, was very careful in his choice of son-in-law. He was, after all, a descendant of Batara Katong, a king of olden times, and it was important for him to have a son-in-law who was equal in status. But now his daughter was in love with a *santri*, a religious man. He was at first disappointed but felt more comfortable when Retno Ginubah told him that Ki Jayengrogo was the son of a great religious scholar, the guru of regents in the eastern part of the island of Java. He felt much better after seeing with his own eyes the man's knowledge of religion and the arts.

Once again, Roro Widuri managed to escape from the tight clutches of her parents and marry the man she wanted. She was at this moment with her grandparents at their home. It was a place where she felt she could be herself. There is a saying that grandparents love their grandchildren more than their own parents love them. At present, she had all the cards in her hands, especially Ki Jayengrogo, the ace in the game of love. He was, in fact, most experienced and an expert in that game. His wife and four concubines back in Wonomarto were often overwhelmed by his prowess and could not match his vigour. Ki Jayengrogo, the champion of sexual relationships, had met his match in Roro Widuri. Still, he was somewhat disappointed with her insatiable passion. He recalled his uncle's exploits with the wealthy widow Nyi Sembodo, from whom he received clothes and provisions for the journey. Although he felt lucky to have a beautiful wife and wealthy and powerful in-laws, in his heart he felt as if he was living in the jaws of a crocodile.

## 5) Suffering in the lion's den

The word *raja singa* (lion king) in Javanese has a double connotation. The first meaning, 'king of the lions', is literal. The second is 'big danger' as in 'the lion is a wild and dangerous beast'. Within the second meaning lies another. *Rajasinga*—in the Javanese language—refers to a most dangerous disease, one that is usually caused by sexual relations with prostitutes. In English, it is called syphilis. Ki Kulowiryo suffered from syphilis, from that one encounter with the shapely *gender* player, whose name was *Asem-sore* (evening sour), which sounds like 'evening sore'. For a minute of enjoyment, she gave an affliction that could cause agony for life.

With the herbal concoction prescribed by Ki Jayengrogo, the pain subsided a little and he could finally sleep. But after a while, he felt another painful stab, woke up with a start and called for Nuripin, who was on watch outside the door. He walked lazily to his master. Ki Wiryo said: "Nuripin, I had a dream." Nuripin replied: "A dream during the day, Kyai? That is daydreaming. There's no meaning to it at all. Even night dreams are lies, so why should Kyai pay attention to a dream at daytime." Kyai Wiryo snapped back, though without energy: "I'll beat you up when I'm recovered." Nuripin continued: "But you haven't recovered yet! You are still sick, very sick, making everyone else sick. Your threat is an empty threat." Said Ki Wiryo in resignation: "All right, all right! You win but listen. In the dream, Jamal and Jamil visited me. They reprimanded me a little but gave some advice. They said I could be cured if I make love with a girl who has not had her periods, or if I make love with an old woman who no longer has periods, or if I make love with a horse. What do you think? Which of the three is the most practicable?"

Nuripin replied: "Indeed, Jamal and Jamil can be trusted, but their advice is extremely difficult to carry out. The first option… where can Nuripin find a girl who has never had her periods? If I succeed in finding such a girl and Kyai enjoys her virginity, Kyai Wiryo will recover, but the girl will be infected and her future destroyed. If her parents learn of the truth, this unfortunate Nuripin will become the object of revenge of the villagers because the people will not dare to fight Kyai. But be warned, Kyai! You can't escape the hereafter. There the fire of hell will torture you. Because of the intense heat, your skin will burn and peel off. You will get new skin, but it will burn and peel off again, then you get new skin, it will be scorched and peel off …" Ki Wiryo retorted in exasperation: "Stop blabbering!" Nuripin continued: "It's true, Kyai. Qur'an chapter 4, verse 56 says that the skin of a sinful person will be burnt and peel off, he will be given new skin, which will be burnt and peel off…" An exasperated Ki Wiryo said:" Pin, I know that! You don't need to repeat that again and again. Blabbermouth!"

Nuripin continued: "Kyai, I'm only warning you! The second option is also impossible. Where can I find an old woman who can be persuaded to cure your disease that way? Such women are usually wise and experienced, and they will only loathe you. As for the third cure…" Ki Wiryo interrupted: "What about it? What is the objection?"

## jayengresmi, jayengrogo and kulowiryo

Nuripin continued: "A lot, Kyai! A horse is an animal. Although you have been following your bestial lust, unfortunately you are still a human being. The rank in life of a human being is much higher than that of an animal's. If Kyai makes love to a horse, it means Kyai leaves the rank of a human being and enters the rank of an animal. It might be all right if it is the rank of a horse, but what if it is that of a dog's or a worm's or a slug's? Ah Kyai, where should I hide my face? I, Nuripin, the servant of a worm! If we have to do it because it is the only way left, you have to think about yourself, Kyai! So far, Kyai has made choices—Nyi Kacer, the young *ronggeng*, and the rich Nyi Sembodo. Now the last option is to make love to a horse. I'm sure even your weapon will not be willing to comply and it will stay weak and lifeless." Both fell silent for a while.

Then Ki Wiryo said: "Nuripin, you are rude and impertinent, to tell you the truth. But this is a matter of life and death. If I have to choose between life and death, I will choose life. And if I have to make love to a horse to stay alive, so be it. I can't choose death! I'm not ready for that yet. I need time to repent, you understand. There is a solution for your last objection. When I made love to Nyi Sembodo, my penis lost its power. Then Kacer made it alive and I could continue for a while. Then it became powerless again and she made it alive again. That was why I rewarded her and ended up the session in her womb. Do you know what it means, Nuripin? I need a temptress, a seductress. With her help, even if my penis has only half its capacity, it might still work to satisfaction. Nuripin, be quick! Bring Nyi Grepet, the lady vocalist, here. She's beautiful and I'm attracted to her. It might work!" Nuripin had more to say, but Ki Wiryo put his index finger to his lips to silence him. He left the room, grumbling under his breath: "What can you say to a *kyai* like that. A horse *kyai*!"

Fortunately, Nyi Grepet agreed to help. She had been interested in Ki Wiryo from the time she helped him dress up for the mask show. She had touched his manhood accidentally, but he only kept silent. She then deliberately held it in her hands. All he did in return was to insert his big toe into her vagina. It was good and she swallowed her saliva three times in a row. Tonight, she will have the chance to be with him, although it would come with a high risk.

The night advanced. Nuripin was ready with a female horse, which he hid in the darkness of a shady tree not far from Ki Wiryo's room. Ki Wiryo and Nyi Grepet were inside, each pleasuring the other to achieve their own goals. Ki Wiryo stripped Nyi Grepet of all her clothes and began to knead her breasts. She responded to all his advances. Her lips pressed tightly to his, she moved her bottom and wriggled with pleasure. Ki Wiryo's manhood came alive, making its master scream out in joy. Nyi Grepet had accomplished her task and he had achieved his first goal. They stood up and still touching each other, moved step by step to where Nuripin was waiting with the beast. Its vagina had been lubricated with a concoction of herbs prescribed by Jamal and Jamil in his dream. Ki Wiryo carefully placed his weapon

---

**opposite left:** *Common* jamu *ingredients.* Jamu *is a traditional Javanese herbal medicine made by mixing various parts of plants, such as leaves, flowers, fruits, roots and bark. Hundreds of herbs and spices are used in* jamu *prescriptions. These include ginger, lime, turmeric, cinnamon and jasmine.* Jamu *has two main uses—to maintain physical health and fitness and to cure disease and ailments. Traditional doctors (and sometimes witch doctors) prepare and mix their own* jamu.

**opposite right:** *These days,* jamu *is easily available in pills, capsules, ointment and powder form. Still, some people will prepare* jamu *the traditional way, which is by boiling the ingredients and drinking the infusion. The main implements used in making* jamu *are a small iron mortar, crusher, grater and clay pot.*

on the horse and with a last burst of energy, assisted by Nyi Grepet and Nuripin, pushed himself into the animal. The horse did not budge. It was painful at first, but the pain slowly vanished and turned into pleasure when the herbs took effect. Ki Wiryo held the horse tightly. Nyi Grepet embraced Ki Wiryo from the back and moved rhythmically with the motions of the horse.

Not wanting to watch the appalling sight, Nuripin closed his eyes but could not block out the sound of 'fish caught in a muddy hole' as well as Nyi Grepet's gasps and heavy panting. Very quickly, Ki Wiryo increased his movements and Nyi Grepet's passion soared. The deed was done and the penis lost its power. The horse was led away and freed in Ki Asrodento's yard. Inside the room, Nyi Grepet asked to be paid for services rendered but had to be satisfied with being paid in cash. She returned to join the gamelan ensemble.

### 6) Widuri's wrath

The wedding festivities continued into the next evening with a *ronggeng* dance show, scheduled to begin after the evening prayer. The dancers came from different villages—Nyi Madu from Kalangbret, Nyi Gendro from Pulung and Nyi Teki from Ponorogo. The show would become the main attraction of the night and would be graced with very important guests from the region of Lembuasto and its surroundings. Ki Jayengrogo would play the most important figure of the show.

In the changing room, Nyi Widaryati handed over Ki Jayengrogo's costume to Roro Widuri with the message to dress up her husband as best as possible. In truth, she did not want him out of her sight. She wanted him to stay in the bridal room and make love to her even though he had done nothing but that the whole day. Although dejected, she helped him and when he was all dressed up, she could not believe her eyes. It was as if her husband was Kamajaya, the God of Love. For a few moments, all she could was stare at him. Finally, she fell on her knees and begged him to make love to her again. Ki Jayengrogo could not consent, as he had been asked twice by Ki Demang to meet the guests. And so he kissed her passionately and left. It was a kiss that made her want him even more.

Ki Jayengrogo sat between Ki Demang Wirocopo and Ki Demang Prawirancono. The three *ronggengs* sat in front of him, waiting to be introduced and to ask his permission to dance. When permission was given, the opening *gambyong* dance was performed. The dance was a success, having captivated the audience who threw presents into three buckets placed there for the occasion. All the important guests had a chance to dance with the *ronggengs* and the groom got his turn around midnight. His dance was expected to become the crown attraction of the night. Ki Jayengrogo displayed superb skills in dancing. Even the *ronggengs* felt the need to dance their very best. He was so good that the audience fell silent as if under a spell, breaking out to cheer whenever the dancers seemed to be in a romantic mood. Roro Widuri watched with envy as her husband danced with the *ronggengs*,

left: *The opening of an officially sanctioned* tayuban *dance competition in Sawo village, Ponorogo Regency. Giving the opening speech and copying a* tayub *dance movement is a well-known dance teacher. In these events, alcohol is never served and men are not allowed to offer money to the dancers.*

who seemed to be fighting for his favours. In the end, it was just too much for her. Unable to contain her jealousy any longer, she grabbed a brick and a stick and attacked the dancers. Ki Jayengrogo could parry the brick and smash it to pieces, but she managed to hit the women with the stick. They ran away into the dark. Roro Widuri did not go after them but ran over to her husband, grasped his legs and wept. Her uncles managed to loosen her grip and then they brought her into the house. Not expecting the show to go on, the spectators dispersed. Widuri's father, Ki Prawirancono, was still seated in the front hall. He did not think the wedding festivities would last its seven days.

Meanwhile, Ki Wiryo left to look for the missing *ronggengs*. When he found them, he brought them to his quarters where he attempted to make love to them. In the *pendopo* of his quarters, he found Ki Jayengrogo who had decided not to return to the bridal room. With him were two male *ronggengs* Wukir and Lobo, whom he had met at the show. For the next few days up to the seventh day of the wedding, Ki Demang's home was a hive of activity that included games and gambling. People were still coming round to bring gifts for the bride and groom. Little did they know though that the groom and his companions were already on their way back home to Wonomarto.

## 7) A nightmare?

After her husband left, Roro Widuri lost her mind. It was as if she was living in a nightmare. She did not care about her clothes or the way she looked. She ate less and spent her days talking to herself and having imaginary conversations with her husband. Her behaviour made everyone, especially her parents, sad.

Ki Wiryo was deep in thought. He could not catch the meaning behind Nuripin's words quickly enough. Was he, Ki Wiryo, the son of a *pengulu*? Who was the *pengulu* and who was his daughter? What a riddle! After a long while, the answer slowly dawned on him. Nuripin once told him that the horse that cured him belonged to Ki Asrodento, the *pengulu* of Lembuasto. In a fit of anger, he grabbed a stone to smash Nuripin's head with it, but the little *santri* was nowhere in sight. Ki Wiryo slumped to the ground in disgust. In the distance, he could hear the faint neighs of a horse.

Meanwhile, Ki Jayengresmi and Ki Jayengrogo had reached the top. They waited for a while for Ki Wiryo and Nuripin but neither came. As the time for the evening prayer was coming to an end, they proceeded to pray. They could not find water to purify themselves and so used clean sand for the purpose. Ki Jayengresmi wondered aloud: "What has happened to them?" Ki Jayengrogo said: "I think they couldn't climb the last part. It was very dark and difficult. I could hardly follow you." Ki Jayengresmi said: "Therefore, my brother, you should take notice of the mercy of God. Don't be led by your vain desires and stop looking for sexual gratification. So far, you are still protected by God. Everything can be obtained easily and all problems can be solved." Ki Jayengrogo said: "Thank you, brother, for your advice. I ask your blessings and support so that I can perform all that is necessary in the right way." They stopped talking and soon were in deep meditation, plunged into remembrance of the Merciful God. After some time, they went down and met Ki Kulowiryo and Nuripin. Soon they reached the road to Kalangbret and Rowo.

## 10 Ki Seh Ekawerdi

Arriving at the village of Gubug, the wayfarers heard from the people that there was a highly learned guru who lived there. His name was Ki Seh Ekawerdi. Ki Jayengresmi remembered that he was one of the nine men in his father's circle of friends and expressed interest in visiting him. A villager told him that the guru was not at home but could be found at the top of Purwo Mountain where he was doing asceticism. And so they went to the hermitage on the mountain where Ki Seh Ekawerdi received them warmly. From him, they received teachings that would guide them through life. In addition, he told them that they could obtain glory on Earth and greatest happiness in the hereafter by being a good public servant and by focusing one's service to God alone. The basis for it was honesty towards oneself and sincere worship.

## 11 Wonomarto and the emotional news about Seh Amongrogo

Back in Wonomarto, Ki Bayi Panurto and his wife were in Nyi Tambangraras' home when Ki Jayengresmi, Ki Jayengrogo and Ki Kulowiryo came with their wives to report the outcome of their travels. From time to time, Nyi Tambangraras would hold offering meals for the safety of her husband and this was one of those occasions. Ki Jayengresmi talked about their encounters with Ki Rogoyuni, Ki Danumoyo and Retno Ginubah, all of whom said that Ki Amongrogo was safe and still in the protection of The Almighty. He also told them that they would be able to meet Ki Amongrogo later at a place called Wonontoko in the region of Tunjungbang. Everyone was sad to hear the news, especially Nyi Tambangraras.

It was a little after midday. Ki Bayi and his wife were sitting in the *pendopo* when *santri* Luci suddenly entered. Behind him were Jamal and Jamil, who were so emotional to be there that they burst into tears. Giving them time to recover, Ki Bayi ordered *santri* Luci get all the family members together to listen to the news they had to share.

above: *The fragrant pink lotus. An aquatic plant that flowers throughout the year, this waterlily is considered sacred as it represents purity in mind and body.*

When everybody was present and their emotions were in check, Jamal gave his report: "From Wonomarto, we visited dangerous and isolated places and met learned hermits and gurus. At Nusobarong, Ki Amongrogo received a sign in the form of a lotus growing in the sky. He saw the sign again and again and concluded that his quest to obtain the perfection of life could only be solved with the interference of Sultan Agung of Mataram. He tried to meet the Sultan but never succeeded. Every time he visited a hermitage, a cave or a place of worship where the king meditated, he would have left by the time he arrived. So Ki Amongrogo tried to force a confrontation with the Sultan by building a big mosque in the village of Kanigoro. We performed magic shows every day and more people joined us. Our followers now number in the thousands. Ki Amongrogo took the title of Kyai Ageng Amongrogo. When these events came to the notice of the Sultan, he sent Ki Tumenggung Wiroguno to Kanigoro to investigate. They concluded that Ki Amongrogo was guilty of breaking the Islamic law and sentenced him to death by drowning at Tunjungbang Bay. Ki Wiroguno and his assistants put Ki Amongrogo into a bamboo basket and threw him into the ocean. When the basket washed on to the beach, it was empty and Ki Wiroguno heard Ki Amongrogo's voice expressing gratitude to the Sultan." Before Jamal and Jamil could finish their story, Nyi Tambangraras fainted and fell to the floor.

The *santris* continued: "When Ki Wiroguno returned to Mataram, he reported the execution to the Sultan and conveyed Kyai Ageng's greetings and expression of gratitude. Sultan Agung then informed the audience present that Kyai Ageng Amongrogo wanted to achieve the perfection of life and that the only person who could help him in that matter was the ruling king of the day. As such, Sultan Agung was not punishing Kyai Ageng for his misdeeds but was helping him attain the perfection of life that he wanted so much, which would ultimately lead him to the Realm of Reverse. That was the reason why Kyai Ageng Amongrogo expressed his gratitude."

## Nyi Selobrangti and Cethi Centhini

FROM WONOMARTO TO WONONTOKO
TO JURANG-JANGKUNG

### 1 The assassins

The news of Ki Amongrogo's death in Mataram quickly spread and Nyi Tambangraras became known as the beautiful young widow of Wonomarto. His death, however, created new difficulties for her and her family. People went to her home every day to ask for her hand in marriage, bringing along dowry that outcompeted each other in their number and value. But her heart was still filled with love for her husband and she declined the offers. Although Jamal and Jamil had clearly said that Ki Amongrogo was put in a basket and thrown into the ocean at Tunjungbang Bay, in her mind she could not accept the notion that her husband had died from the punishment. The night before Jamal and Jamil came, he had appeared to her in a dream and there was no sign in it that he would leave her forever.

Over at the village of Panataran, west of Wonomarto, there was a young man who also did not want to marry. He was Ki Sawojajar, the younger son of Ki Menak Pasagi, the late chief of the village. When Ki Menak fell in battle at the invasion of Giri, the Sultan of Mataram appointed his eldest son, Ki Kudosrenggoro, to be the new village chief. Although he already had two wives, his handsome younger brother was still not married. So when he heard about the beautiful widow of Wonomarto, he sent an emissary to ask her to marry his brother. However, his proposal fell on deaf ears. Who was Ki Bayi Panurto who dared to refuse him? It made him so mad that he sent two assassins to kill Ki Bayi. Ki Jayengrogo could see danger ahead, but Ki Bayi did not want to prepare for a violent clash. Instead, he wanted to place his fate in God's hands, saying that he would be safe in His protection if it were not his time to die yet.

*opposite: In the courtyard of the Cetho temple, located on the sacred Lawu Mountain, lies this extraordinary composition of fertility symbols. They comprise an enormous phallus pointing to a frog (inside the inverted triangle) and a turtle (at the base of the triangle). The temple was built in the last period of the Majapahit kingdom.*

## Jayengresmi and Jayengrogo

FROM WONOMARTO TO ARDIPOLO TO ARDISALAH

One night, Nyai Malarsih had a dream. She dreamt that her daughter and her husband Ki Amongrogo were visiting her as she was sitting in the *pendopo*. When she woke up, she felt great disappointment and sadness and broke down in tears. Ki Bayi Panurto called for his sons, Jayengresmi and Jayengrogo, and sought their opinion as to what to do. Still weeping and with a broken voice, she ordered them to look for their sister. It was an order they could not refuse for she had borne them for nine months and ten days. They asked for their parents' blessings and went home to take leave of their wives, promising to return as soon as possible.

### 1 Nyai Tilarso

Ki Jayengresmi told his brother of his plan to visit an old friend called Ki Malangkarso, as he might have some information about their sister. Ki Malangkarso was a learned religious teacher who lived at Ardipolo, about a three-day journey away. They walked south until they reached Sindurejo village at nightfall and rested near the house of Nyai Tilarso, a widow with two daughters.

That evening, the widow's old maid Nyi Pucangan was opening the gate when she noticed the young men sitting on a bench nearby. She asked: "Well, young masters! What are you doing here?" Ki Jayengresmi answered: "We are wandering *santris* overtaken by night and are looking for a place to stay for the night." She replied: "If so, I'll ask my mistress to give you lodgings. Please wait for a moment." She went in and came back with her mistress. On seeing the men, Nyi Tilarso immediately agreed to let them stay for the night and even asked them to stay longer. They went inside and she

opposite: *A women's rebana band. There are also men's and mixed rebana groups. These days, women's groups are hired to perform during special occasions such as the* siraman *(holy bathing) ritual held the day before a wedding and the celebration of a baby's first forty days of life. The songs performed in rebana recitals, called* singir, *are in praise of God and the prophet Muhammad.*

## Nyi Turido and Nyi Rarasati
### FROM WONOMARTO TO ARDISALAH

### 1 Batara Kala

Nyi Turido and Nyi Rarasati—the wives of Ki Jayengresmi and Ki Jayengrogo—waited for days and days for their husbands to return. They had said they would be away for only a few days, but it was now more than a week and there was still no news of them. They decided to look for their husbands themselves and one night, slipped quietly out of the village. No one saw them leave.

Passing through fields and mountains and ignoring fatigue and danger, they came to a forest where they heard all kinds of sounds even though they could not see anything. They knew the place was haunted and fear crept into their heart. But then they realised that death in a haunted forest was preferable to being separated from their husbands and the thought calmed them down.

Suddenly, a monstrous creature appeared in front of them, roaring vociferously. It was a demon of gigantic size, as tall as a mountain. In a thundering voice, it growled: "Well, Turido and Rarasati, prepare to die! I have not eaten for many days. What luck! Now two beautiful girls have come my way! You must be very tasty!" For a moment, Nyi Turido was afraid, but she quickly regained her senses and retorted: "All right, demonic grandfather! It is better to give satisfaction to a man-eating demon than to be an abandoned wife. All right, have your way. I am ready."

Just as suddenly as it appeared, the demon became friendly and his countenance was no longer ferocious. He said kindly: "Don't be afraid, my granddaughters. I am Batara Kala. I took on a demonic appearance to test your resolution. Now I truly know where your hearts are. Your husbands are doing penance at the top of Ardisalah

opposite: *Leather puppet figures of the gods Batara Guru (left) and Batara Kala in the story of Murwokolo. Batara Kala was Batara Guru's mistaken sperm (Kama Salah), which fell into the sea after Goddess Uma rejected Batara Guru's passion of lovemaking. Kala, who became a giant ogre, wishes to eat human flesh. This story is usually played during the Ruwatan ceremony, a purifying ceremony held to protect children with certain conditions from disasters.*

Mountain, southwest from here. Continue your journey. I will protect you." And with that he disappeared. Nyi Turido and Nyi Rarasati were relieved and feeling hopeful, they pushed forth.

## 2 Ki Paragen

The women walked on until they came to another wild forest. In it, they found a hamlet. It was the home of Ki Paragen and a few followers. Nyi Turido asked for directions, but instead of helping them and giving them honest answers, Ki Paragen tried to make them stay and marry him. To get rid of him, she offered: "I have a riddle. If you give me the correct answer, I will stay." He agreed to the deal and she gave the riddle: "Where were we when the Universe was not yet created?"

Laughing loudly, Ki Paragen answered: "At that time, only light existed. So we were in heaven." Nyi Turido replied: "You are wrong! It is apparent you are a false and foolish cleric, one interested only in chasing sexual passions." With that, the women turned around and walked away, leaving Ki Paragen stunned and perplexed.

## 3 Ni Endang Rarasati

They continued walking until they came to yet another forest. Realising they were lost as they had been moving around in circles and without direction for some time, they called out for help as well as their husbands' names. Finally, a lady hermit by the name of Ni Endang Rarasati appeared before them and said: "Well, my dearest. Your husbands are doing penance at the top of Ardisalah Mountain, southeast from here. There is still one more test for you to pass. Be careful!" Then she disappeared.

Nyi Turido and Nyi Rarasati followed the directions given by the lady hermit. Along the way, there was a thunderstorm and it rained, but they did not pay attention to it. Instead, they pushed on resolutely all the while pronouncing prayers. At long last, all the difficulties and troubles vanished and to their relief, they saw two figures sitting in deep meditation. They were Ki Jayengresmi and Ki Jayengrogo.

They tried many ways to wake them up but were not successful. Finally, Nyi Turido loosened her hair knot and wiped her husband's feet with her hair. Seeing her loyalty and devotion, Ki Jayengresmi emerged from the meditative state and so did Ki Jayengrogo. The women were estatic and embraced their husbands. A happy get-together followed.

opposite: *This pathway leads to a meditation place located east of Semeru Mountain in East Java. Followers of Hinduism and ancient Javanese beliefs come to this place to meditate. Nearby is Senduro temple, the second biggest Hindu temple in Indonesia after Besakih temple in Bali.*

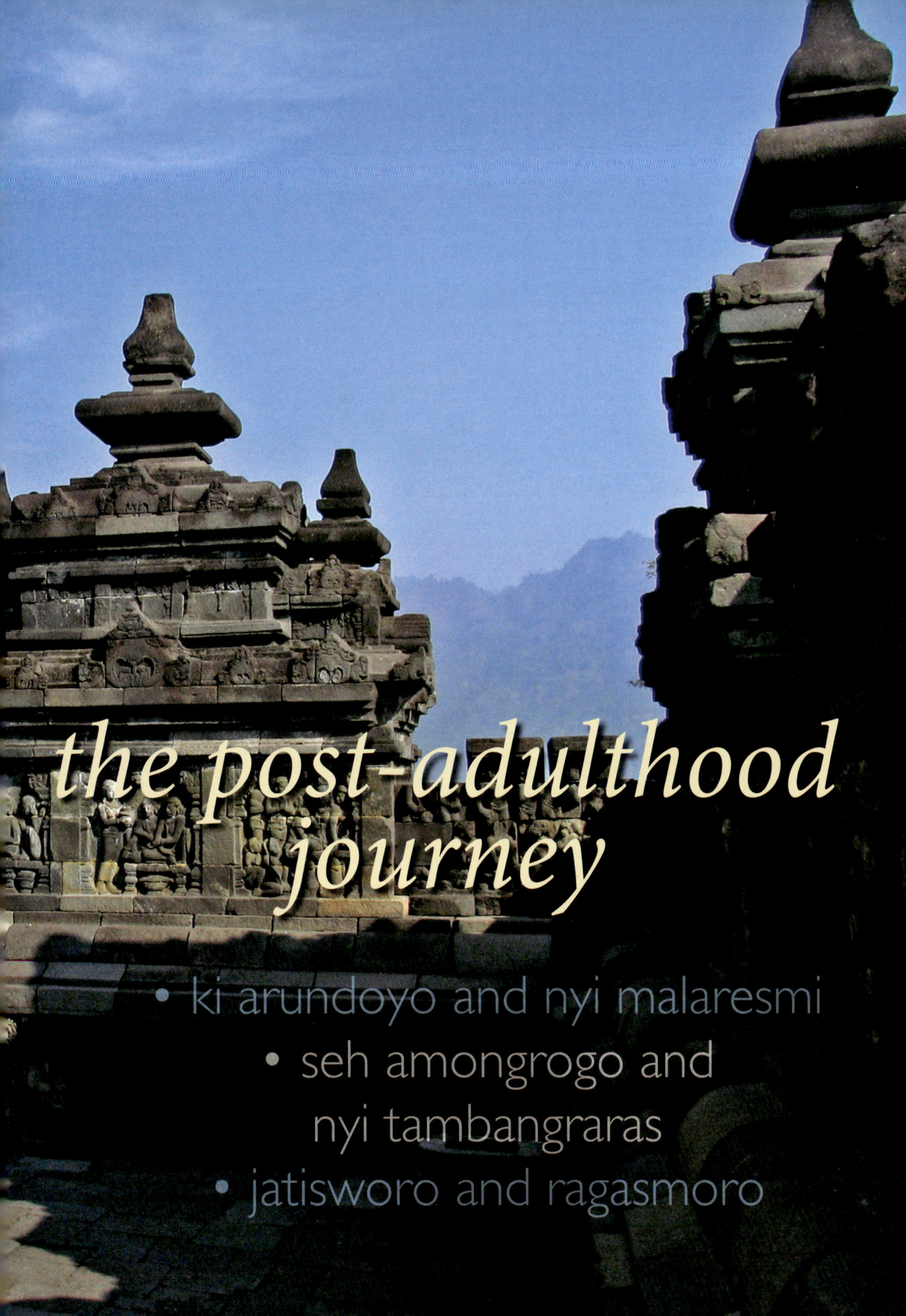

# the post-adulthood journey

- ki arundoyo and nyi malaresmi
- seh amongrogo and nyi tambangraras
- jatisworo and ragasmoro

## Ki Arundoyo and Nyi Malaresmi

### FROM WONOMARTO TO WONONTOKO AND BACK TO WONOMARTO

# 1 Ardimuncar

"Kyai?" Nyi Malarsih called to her husband. Replied Ki Bayi: "Yes, Nyai! What is it? Ki Montel brought us good news and you looked delighted, but now you are so gloomy again. What is the reason?" She kept quiet for a while and then said: "Kyai, Ki Montel's news is the reason. The letter he brought from Ki Amongrogo indeed brings joy. We should accept Centhini's marriage to Ki Montel with happiness. Jayengresmi and Jayengrogo's message is also very important. But, Kyai…" Ki Bayi asked: "But what, Nyai?" Nyi Malarsih continued: "Kyai, our sons' message that they will not come back makes me sad. I also want to see Centhini. She has never been separated from our daughter. Now that she's married, for sure they are apart." Nyi Malarsih took a deep breath and began to weep.

Feeling sorry for her, Ki Bayi said: "My dear wife! Listen, I'll look for the children. According to Ki Montel, it takes only between three and five days to get to Ardipolo, so I'll be back in ten days." Nyi Malarsih replied: "Kyai, this isn't a good idea. None of our children are here. Even our daughters-in-law are gone. Only Kyai is left. If you go, I'll be very lonesome and will die very soon. Take me with you. I don't care if I get hungry on the way or die from exhaustion, as long as I'm with you, my husband."

Ki Bayi was very moved by his wife's devotion. She was right. He could not leave her, not even for a minute. Finally, he said: "All right, Nyai. If you want to, you can come with me. Listen, I have a plan. I'll take the name Mas Arundoyo, my name when I was young, because I want to visit my old friends Ki Adimuncar and his brother Arundarso in the village of Ardimuncar. They only know me by that name. You must

opposite: *A page from a 200-year-old* wuku *(Javanese almanac) book from the Surakarta royal library. In the* wuku *system, there are 30 weeks in a year, each with 7 days. A person whose birthday falls under a particular* wuku *will have certain attributes said to determine their destiny. Calculating the* wuku *can only be done by experts. The picture shows the* wuku *Watugunung with its tree and bird attributes. This* wuku *has the gods Batara Antaboga and Betari Nagagini as its protectors (not shown).*

change your name, so that no one can identify you. Take the name Nyai Malaresmi. Don't bring too many things. The journey will be difficult and we have to pass through forests and mountains." She got up to prepare for the journey. There was ease in her heart; her husband's promise to take her along had given her extraordinary strength.

They slipped away from the village before dawn, their steps light in anticipation of meeting their children. No one knew of their departure. They rested for a while after the midday prayer. By late afternoon, they arrived at a field full of green vegetables and found a *santri* who took them to Ki Adimuncar. How happy he was to see Mas Arundoyo and his wife! He introduced them to his wife and ordered a *santri* to inform his brother of their arrival.

After dinner, Ki Arundoyo explained why he was travelling: "My brothers, forgive us if we have troubled you. The reason for our travels is to look for our children. I hear my sons are in Ardipolo and my daughter is in Wonontoko with her husband, Seh Amongrogo. Do you know where these villages are?" Ki Adimuncar replied: "Indeed, I do. About ten days ago, a *santri* from Wonontoko by the name of Ki Montel stayed with me for the night. He said he was on his way to deliver a letter from Seh Amongrogo to his father-in-law at Wonomarto, Ki Bayi Panurto. Do you know him, brother?"

Mas Arundoyo smiled and said: "Of course, I know him! I am Ki Bayi Panurto and Seh Amongrogo's letter is the reason for my travel. I want to see my children and where they are staying." Ki Adimuncar added: "Well, brother, according to Ki Montel, Ardipolo is about two days travel from here and Wonontoko, three days." Mas Arundoyo asked: "Can they be reached from Bustam? I want to see Ki Arsengbudi. I hear he is living there." Ki Adimuncar replied: "Yes, they can. In fact, I think Bustam is even better as it is located roughly midway from here to Ardipolo and there's no need to turn anywhere." Said Mas Arundoyo with finality in his voice: "If that is the case, I ask leave tomorrow so that I can get to Ardipolo as soon as possible."

## 2 Bustam

The late afternoon prayer was over and Ki Arsengbudi was sitting with his wife, Nyi Wiyadi, in the *pendopo*. Ki Arsengbudi said: "Well, my dear wife! I see you're in a good mood today. It's unusual for you to serve so much. It's as if you are expecting guests." Nyi Wiyadi replied: "I don't know why myself. I'm just in the mood to cook. But, Kyai, I don't do this very often. It is all right with you, isn't it?" Ki Arsengbudi said: "I'm fine with it but this much? Even if the whole household eats the food, I think it will not be finished. Or does that mood of yours also tell you that we will have guests?"

Just at that point, a *santri* came to inform them that there were visitors at the gate, a middle-aged couple. Ki Arsengbudi told him to bring them in. To his wife, he said: "Your intuition is amazing, my dear. We do have guests indeed. Is that also why you prepared something special?" She replied: "Indeed, Kyai! I cooked chicken dishes and white rice. They are special, Kyai, but can you tell whether our guests are special or just ordinary people?" Ki Arsengbudi said: "Well, judging by the care you took with the food, I think they are special because Allah only bestows His favour to people in accordance to their merits."

They heard the greetings of the guests just outside the *pendopo*. Ki Arsengbudi returned the greetings and hurriedly went out to welcome them. When they shook hands, he looked at Ki Arundoyo and said: "Forgive me, Kyai! I'm not sure, but are you my brother Arundoyo?" Mas Arundoyo smiled and replied: "Yes, brother! I am your brother Arundoyo." Ki Arsengbudi cried out: "God be praised! Well, it has never crossed my mind that you will come to my house. Nyi, Nyi, come out!" Nyi Wiyadi appeared and her husband said to her: "This is brother Arundoyo, whom I've told you about many times. Welcome him properly!" Nyi Wiyadi came forward with folded hands and said: "Welcome, brother!" Mas Arundoyo said: "Thank you, sister. This is my wife, your sister Malaresmi." Nyi Wiyadi welcomed her with folded hands. Ki Arsengbudi said: "Welcome to you, too, sister. We were just talking about you, brother. Allah has really blessed you, brother Arundoyo. Please come inside. And you, Wiyadi, serve everything that you have prepared for our beloved guests."

The sun had just set and it was time for the evening prayer, which interrupted their conversation for a while. When the prayer was over and he saw the dishes prepared for them, Mas Arundoyo thought to himself: "Just now, I saw my favourite vegetables out in the fields and now my favourite dishes are served to me. How great is Allah's mercy to me!" Nyi Malaresmi thought to herself: "Well, Malaresmi! You say you love your children. But once you are served with good food, you seem to have already forgotten them. Aren't you ashamed of yourself?" Bowing low, she wiped her tears away. Mas Arundoyo said to his host: "Forgive your sister, brother! She is thinking of her children. You must know that my visit here is not only to see you both but to see our sons in Ardipolo and our daughter in Wonontoko." Ki Arsengbudi replied: "It is us who should apologise, brother! It isn't surprising for a married woman's heart to go first to her children, then to her wealth and last of all, to her husband. Tomorrow, I will get some people to accompany you. The road to Ardipolo goes through the Jembul forest, which is haunted by evil spirits."

## 3 The Jembul forest

"Kyai and Nyai, we will be going through the haunted forest of Jembul. The spirits in there will try to mislead us, to make us lose our lives so that they can take our souls to their world," said Ki Putih, the oldest amongst four *santris* tasked to guide Mas Arundoyo and his wife through the forest.

Mas Arundoyo asked: "How do we not fall for their tricks?" Ki Putih replied: "You will see and hear things that may attract your attention. If you react to them, whether by praising or showing disapproval or doing something that relates to it, you will fall into their trap. You will be led astray for days until you die. Therefore, whatever

# the post-adulthood journey

happens, whatever you see or hear, don't react or respond. With God's permission, we will be safe." After a while, they entered the forest and as they reached its centre, the atmosphere became strangely quiet, eerie and fearsome. There were no animals or people to be seen. Suddenly, they heard loud noises of people talking; some were asking for directions to Ardipolo and others were responding. Then they heard loud sounds, like those of people chasing an animal. Mindful of Ki Putih's warning, they kept silent; they did not respond or react and only prayed for their safety. Nyi Malaresmi did not dare to breathe. Next, there appeared a group of people walking very fast. As they walked by, they left the things they were carrying on the side of the road and disappeared into the bushes. No one in the group paid any attention to them.

It was almost midday when they reached the edge of the forest. They rested, ate the lunch that Nyi Wiyadi had prepared for them and then performed the midday prayer. Ki Putih then said: "Kyai and Nyai, Ki Arsengbudi instructed us to return once we pass the forest. There is no danger from here on. Give us permission to return so that we will be out of the forest before nightfall." Ki Arundoyo expressed his gratitude and asked them to convey their greetings to Ki Arsengbudi. He also asked them for further directions. Said Ki Putih: "This way leads to Ardipolo. There is no other way. You cannot miss it."

The *santris* took leave and Kyai and Nyai Arundoyo began the walk to Ardipolo. Not long afterwards, they met people returning with firewood they had collected. Ki Arundoyo asked for directions to Ardipolo. They said: "Kyai has passed the side path that leads to Ardipolo. You have to go back. This road goes to Gunungsari, the village of Ki Cariksutro and Ki Carikmudo. Ki Arundoyo replied: "It is God's blessings. We also want to visit them." Pointing to some bushes, the oldest of the men said: "Then you are in luck. Gunungsari is just behind those bushes."

right: *The Javanese believe that bad spirits live in forests and will pray for protection and safety should they need to enter one. In fact, big trees are considered to be the abodes of these spirits and it is not uncommon to find offerings placed under them to signal the people's 'peaceful intent'.*

## 4 Gunungsari

Long before it was time for the late afternoon prayer, they reached the rice fields of Gunungsari. While walking, Ki Arundoyo told his wife that Ki Cariksutro was a religious teacher and had four wives and that his brother, Ki Carikmudo, had two wives. She could not help but smile. By chance, they saw two *santris* working on the field. With the assistance of Setronoyo and Setrogati, for those were their names, they soon arrived at the gate of Ki Cariksutro's house.

At that time, Ki Cariksutro and his wife were sitting in the *pendopo*. He was telling her about a *prenjak* bird (a species of wren-warbler) that had been flying in and around the garden the whole day. They were very sure that visitors would come their way. They were still talking when Ki Setrogati informed them of guests at the front gate. Ki Cariksutro stood up and when he saw Ki Arundoyo, he thought he looked familiar but was not very sure if he was his friend from his younger years.

When they had exchanged greetings, Ki Cariksutro asked: "If you don't mind, Kyai, can I ask your name?" Ki Arundoyo smiled and answered: "Call me as you like. Please guess!" Ki Cariksutro said: "When I was young, I had a good friend called Arundoyo. He was once hurt by a lance and I had to carry him away." Ki Arundoyo replied with a laugh: "Stop opening old wounds! I am that Arundoyo." Ki Cariksutro was amazed and asked: "Well, brother Arundoyo! I never thought we'd meet again. I recall you married a girl from Tuban. How is she now?" Ki Arundoyo replied: "Well, this is that wife of mine. She's always with me, wherever I go." Ki Cariksutro quickly gave his greetings to Nyi Malaresmi and then ordered a maid to call his wives. He also asked Ki Setrodremo to fetch his brother Ki Carikmudo, who lived nearby in the village of Kalisari.

The joyous meeting of old friends was celebrated with an evening of music and dance. Later, when everyone was resting, Ki Arundoyo told of his quest to see his children at Ardipolo and Wonontoko. With some remorse, Ki Cariksutro said: "Forgive me, brother Arundoyo, for being so inconsiderate. We didn't know that both of you have lost your children and are in distress. But don't worry! I know Seh Malangkarso, the religious teacher at Ardipolo. My brother and I will take you there tomorrow. Ardipolo isn't far away and we might get there before the late afternoon prayer."

So at dawn the following morning, the four of them left. Accompanying them were two *santris*, one walking ahead to lead the way and the other at the rear carrying provisions. At midday, they arrived at a pool called Sendang Beloro; it was where wayfarers and people from surrounding places would gather to collect drinking water. Food stalls had been set up on one side of the road and the place was bustling with activity. There were also houses on both sides of the road, which made the area look very populous. Ki Arundoyo and his companions stopped to pray and had lunch near the pool. From where they were, they could see the village of Ardipolo on the slope of a mountain. Ki Arundoyo thought to himself: "It's amazing… a village in the midst of a forest looking like one near a capital city!"

| the post-adulthood journey |

## 5 Ardipolo

That afternoon Seh Malangkarso was having tea with his wife, Nyi Malangresmi, when he said: "Nyi, I've noticed butterflies fluttering around the house since morning. Now they've entered the *pendopo* and are in the *pringgitan*. I wonder whether we will be having honourable guests." Nyi Malangresmi asked: "What do butterflies have to do with guests, Kyai? It's usually the *prenjak* bird that announces the arrival of guests, not butterflies." Ki Malangkarso said: "That's why I think the butterflies are telling us something different because they don't usually do that. Never mind! Let's wait until it's time for the evening prayer and we'll see whether we have guests or not." Just then, Santri Basariman informed them of guests at the gate: "They are your uncles Ki Cariksutro and Ki Carikmudo with two *santris*. There is also a couple with them. I don't know who they are." Ki Malangkarso exclaimed: "What did I say, Nyi? We have guests! Spread the fine mats and prepare food and drinks. And you, Basariman, invite them in and call Ki Modang, Tresnorogo, Amongsari and Pariminto to meet them."

When everybody was present and comfortably seated, Ki Arundoyo asked Ki Malangkarso: "Forgive me. The reason I'm here is to inquire about my sons Jayengresmi and Jayengrogo." Ki Malangkarso replied: "Uncle! Brother Jayengresmi and Jayengrogo were here, but they didn't stay long. After giving Ki Montel their message, they went to the top of Ardisalah Mountain to make penance." Ki Arundoyo said: "If so, give us leave to go to the mountain." Ki Malangkarso said: "Uncle and auntie! I beg you to stay here for a while. The road to Ardisalah is very difficult. There are valleys to pass and steep footpaths, which become very slippery when it rains. Tomorrow, I'll ask Ki Tresnorogo and Ki Modang to go to the mountain and ask brother Jayengresmi and

Jayengrogo to meet you here." Ki Arundoyo agreed, but added that in case they were not there, they should proceed to Wonontoko to see Nyi Tambangraras. They spent the night discussing religious matters, in particular the *shariah*, *tariqah*, *haqiqah* and *makrifah*. Ki Arundoyo thought that the knowledge held by his host was the same as that of his son-in-law, Ki Amongrogo.

## 6 Ki Sangularas

At the break of dawn the next day, Ki Tresnorogo and Ki Modang were already on their way to Ardisalah Mountain. They walked quickly and by midday were at Cimame Hill where they rested in the forest of Cemara-ringgit. When they resumed their walk, Ki Modang thought they were lost because the path ended there. Unable to go further, they decided to climb the steep slopes just the same. It was many times more difficult, but they did not care.

Later, they stopped at Ardi-pasar without knowing it was the abode of Ki Sangularas, an ascetic who was already in the incorporeal world. As they began to climb, heavy winds blew and rain fell suddenly. The clear sky turned black and they could not see in front of them. Just as suddenly, the rain stopped and in front of them stood a gigantic demon laughing loudly. In a thunderous voice, he said: "Hey you, Tresnorogo and Modang, good-for-nothing human beings! Today will be the last day of your life because I'm going to eat you for dinner." Ki Tresnorogo came to his senses. Feeling the danger he was in, he held his iron staff firmly in his hands and said: "You evil demon! Do not think that I am an easy prey. I will defend myself and you will find a worthwhile opponent in the fight of life and death." The demon laughed again, but this time the laughter sounded friendly. Not only that, his appearance changed into that of a kind ascetic. He said: "Well, Tresnorogo and Modang! I am Priest Sangularas. What I did was meant to test your resolution. Now I will take you to Ki Jayengresmi and Ki Jayengrogo. Follow me!"

They passed ravines and valleys as though they were flying and in the wink of an eye arrived at the top of Ardisalah Mountain, where they met Ki Arundoyo's sons. When Ki Tresnorogo asked them to leave the mountain to see their parents, Ki Jayengresmi said: "Ki Tresnorogo and Ki Modang! I beg your pardon, but convey this message to my parents. We cannot leave as we are not allowed to meet them yet. We will meet them later at Wonontoko together with Ki Amongrogo and my sister Nyi Tambangraras." They then disappeared from sight.

A strong wind carried the *santris* back to Ardipolo. It was almost dark when they got there, but it was only after the evening prayer was over that they could tell their story: "Ki Arundoyo, we have met your sons. But they said they are not allowed to meet you yet. Only later at Wonontoko will they meet you together with Ki Amongrogo and his wife. Also, their names have changed. Ki Jayengresmi is now Seh Raras and Ki Jayengrogo is Seh Resmi."

opposite left: *A mat made of woven pandanus leaves. In East Java, the tradition of pandan mat making is a long one and the art has been passed through the generations. Good quality mats are made from the leaves of trees that are at least two years of age; such mats have smooth surfaces and are very comfortable to sit on. Mats are either checkered or plain with borders; some are more elaborate with floral designs. In the past, people mostly sat cross-legged on the floor, instead of on chairs. The tradition of sitting on the floor is still found today, mostly in the villages.*
opposite right: *A mat seller plies his wares on a street.*

garden and shouted: "Nyi! Nyi! Come quickly!" Caught unawares, Centhini dropped her bucket and its contents spilled to the ground and she cried: "What's the matter? Now look what you've done!" Her husband took her hand and pulled her: "Don't bother! Look who's waiting outside the garden!" Centhini cried: "Release my hand so I can see clearer!" But before she could say anymore, she saw Nyi Malarsih. She pushed her husband aside and ran towards her. She fell to her knees, embraced Nyi Malarsih's legs and wept: "Nyai …Nyai!" She only managed to utter those words. Thereafter, she was speechless. Tears flowed down her cheeks. Nyi Malarsih could not speak either. She kneeled down and embraced her loyal and devoted maid. Finally, Ki Arundoyo spoke: "Nyai and you, sister Centhini! Calm down! Let's go to Ki Mangunarso. I'm sure he's waiting for us."

It was true. Ki Mangunarso was already waiting. He met them in the front yard and invited them to sit in the *pendopo*. Centhini promptly served hot drinks and snacks, whilst Ki Montel was ordered to call Ki Anggungrimang and his wife to meet the guests. Ki Arundoyo was deep in thought. When he saw Centhini, he was sure his daughter and her husband would also be there, perhaps his sons, too. But he had been sitting there for a while and none of them had appeared. Unable to hold back anymore, he asked: "My son, Mangunarso! I left Wonomarto hoping to see my children, but none of them have come even after we have enjoyed your hospitality. Do they live in another village?" Reluctantly, Ki Mangunarso said: "Uncle and auntie! I beg you to be patient for a little while more. The time for the evening prayer is almost over. Let's pray first and after that I'll answer your questions. It's a long story." Ki Arundoyo and Nyi Malaresmi felt reassured and became calmer. Meanwhile, Ki Anggungrimang and his wife Nyi Rancangkapti arrived, but it was only after dinner that the story was told.

below: *This is the teakwood interior of Giri mosque. The mosque is located in the Sunan Giri graveyard complex, which holds the graves of Sunan Giri Parapen and his family. People believe it was built during his rule. According to a source, it was renovated in 1860.*

Ki Mangunarso started off by saying: "Uncle and auntie! I will begin by introducing my family. There are three of us. The eldest is my brother Jayengresmi, your son-in-law and husband of sister Tambangraras. He is now known as Seh Amongrogo. The second is myself; I'm now known as Mangunarso. The youngest is Rancangkapti, now the wife of brother Anggungrimang. We were separated when Mataram invaded Giri. My brother fled to the west and ended up at Karang in West Java, whilst we both went to the east. We were later adopted by Ki Hartati, a merchant from Pekalongan. When he died, we went to Sokoyoso to study with Kyai Ageng Sokoyoso. My brother Anggungrimang is Kyai Ageng's son."

| **ki arundoyo and nyi malaresmi** |

Ki Arundoyo asked: "My son! Your brother and sister are married. Where is your wife?" Seh Mangunarso replied: "Forgive me, uncle! I'm not married. I've not been able to find a suitable wife." Ki Arundoyo then realised that Ki Mangunarso was an *ulama wadat* (celibate scholar). For a moment, nobody said a word. Then Ki Mangunarso continued: "Concerning brother Amongrogo and sister Tambangraras, they are incorporeal and live at Jurang-jangkung in Pulau Batu Palanggatan. Brother Jayengresmi and Jayengrogo presently live on Ardisalah Mountain and they have been reunited with their wives. If uncle and auntie want to see them, we have to use the spiritual approach, not the physical way. We have to meditate at Jurang-jangkung for some time until Allah gives them permission to meet us. Therefore, I beg uncle and auntie to prepare yourself mentally and physically and purify yourself." Ki Arundoyo said: "If that is the case, we will do as you have suggested."

## 9 Jurang-jangkung

When they were physically and mentally ready, Ki Arundoyo and his wife set off for Jurang-jangkung. They were accompanied by Ki Mangunarso, Ki Anggungrimang, Ki Malangkarso, Montel, Centhini and some *santris*. Along the way, they stopped at the Kalampeyan pool. Ki Anggungrimang and Ki Malangkarso stayed at the pool while Ki Arundoyo, Nyi Malarsih, Ki Mangunarso, Montel and Centhini continued to Jurang-jangkung. At Jurang-jangkung, Ki Mangunarso showed them the place where they should pray and meditate. He and Ki Montel then returned to the pool, leaving only Centhini to attend to Kyai and Nyai Arundoyo. Centhini promptly burnt incense, while Kyai and Nyai Arundoyo took ablution to perform the evening prayer. The aromatic smell of incense soon spread all over the valley. Centhini joined the prayer.

For three days and nights, the three of them meditated and prayed for permission to meet Seh Amongrogo and his wife, as well as their sons and their wives. Kyai and Nyai Arundoyo fasted every day even though they received food and drinks from the Kalampeyan pool. Finally, after the evening prayer on the third night, Seh Amongrogo and Nyi Tambangraras were permitted to meet them. They stopped first at Ardisalah to pick up Seh Raras, Seh Resmi and their wives.

It was almost midnight when Ki Arundoyo saw a bright spot in the sky moving towards them. Within that light, he saw Seh Amongrogo, Nyi Tambangraras, his sons and their wives. In that moment, all his grief vanished. When they made homage to him and Nyi Malarsih, he felt as though they had never left Wonomarto at all. Seh Amongrogo said: "God be praised! God has allowed us to meet father and mother. What do you want us to do for you, father?" Ki Arundoyo replied: "If Allah permits, I want all of you to come home with me to Wonomarto."

Ki Amongrogo said: "Father and mother! Nyi Tambangraras and I are already incorporeal and we can't do that. We can only meet in this way. However, brother Jayengresmi and Jayengrogo and their wives will return to Wonomarto to continue the family line." Ki Arundoyo said: "While your mother and I want things to be as they were before at Wonomarto, if Allah decrees otherwise, I will not dispute His wish." Ki Amongrogo added: "We will meet once more because Ki Malangkarso and others want to meet me. Now, I would like father and mother to stay at Wonontoko with brother Mangunarso or Anggungrimang. Brother Jayengresmi and Jayengrogo will join father and mother later on." The bright spot began to dim and at length, disappeared. Dawn was breaking. Ki Arundoyo asked his wife and Centhini what they had seen. They admitted to having seen the same as him. So he concluded that his prayer to see his children had been answered. They prayed and then left to join the rest at the pool.

Ki Malangkarso's hope of meeting Seh Amongrogo was fulfilled several days later. This time, Ki Jayengresmi, Ki Jayengrogo and their wives did not go back with Seh Amongrogo. They stayed on at Wonontoko with the intention of returning to Wonomarto. Back at Wonontoko, Ki Mangunarso remarked that twelve years had passed since he left Giri. Ki Arundoyo then told the story of his hermitage at Wonomarto, which had its beginnings in the hermitage of Tegal Pucangan founded by his forefathers. The last memorable event at Wonontoko was the congregational prayer, which was led by Seh Amongrogo.

## 10 A happy reunion in Wonomarto

Ki Arundoyo and Nyi Malaresmi stayed for a few more days at Wonontoko, alternating their stay between Seh Mangunarso and Seh Anggungrimang. On the evening before they departed for their home in Wonomarto, Seh Amongrogo and Nyi Tambangraras came to bid them farewell and once more to remind their father to allow Ki Jayengresmi and Ki Jayengrogo to finish their penance at Wonontoko. Accompanying the couple on their return journey to Wonomarto were Ki Montel, Centhini, another *santri* by the name of Ki Martoduto as well as four *santris* belonging to Ki Anggungrimang—Saloko, Polokarti, Kartipolo and Nurwitri.

Meanwhile, at Wonomarto, everyone in the village—including Ki Wiryo—were hoping and praying for the safe return of Ki Bayi and Nyi Malarsih. They were concerned because the prosperity of the village had declined considerably during their absence. One day, when the food offerings had been made, several people stayed behind to discuss the possibility of their return. A villager by the name of Ki Sembagi said that there were no signs yet of that happening. However, his son Ki Luwaran was positive that they would be back that night or at the latest, the next day. Ki Sembagi was very cross with his son's impudence. But the fact was that Ki Luwaran had received news that the old couple were spending the night in the village of Seruni, which was why he so adamant over the point.

Indeed, Ki Bayi could have made it to Wonomarto that night but he chose not to as he did not want to wake the villagers up and cause confusion. Since he also did not want to disrupt the people by arriving in the morning when they would be at work, he

opposite top: *The photograph shows a* kenduri *(ritual gathering or feast).* Kenduris *are held to celebrate happy occasions. A common meal would be prepared for all the villagers to share. Before the feast, communal prayers would be performed. Guests will also bring home some of the food as a token of blessings from God.*
opposite bottom: *The food is ready and about to be distributed for a* kenduri.

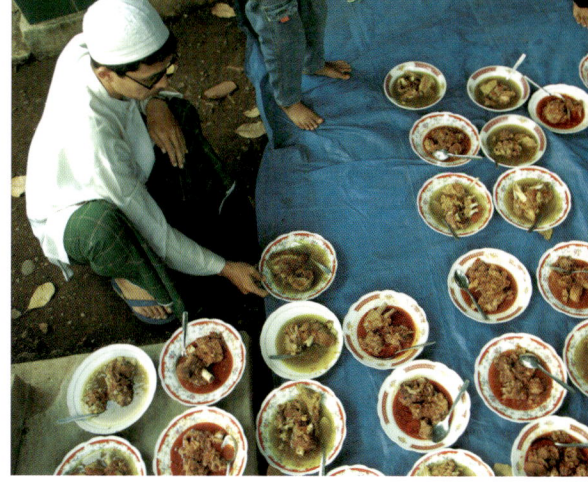

decided to stop at Pagutan, Nuripin's village, where he waited until the evening. He only entered Wonomarto at nightfall as the people were preparing to go to the mosque for the evening prayer. Just as Ki Kulowiryo was lighting up the mosque, Ki Bayi appeared. It was a happy reunion that spread throughout the village. People everywhere kindled all kinds of lights and the evening prayer was especially memorable. When he got home, Ki Bayi told the story of his journey and his meeting with Seh Amongrogo and his children. He did not finish the story as he was tired from his long journey and promised to continue the next day.

    Nyi Centhini and Ki Montel stayed at Wonomarto for one week. During that time, they visited her family. During that time, too, Ki Bayi related the rest of his journey. He also felt the urge to see his sons at Wonontoko. One afternoon, after the Friday prayer and as he sat in the *pendopo* receiving guests, Ki Montel and Nyi Centhini came forward to take their leave. They were given presents and cash contributions to begin their family life. Nuripin and eight of his subordinates accompanied them to Wonontoko and were back in Wonomarto ten days later. Life at Wonomarto went back to normal and the village became even more prosperous than before.

## Seh Amongrogo and Nyi Tambangraras

FROM JURANG-JANGKUNG TO PULAU BESI PUROSANI AND BACK TO JURANG-JANGKUNG

### 1 The hermitages of Wonotawang and Wonosonyo

After the evening prayer one day, Ki Mangunarso sat in the mosque of Wonontoko with Jayengresmi, Jayengrogo, Anggungrimang and their wives. They were discussing the building of hermitages for Ki Jayengresmi and Ki Jayengrogo. For Ki Jayengresmi, he proposed that it should be located in the forest of Wonotawang, south of Jurang-jangkung; for Ki Jayengrogo, he proposed that it should be built in the forest of Wonosonyo, located east of Jurang-jangkung. Just then, Seh Amongrogo and Nyi Tambangraras appeared. They approved the choice of the locations as they were close to Jurang-jangkung. Seh Amongrogo then told them to return to Wonomarto as soon as possible because their father was ill. He also told them that they would be visiting hermitages and places of worship throughout Java. His brothers and sisters then paid homage with folded hands and he left them to continue with their deliberations.

### 2 Pulau Besi Purosani, the island of black marble

Seh Amongrogo and his wife visited hermitages and holy caves set in mountains inland and by the sea, enjoying very much the changing scenery. Finally, they arrived at Watingkup Bay at the very end of Banten on the west of Java island, south of Pulau Kelapa (Coconut Island). The wild and restless rolling and tossing of the waves combined with the sharp protruding peaks of coral reefs created a composition of horror and fear. Seh Amongrogo, as *insan kamil* (perfect man), wished to change the dreadful atmosphere to one that was tranquil and peaceful.

opposite: *A hermitage in Sokaraja, Banyumas Regency, Central Java. Accessible via steps from a river, this small place of only 3 square metres is mostly used by ascetics in the weeks leading up to the holy month of Ramadhan. They spend their time in deep meditation to purify the body, soul and mind. On other days, the place is used by the locals who go there to pray.*

He therefore created an island of black marble on the bay. Shining brightly in the sun, it was an island of enchantment, rich with gold and precious stones in natural shapes and forms, as well as finished jewellery. The wild breaker waves became calm rippling whitecaps, which made sailors feel secure. That was perhaps the reason why the island became known as the island of Balitung. It was not surprising that sailors—who at first went there to obtain water supplies—would go back to collect gold and other things the island offered, such as clothes, weapons and food, which were free for the taking. The island of black marble became renowned throughout the world.

## 3 Ki Datuk Rogorunting

Now to the east of Java lies the island of Sumatra.[1] On that island lived a man by the name of Ki Datuk Rogorunting. He was known to be the most powerful and learned scholar around, at least according to Ki Datuk himself. Some say he lived in Bangkahulu, others say his home is in Palembang. But where he lived was not important. Of more importance was the fact that he was an experienced and powerful guru.

One day, Ki Datuk sat in the *pendopo* of his house with 85 disciples to discuss the black marble island and its owner, Seh Amongrogo. He wanted to subjugate Seh Amongrogo and take possession of the island and had thought of a sly trick. Since Seh Amongrogo was known never to refuse the requests of people, he would ask for Nyi Tambangraras to be his wife. Surely, this would be a test of his generosity. If Seh Amongrogo did not give his wife to him, it would only prove that he was not really a generous person. Ki Datuk's disciples, on the other hand, were only thinking of the material things they could get. Ki Datuk explained that it would not help to ask for worldly things; doing so would only benefit Seh Amongrogo as he would attain heaven, while those hankering for worldly riches would be tortured in hell.

With that plan in mind he made preparations to set sail for Watingkup Bay, at the utmost end of Banten. He brought all his books with him just in case Seh Amongrogo wanted a contest in scholarship and knowledge. He also ordered his followers to bring along their weapons, just in case Seh Amongrogo did not agree to surrender peacefully. With a heart full of disdain and vanity, he got on his boat. But that contempt and arrogance quickly vanished when a thunderstorm raged and tossed the boat brutally in the midst of the ocean. Ki Datuk and his followers were thrown into the water and all their books and weaponry were lost. When a merchant ship bailed them out of the water, they did not have a single thread on their body and had to beg for something to cover their shame. On the island, Seh Amongrogo smiled and said: "Crime doesn't pay. Whoever commits crime should be punished."

---

1 In the original manuscript, it was written that Sumatra lies to the east of Java. In reality, the island of Sumatra lies to the northwest of Java. It is probable that the writers had incomplete information about the geography of the region in the 1800s. Further research is also needed to determine whether 'Bangkahulu' mentioned here is Bengkulu or Bangka that can be found on Sumatra today.

Since the ship was heading for the same island, the captain agreed to take them there but added that they would have to fend for themselves as he would be busy loading his ship with riches. Ki Datuk did not mind doing so since he had already resolved to take possession of the island once he landed there, if necessary by killing Seh Amongrogo. Forgetting all that he had said about becoming too attached to worldly objects, when he got to the shore, he quickly chose some clothes to make a good impression on Nyi Tambangraras. He saw a *pendopo* and walked fearlessly towards it. Behind him were his men, who had helped themselves to weapons—so fully armed were they it was as though they were going to battle.

Meanwhile, Seh Amongrogo was sitting in the *pendopo* with his wife, looking at Ki Datuk and his 'army' with pity and humour. He prayed to God to make him and his wife invisible to them. Since Ki Datuk could not see anyone in the front hall, his first thought was that Seh Amongrogo had fled out of fear. He checked every nook and corner and finally called a challenge: "People say Ki Amongrogo is friendly to all his guests. I have come as a visitor, but why is he hiding?" Seh Amongrogo, who was still invisible, answered: "I hear that my guest is a learned guru. Why then is he still so blind and mindless?" Ki Datuk was shocked to hear the voice coming from so near to him. He gripped his hand tightly on the handle of his sword and turned around but there was no one there. He then ordered his followers to stand around him. A witty laugh was heard, followed by a friendly voice: "Welcome, my friend. It is not nice to visit armed with weapons. One might think you are criminals fleeing from the police. Please, have a seat. I've been waiting for you for a while."

Seh Amongrogo and his wife then revealed themselves. Ki Datuk was flabbergasted to see them sitting on a double chair. He looked around; his men were already sitting on mats as though making their audience with a regent. He looked back at his hosts and saw them beckoning him to sit on an empty chair that had appeared in front of them. As if controlled by some power, he proceeded to sit. He was worried and his mind was full of questions.

Said Ki Amongrogo: "Welcome, Ki Datuk Rogorunting. I hope you didn't have any trouble getting here." Ki Datuk was amazed that he knew his name and in his heart, he felt he had already been defeated. But he told himself that in deceit and trickery, there was no proof yet that Seh Amongrogo could outwit him. He said: "So, you know my name. I am indeed the great Ki Datuk Rogorunting, the guru of all gurus in Sumatra. You, Seh Amongrogo, are known to be a generous ascetic. You never let people go empty-handed. I have come to ask you one thing." Ki Amongrogo said: "Only one thing? I think you need more than one thing." Ki Datuk replied: "Only one thing. If I ask for more than one thing, let God curse me and punish me severely." Ki Amongrogo added: "Those are your own words. Don't blame me if they come true!" Ki Datuk said: "I won't. Now listen! Despite my great stature, I'm still single. Therefore I ask for your wife to share my great fortune. If you don't want to give her to me, you prove yourself to be insincere. What do you say?"

But Ki Amongrogo already knew the trick that Ki Datuk would play. He looked at his wife for a moment, then said: "All right! Take my wife!" Nyi Tambangraras could read her husband's order from the way he looked at her. She said to Ki Datuk before disappearing: "Ki Datuk, I wait for you at the beach." Ki Amongrogo said: "You heard what Nyai said. She is waiting at the beach. You may go! Don't let her wait too long." Ki Datuk turned to look at the beach. He saw her sitting on a rock, a few feet away from the waterline. He was so delighted that he forgot to ask his leave. He ran to the beach, with his men trailing behind him.

With his special powers, Ki Amongrogo then instructed all the ships to depart, so that not one ship was in sight when Ki Datuk got to the beach. Although he was out of breath, he could think of only thing—to ask his adversary for a ship to return home. He ran back to the *pendopo* and begged for a ship filled with gold and other goods. Seh Amongrogo reminded him that he had broken his promise: "Aren't you afraid of the curse of God?" Ki Datuk shouted angrily: "Damn you! Who cares about God's curse? I need a ship!" Ki Amongrogo: "Ki Datuk, you are a brute. You ask for it! All right, look at the beach. There is your ship and Nyai is already on board with all that you want."

Ki Datuk turned his gaze to the beach. A three-master was anchored there and Nyi Tambangraras was waiting on the bridge, waving goodbye. He quickly ran back to the beach, again forgetting to ask for leave. Mustering all their strength, Ki Datuk and his men swam to the ship and climbed to the deck. There on a carpet, they saw food and drinks set out, even alcoholic drinks that sailors seem to like so much. Ki Datuk took a gulp and felt his strength return. Not only that, all the objects he and his disciples desired were neatly piled on the deck, ready to be brought back to Bangkahulu. How happy he felt. Nobody was injured and the whole episode was ending well. Thus with more gusto they continued with their feasting and drinking. Ki Datuk would sometimes glance at Nyi Tambangraras, who was sitting calmly on the bridge counting beads while pronouncing God's beautiful names.

All this time the ship was moving where the wind blew; there was no one at the helm. On seeing this, Ki Datuk ordered one of his men to steer the ship towards Bangkahulu. Suddenly, the calm of the sea changed. Ki Datuk realised they were in the same spot where they had lost their ship. All feelings of drunkenness disappeared and everyone went to their posts. A whirlwind spun the ship like a top and not long afterwards, the ship disappeared from the surface of the sea. Once again, Ki Datuk and his men were thrown into the sea, where they lost consciousness and floated as though dead. Just then, the whirlwind died as suddenly as it came. The sea became calm; boats and ships of all kinds and sizes were sailing as though nothing had happened. Again, they were rescued and yet again given cloth to cover their nakedness.

Ki Datuk was the first to gain consciousness. He asked the captain to take them to Bangkahulu, promising to pay the fare when they got there. One by one his followers became conscious. By the time they reached Bangkahulu, they were all well. They were also conscious of their semi-nakedness, as the cloth they had on only brought them disgrace and humiliation. They ran to the hermitage as quickly as possible and proceeded to make themselves presentable. Although Ki Datuk paid the fare, the story of him running through the streets without any clothes became more vivid and deplorable by the day.

The story about Ki Amongrogo, on the other hand, was very different. When the whirlwind made the ship its plaything, he picked up his wife and together they returned to the Realm of Silence. Their home on the island changed back to its original state—a coral reef protruding to the sky—and the ocean became wild and stormy again. On his way back to Jurang-jangkung, Ki Amongrogo passed through Parangtritis beach where he found a young man called Ki Ragasmoro doing penance. After passing a test with flying colours, Nyi Tambangraras—who had been calling herself Nyi Selobrangti since she left Wonomarto to look for her husband—took him as her disciple. The three of them then headed back for Jurang-jangkung.

## 4 On the way to see Ki Bayi Panurto

Ki Jayengresmi and Ki Jayengrogo had been staying at their respective hermitages for four months. They had three *santris* each to serve them. Every now and then family members from Wonomarto would visit to bring news about their father, who had been ill for some time.

One Friday morning, the brothers and their wives went to Wonontoko to join the congregational prayer. Ki Anggungrimang and Nyi Rancangkapti were also there. The congregation that day was very big. Seh Amongrogo, Nyi Tambangraras and her disciple were amongst the devotees, but they did not show themselves until the prayer was over. Seh Amongrogo advised Ki Jayengresmi and Ki Jayengrogo to return to Wonomarto because their father was seriously ill. He and Nyi Tambangraras would join them later on.

They quickly formed a team of fourteen people. It was to be led by Ki Mangunarso. On the way to Wonomarto, they stopped at Ardipolo, where Ki Malangkarso welcomed them with a *rebana* recital and dance performance. Amongst the people in the team

below: *This mosque, located in the middle of a rice field in Central Java, belongs to a* pesantren. *The* tajug *roof is typical of Javanese buildings, although this is much smaller in scale and not as elaborate as those of larger mosques. The small dome on top of the roof is characteristic of Islamic buildings.*

were Ki Modang and his young wife, Nyi Pelangi, who was also a dancer. She wanted to dance that night to attract Ki Jayengrogo's attention. They had flirted some time ago when Ki Jayengrogo first came to Ardipolo. Now, she wished to extend their flirtation into something more intimate. But she was wrong to think that he would reciprocate for the present Jayengrogo was not the same person of several months ago. Having made penance at Ardisalah—which had increased tremendously his knowledge of religion and faith in God—Ki Jayengrogo was also able to control his sexual desires. Moreover his wife, Nyi Rarasati, was present and watching his movements closely. Unaware of these changes in Ki Jayengrogo, Nyi Pelangi became more infatuated with him. That night, Seh Amongrogo came to give a discourse on the *takdir* (decree) of God in the Islamic faith. At length, Ki Malangkarso and his wife joined the team. They would be leaving next morning.

## 5 Calamity in Jembul forest

Nyi Pelangi was allowed to join the group because she had said to her husband that she could not stay apart from him for long. Who was the man who wouldn't be thrilled to hear such an admission from a young wife? But in her mind, it wasn't her husband she wanted but Ki Jayengrogo. So that first night which they spent in a forest, Nyi Pelangi chose to sleep apart from the others, thinking it would give her a chance to creep to him and drag him to the bushes. But she slept through the night and only woke when she heard the call for the morning prayer. The opportunity she was waiting so passionately for had quietly slipped away.

They spent the second night with Ki Cariksutro, who kept them entertained with dance and *rebana* recitals. In addition, Ki Mangunarso gave a discourse about *tariqah*, *haqiqah* and *makrifah*. That night, the men slept in the mosque and the girls in the house. Nyi Pelangi had no chance to get to Ki Jayengrogo because Ki Cariksutro's *santris* were sleeping on the verandah and were blocking the door. Once again, she could not realise her plans.

The next morning, Ki Cariksutro, his first wife, Nyi Wilopo, and one of his disciples, Ki Secodarmo joined the team. The route would take them through the haunted forest of Jembul and sure enough, strange things happened when they reached the centre. They heard the sounds of hunters rounding up animals but could not see a single person. Then they heard the footsteps of people walking past them; they were carrying all kinds of things, which they put down nosily on the side of the road. Everyone in the group was warned not to pay any attention to the sounds but to pray for their safety.

However, Nyi Pelangi did not take note of the warning. Disturbed by her failures of the nights before, she did not pray for safety and instead fantasised about making love to Ki Jayengrogo. Her walk was not straight and she was swaying to the right and left. Ki Modang thought she was tired from walking for so long. Suddenly she screamed, her body convulsed, her eyes rolled and she fainted. There was much confusion. Efforts to revive her were not successful. Ki Mangunarso then said a prayer to ward off the attacks of the spirits. After a while, she opened her eyes and saw that her cloth was stained with blood. While she was washing it, she told her husband that she was raped by a tall man with a weapon so formidable that the experience was torturous. Apparently, the blood was menstrual blood, but she still felt the pain. Ki Mangunarso reprimanded the man and he did not appear again. Everyone became more careful after that incident.

By late afternoon, they were at Bustam village where Ki Arsengbudi lived. They spent the night there and watched an entertaining *rebana* recital and dance show. They also held discussions about *tariqah, haqiqah* and *makrifah*. Before turning in, Ki Arsengbudi announced that he and one of his devotees, Ki Iman Seco, would join them and go to Wonomarto to see his old friend, Ki Bayi.

## 6 God's decree and God's will or help

From Bustam on, Ki Arsengbudi led the way since he knew the region very well. There were no mishaps and by the time the late afternoon prayer was to be performed, Ardimuncar Mountain was already in sight. After prayers, they headed towards the mountain and soon reached the rice fields and vegetable gardens belonging to the hermitage of Ardimuncar. Ki Somurco, one of Ki Adimuncar's disciples, was watering the rice fields and applying manure to the vegetables. Ki Putih, another of Ki Cariksutro's disciples in the group, asked: "Well, brother Somurco, how are you?" Ki Somurco was startled to hear someone addressing him. He looked up and turned to the direction of the voice: "Aha, brother Putih! I am well. Thank you for your blessings. And how are you, brother?" Ki Putih said: "I'm well, too, brother! I have a group of visitors who want to see Kyai Adimuncar." Ki Somurco looked at Ki Arsengbudi and the people with him. Ki Arsengbudi said: "It's true, Ki Somurco. I want to see your master. Is he home?" Ki Somurco replied: "Yes, Kyai. He's at home." Ki Arsengbudi said: "If so, please tell Kyai that his brother from Bustam wants to see him." Ki Somurco picked up his hoe and hurried home.

The group spent the night at the hermitage. Ki Adimuncar and Ki Arundarso were very happy to see their old friends, whom they rarely met. Ki Arsengbudi told Ki Adimuncar that there were two groups on the way to Wonomarto—the first consisted of the family of Ki Bayi Panurto; the second group comprised Ki Bayi's friends whom they had met along the way and wanted to come along. Ki Adimuncar said: "If that is the case, I will join you. Ki Bayi stayed the night here when he was looking for his sons and daughter. It is now my turn to visit him."

That night, Ki Mangunarso gave a discourse about *kodrat* (God's decree) and *iradat* (God's will or help), which found much approval from the older *ulamas* (learned people recognised as expert in Islamic law). The night was closed with a *rebana* recital and dance show. Nyi Pelangi danced and sang a song with lyrics taken from a religious teaching:

# the post-adulthood journey

*Agampang wong sembahyang, nora ngel wong angaji, pakewuhe wong angesang, angadu sukma lan jisim, akeh wong bisa celathu, jatine nora nana, lir wong dagang madu gendhis, nggih punika lampahe wong sarengatan.*

**To perform the prayer is easy; to read the holy book is not difficult either. What is difficult in this world is to pay attention to either the body or the soul. A lot of people can just talk, without any truth in it, like the words of a vendor of honey or sugar. That is the way of the followers of the law.**

The next morning, the group that left Ardimuncar for Wonomarto was bigger. This was because Ki Adimuncar, his brother Arundarso and Ki Somurco had joined them.

## 7 The Seloko-kas forest

It was time for the late afternoon prayer, but there wasn't any water to make ablution. When they finally found water and prayed, Ki Adimuncar asked his *santri* where they were. Ki Somurco replied: "The river we took ablution in is called the Gareswangkit River. It cuts through the Kamal forest. The centre of the forest is haunted by ghosts and spirits." In the past, the Kamal forest was the hermitage of Priest Kiliraja, the older brother of King Kelatbahu whose sister was the lady priest of Wonontoko. The story goes that the forest became dangerous when bogeys—tigers in human form—began to haunt it. Ki Adimuncar remarked: "I think you just made that up." He turned to Ki Mangunarso and said: "What do you think, my son? Shall we stop here where there is water or shall we push forth until nightfall? Ki Somurco says the area further in is the forest and that it's haunted. Also, there might not be any water further in."

Ki Mangunarso replied: "If you ask me uncle, I prefer to push further until nightfall. Concerning the ghosts and spirits, we should not worry about them because God is the best protector. Our lives are in His hands and its better to build up our faith in God and His protection (Q, 22, 78)." His reply encouraged the group to continue. They relied on God's help and protection. What Ki Somurco said was true, for at nightfall they were in the Seloko-kas forest, deep in the centre of the Kamal forest. Ki Adimuncar was amazed to find in the middle of the dense forest a natural garden with plenty of water and flat stones to sit on, so clean as if they were swept every morning and evening. The group decided to rest there and began to make themselves comfortable.

Suddenly, a group of people appeared and asked permission to spend the night in the same place. Ki Montel told them: "It's all right with me, as long as your group doesn't mix with ours." Ki Mangunarso interrupted: "Don't discriminate, Ki. We are all in a strange place. It's best to protect each other." The leader of the group expressed his thanks and asked permission to leave them for a while. They came back with all kinds of fruit, which they offered to Ki Mangunarso and his companions to express their gratitude for being allowed to stay. In reality, the strangers were the bogeys returning to their dwelling place. Ki Adimuncar was truly impressed by the fruit as he thought he would have to sleep on an empty stomach. But Allah is All Merciful; He gives His sustenance to whosoever He pleases. So in this case, even strange people were conveyers of His grace. While waiting for sleep to come, the devotees were either praying or remembering the beautiful names of God or reciting the holy Qur'an. One by one, they fell asleep, their snores alternating with the snores of the strangers. Ki Montel stirred and when he opened his eyes, what he saw was beyond his imagination—there were tigers of all sizes lying amongst his companions! He quickly woke up Ki Basariman, Somurco and Secodremo. They, too, saw the tigers and screamed, which woke up the others with a jolt. But before anyone could realise what had happened, the tigers were already out of sight. As dawn had broken, Ki Mangunarso gave the sign for prayer. Ki Montel made the call to prayer and when the prayer was over, they continued with their journey.

There were still the dangerous forests of Tunggorono and Pandegan to pass through but the experience of the previous night made them more vigilant and careful. When they finally cut through Rimbi and Pikun forests, they could see the edge of the village of Kepleng. This time, Ki Jayengrogo had no intention of stopping there even though he saw, at the pool, a woman he was once acquainted with. She was Si Enduk Watiyah, who by then was a mother of two children. The group knew that Wonomarto was very close by and they would be at Pagutan, Nuripin's village, in a day or two. They spent a night in Pagutan and the very next morning, Nuripin and Montel went to Wonomarto to inform Ki Bayi Panurto of the arrival of his sons and a group of visitors. Ki Bayi ordered Ki Wiryo to meet them at Pagutan and asked his other brothers to prepare a great welcome for them. Ki Bayi was so happy to see them all that he recovered quickly.

left: *The outskirts of Wonomarto village.*

## Jatisworo and Ragasmoro

### FROM CAMPA TO JAVA AND BACK TO CAMPA

# 1 The contest between two brothers

Over in the kingdom of Campa—historically believed to be in the region of Cambodia, Vietnam and Thailand—the ruling monarch had two sons. Their names were Ki Jatisworo and Ki Sajati. When King Pratokal invaded Campa, its ruler fell in battle and his sons were driven away in different directions.

One day, Ki Jatisworo heard a voice from out of nowhere saying that if he wanted to be reunited with his younger brother, he should befriend Seh Amongrogo who had supernatural powers. So Ki Jatisworo set out to look for Seh Amongrogo. At the same time, he built up his own powers until they were of a very advanced stage. He explored the island of Java and traversed the entire length and breadth of Sumatra but did not hear anything about Seh Amongrogo. If the man was so powerful, why hadn't anyone heard about him? Ki Jatisworo doubted Seh Amongrogo's existence and resolved to put him to the test first before befriending him. But he could never find this mysterious and unknown powerful man. At his wits' end, he finally sat down on a flat stone in the midst of a jungle and grumbled to himself: "Was what the mysterious voice said a lie? It said I had to befriend Seh Amongrogo, but I still haven't met him. Was the mysterious voice a lie?"

Suddenly, he heard laughter and someone say: "It is impossible for a mysterious voice, which is usually God-inspired, to be a lie. If there is a name, then there should be a man behind that name." Although Ki Jatisworo was rather offended to learn that there was someone out there who was able to approach him without his knowledge, he realised the person must be a supernaturally powerful hunter to be able to do so! So he

*opposite: The meditation and prayer room in the Princess Campa tomb complex in Trowulan. It is believed that the long relationship between Campa and Java goes back to even before the Majapahit era. Some sources say it began during the reign of King Indravarman II of Campa kingdom who came to power in AD 854. The tomb keeps alive the memory of this close relationship, as the princess married the last king of Majapahit. People visit the tomb to pay their respects to the princess.*

replied respectfully: "My brother, a voice ordered me to meet Seh Amongrogo if I want to find my brother. I have searched everywhere for him but have not been successful." Just then, Seh Amongrogo, Nyi Selobrangti and Ki Ragasmoro made themselves visible. Seh Amongrogo continued: "You have been looking in the wrong places, my brother! I am Seh Amongrogo. This woman is my wife and the young man is her disciple. If you want to befriend me, let us sit and talk comfortably." Ki Jatisworo happened to look around and, strangely, he only just noticed a beautiful house nearby. It was located in the middle of a pond, which was surrounded by a beautiful garden.

In his heart, Ki Jatisworo admitted that the person claiming to be Seh Amongrogo had reached the stage of *waliyullah* (friend of God). Yet his mind was not satisfied and he had to test him. So he said to Seh Amongrogo: "Sir, you can only be my brother if you pass my test." Ki Amongrogo replied: "Be my guest. My wife will represent me this time. Ask your question." Ki Jatisworo asked about the meaning of *Islam* (surrender to God) and *kafir* (disbelief). Nyi Selobrangti answered to his satisfaction.

Ki Amongrogo then said: "It's now my turn to put a question. This will be done by my wife's disciple." Ki Ragasmoro asked: "Who are your ancestors?" Ki Jatisworo answered: "My ancestors, and yours, are dogs." Ki Amongrogo said: "Wrong! Your ancestors are spotted dogs."[2] Ki Jatisworo admitted that Ki Amongrogo had guessed correctly. He felt angry and said: "So far, you have been represented by other people. But this time, you yourself must oppose my power." Feeling ashamed, he left without saying goodbye.

## 2 Wonocondro

After travelling for some days and suffering from hunger and thirst, Ki Jatisworo arrived at the hermitage of Wonocondro. The ascetic who lived there was called Ki Rogomono. He welcomed Ki Jatisworo with open arms and asked him to help him train the disciples at the hermitage.

That night he had a visitor in his room. It was Ni Sakati, the hermit's daughter. She had fallen in love with him the moment she set eyes on him. The ordeal of his days of wandering around looking for Seh Amongrogo, the extreme exhaustion and the relief he felt from meeting Ki Rogomono made him fall into her amorous embrace without any resistance at all. But he was haunted by the thought of that encounter with her. Indeed, it was punishment for not asking leave from Seh Amongrogo. The next

---

2 There is a story that says the *kalang* people are the offspring of a spotted dog. A princess was banished to live in a forest by her father, the king, because of a minor mistake. Her only companion was a spotted dog called Belang Wayungyang. She spent her days spinning and weaving cloth in her hut, which was built on poles for protection against wild beasts. While weaving one day, she dropped a tool. There and then, she made a vow that she would marry whatever or whoever retrieves the tool for her. If it were female, she would make it her best friend. It so happened that her dog brought the tool to her. She kept her word—they married and had children. As they lived in the forest, their descendants were called *kalang* people which, perhaps, means 'the wood people'. It thus appears here that Jatisworo and Ragasmoro were *kalang* people (See story on the *kalang* people on p125–126).

day, he ran for his freedom from the control of passion, pushing through valleys, ravines, wetlands and highlands. Eventually, he came to a beach where he found a cave.

## 3 The jewel in the cave

In the cave, he found an ascetic called Seh Boko, who knew everything about him. Ki Jatisworo was fascinated by his knowledge. He felt that Seh Boko could help him locate his brother and asked to become his disciple. Seh Boko said: "If you pass this test, I will take you in as my disciple and advise you where to find your brother. At the moment, he is well and under the care of a powerful protector." Ki Jatisworo replied: "All right! What is the test?" Seh Boko: "There is a jewel in this cave. Find it and bring it to me." Ki Jatisworo agrred and said: "All right! Give me your blessings, holy one."

above: *This is the many-chambered Putri Kencono cave, located in Kidul mountain area in Central Java. Discovered on 1 January 1991, it is 125 metres deep and filled with stalactites and stalagmites. It is one of hundreds of caves in the region, many of which remain to be discovered.*

He went further into the cave, which proved to be very deep and dark. He could not see anything. However, by virtue of the spiritual power that he possessed, he 'saw' a door set flush against a far wall. The door opened for him and he walked into the next chamber. The further in he went, the more difficult it was for him to make out the doors but still he was able to find them and venture deeper. Finally, after walking through nine doors, he found the jewel. It was shining brilliantly in the dark. He quickly grabbed it and brought it to Seh Boko. The ascetic thanked him and advised him to return to Seh Amongrogo. He added: "Your brother is under Seh Amongrogo's protection at present. Do not test him, but go to him humbly and respectfully. Your brother is now called Ki Ragasmoro."

## 4 Campa

But Ki Jatisworo still could not find Seh Amongrogo. Like he did the first time, he went everywhere. The place where he met first Seh Amongrogo was no longer there and the house in the pool was also not to be found. Feeling hopeless about the situation, he sat down to meditate and pray. Suddenly, Seh Amongrogo, Nyi Selobrangti and Ki Ragasmoro appeared. He fell to his knees and paid homage with folded hands. Ki Amongrogo said: "Ragasmoro! Join your brother and take back your country!" As they embraced each other, Ki Amongrogo and his wife disappeared from sight. The brothers returned to their land, attacked King Pratokal and killed him in battle. Ki Jatisworo ascended the throne and his brother became high priest of the land.

# the arrival

- ki bayi panurto and nyi malarsih
- seh amongrogo and nyi tambangraras

# Ki Bayi Panurto and Nyi Malarsih

## The perfect demise

Feeling that the end was near for Ki Bayi and he was waiting for them, Seh Amongrogo and his wife went straight to Wonomarto. All his other children were at his deathbed. Nyi Tambangraras went straight to the foot of the bed and knelt there. Just then, Ki Bayi opened his eyes and saw that his family was complete. Seh Amongrogo whispered in his ear all that he needed to know to begin the journey to Eternity. Ki Bayi acknowledged his understanding with his eyes and began to apply what he had just been told. He saw a light. It was as if it was waiting for him and it was lighting up the dark alley ahead. He looked at the light [the soul in light form] and with his eyes, followed it as it slowly moved from his feet to his forehead where it stopped for a while as if to bid farewell to the body. The light then gradually subsided and disappeared into serenity.

After a few moments, Nyi Malarsih became aware that her husband had passed on. Whatever energy that seemed to keep her alive began to leave her and she fell on her daughter's lap. Ki Jayengresmi carried her body and placed it gently beside her husband's. Weeping and crying filled the house. Santri Luci beat the drum in a way that told the villagers that Ki Bayi had gone, but they only knew of Nyi Malarsih's passing when they paid their respects to Ki Bayi. All the rituals and offerings were carried out immaculately according to religious rules and on the advice of Seh Amongrogo.

At a meeting several days later, it was agreed that Ki Jayengresmi would succeed his father as head of the religious school of Wonomarto, whilst Ki Jayengrogo would administer the social affairs of the tax-free domain of Wonomarto. Seh Amongrogo and Nyi Tambangraras returned to the Realm of Silence.

opposite: *Detail of wood panelling from the tomb chamber of Sunan Giri Parapen. Approximately 60 by 40 centimetres, the relief depicts flowers, which is considered to be a symbol of peace for the souls of the dead.*

# Seh Amongrogo and Nyi Tambangraras

## 1 The hermitage of Ngandongrukmi

Seh Amongrogo said to his wife in the Realm of Silence: "My dear wife! It would be nice if we could save the lives of other people of this world and help them attain happiness in the hereafter. Indeed, we have a good life and are enjoying all the blessings of The Merciful One, but I will only be satisfied if we can share those blessings with others." Nyi Tambangraras replied: "What do you want to do, Kyai? I will agree with all your wishes and plans." Ki Amongrogo replied: "My dear, I would like to descend to the world of the human race and lead them to security. But to do this, we have to live amongst them as king and queen. Only then will we be able to enforce the law and defend the faith." Nyi Tambangraras only nodded. He continued: "Let us see the Sultan of Mataram to discuss my plans. At present, he is living as a hermit at the hermitage of Ngandongrukmi."

Let us now talk about the sage at the hermitage of Ngandongrukmi, which was located on the slopes of Telomoyo Mountain. He was known wide and far to be a generous and powerful sage, one able to fulfil the wishes of those who come to him for help. There was only one exception—he would not help people if doing so would lead to hostility, hatred and killing. This sage was known as Priest Anyokrokusumo Sidowakyo. Even the Sultan's right hand man, Tumenggung Wiroguno, did not know who the priest was and sought his advice on how to gain the Sultan's favour. To that

opposite: *This is the middle of three main doors of the Giri Mosque. The calligraphy above the door is from Surah (chapter) Al-A'raf, verse 29 in the Qur'an. It reads: "Say: My Lord hath commanded justice; and that ye set your whole selves (to Him) at every time and place or prayer, and call upon Him, making your devotion sincere as in His sight: such as He created you in the beginning so shall ye return."*[1]

---

1 Taken from the Holy Qur'an. Translated and interpreted by Abdullah Yusuf Ali, a widely respected figure whose work has been reproduced more than thirty times around the world. He was born in India in 1872 and died in London in 1953.

# the arrival

above: *Telomoyo mountain, located on the border of Magelang and Semarang regencies in Central Java.*

question, the priest replied with a smile that honesty and devotion was the answer. Priest Anyokrokusumo had two disciples who acted as his assistants. Unknown to them, too, their master was the king himself, the ruling monarch of Mataram, Sultan Agung Anyokrokusumo.

One quiet evening, the priest felt that two spirits would be coming over to see him. He immediately sat down to meditate and in an instant knew who they were and why they were visiting. Soon enough, their greetings were heard from outside. He greeted back and Seh Amongrogo and Nyi Tambangraras, enclosed in a brilliant light, entered the room. As they approached the priest respectfully, he invited them to sit. And then he said: "Welcome, my honourable guests. Frankly, I am amazed that you still desire that which matters most for lower grade human beings. But all right, tell me what you want and I will try to help you." Seh Amongrogo said: "I notice that my visit to see your majesty is no secret for your majesty. We want to lead people to the right path. If your majesty has no objection, permit me to succeed your majesty as king so as to enforce law and defend the faith."

Priest Anyokrokusumo replied: "I am quite surprised with your request but will try to meet it. Do not blame me if you find life a bit rough later on. This is because the life of a human being is akin to crossing an ocean of sin and suffering. Many people fail even though they have accumulated sins and suffered much misfortune. Take your own father, the honourable Sunan Giri, for instance. The glory of life did not free him from greed, from desiring political power and wanting to be called the vicegerent of God, even though that was already assigned to me, the ruling monarch. Why didn't he want to believe that? Moreover, my emissary was my brother-in-law, Pangeran (Prince) Pekik, who was closely related to your father. Therefore, do not harbour any bad feelings for him, as he was only carrying out the order of his king. When you become king, do not take revenge. Become a king who has only the interest of the people at heart."

Seh Amongrogo humbly replied: "My wife and I understand, sire. Now we surrender entirely to you." Priest Anyokrokusumo explained further: "All right, but let me remind you again for the last time that the suffering is incredibly great. The process is like this. You will have to take the guise of a male and female maggot. I will eat the male maggot and I'll give the female one to Pangeran Pekik. You will be born as my son and will succeed me as king, whilst your wife will be born as the beautiful daughter of Pangeran Pekik, worthy to be queen of the land. This is the plan I can offer you. After your rebirth on Earth, everything will be your responsibility. I will have no say at all."

## 2 The wonder maggots

Ki Amongrogo and his wife accepted all the conditions proposed by the king. When they had changed themselves into a male and female maggot respectively, the king brought them home to the palace. Early the next morning, he summoned Pangeran Pekik and his wife, Ratu Pandan, to the palace. After explaining Seh Amongrogo's intention to succeed him as king, he took out the wonder maggots and fried them on a very hot pan. They heard cries of pain. They were so terrible that the Queen and Ratu Pandan quickly left the scene.

Time advanced with giant steps. Sultan Agung had a son and Pangeran Pekik had a daughter. The children married each other. When the king died, his son ascended the throne and was called Sunan Mangkurat. Because he had spiritual eyes and could see beyond what his officials were doing, there were many among them whom he found guilty of crime. He punished these people severely. However, the common people did not understand their king's behaviour, which they saw as being unnecessarily heavy-handed. Therefore, they urged Pangeran Adipati, Sunan Mangkurat's eldest son, to rebel. Not wanting to upset his father, the prince ordered Raden Trunojoyo, the son-in-law of Panembahan Romo, to act on his behalf. He acted swiftly and Sunan Mangkurat was forced to leave the palace. The king died in exile in a place where the soil was fragrant. As such, he was also known as Sunan Seda Tegalarum (the King who Died at the Field of Fragrant Soil).

With this, we could say that Seh Amongrogo and Nyai Tambangraras had arrived at the end of every human being's journey, a journey that begins at birth and ends at death. But was it the end of the journey or the beginning of a new journey?

*Wa'llahu a'lam*! Only God knows!

# GLOSSARY

**Alam Walikan** the Realm of Reverse

**Alhamdulillah** 'God be Praised'

**Allahu Akbar** 'God is the Greatest'

**amreta** the elixir of life

**Asyar** the late afternoon prayer; this is the third of five obligatory prayers that Moslems have to perform daily

**bagor** mask dance

**bai'at** the declaration of devotion

**batara** god

**cethi** maid servant and/or maiden companion

**dalang** puppeteer in a **wayang** show

**Dzat** Essence

**Dzatullah** the Essence of God

**emprak** magic show

**endang** female attendants

**gamelan** traditional musical ensemble in Java and Bali, comprising drums, gongs, metallophones and xylophones; from *gamel*, which means 'to strike or handle'

**gemblak** an ascetic who possesses spiritual and physical powers; also called **warok**. He maintains his powers by not having sexual relations with women and fulfill their needs with young men known as **jathil**.

**gunung** in the Javanese language, this refers to both mountains and hills

**Hadith** the collection of the traditions of the prophet Muhammad; contains the words and deeds of the Prophet

**hajat dalem** rice offerings for the king

**haqiqah** the ultimate truth in mysticism/the ultimate knowledge where the creature is able to see the true nature of the Creator (God) and the creature

**iman** faith

**insan kamil** perfect man

**Insya Allah** 'God willing'

**istighfar** the plea for forgiveness, which reads *Astaghfirullah* (I ask Allah forgiveness)

**Islam** surrender to God

**Isya** the evening prayer; this is the last of five obligatory prayers and is to be performed between dusk and the next **Subuh** prayer

**jathil** young male who serves as the **gemblak** or **warok's** companion

**joglo** type of house defined by its steep roof supported by four main pillars; usually the abode of the wealthy

**kalimah sahadah** the Islamic creed and declaration of faith, which reads "There is no God but Allah and Muhammad is His messenger"

**kekawin** poem written in Old Javanese, the language used from approximately the 8th to the 15th centuries

**kyai (ki)** a form of address for men, usually reserved for scholars, those learned in religious matters and those of the older generation; also used for certain objects of veneration, such as gongs and canons

**khusnul khatimah** the perfect death

**kiblah** the direction of the Ka'bah in Mecca; the Ka'bah is a square building that contains a sacred black stone

**luyut** to pass out in God's consciousness

**Maghrib** the sunset prayer; this is the fourth of five obligatory prayers and is to be performed between sunset and the performance of the **Isya** prayer

**makrifah** the highest knowledge in mysticism, which is the consciousness of the union of the Creator and creature

**mangunah** magical power

**mas**  a general polite term for addressing males

**masjid**  mosque

**mighrab**  niche in the wall of mosques; faces the direction of the Ka'bah in Mecca

**ni**  a form of address for young girls and those not married

**nyai (nyi)**  a form of address for married women; also for those who are divorced or widowed

**Pangeran**  a form of address meaning 'Prince'

**pendopo**  the front hall used for receiving guests; a typical feature in a *joglo* house

**pengulu**  religious official; also has the authority to administer wedding rites

**pesantren**  religious school of Islam

**pesinden**  female singer in a gamelan orchestra

**pringgitan**  narrow passageway that links the *pendopo* of a *joglo* house with the private back area

**Raden**  a form of address for a person of noble rank

**rebana**  Javanese drums; includes the tambourine

**ronggeng**  paid female dancer

**salam**  the Islamic greeting which is used when saying 'hello' or 'goodbye'; in Arabic, the word means 'peace'. *Salam* is short for *Assalamualaikum*, which means 'Peace be upon you'.

**salat**  prayer, both obligatory and optional

**Salat Tasbih**  optional prayer of glorification

**santri**  disciple and/or attendant

**Seh**  a form of address accorded to a religious teacher of Islam or spiritual master

**Sekaten**  festival celebrating the birth of Prophet Muhammad

**sengkalan memet**  concealed chronogram

**shariah**  the Islamic law; comprises the moral and ethical rules governing aspects of everyday life

**singir**  songs of praise of God and the prophet Muhammad

**sraddha**  offerings for the deceased

**Subhanallah**  'Glory be to Allah'

**Subuh**  the morning prayer; this is the first prayer of the day and is to be performed between dawn and sunrise

**Sunan**  a form of address, meaning 'the highly esteemed one'; also refers to 'king'

**Tahajjud**  optional late night prayer

**tariqah**  path in mysticism through spiritual practices and guidance to seek *haqiqah* (the ultimate truth)

**tawhid**  oneness of God

**tayuban**  *ronggeng* dance show

**ulama**  religious scholar and/or learned person recognised as an expert in Islamic law

**wali**  the Arabic meaning is scholar or friend [of Allah]; also means 'saint' in the Indonesian language

**waliyullah**  in the spiritual tradition of Islam, this is a 'friend of God' or holy person

**Wali Songo**  the collective name for the group of nine holy saints responsible for the early spread of Islam in Java

**wangsalan**  a type of riddle hidden in words

**warok**  see *gemblak*

**wayang**  shadow play, a Javanese art form in which puppets are used

**wuku**  the Javanese almanac

**zikr**  remembrance of God

**Zuhur**  the midday prayer and the second of five obligatory prayers

# INDEX

## A

Adiwijoyo, Sultan  34, 140, 141, 142
Ageng Banyubiru  147, 148, 149, 150, 151
Ageng Selo  48, 49, 50, 103, 141
Ageng Tarub  103, 141
Aji Saka  21, 26

## B

Babad Tanah Jawi  10, 26, 147
Bajangkaki Mountain  309, 312
banyan tree  9, 36, 37, 67, 88, 89, 90, 112, 172, 187, 211, 241, 265, 302, 303
Batara Kala  223, 347
Batara Katong  304, 306, 327
Borobodur  2, 14, 91, 96, 97, 99, 121, 153
Brawijaya, King  39, 40, 44, 73, 92, 102, 139, 140, 141, 146, 149, 257

## C

Campa  39, 40, 139, 379, 381
Condrodimuko crater  257, 258

## D

Dalil  114, 201, 231
Demak Mosque  16, 17, 50, 52, 140, 269
Dewaruci  22, 26, 156, 157, 158
Dieng temples  2, 82, 83, 187, 248
Dlepih Mountain  254, 255
dragon  41, 44, 45, 46, 47, 48, 56, 58, 74, 157, 206, 208, 209, 210, 282, 284, 323
Dzatullah  194, 224, 232

## E

elixir of life  16, 41, 157, 158, 210

## G

gamelan  11, 16, 17, 42, 105, 109, 110, 162, 169, 173, 209, 210, 223, 224, 271, 272, 273, 286, 287, 288, 289, 292, 295, 296, 297, 319, 322, 326, 330
Gua Bidadari  240

## H

Hadith  114, 115, 201, 231, 235, 394
haqiqah  123, 124, 215, 219, 226, 359, 372, 373, 376, 377

## I

Ijmak  114, 115, 201, 231, 235
Indrokilo Mountain  93, 245

## J

Jamus Kalimosodo  104, 105
jathil  159, 160, 161, 162, 163, 164, 165, 166, 167, 178
Joko Bodo  146, 147

## K

Kadis Markum Baslam  75, 76, 77
kalang  125, 126, 306, 380
kalimah sahadah  16, 17, 57, 105, 227
Kamajaya, god  111, 257, 273, 330
Katim Tayi  170, 171, 172, 173
Kaurava  157
kekawin  18, 156
Kelud Mountain  40, 237, 246, 247
King Darmokusumo  104
Kota Gede  97, 98, 124, 142
kris  9, 69, 100, 136, 201, 219, 243, 301

## L

Lawu Mountain  119, 158, 255, 256, 257, 258, 290, 337
Limusbuntu cave  88
Lokopolo-Kawi  115
Lorojonggrang temple  122, 123

## M

Mahabharata  14, 19, 21, 22, 41, 89, 104, 158, 252
Majasto  146, 147, 148, 149
Majapahit  9, 15, 16, 39, 40, 41, 44, 52, 53, 55, 71, 78, 86, 92, 100, 102, 130, 139, 140, 141, 146, 149, 219, 256, 257, 290, 304, 337, 379
makrifah  123, 124, 153, 203, 215, 226, 231, 232, 359, 372, 373, 376, 377
Malam Maksiat (Night of Sin)  293, 294, 297
Mandhara Mountain  16, 41, 158

Martabat Tujuh (Seven Stages of Creation)  59, 174, 228
Mataram  13, 14, 17, 20, 22, 33, 34, 35, 38, 43, 48, 49, 97,
    98, 100, 103, 104, 111, 112, 115, 116, 124, 125,
    126, 129, 135, 137, 138, 139, 140, 142, 143, 151,
    169, 170, 203, 237, 255, 262, 263, 264, 265, 281,
    303, 307, 322, 335, 337, 341, 362, 377, 387, 388
Menakjinggo, King  78
Menak Sopal, Prince  318, 319
Mendut temple  91, 96, 97
midodareni  103, 205
Mount Bromo  2, 69, 70
Murwokolo  109, 110, 111, 223, 347

## N

Ngebel lake  248, 249, 250
Night of Power (*Lailatu'laqdr*)  104, 136
Nusobarong island  241, 242
Nyai Loro Kidul  43, 102, 255, 340

## O

origin of man  228

## P

Pajajaran kingdom  57, 60, 61, 62, 63, 112
Pajang kingdom  34, 138, 139, 140, 141, 142, 211
Panataran temple complex  40, 41, 337, 338
Pandava  110, 157
Panembahan Senopati  43, 98, 124, 255
Pangeran Pekik  20, 34, 35, 67, 181, 389
Partodewo  109, 110, 111
pesinden  209, 210
Prambanan temple  2, 14, 15, 26, 122, 123
Probodalem cave  253, 254
Prophet Muhammad  11, 17, 21, 22, 62, 114, 129, 136, 173,
    222, 235, 295

## Q

Qiyas  114, 115, 201, 235

## R

Rajegwesi Mountain  332, 333
Ramadhan  17, 52, 104, 136, 367
Ramayana  10, 14, 15, 18, 19, 21, 22, 23, 338

Ratu Mas Trengganawulan  44
Realm of Reverse (Alam Walikan)  283, 285, 335, 341
reincarnation  20, 258
ronggeng  25, 98, 177, 270, 271, 272, 273, 274, 275, 289,
    291, 292, 293, 296, 297, 298, 329, 330

## S

Sahadah Quraisy Mataram  169, 170
Sang Hyang Sedyo Suksmo  225, 226
sastra cetha  115
Seh Domba  15, 130, 131, 134
Seh Lemah-abang  54, 55, 124
Selomangleng cave  280, 281, 282
sengkalan memet  52, 284
shariah  123, 124, 136, 153, 174, 203, 215, 219, 220, 226,
    227, 231, 263, 308, 359, 376, 377
Singosari  68, 69, 111, 284, 318
South Ocean  43, 46, 47, 77, 89, 102, 255
Stone Mosque  88, 89
Sultan Agung  13, 17, 20, 22, 26, 35, 111, 124, 141, 142,
    143, 255, 265, 281, 307, 322, 335, 388, 389
Sunan Giri Gajah Kedaton  34, 54, 55
Sunan Giri Parapen  26, 33, 34, 35, 57, 58, 63, 67, 69, 72, 83,
    122, 180, 203, 362, 385
Sunan Kalijogo  15, 16, 17, 52, 53, 89, 105, 132, 135, 149
Sunan Ngampeldenta  34
Sunan Tembayat  15, 54, 130, 131, 132, 135, 136, 147

## T

tariqah  123, 124, 215, 226, 359, 372, 373, 376, 377
tasawwuf  149, 153
Tengger  69, 70, 179, 244
Tunjungbang Bay  19, 26, 237, 242, 255, 307, 324, 335, 337,
    340, 341, 377

## W

Wali Songo  15, 52, 54, 89, 131
wangsalan  58
warok  160, 161, 162, 163, 164, 165, 394
wayang  14, 17, 105, 109, 110, 156, 223, 252, 256, 257,
    271, 274, 289, 301
Wijoyokusumo flower  89, 90
Wonontoko (Realm of the Dead)  74, 150, 187, 188, 283,
    285, 335, 337, 339, 340, 341, 345, 353, 354, 355,
    357, 359, 360, 361, 364, 365, 367, 371
wuku  56, 139, 353

# acknowledgements

**In projects** such as *The Centhini Story*, there are always too many people to mention and too many people to thank. But to everyone who gave their ideas, their time and encouragement, I would like to express a big Thank You. This project has been a piecing together of many different inputs and each contribution has added even more value to this book. I need to make mention those who have been critical to *The Centhini Story*, without whom this project would still be on the starting block.

I feel very fortunate to have had the unstinting support of P.T. Astra International and P.T. Indofood Sukses Makmur. As leaders in industry, they have demonstrated their commitment to the wider community many times and in so many different ways including, in this case, the area of cultural preservation. A very special thank you to Bapak Aminuddin and Bapak Dindin Machfudz of P.T. Astra International, and Ibu Jennifer Mandagi and Bapak Indra Josepha of P.T Indofood Suskes Makmur for their faith and trust. I cannot thank you enough for the encouragement you have provided. A big thank you, too, to John Slack for his long friendship and genuine love of Indonesia.

Thank you to Marshall Cavendish—Violet Phoon, David Yip, Melvin Neo and their talented team—for their courage in committing to this project. A very special thank you to Lee Mei Lin with whom I have built a special bond and respect for her dedication, her professionalism and her drive to interpret and edit *The Centhini Story* so as to allow all unfamiliar with Java to be captured by its mystique. I hope, Mei Lin, when you look past the difficulties encountered along the way, that you have had as much joy as I have had in working on this book.

To my darling husband for being my strongest anchor and greatest supporter of all my crazy ideas and my beloved parents who have always taught me to work hard and pray hard to make my dreams come true... thank you.

To the families of Pak Wito and Pak Fendi, let me apologise for taking away from you the precious family time that they have sacrificed for this project.

And finally, I would like to thank everyone else whom we have come to know along the way... for pointing Pak Wito, Pak Fendi and myself in the right direction when we needed to find our way.

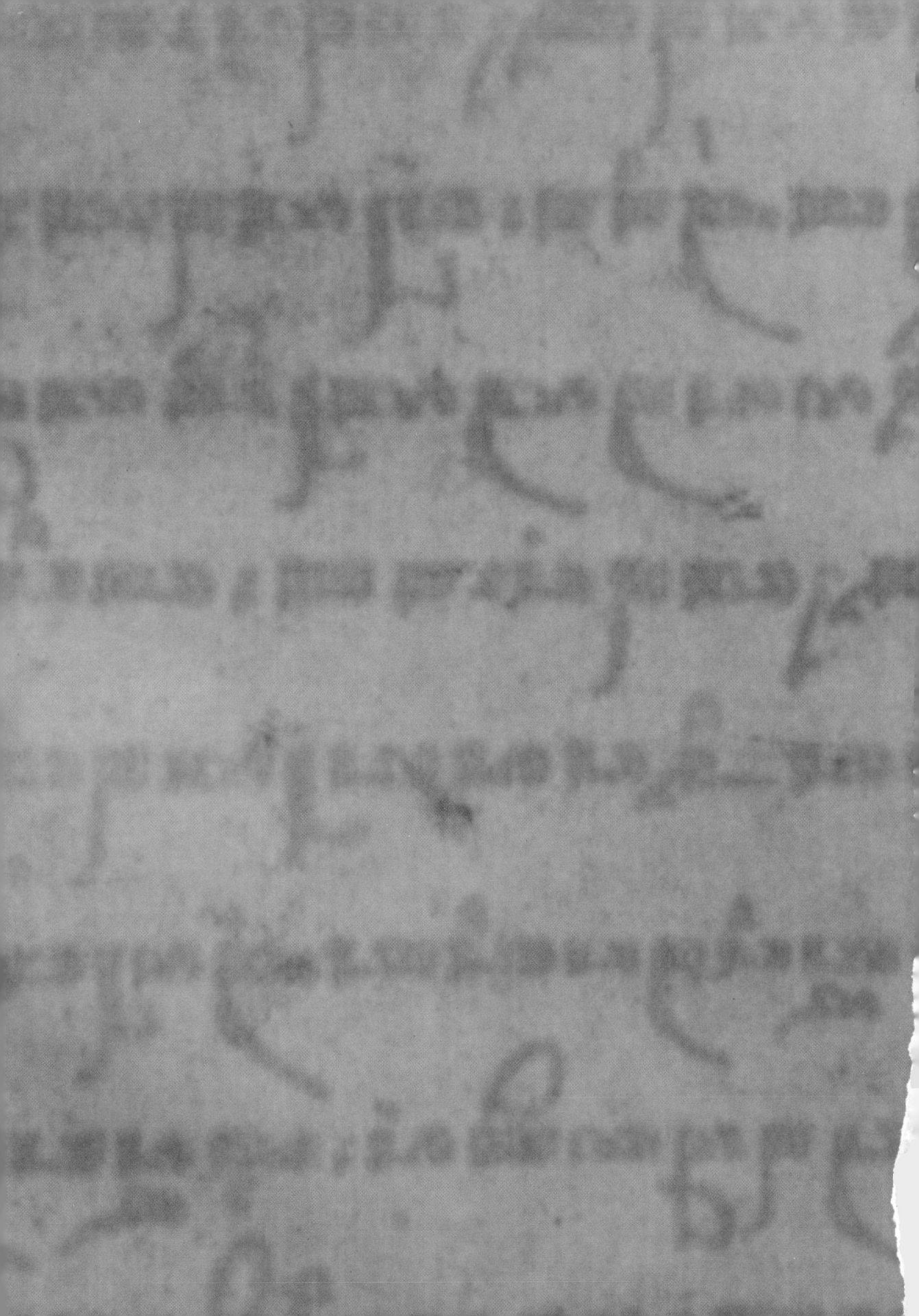